Tara, Princess of Wales

"This is a tremendously entertaining piece of writing-impeccably researched and consistent in the vivid fictional world it depicts…indisputably a good read."
—*Deborah Futter, Doubleday*

"TARA is a rich, detailed story, certain to be successful."
—*Diane Reverand, Villard Books*

"…a strong period saga, and a delightful heroine in Tara."
—*Monica Harris, Dell*

"There's clearly a strong historical imagination at work here, and Tara is a protagonist who is very easy to pull for…Brinckloe has found a fascinating time and place to develop his hero."
—*Rebecca Salutan, Simon & Schuster*

"There is no question it is a worthy publishing project."
—*Sharon Madison, Bethany House*

"The story is well-crafted…"
—*Anne Hamilton, Warner Books*

"I found this novel to be commercial in the very best sense of the word."
—*Mary Cunnane, W.W.Norton*

"I was impressed with Brinckloe's grasp of the historical background to TARA…the novel and author show great promise…"
—*Leslie Meredith, McGraw-Hill*

"Several of us here have had an opportunity to look at TARA. It seems like a compelling project."
—*Monica Speidell, Houghton Mifflin*

"The research is excellent, and the tale balances action and dialogue to make a well-paced commercial story."
—*Richard Curtis, author of over 50 books, and head of a leading New York literary agency.*

Tara, Princess of Wales

The Breathtaking Tale of a Magnificent Woman Warrior's Battle to Lead Her Nation

William D. Brinckloe

Authors Choice Press
San Jose New York Lincoln Shanghai

Tara, Princess of Wales
The Breathtaking Tale of a Magnificent Woman Warrior's Battle to Lead
Her Nation

Authors Choice Press
an imprint of iUniverse.com, Inc.

For information address:
iUniverse.com, Inc.
5220 S 16th, Ste. 200
Lincoln, NE 68512
www.iuniverse.com

ISBN: 0-595-12507-7

Printed in the United States of America

Dedicated to My Wife

…Sailing Partner,
…Fellow Historical Researcher,
…Editor-in-Chief,
…Head Cheerleader,
—and Dearest Love

ACKNOWLEDGEMENTS

Julie Brinckloe–Cover Design
Josephine Brinckloe–Background Painting
Olivia Yates–Final Proofreading and Editing

CHAPTER 1

It was the deep of night, and the chill mists shrouding the rugged hills showed ghostly white in the waning moonlight. The far valley was a dark slash in the gloom, and to the west stood the ruined holy place of Dond, where the spirits walked, stark against the brooding clouds.

Inside Menevia Castle, old Sir Gruwent paced restless as a lion, his thoughts directed upward, to the birthing chamber above, where frail Queen Gwenwed lay waiting in travail. The loyal knight had waited through two devastating miscarriages and the delicate Queen's problem in conceiving or carrying to term, and thus his prayers had grown all the more desperate for an heir to the throne of Dyfed Gwlad. At the Great Hall hearth, Atheurin, the King's Bard, shared the long emotional vigil. The scramas axe in his belt seemed incongruous on one so slender, but a closer look at Atheurin bespoke a deep reservoir of inner resolve.

"Pray Lug a fair and strong prince be born tonight!" Gruwent intoned the wish gravely, but his husky tone betrayed his pent-up emotion.

"There will be no prince." Atheurin spoke in the softest whisper. If the old Seneschal heard, he gave no sign.

Of a sudden, one of the caethwas messengers burst into the Great Hall, atremble with excitement, causing the torchlights to flicker in his wake. "O Sire," he gabbled, "the King prays you attend him above!" The Seneschal and Bard exchanged hasty glances, then turned as one and followed the slave up the worn stone stairs. At the top King Llywarch awaited them, standing in the chamber door with his noble head cast down as if scarcely noting their arrival. The King's hair, cut in a Saxon fringe, showed but a hint of silver. He stood fully as tall as the cadaverous Gruwent, but nigh onto threescore winters had failed to diminish his robust frame.

"Sire!" cried the Seneschal, unable to contain his fretting. "Have we a prince at last?"

The King acknowledged the anxious question with a fleeting ghost of a smile. "Nay, my old friend," he said scarce above a whisper. "The Queen has birthed a lass."

For a moment it seemed he would say more, but the moment passed in silence. Both courtiers understood well his intense disappointment at the dashing of his hopes for a gallant young prince to bear Menevia's scarlet banner and bring back the days of its glory. Both knew how he had longed for an heir who might be able to relieve Dyfed's people of the twin scourges of hunger and pestilence, as he had labored unsuccessfully to do. At last Llywarch spoke again, gravely but with unmistakable pride. "Her Ladyship has given our land a Princess," he told them. In his mind's eye he saw the drawn face of his Queen, and his countenance softened with affection, and with regret and sorrow for her, for himself, and for his kingdom.

But if the King and Gruwent were disappointed that the Queen had delivered herself of a girl-child, the bard Atheurin, though showing not a hint of his inner thoughts, was strangely silent amid the groundswell of commiseration throughout the Court.

The supper King Llywarch served when Bishop Asser came to perform the baptism was a special occasion, for it was his beloved Queen's first appearance since the birthing. With just the three plus Gruwent at table, the lovely Gwenwed had no need to retire whilst the men savored their mead before the crackling fire.

"I chatter excessively, Milady," apologized the Bishop when there came a break in the conversation. "Pray tell me of the little lass we bring to grace in the morn."

Queen Gwenwed was far too slender, and her color unnaturally high, but she was a woman of striking beauty. Her dark lustrous hair was worn in a simple style, and her soft brown eyes were warm and honey-liquid in the firelight. On her right hand glistened the brilliant signet ring Llywarch had placed there many years before in Eire, from whence he stole her after she had stolen his heart. Her face grew radiant as she replied. "Wait until you see her hair, Grace! It must be a gift from her lovely grandmother in Meath, whose fiery red tresses were my Sire's greatest pride."

The Bishop chuckled at the thought. "And what must we name your fiery wee Irish Colleen, then?"

The Queen frowned. "I seek a name to keep alive the memory of my bonny home, on a grassy mount in County Meath," she said, "but try as I will, none comes to mind."

"A castle on a hill, is it?" asked the Bishop, seeking to be helpful. "Then would you fancy such an old Celtic name as Y Foel Famau—Hill of the Mothers? Or perhaps the name of your ancestral mount, Milady?"

The Queen laughed with delight, brightening the room with her happy smile. "Why bless you, your Grace. Tara! Tara Hill. A beautiful place it was, and in sooth a lovely name for the Princess."

The King stood on the parapet with his Seneschal the next morn, watching Asser's caravan wend its way back to Saint David. Both men stood in reflective silence, until Llywarch broke their meditations with a question. "Think you our land is secure from attack, old friend?"

Gruwent searched his memory. Long ere his time, Vikings had harried the Cymri coast, but after Rhodri became High King and pressed all the minor kingdoms to act in concert, those depredations dropped to bearable level. He hesitated to speak, lest he remind Llywarch of his now subordinate status under Rhodri's suzerainty.

"You credit Rhodri's unifying the Cymri kinglets with holding the pirates at bay," said the King perceptively. "It is not the Vikings I fear, but Alfred."

Gruwent pondered the matter. Alfred was a powerful Saxon king, stopping the Danes at Wilton, and withstanding their incursions ever since, but they remained a dangerous foe. "Surely the Danelaw keeps Alfred busy, Sire," he said. "Time enow to fret when the Danes are a threat no more."

"And that time may be nigh." Llywarch sighed. "The Danes came as Norse warriors, but they are become farmers and husbandmen, preoccupied with tending their own crops and flocks. Any day I look for the two sides to come to terms, leaving Alfred free to strike at us."

Llywarch's words were ominously prophetic, for scarce a week later the High King's courier brought word that at Wedmore the Danish jarls had sworn allegience to Saxony.

During his years in the stables, Mathias had ridden many a child at his pommel, but there came a day his red-veined face glowed with pride at taking the little princess on her first ride. As always, Mathias had on worn leather britches exuding an unmistakable paddock aroma, one that always would evoke in Tara bittersweet memories of her youthful days at Menevia Castle.

"The wee Princess will make a bonny hunter, Sire," he reported. "Best we get her a steed of her own."

"Time enough when she can mount unaided," said the King. "She can scarce walk yet." But when they turned homeward he took her up on Bruh, and father and child shared the first of their rides together.

Llywarch took Tara thus many a morning thereafter, though astride a gentler mount than his stallion. Queen Gwenwed was sorely torn, sensing that their growing camaraderie would help the King accept Tara as his heir, but haunted by the constant danger of mishap.

There came a morning when Tara arrived at the stables to find Sire waiting. "We've a surprise for you, Milady," he beamed. She saw at once what was different. In place of the usual placid palfrey, their steed was Bruh, his big grey stallion. "Bruh!" she cried, her eyes alight. "We're riding Bruh!"

At that moment Llywarch heard a rising hubbub from the Castle, and looked up to see flames streaming from the storeroom. Dropping Bruh's halter, he raced up the hill. Tara, forgot in the confusion, was uncertain what to do, finally turning to run on stumbling baby feet down the road toward the town. Snorting, Bruh trotted after her.

The normally bustling Moot was deserted. The village women had shepherded their bairns into their cottages, and the men were running in from the fields with staves and pitchforks. In the square stood a mastiff, stiff-legged, a stream of saliva drooling from its open mouth. Catching sight of the little girl, it moved uncertainly in her direction. As she turned back in alarm, the beast snarled ominously and began to run unsteadily after her.

"Bruh!" she screamed in terror. Tripping on the path up from the Moot, she sprawled in the dirt. The great stallion's ears pricked up, all senses alert. The babel tickled in its memory the battle sounds of long-forgot border campaigns, and Tara's panicked cry galvanized it to action. Too late the rabid dog sensed the deadly hooves slashing above it. The stallion reared up, snorting its angry battle cry, and lashed out again and again until naught remained in the dirt save mangled flesh and bones.

The villagers poured forth, and eagerly escorted horse and child up to the castle. They were happy and excited, but there was wonder in their faces, and many crossed themselves or made the old signs. Someone struck up the song of Taliesin, who tamed the wild beasts, and the rest took up the ballad as best they knew.

"And what is your explanation then, my Lord?" asked Gwenwed gently when the two were alone at last.

"That we were mightily blessed by good fortune, that is all."

"Might it be that the gods save her for a high purpose?" she ventured, pressing him to look closer at the fateful event.

Llywarch threw up his arms in exasperation. "I know not if such purpose there be! Nor do you. I do know she is too active for her years, and we are most fortunate that she escaped unscathed." But an unanswered question—just what strange influence had made him select Bruh for the ride that fateful day?—impelled him to summon Atheurin.

"My Lord," announced the Bard in his low musical voice, "I have sought guidance at the sacred burial mound, consulting the Vates. I summoned up Bodb the foul raven goddess, who plotted to take the princess but was foiled, and the tarbfeis of the great white bull was shown to me. There are the signs that this babe has the flaithes power, which comes but once in an hundred years. She may have the vaunted female force without which no reign may prosper." He hesitated a moment, his words hanging in the air, then looked off at some invisible place in the distance and spoke once more. "She has been spared by the gods for the high cause she is destined to serve one day."

Atheurin stopped then, and walked to the center table, placing an object before the King. "This is yours, Milord, to hold in trust for the Princess—the golden Torc of Queenship which will go around her neck one day. It appeared before me on the altar slab in the sacred cromlech of the Old Ones, amid the Standing Stones. It is a holy relic of the ancient Druidic gods, older than any man may know." He bowed low and turned away from the King. Without waiting for dismissal, he walked to the far door of the chamber and was gone.

Llywarch wondered if his fears of the Saxon King, Alfred, were a misreading, since naught had transpired to support suspicion of Saxon invasion plans. Almost naught, that is. There had been strange happenings: a goatherd found on Caldey Isle with his throat cut...a fisher boat lost off Skomer Isle without trace on a fair day...Saxon lion-head ships sighted thrice off Saint Gowan's Head...and outlaws with a wild tale of soldiers sprung from the sea to slay half their number.

Could such small things mean Saxon spying? Llywarch thought to tell the High King of his fears, but there was scant real evidence and he refused to appear as a frighted woman—until there occurred an event to end all doubt.

The Eorl of Tenby, whose cantref lay in the coastal lowland, reported strange beasts marauding his flocks and terrifying his shepherds, and called on Llywarch for aid. Llywarch summoned Tellicho, Captain of the Guard and sometime military strategist, for a talk.

The squat, powerfully-built guard captain wore a leather byrnie denoting his office, cross gartered hose, an undyed mantle showing the outline of his sword scabbard beneath, and on his bullet head the iron-framed helmet without which he was never seen. When he heard Tenby's concerns, he asked to take a detachment to the Eorl's cantref and ferret out the problem.

On their arrival, the distraught Eorl poured out a confused account. "So you see, Captain," he summed up, "strange happenings are afoot. It's more than mongrel dogs or wolves, sure!"

"And what else could they be, Eorl Tenby?" asked Tellicho wryly. "What other animal can drag off a full-grown sheep? Unless you think outlaws are pilfering your flocks."

"Nay, Captain, their outlandish tracks are not human. Beasts they be, but not of this world."

When Tellicho was in the presence of nonsense, his voice became a bass rumble. It became so now. "Not of this world, Eorl? Your flock is being stripped by werewolves?" He had a shrewd idea what could be happening, so late that afternoon he led his force stealthily out onto the moors, and at dawn they were back, troopers prodding along two dispirited prisoners.

"What we have here," Tellicho told the Eorl, "is a Saxon attempt to make you think your coastland is bewitched. The howls you heard were blasts from a conch shell. We surprised five intruders, and contrived to keep these two of them alive." He drew from his pouch two crude boots with odd iron triangles strapped to their soles. "Here, Eorl, are your werewolf tracks."

"Saxons, by Lug! I can scarce credit it!" A thought hit the Eorl. "Does this mean they plan to invade Tenby?"

"I'll be bound they reck fear will chase shepherds away from the coast. But their plans are not for a Captain of the Guard to ponder. I misdoubt the High King will hear of it soon enow."

Tellicho's news came as less than a total surprise to Llywarch. "This is a key to Alfred's strategy," he told Gruwent. "He will invade along the south coast, near Tenby."

"But why chase lowly shepherds off? They cannot stem an invasion."

"It is what they see, not what they do. He hopes for a surprise landing at Tenby. That was how he bested the Dane, when they thought him mired in the bogs. Tellicho must leave for Brecon as soon as may be and lay this before Rhodri." In the event, Llywarch's message was not dispatched. The next day brought an exhausted courier from the High Court, bidding all the kings assemble urgently in Brecon, to plan defense of the realm against King Alfred of Wessex, who was suspected of readying a massive attack on Cymru.

"Which route will you take to Brecon, Sire?" asked Gruwent.

"Tellicho would have me take horse to Loughor where we meet Rhodri's escort, but I favor taking ship, not pounding my aging bones on a long overland trek in the saddle."

"The risk of pirates is ever-present. I hold with the Guard Captain."

"When you say 'pirates' have you in mind real pirates, or Saxon spies mumming as pirates?"

"Saxon pirates, Sire. If you credit Tellicho's prisoners, Saxons are the only pirates in the Channel."

"Then as Saxons they dare not risk discovery, lest we divine their intentions. We have naught to fear from Saxon seamen, old man. We go by sea to Loughor." The King turned to leave, but a thought struck him. "No word of this to the Queen, mind. Let her believe we take horse, as must all the Court believe—and the Saxons."

But even news of a land trip terrified the Queen, to the point that she summoned Atheurin. "I would speak of the King's trip," she began, the moment he entered the bower. "Have you read the augers? Will they have a safe journey?"

"Aye, my Queen. The little princess will bring him safe home."

"Tara? How may she keep him safe? A babe of four cannot abide a hard three-day ride!"

"The King will go by sea. He must go by sea."

The Queen's eyes widened in alarm, and she was about to question Atheurin further when Llywarch entered. He stopped short in surprise. "What is afoot Lady, to bring the Bard hence?" He did not look entirely pleased.

"Atheurin says Tara must accompany you to Brecon, Milord."

"You would have our little lass endure three long days in saddle?"

"Atheurin says you needs must go by sea," she replied in a tremulous voice. "Though it be a hazardous venture."

Llywarch did not hide his dismay. How had they caught wind of his secret plans? "You spoke with Gruwent, then?" he demanded.

Of a sudden all was clear to Gwenwed. He was going by sea, but had kept it from her lest she worry. Best I let him think I know, she decided. "I knew you would go by sea—and Tara must be your talisman."

"I will not take the child!" Llywarch looked his outrage.

To that his Queen had an unanswerable argument. "My King, is it not your duty to present an heir at the High Court so soon as the heir be old enow for presenting? Have you not waited overlong already? Rhodri will not take it lightly if your retinue arrives without the heir. Think you not that would be a grievous slight?"

"What? But she is not my..." He broke off short, as the rightness of the Queen's words struck home. Tara was in sooth his heir—mayhap the only heir he would have. By long-established custom, failure to present her now would be a near unpardonable rudeness, and more.

"Very well, Milady...you have cobbled up an unanswerable argument. We will take Tara, and we will proceed by sea." He smiled ironically. "The Princess shall keep us all from harm."

The captured Danish longboat glided smoothly over the sheltered waters of Milford Haven, but when they rounded Saint Gowan's Head into the Hafren Channel the craft heeled and began to drive through the heightened waves. The lively breeze ruffled Tara's hair, the sun tinting her red curls with fiery gold, and the wave-tops glinted like sparkling jewels. But the King and his sailing master had no eyes for beauty. They were straining to make out a strange craft on the horizon astern.

"I ken she's made us out, Sire," said the sailing master. "Her bearing does not change. And by her sail she's a Northman, or very like."

"Can you stay ahead of her?"

"Nay, your Majesty, not in these light airs. She be a 16-oar craft to our eight."

"How far off does Tenby lie, then?"

"Mayhap three hours—but they'll be on us afore that, give t'wind holds light. In a stiff blow we could keep ahead."

The pursuing sail lifted all too swiftly above the horizon. His eyes desperately sweeping the empty expanse of sea ahead, Llywarch made out an indistinct shape through the haze. "Aye, Sire," said the sailing master to his unspoken question. "Yon's the Caldey Isle."

"Think you we can reach it before the Northman?"

The sailing master squinted aft, then ahead. "Happen we can, your Majesty, but naught's there save shepherds."

"Better than being o'ertook at sea. Our men are fine soldiers, and we can put up a better fight on shore." And have a better chance to hide Tara away in some rude cave. "Give off trying for Tenby. Head for Caldey."

Their pursuer gained inexorably. Now bossed Norse shields loomed up above the waves, lashed to the gunwales. Caldey Isle was growing in size, but with maddening slowness.

The King scanned the horizon desperately for any hint of wind, but could see naught save a small dark cloud over the far shore. It struck him that it had not been there when first he looked, and he stared fixedly at it, willing it to grow and to head their way, but it did not change.

The sailing master called him to look aft again. "She be a Skuldelev boat, Sire," he announced grimly. "She be near double our size, and I wight she carries a full cargo of men."

"So if she overtakes us, then we have no chance?"

"Nay, Sire. No chance."

Llywarch peered again at the cloud. It was spreading and darkening, and he stared with deadly intensity at it. Suddenly a dash of spray blew across his face. O Teutates, he prayed, bring us the wind!

The sailing master took his arm, forgetting he laid hands on a king. "Look Sire," he shouted.

In the distance, close to the shore, appeared a line of darker water, breaking up the sun's reflections. As he watched, the dark line began marching across the water toward their craft.

"We'll get it afore the Northman, Sire," cried the sailing master, a look of vast relief on his seamed face. "We'll get a lift toward the Caldeys that the Northman won't feel for a time."

The wind line was very close now, and the sail began to flutter. Suddenly the squall hit, and the boat heeled under the blow until it lay nearly on its beam ends. For a moment it hung there motionless, then righted somewhat and came alive, driving powerfully through the waves.

"She be a fair beauty of a sailor," shouted the sailing master exultantly. "We have t'wind and our Northman's got none!"

As they came abreast of the forbidding rocky bluff of Caldey Isle, and the steersman put the great steering oar down to tack into the island's lee, the King looked back. The wind was nearing gale strength now, and hauling around to the east. As he watched in wonder, the Viking craft slowly turned away, until only its beaked stern could be seen.

"She must run downwind before t'blow to save herself!" The sailing master's shout rose exultantly over the howling of the wind. "She'll founder else!"

Llywarch and Tara stood together on a red sandstone promontory while lookouts scanned the horizon around. The pursuer was not in sight. The wind was moderating, and veering back around—the wind the gods had called up to save them. Was it indeed a godly intervention, he wondered, or was it blind fortune?

The sailing master stood before him, his face shining as if he had witnessed a miracle. "The ship can get underway again, Sire," he said. "The wind be fair for Tenby, and for Loughor as well, though t'would be chancy to head for Loughor with the Northman about."

Llywarch felt a sudden inexplicable surge of confidence. "Underway, then," he ordered. "Make for Loughor."

As the longboat surged along under the fair wind for Loughor, Llywarch was struck by the scene that he recalled only now. In the heat of the chase it had not registered on his overtaxed brain, but thinking back, he saw again Tara's face when the wind first struck with full force and heeled the ship over until its lee rail was awash. She had been standing straight and tall, looking ahead as if savoring the wind and spray ahead. Her expression had been fearless. No, not quite fearless, rather calm, as though she welcomed the tempest as a friend.

And she had been laughing.

CHAPTER 2

It was dark when the dim lights of the landing stage came into view through the mists, and Llywarch's storm-drenched coterie crossed the drawbridge into the old fortress of Loughor.

"Od's blood, but you be a stout seaman," said King Brechnor of Ystrad Towy who would be joining forces with him for the final leg of the trip. "The Dane's storm-god Thor, that rules the raging seas, took you into his arms this foul day! Let us lift a toast to him."

Llywarch wearily raised his flagon, but with his own unspoke toast: I drink to Atheurin, he thought—and to Princess Tara.

The escort from the High Court arrived silent and preoccupied. "There has been a grievous development, Milords," announced the captain solemnly. "The High King is dead."

"Dead?" Brechnor and Llywarch spoke nearly as one. "And his successor?" asked Brechnor after a moment of silence. "Belike his son, Cadell?"

"Prince Cadell of Morgannwg succeeds him, Sire. The funeral and coronation ceremony takes place three days hence."

"We'll have a busy time," murmured Brechnor. "Best we get what sleep we can tonight."

Llywarch spoke little at supper, for wondering whether young Cadell could cope with the Saxon threat. These were uncertain times for an untried leader. The gods weave their webs, he mused, and kings can but puzzle out through the impenetrable mists what part they play, and hope their actions at least do not worsen the defense of the realm.

Brechnor was king of Dyfed's neighboring glwad, Ystrad Towy, and welcomed the chance to talk with his old friend as they rode along the ill-kept trail to Brecon. "Young Cadell is the older son, I believe," he stated, "so there's little choice of heir."

"Has he experience in the field?"

"He was garrisoned on Rhwng Gwy a Hafron's border, but in recent years that would mean scarce more than gaming and wenching. If he has other experience, I've heard naught of it."

"It comes to me that Cadell has children. What are they?"

"Two boys, unlike as morn and eve. The elder, Clydog, near twelve years and a spawn of the devil. The younger, Hywel, seven or so and a gentle lad. And there's the Lady Meuriga."

"So Clydog will be Cadell's heir one day, for good or ill. How is he devil's spawn?"

"He's squat and overfed, with scarce any neck. And the things he does! One morn he dropped Hywel's pup in scalded water, and laughed to see the poor dead brute they fished out. Another time he slipped a poison snake in his nurse's pallet, and the poor crone died of a fit."

"And one day he succeeds to the Kingship."

"Aye, but that lies in the future. A matter more of the moment is his betrothal."

"What hapless maid would promise to so misbegotten a beast?"

"Some wretched lass must soon, once Cadell dons the crown."

I will guard Tara closely, lest he try his devilish tricks on her, thought Llywarch grimly.

When they reached the Brecon Keep, an elderly knight hobbled stiffly out to greet them. "You find us somewhat at odds," he said, in an old man's voice. "But we do our best. Let me show you to your chambers. Prince Cadell awaits you in the Great Hall when you are ready."

The Great Hall of Glamorgan Castle was a vast chamber. Behind the King's place was a huge arched fireplace containing a crackling file. Over it was the Glamorgan Tapestry, Macsen Wledeg bravely holding aloft the red dragon banner, and on each side an alcove for gleemen and jongleurs. The Hall was alive with a confused cacophony of talk.

Llywarch proceeded straight toward the Uwch Cyntedd where Cadell stood. "Greetings, Sir Prince," he said. "I am Llywarch of Dyfed."

Cadell, sober of mien, extended his hand warmly. Diagonally across his dark tunic was a black mourning sash. The throne chair beside him held Rhodri's ceremonial sword and buckler, and in a velvet-lined box on the table gleamed the jewelled crown of Cymru.

"You were good to be with us on this occasion, Sir King. I play host to a sad occasion, but one bright spot is the chance to welcome our loyal friends and subjects."

"I was your Sire's staunch supporter in all he did," said Llywarch gravely. "And I am proud to swear allegiance to his son, and hold to him as liege lord and suzerain." He took the Prince's hand and solemnly touched the big signet ring to his lips.

Tara reminded him of her presence with a tug at his tunic. "My Lord," he said in some confusion, "I beg leave to present my heir, the Princess Tara."

From his great height, Cadell looked down at her in surprise. "Why, what a bonny lass you be, Tara. Welcome to Brecon, Milady."

Llywarch looked proudly down at her. "Will you say a greeting, Tara?"

Tara made a careful curtsy. "I am glad you asked us to sup with you, King," she said in a firm voice. "Is it time to eat?"

Llywarch spoke over the general laughter. "Nay, Tara, you will not be eating with us. The handmaiden will take you to sup in our chambers."

"Not so," said Cadell at once. "Not after she does us the honor to travel so far for our crowning. She must join us all here, in the Great Hall." With a sweep of his bejeweled hand he indicated a nearby table, gallantly escorted her there, and saw a place set to accommodate her.

Llywarch watched, at a loss for words. From an adult, a remark such as hers would be rude and coarse, but Tara made it sound unrehearsed and natural. In fact, he concluded, just right. Whence comes her unconscious gift of understanding, he wondered. How can so small a babe, in her innocence, have this gift of knowing? Could Gwenwed have the right of it? Could the gods indeed hold her special? His brow furrowed as he tussled with this foreign thought.

From the long head table, Llywarch could make out Tara at her place, sitting so confidently erect, devoting herself happily to the special supper Cadell had commanded. He was surprised and pleased at her orderly manners. Who may her seatmates be, he wondered. On the near side sat a young maiden of nine or ten years, doubtless the young princess, who seemed to enjoy Tara, for she laughed frequently as they talked. Tara's body masked his view of her other seatmate, until she threw back her head in laughter and Llywarch realized with a sudden sinking feeling just who it was.

Prince Clydog was in foul humor. He had objected to donning court garb, slapping his nurse constantly as she essayed to dress him. It had taken two stout squires to drag him from his arboretum, one actually twisting his ear painfully to move him along. And when he reached the Hall, they brought him at once to his father, which prevented him from showing his displeasure as openly as he wished. Now he must sit next to this abominable slip of a girl, who not only caused his place to be pushed down to make room but had been served with special food while he had to wait. And when he told her how rude she was to sup before he was served she paid him no heed. Suddenly he thought how he could get even, and slyly undid his pouch to withdraw what he'd hid in there for safekeeping when the squires laid hands on him.

Llywarch was just setting down his mead flagon when his eye was caught by a disturbance erupting at Tara's nearby table, and was dismayed to see her standing on her chair and slapping at her tablemate. Slapping Prince Clydog! An instant later, menials swarmed around the group and he could see no more of what was happening. He sprang up, crimsoning in embarrassment.

Cadell reached the scene first, and snatched up the shrieking Clydog. The boy struggled to pull free, his face contorted with rage, but the Prince shook him violently until he quieted. "Go to your chamber at once," he commanded. "I'll see to you later!" He handed Clydog over to an attending squire, and turned away. Llywarch attempted vainly to speak with Cadell, but he stomped angrily back to the head table. As Clydog was dragged protestingly out, he directed at Tara a venomous look that left Llywarch with a sharp thrust of unease.

"It was that boy's fault, Sire," insisted Tara, when they were back in their chamber. "He started it!"

"What did he do, lass?"

"He put a little green snake on my plate—right atop my loin!" She looked at her Sire indignantly, as if for support. "He was mean, Sire!"

By the gods, thought Llywarch in horror—a snake! He recalled Brechnor's dire tale of Clydog's poisoned nurse. "It didn't bite, did it?" he demanded urgently. "Did it bite at all?"

"O no, Sire, it wasn't but a wee snake. It didn't know how to bite yet. Mathias found me one just like it in the wood."

"What did you do then, lass? Why were you standing up on your chair? Did he hurt you?"

"I picked it up to put it over on his plate. Then he got up, so I got up. Then he hit me, so I hit him, and the snake fell out of my hand and dropped down inside his tunic."

"You tried to drop it down his tunic? Think now, Tara!" He knew not whether to laugh or groan. He took her on his lap and held her close. Would that Gwenwed were here!

"O no, Sire! It fell when I slapped him. It was his fault, cos he hit me on the head first."

"Yes, Princess," said her father resignedly. "Mayhap it was at that." And let's hope Cadell thinks the same, he prayed.

Tara was not finished. "Then he yelled, and all the Sires laughed, so I laughed too. And that's all that happened, Sire—just the snake and then hitting me."

And more than enow, said her father to himself. Of any she might have fought with, it had to be that foul creature. What the outcome would be only Lug could know, but naught good could come from it.

It was well for the King's peace of mind that he could not foresee the unfortunate chain of events this night had set in motion—events destined to change their lives profoundly.

Picking the little princess up in his arms, he hugged her and tucked her gently into her pallet. Then he retired to his own, and put his mind resolutely to the pressing problem of how to defend against the inevitable invasion of Cymru by the mighty Alfred of Wessex.

The coronation was held in the cloistered chapel of Saint Augustine, and the court officials and visiting notables fell silent as the interminable service of Dedication to Kingship dragged out. Prince Cadell's long white robe was heavily brocaded in gold, and about his neck was a massive torc of linked golden medallions. Over his shoulder was draped a scarlet robe emblazoned with the red Cymru dragon, and empurpled pennons hung from his jewelled scabbard. His neatly coiffed head was bare, awaiting the crown.

The Archbishop finished at last, and Cadell of Morgannwg was crowned High King of Cymru. The torches were snuffed and the nuns of Saint Catwg began the tuneless dirge of hope and lament for Rhodri's soul. Slowly the funerary chariot was trundled in before the altar.

In the hush that followed, Llywarch thought back to the accession of Rhodri as first High King of Cymru. Feelings had run high over bending the knee to a distant Lord, but Cymru was stronger for the union he imposed so forcefully, and it was essential now with Alfred poised to attack. Even this moment Saxon levies could be loading baggage trains, buckling mail coats and sharpening lances to strike Cymru, whilst they sat unready, busy with these ceremonies.

Next morning the Council was in session scarce an hour when divisions erupted. The south gwlads of Dyfed, Ystrad Towy, Gower, Morgannwg and Gwent, reckoned the danger coming from across the Hafren Channel or the Saefern, while the northern gwlads of Powys, Gwynedh and Rhung Gea a Hafren saw it much higher up, from Mercia. These differences, in the main from self-interest, could split them apart, and Cadell was no Rhodri, to knock heads together.

Tempers were flaring, with reason a casualty, when Cadell rose to call for silence. "Let us all have done, and foregather in the Armory for ale," he said quietly. At the Armory, Llywarch joined a group of southern nobles.

"The northern kings count themselves proof against thrusts from the south," Brechnor was saying. "They see us blunting the attack whilst they save their strength for their own purposes."

"And mayhap any churl could guess those purposes," said the fiery Prince of Gwent. "We lie occupied and weakened from the Saxon thrust, and they make free to pillage our borders!"

"You read what is not there, Geoffrel," said Llywarch quietly. "It shows plain on Liathan's face when he schemes. Their lands are far from Chippenham, and they see not the peril we do."

"They think these be but outlaw forays," said Brechnor. "If we handed them the spies Llywarch nabbed at Tenby, they'd sense the danger themselves and be as eager as are we."

Discussions went on around the Armory into the night, naught settled but tempers cooling and giving reason more sway, until the lateness of the hour made an end, and the conferees retired to their chambers.

Llywarch was settled into his pallet when there came a pounding at his door. It was Tellicho, dog-tired and dusty from the trail. His garments were stained with sweat and his face drooped with fatigue, but his eyes were alert with suppressed tension, and Llywarch's stomach knotted with unease.

"God's wounds, Tellicho, you're dead spent! What ill tidings drag you to Brecon? Take seat, man! Unbuckle your arms. You look but half alive."

He led the protesting Captain to a bench and saw him well seated, his ministrations likely a subconscious effort to put off hearing urgent tidings he had little wish to entertain. But Tellicho refused to settle back until his message was delivered. "We have disturbing news from Saint David, from the Cathedral. I rode to tell you before the news reaches the new High King."

Saint David? The Cathedral? What tidings from there could affront the High King—or could impel Tellicho to ride day and night? "What of the Cathedral?" he demanded.

"Bishop Asser has left Dyfed gwlad. He has left Cymru. He has gone over to Alfred—defected to the Saxons!"

Stunned at the bitter news, Llywarch sank back heavily into his seat. Asser gone? The man he'd trust with his life, a turncoat traitor? "No! I credit it not! You must have heard amiss."

"I heard it aright, Sire. He is gone. His messenger came with the tidings. No mistake."

"But Bishop Asser is no man to go over to the enemy. He has no cause to leave us." Cause? He must have had a compelling motive to take this incredible step. "What reason did he give?"

"None he gave to us, Sire. But I waited not to pettifog with the friar he sent. I came at once, lest news reach the High King's ears first."

The High King's ears? Yes—his spies would be agallop to report. He'd waken with the news. And the King of Dyfed's first dealing with his new suzerain would be the stirring of this devil's brew of underhanded dealing with the Saxon.

High treason!

Cadell started the second day's meeting speaking of yesterday's differences, urging all the Council to agree that any Saxon drive must come from the south. He enumerated Alfred's forces and analyzed how an experienced commander must deploy them. Had Llywarch not been so preoccupied, Cadell's calm grasp of the situation would have impressed him. If Cadell had heard aught of Asser's perfidy, he gave no sign. He led the discussion skillfully on, in a catalog of Saxon strengths and weaknesses, analyzing the forces available to Cymru gwlad by gwlad, setting forth the contribution each could make, and outlining so comprehensive a defense strategy that Llywarch almost forgot his fears in concentrating on the stern business at hand.

"Then we agree that the Saefern is key to Alfred's invasion plans. Since he's not like to venture as far from his base as Mercia, he must needs cross the Saefern or the Hafren to have at us. Our task, then, is to learn when any force more than garrison strength crosses, and to strike whilst his army is in the turmoil of a water passage. He'll not guess we would venture into his own demesne to attack, for he thinks the Cymri fear him too much.

He paused for comments, and hearing none went on. "We must not singe his beard by snapping at the fringes of his patrols, lest we stir up the invasion we seek to prevent. We need no hotheads. But the future of the realm demands that we stand firm against any real attack."

It was time now to speak of the happenings at Tenby. "Milord," began Llywarch, "I would speak of what we uncovered on Carmarthan Bay." He related the strange tale of the Saxon spies Tellicho had taken. "My thought is that we make as if deceived, and leave off tending flocks near the moors for a time, whilst mounting a secret force there. If Brechnor joins me as one, we'll throw Alfred back into the sea, and at least blunt one claw of his pincers."

The talk turned then to the other claw, where the bulk of Alfred's forces might deploy on the eve of any invasion. We're of one mind now, at least for a time, thought Llywarch with satisfaction. Let us hope these weighty matters may hold Cadell's full attention.

But in this hope he was soon to be disappointed. No messenger approached Cadell during the meeting, but at its end he raised his hand for attention. "I must needs tell you of grave tidings that have just come to our ears. The high prelate of Dyfed Gwlad, Bishop Asser, has treacherously deserted to Alfred."

There was utter silence in the chamber. Llywarch looked stonily about him, but all eyes were averted and none met his.

"I decree this Asser is a traitor to the realm, and charge all my subjects to treat him as enemy." Cadell let his solemn words hang in the air for a time. Then he broke the tension by changing his manner, and spoke jovially. "And now we have tarried too long. Hie we to the Armory, and let us broach a cask to the health of the realm."

Llywarch felt eyes on him now, privately assessing his reaction to the High King's grim proclamation. Ignoring their glances, he brushed past them to the head place and Cadell.

"The tidings came to me late in the night, Sire," he explained. "I've scarce had the time nor wit to digest them and puzzle out the why of it. No hint did I have of any such move in the offing."

"I'm sure you could not have," said Cadell dryly. "There can be but one reason for such base treachery. Alfred made Asser an offer so tempting he had no further thought for Cymru."

"But he was ever a good and loyal friend! Cymru was his land, as good as if he had been born Cymri."

"Ah, but he was not born Cymri, was he? He came to you from Saxony, and we see now what master he served, e'en as he snaked his way into your counsels and your trust."

"Can you think all was plotted and foreseen in his mind ere ever he came to Dyfed?" Cadell's cold accusation echoed Brechnor's thoughts, and yea, even those of his own guard Captain, but Llywarch could not read it so unchallenged. "Sire, I knew Asser close over the years, and he was ever a good and honest friend. I cannot credit so base a scheming."

"Better you start to credit it, then." There was scant friendliness in Cadell's tone. "You'd do well, my King, to disavow this turncoat at once, lest his evil deeds cast blight on you as well."

With what seemed a conscious effort, he changed his tone. "This talk takes a direction that does disservice to the twain of us. I have no slightest question of your loyal devotion to Cymru. We must reck how others read your position, what we must do to end the breach. All must read a positive signal of my confidence in you." His look suddenly was warm. "Not only would I retain your friendship, but I cannot do without your strong hand when Alfred lands at Tenby."

"Sire," said Llywarch awkwardly, "my gratitude…"

Cadell raised his hand impatiently. "No stiff thanks. Cymru has need of you. But we must conjure up an earnest of my support so strong none here can mistake it."

Llywarch was uncertain what response to make. For a moment Cadell was silent, his foot tapping impatiently as he considered the problem. Suddenly his face cleared and he spoke.

"I have it. My eldest son and my heir is overdue to announce his betrothal, and whilst many young maids have been considered, none is yet selected." He looked speculatively at Llywarch. "What say you to an announcement that can leave none in doubt of the strength of our relationship?"

"And that announcement, Sire?" Llywarch hoped he was wrong about Cadell's meaning.

"Say we go now to the Armory, where I proclaim to the assembly that Prince Clydog of Brycheinoig hereby is affianced to the lovely young Princess Tara map Llywarch of Dyfed." He paused to look at Llywarch, with a disturbing hint of challenge in his eyes.

Great Lug, thought Llywarch in horror, his worst suspicions realized—not Clydog! Just the thought of his bonny little lass sentenced to marry that accursed monster was near more than he could stomach. I must reject the offer, however kindly meant, he decided. I will tell Cadell my daughter is promised to the Church. No, no! Not the Church, for that would put me square in league with Asser. Then how if I say she's already promised? But it would be little short of insulting to make such response to this seemingly generous proposal. No, I must tell him straightaway it cannot be, giving no reason. But what, then, when he demands the reason? Then I am left with naught to say but to recite all Brechnor has told me of his accursed son.

And belike be stripped of my lands were I so rash as to respond thus. Nay, far more than rash—naive, and belike disloyal as well. Betrothals are made for purposes of state, to advance the fortunes of a kingdom, to safeguard the realm. Cadell is simply proposing an alliance to strengthen Cymru in its hour of supreme peril, and he looks to me to understand, and to be practical as well. With a bitter sigh, imperfectly hid, Llywarch did what he had to do.

"The Princess Tara is honored, as are all in Dyfed, your Majesty," he replied, keeping his voice calm while writhing within. "For myself, my Queen, and my subjects, we are proud to accept your office."

"Then that's done," said Cadell abruptly. "Now we join the baying hounds who think to scent blood."

The betrothal ceremony was held with unprecedented speed, the very next day, in the Palace Chapel. Llywarch instructed Tara to kneel at the altar beside Prince Clydog, to pay homage to the new High King. To mollify her outrage somewhat, he arranged for the Princess Meuriga to attend her. The Archbishop was urged to expedite things, in view of Tara's tender years, and the shrewd old prelate got her to the altar and away with gratifying speed. The awful compact now was a public commitment, and King Llywarch's honor was pledged to the union of Clydog and Tara—a union he swore privately never would be consummated.

After the ceremony the celebrants repaired to the High King's chambers for the signing. "I have consulted the court Bardi," said Cadell, "and the augers are favorable for the Prince's birthday twelve years hence, when he will be twenty and four." He glanced at Llywarch for agreement, his eyes strangely sympathetic. "What say you?"

Twelve years hence—when Tara would be but sixteen. Twelve years more of freedom, then sentenced to a marriage of horror with this monster. Twelve years to cobble up an escape from this compact—and find it I shall, he vowed. "Certainly, Sire," he replied. "My Tara will have reached her sixteenth year—a suitable time for the marriage."

Sir Oresten brought the book, and both rulers affixed their marks. As Cadell turned to leave, the old knight respectfully bade him bide for a moment. "The Prince and Princess must sign the Compact as well, Majesty," he reminded.

At the moment, Clydog was gorging on sweetmeats brought for the betrothal party, and Tara and Meuriga played with their dolls on the window seat, but Sir Oresten managed to coax them to the table. He tendered a pen to Clydog, indicating where he must make his mark, but the Prince petulantly threw down the pen. "I hate that silly princess," he shouted. "When she's mine I'll lock her in her room and never let her out!" He caught sight of Tara, being brought up in her turn. "Hear that, you ugly little baby?" he screamed, poking a grimy finger at her.

Taken aback by the unexpected assault, Tara clung to her Sire's hand. "What's the matter with him, Sire?" she demanded. "Why does he act so crazy?"

"It's naught, lass. He's excited. He doesn't know what he says."

"Yes I do!" shrieked the red-faced Prince. "She'll be all mine, and I'll do what I say. Do you hear that, you silly little gel?" He thrust his contorted face up against hers, as if to ram the words down her throat.

Cadell, keenly embarrassed, grasped his son's arm so tightly that the boy yelled. "'Fore the gods, Clydog," he growled, "mind your manners, or it's the rod for you, Prince of the Realm or no! You tell Tara you meant not what you said, and give her the betrothal kiss."

Tara caught his last words, and announced firmly, "He can't kiss me! He makes me sick inside me. He can never kiss me! He's crazed!" Swiftly she ran back to the window seat.

Now is my time to speak, thought Llywarch, lest I choke Clydog's fat neck. "We'd best call an end, Sire," he urged. "My little maid of four years knows not what she says. Best let her place her mark another day."

Cadell assented, but added," Though I would avouch your fair little maid knows well enow what she says. You be Lug-blessed with so resolute a princess." The look he turned then on Llywarch was thoughtful, and tinged with sadness. "Mayhap she can mold our Prince into a proper man once they're wed. Now let us call the ceremony well ended. She can sign later."

Courteously he escorted Llywarch to the door. He stopped just outside, and pulled Llywarch aside to speak in private. "We welcome the distinguished lineage of Dyfed Gwlad to pump new blood into the regal line. The gods put heavy tasks on us at times, Llywarch, and we wat not always why they burden us so. Kings have heavy duties of which commoners do not dream. It is part of the warp and woof of royalty, and we cannot shed our responsibilities. We do what we must, for the future of our realm and the sometime happiness of those who entrust us with the crown. If we cannot believe that our own actions preserve the realm, then our very lives are for naught." He took Llywarch's arm. "Let us go now, my friend. There is much to be done, and the gods grant us so little time to accomplish it all."

CHAPTER 3

The wiry welsh pony galloped at breakneck pace, its rider a red-haired lass of eight or nine years who spurred it furiously to coax more speed along the woodland trail. Her long coppery hair, escaped from its binding, streamed uncontrolled behind her, glinting in random golden reflections of the sunlight beams through the leafy mantle overhead. The route was well trod and easy to mark, but on reaching a murky woodland pond the rider abruptly pulled her mount aside to plunge through a tangled mass of tall cattails and disappear from view.

The next moment another rider came along the trail—a well-favored lad of about twelve on a piebald mare, peering closely at the ground. His garb, neater than the shapeless undyed wool garment worn by shepherds and tillers of the soil, marked him a grwda or freeman. Aneoch, in training as squire to Princess Tara and seldom able to control her, this time had been forced to fling a saddle on his old mare and set out in frantic pursuit.

At the pond he noted the trampled reeds, wheeled his horse into the tall grasses, and shortly came upon his kneeling quarry examining something on the ground while her pony foraged for sprigs of grass in the moss. Without looking up, she called to him. "Where were you Aneoch? I thought you'd never get here. Want to see something?"

"The King would take switch to you did I tell how you disobey his orders never to ride out alone. One day you'll get lost and die of hunger, or a beast'll gnaw your bones," he growled. But his interest was piqued at what she'd found. "What is it there?"

"A real unicorn horn. A unicorn's horn is magic. With this horn I can have anything I wish for. Look." She lifted the object for his inspection.

"It's but a cast bit of antler from a rutting deer," he said scornfully. "There's many about."

"You take it then," she said, tossing the horn at him. It flew wide, and she sprang up. "Catch me before I reach the stable." She mounted the pony and was off the way she came, Aneoch scrambling after her.

"Macushla, you will send me to an early tomb, the way you tangle your beautiful hair," said the Queen, smiling affectionately. "Promise you'll take better care next time, or we'll have to put you in braids."

"I promise. Why don't you ever ride out with me, Mama?"

"Oh dear, my riding days are over."

"When I am Queen, I'm going to ride, and wrestle, and sword-fight, and be the best warrior in Dyfed."

The Queen's expression turned serious. "I'm glad you speak of when you are Queen, for you have much to learn first. You must know the old gods and the plans they have for you." She took Tara onto her lap, wincing with the exertion. "Atheurin will tell you of the old Celti gods, Macushla. He hears what they say, and you may have the power also, but the learning will be hard."

Tara made a face. "I learn from Father Padrig, Mama, of Jesu and the Roman Church and Saint Brychan and Saint Tielo. I like the part about Saint Tielo slaying the dragon, and Saint Cybi hiding a goat under his cloak and Saint Bueno praying water from a rock." She made a pout. "Mama, I can't learn any more! When will I ride or play with Anny or ride with Sire in the wood?"

"Atheurin will teach you, out in the woods. Where would the old gods be but in their forest holy places?" Gwenwed lowered her voice and spoke conspiratorily. "But we're not telling Sire, Tara. This is not for men to know."

"List to a story, Princess," said Atheurin on his first day of teaching with the young Princess. He sat on a weathered chestnut log, his deer-skin britches cut off high, a linen tunic open at the throat, his curly hair a glowing mixture of browns and golds. "One day, a great Roman ruler of thirty kings, Macsen Wledeg, saw in a dream a ship of ivory and gold that bore him over the seas to Cymru. He came upon an isle where sat a maiden wearing a white silken vest and a bejewelled frontlet on her hair. But when he would sit with her he awoke, to see only the trees of the forest around him."

"But did he not see her again?" asked Tara in distress.

"He built a fine ship and sailed to Cymru where he found her in Aber Seint, which the Romans called Segontium and we know as Caernarvon. Her name was Elen Luyddog, and he made her queen, and they founded the clan from whence sprang Ambrosius and Myrddig Emrys and Uther Pendragon, and the mighty King Arthur who defeated the Saxon at Banesdown to found the line of the Cymru kings."

Tara was lost in her thoughts on the Queen Elen Luyddog. Am I like her, she wondered. Did she ride out on a great stallion, or stay back in the bower like Mama?

"You think of Elen," said Atheurin.

Tara looked at him in amazement. "How could you know?"

Atheurin laughed. "I knew Elen would be the one to take your fancy. When Macsen Wledeg was killed in battle, Queen Elen took the field against the Picts and drove them back. And at Cym Rosita amid the standing stones she built a church, where the great arm of Dyfed meets the Irish Sea. And all her deeds were done because the gods held her blessed."

Tara's head was too full for speech. She sat quiet, lost in thought of a heroic maiden who combined bewitching beauty and redoubtable valor on the field of combat. So will I be, she vowed.

Another day Atheurin spoke of the old gods. "The three great Celti gods are Esus, Taranis and Teutates. Esus is god of all man, and Taranis the storm-god. And Teutates is many gods in one. And under these are lesser gods. Lug, god of the harvest. The earth herself is a goddess, Matrones. Anu, mother of all gods. Eochaid Ollathair, god of the Otherworld where go slain warriors. Sometimes he is Aed, god of fire and lightning—his flashing sword is the Claidheimh Soluis. And Dond is god of the Underworld; his mound is atop Presceli Mountain. His minion is Bodb, the foul raven goddess, who seeks to take the sick or injured in her icy hands."

"I rode with Sire up the Presceli Hills," said Tara, picking up on the one familiar word. "And he told me the goblin folk live there."

"The Tylwyth Teg," said Atheurin. "They are older than the Celts. Their temple is Evan Cromlech, old when Jesu was a babe. One day you will hear them whispering down in their cromlech, I promise you."

Despite the double burden of instruction from Father Padrig and Atheurin, these days were as happy as Tara would ever know. Alight with the glow of health, she already gave promise of future beauty and resolute bearing. Her lustrous red locks, brushed into burnished gold by her nurse, fell into a long thick mass of tangles in response to her lively movements. Her sunny disposition gave pleasure to all she encountered when she rode out. She explored to the west, where the road to Saint David's wound through the woods to break out on Saint Bride's Bay. North lay Treffgarne Gorge, with the peaks of Castle Rock and Lion Rock lost in the mists. East was the stockaded ringe motte fortress of Llawhaden, with its grassy dry moat she could tumble down. Her favorite was south, to the broad Cleddau River estuary, where fishermen in tarred coracles caught the fighting salmon and sailors brought in silvery hordes of red-eyed herring that the women would slit and gut for smoking in the smouldering oak-chip fires.

Tara and Atheurin were in the glade one morn, when of a sudden he hushed her while he listened. "The gods," he said tensely. "They call you to the sacred place. You must ride out at once!"

"But why?" she asked, bewildered, and frightened at his tone. She dropped her eyes in confusion, and when she looked up an instant later he was gone. Slowly she mounted her pony, not knowing what else to do.

The pony seemed to know the way, for no sooner was Tara up than he started out. At first she could not make out where he headed, but as the trail unfolded she knew—Presceli Top.

Over an hour of steady riding had passed when she felt a sudden need to pull up in a small clearing and dismount, thinking the both of them needed to rest. There were no bird sounds or small rustlings in the undergrowth, and she felt a vague unease at the stillness. Then she heard an alien sound—the hushed voices of men. Cautiously, her heart pounding, she led the pony to the edge of the clearing and peered through the trees.

The horrifying sight filled her with terror. Two rough-clad men were butchering a stag, and as she stared, transfixed, one lashed a severed hindquarter to a big plowhorse.

Poachers!

Poaching was a hanging offense, she knew, and if they caught sight of her…! She stiffened in horror and pulled lightly on the reins to turn and creep away, but at that moment the big farm animal lifted his head and snorted, and her pony whinnied in response. The two men looked up, startled, and caught sight of the terrified girl. One ran furiously toward her, and as she turned to run she caught the lingering sight of the other slashing the meat from the horse and throwing himself astride it.

She wheeled the pony in a panic, and spurred it down the trail. For a minute she thought she'd eluded pursuit, until she heard the big horse pounding behind her.

Her wiry little pony could outrun the ungainly farm animal easily if it were fresh, but it was near played out. She stayed on the trail, praying a miracle. She had a momentary thought to turn into the wood, but abandoned the idea as she realized the poacher would know these parts better than she. Glancing back, she caught sight of him momentarily whenever the trail straightened. He was not gaining yet, but her pony's heaving flanks and gasping breath told her she was lost if no escape path offered. She called for Atheurin in silent prayer, but there was no answer.

The trail turned sharply right, and her desperately darting glance spied a small opening at the bottom of the thorn hedge on the left side. She could not tell if it was a tunnel, or but an alcove too small to hide her. Seizing at the forlorn chance it offered, she slid off the pony and scrambled frantically into the opening just as her pursuer reached the turn.

He must see me! He can see my feet sticking out. He's not fooled. In an instant he'll grab my feet and drag me out!

But miraculously he kept on, chasing the pony he could hear but no longer see. The thorns grasped viciously at her tunic, and she pulled herself free to thrust deeper into the opening. Then of a sudden she was through.

Standing erect and majestic before her eyes in the shaded clearing, three great megaliths towered higher than the war-plumes of a mounted knight. Across them lay the immense capstone, enormous against the clouds. She gathered her courage to approach, and could see between the columns a dark opening into the ground. Tiptoing closer, she peered in, but all was blackness. Atheurin's words came back to her then: "…one day when you are out past the hills you'll hear them whispering down in their cromlech…" Perhaps in her imagination, it seemed she did hear the rustle and whisper of their ancient tongue.

Then, knowing she had naught to fear, she climbed down into the chamber. The sounds, if sounds they had been, ceased. She stood on an earthen floor as smooth as if trod for untold centuries. When her eyes adjusted, she saw before her in the dim light a massive altar fashioned foursquare from one massive block of stone. She laid her hands upon it, and it was warm to her touch as though other hands had just drawn away. Her eyelids felt unbearably heavy, and as if in response to a silent command she lay down on the packed earth.

Strangely, for it was dark, she saw movement in the far recesses of the cavern. She felt eyes upon her, but they meant her no harm. Then within her sounded a voice, as deep as the sea and as old as the purple Presceli hills. *You are of us, and we are of you. Always we are with you, and always we will hear your call.* And while she was trying to puzzle out the inner voice, it went silent and spoke no more. Without knowing how, she understood.

Atheurin was shaking her gently, and she sat up groggily, slowly remembering where she was. "How did you find me?" she marvelled.

"It was writ. This morn I caught a hint of it, and knew the gods might call you to their ancient holy place of the Tylwyth Teg. I knew danger lurked here, but whom the gods have plans for they hold safe from harm. I saw your escape, and though the gods guided you, your courage was needed as well to save you. Your actions would credit one twice your age."

Tara felt herself unable to respond, but she was suffused with pride and pleasure at his praise. Not even the fact that the pony waited on the trail surprised her. Naught having to do with Atheurin ever would surprise her again.

Since Tara had got a pony of her own, rides with Sire had become infrequent, so she was happily surprised one morn to hear him at her chamber door. "Come, Princess," he cried, and his tone told this was no ordinary day. "We're off to the stables."

Tellicho handed her a bundle when she arrived, and excitedly she ripped off the wrappings, It was a miniature hunting bow of shining straight-grained elm, with a chased silver grip, its ends curving to the nocks like the flight path of a soaring seabird. She thrummed the bowstring ecstatically. "O Sire," she whispered ecstatically. "Is it truly mine?"

"Cadog fashioned it for you," said the king, and the grouped stablemen waited for her to speak. "O goodman Cadog," she began, "It's just beautiful…it's…" She couldn't find words, and stared dumbly at her feet.

"Go you with Dorchas, lass," said Llywarch quickly. "He will show you how to use it, before the hunting horn blasts."

Tara had been on hunts as a spectator, but hadn't thought how different it would be when she found herself perched on a stand high in the trees to await the beaters. Durchas had showed her how to hold the bow and nock the arrow, but in the small time available she'd sprayed her arrows all about, and knew she was woefully unready.

"Hist to the trail," whispered the gamekeeper, pointing. They were up from the ground, in a rude platform secured between the tree limbs. She wanted to ask what they hunted, but stayed silent. Her muscles were stiff with the waiting, and she longed to be home. The gamekeeper's hand grasped her shoulder urgently, and she tensed with excitement.

A deer stood at the edge of the glade, its erect ears turning this way and that. "Let fly!" hissed Durchas. She drew with all her strength, shut her eyes tight, and let go.

There was a small thrashing in the copse, and she opened her eyes. The deer was down on its forelegs, trying vainly to rise. Quickly Dorchas dropped to the ground and clubbed it, and it slumped to the ground. She could see now that the small lifeless thing was but a fawn, and felt a sickness in the pit of her stomach, that she had brought death to this gentle creature. Then she saw the large arrow protruding from its chest, and knew the truth.

"It's all right, Macushla," said Gwenwed, cradling Tara in her lap and stroking her hair. "It's harder for women to see death. The deer is with Jesu now, and in blessed peace. Girls were never meant to hunt!"

Even in her distress, Tara found her mother's last words disturbing. "Mayhap girls are not meant to hunt, but I'm not a girl." She sensed an important crossroads in her life, and wiped angrily at her tears. "I'm a princess! A princess must be a good warrior and hunter." But I wish I were no princess at all, she thought fervently. I wish I were a prince!

Tara finally wormed from Durchas that her arrow had flown wide, and thereafter archery training competed with Father Padrig and Atheurin for her time. As the weeks dragged by, she learned to harness the full strength of her developing sinews, and dragged Aneoch incessantly into the wood for hares until she bagged more game than she missed.

"Come into my chamber with me, Tara," said her mother one eve as they sat in the bower. She lay on her pallet and placed Tara's hand on her stomach. "Do you feel aught?" she asked. Mystified, Tara held her hand still, and shortly felt a small movement. "Whatever is it, Mama?" she demanded. "Are you sick?"

"That's your baby brother, Machusla, who will come into the world if the gods are kind." She pulled Tara close. "If Jesu wills it." Much later, Tara was to recall her mother's prophetic words, and wonder if Jesu had reasons good enow for some things he let happen.

During the session with Atheurin next day, Tara thought of naught but her mother's words, until he gave over his teaching in resignation. "Very well, Princess," he said. "What lies on your mind?"

"I will have a baby brother!" she blurted out. Then the significance of her Mama's words struck her, and her face fell. "If it be he stays alive," she added somberly.

"Prepare yourself for sadness, Princess," said the Bard, sympathy etched on his face. "The gods have no plan for a prince as heir to the kingdom. They have chosen you as heir." He paused a moment. "The Queen knows, and would not have it different. Don't cry or fret over what must be." He reached out compassionately, as if to take her hand, but drew back.

Gwenwed took to her bed, conserving her fragile strength for the coming ordeal, and Tara began to go with the King on his morning rides. He spoke for the first time of wishing to improve the lot of his subjects, and she sensed his deep longing.

"But if the people hunger, Sire, why cannot you feed them from our storerooms?"

The King smiled. "Our small stocks would be gone in a trice if we made shift to feed the people."

She began to realize the breadth of Dyfed, and the number of hungry mouths. "Then what's to be done, Sire?" she asked in distress.

"The fields must be made to grow more crops. The livestock must fatten more. The how of this will be the task of the young Prince your mother carries." His eyes were shining. But the babe will not live, thought Tara in great distress, and knew not how to tell him.

The King was to know soon enough. Within the week, the midwives were summoned urgently to the birthing chamber, and through the night they labored, first to deliver the infant from the weakened mother, then to blow desperately on the spark of life that flickered in the tiny body. As morn broke over the Presceli hills they brought the lifeless bundle to Llywarch, and the grief-stricken monarch went sadly in to comfort his Queen.

It was some ten days later, a bleak period filled with grief and fore-boding, with the Queen's condition far too precarious for visiting, that Tara was brought to Sire's counting room. It was the first time she'd seen him since the sad day, for he had been in tireless attendance upon his beloved Gwenwed, and she was shocked at how drawn his face had become. She felt an instant of panic, suddenly frighted that she might lose them both, but put the thought aside resolutely as she knew Atheurin would wish her to.

Llywarch was garbed in a simple blue tunic caught up at the waist with a leathern belt, with no decoration to relieve the plainness. Save for his indefinable air of authority, he might have been a minor court worthy. He beckoned her to a seat, but his eyes were on the portrait of King Ceorle over the fireplace. He was silent so long she thought he'd forgot her.

"Tara," he began at last. "The time has come for deciding." He was looking at her as if at a stranger. "How many years do you have, lass?"

"Near nine, Sire," she responded, surprised at the question.

"Just so. You are nine years of age, and heir to our throne, for it seems there may be none other. Time you got on with your training as Princess and future Queen. Come to me—let me see you, child."

She arose from the bench and stood before him, mystified and awed at the attention. He ran his hands over her arms and the taut muscles of her thighs. "Good, good," he said. "You are strong and healthy. Durchas says you grow expert with the bow, and Mathias finds you a fine horsewoman. Even Aneoch says you are devilish hard to best at catch-as-catch-can. We find it unfortunate that you're not a lad, but you are of good stuff. We must build on what we have."

Tara bridled at his last comment. "But I'm full as good as any lad, Sire! Aneoch's brother is a lad, and nine already, but he cannot best me at wrestling. He's bigger, but I'm quicker, Sire, and he cannot hold a grip on me. I wish you'd see us wrestle."

"Perhaps I should do, Princess, and that bears on what I have to tell you. The time has come for you to be trained as Prince of Dyfed—to become as a lad and be trained so. If you are fated to rule Dyfed after me, it will be best if I admit as much."

Tara was enormously excited to think of becoming a splendid Prince, and she ached to say so, but the sense that momentous events were setting in motion held her silent.

"I will send you to Aber Castle in Mathry Cantref, under charge of the uchelwr who rules there, my subject the Eorl Skomer. You will be page, and later squire, to his household, to learn all matters becoming a Prince. We will make you ready, for you must leave soon."

Tara's world was spinning with this devastating news. Suddenly she was being sent off to some foreign land, under some strange uchelwr she knew naught of. Leaving the palace…the stableyard…her nurse…Aneoch, and Mama…her Mama! The enormity of this banishment was too overwhelming for understanding.

The King was going on as though this agonizing turn of events was but an everyday matter. "Aneoch will go along to attend you, but mind you, he's no longer squire to you, and you but a page. He's a companion, to ease your first loneliness, and will return here when you're settled in. Cadog will prepare your accoutrements, and Sir Gruwent see to your outfitting."

He took her up in his lap, and his strong arms wrapped about her. "I know you think this a mighty change for you, little lass, but you'll find it the making of you."

Tara was on pins and needles to tell Atheurin the terrible news turning her world upside down, but he showed no surprise. "This is but what you knew already, Princess," he said calmly. "Have I not been telling you all these years that you are marked to be ruler of Dyfed?"

"But you never told me I'd be sent off to some distant cantref! Why can't I learn paging and squiring here at the palace?"

"That's a bit hard to explain, Princess. Your father's courtiers would not be as stern in your training as strangers, so you'd not learn as well in your own castle. The finest Rhenish blade would not hold near so keen an edge were it not tempered in the flame. And it's the same with men. And with maids," he added hastily.

"But I'll hate it! I'll have a horrid time, away out on a black cliff that's pounded night and day by the dreadful Irish Sea!" Tara, who knew naught of black cliffs or the temper of the Irish Sea, was drawing on her nurse Brigidea's dramatic imaginings, but no need to let Atheurin know as much.

He laughed aloud. "Black cliffs? Dreadful Irish Sea? And what mad jongleur told you that? Mathry is a bonny place, mayhap more than your Menevia. Bards forever sing praises to the wild beauty of its blue waters and snow-white shores. You'd best wait and see for yourself before deciding how awful it is."

"But I'll be leaving everyone I know—except Anny, and he doesn't count." Her words brought a final shock too great to be borne. "I'll be leaving you!"

"No, Princess." His voice was soft and soothing. "Have I not told you I will always be there when you need me? Carreg Samson cromlech, much like the cave where you hid from the poachers, lies but a short ride south of Aber Castle where you'll be. One day when you ride out, you'll find it, and will know it by its six upright stones. And whenever you are there, you will not be alone."

With that assurance Tara had to be content and it did make her feel better about the project. It was clear she could not be a Queen without learning warlike skills—and had she not longed only the year past to become like the great Elen Luyddog? She fell asleep many a night on a pallet damp with tears, but in her waking hours the pain was dulled by the furious activity of making ready for her mission.

And furiously active the days were. Once the King's decision was made, with Tara a full year past the age a new page should be sent off, he tried to catch up by rushing the preparation. Cadog worked late into the night, fashioning a leather byrnie and mailed coat to the Princess's small but sturdy frame, beating metal into a small helmet, and selecting the choicest hickory for lances and quarterstaves. Sir Gruwent was no less busy organizing the steward, the chamberlain, and the groom of the rein in preparing her attire and personal effects. The King decreed she must wear masculine garb, partly to salve his wounded pride that he could not send a lad, but more for the practical reason that none knew how a female page should dress. He directed Brigidea to crop off her long hair, but these orders came to the ear of Gwenwed, who forbade it resolutely.

"You go too far, Sire," she said gently. "Tara is to be a Queen, not a King, and we need not pretend she is a boy. She can braid her hair, and bind it tight about her head when there be need, but I will not have her shorn like a trooper to suit Skomar's masculine fancy."

It was the stiff-necked Gruwent who gave Tara the most comfort about her approaching ordeal. "You are miserable now, I wat," he said, "And would give all if you could put by this frightening mission." She nodded wordlessly. "I have sensed as much, Princess, but you should know that the two lads who will page beside you are equally affrighted. I was such a page as a young lad, and the thought of it struck me dumb with terror. You'll see in the eyes of the two lads going with you wetter tears than yours."

"What two lads, Sire?" That she would not go alone was a welcome bit of news. If they were no more agile than the stableyard boys, she would hold her own well enow. She had pictured herself thrown into a band of dour and ferocious knights, so it was at least some consolation to learn that her misery would be shared.

"Eorl Tenby's lad Rhiall will be esquiring with you, and he scarce eight years. The other is son of a Fishguard uchelwr in the north; Cadfan, they call him, after the old ruler of Gwynedh, and he's little older." He smiled sympathetically, and Tara realized that never before had she seen the old Seneschal smile. "You will be oldest by a year, and by all odds the biggest. You may find yourself mothering the brood betimes, as well as jousting with them."

She thought he'd finished, but he went on. "Give your new life half a chance, and you'll find many things to like. A page's life is hard, but exciting withal, with a measure of frolicking and fun. And all the while, you'll be learning the skills a King must know."

She felt his eyes full upon her. His words were odd, she thought. Did he misspeak, to talk of when she would be King, meaning to say Queen? But when she met his serious gaze, somehow she knew he did not. He had said what he meant.

Inevitably, the morn of her departure arrived. The Queen had called her to the bedside the night before, and bade her farewell in words Tara found hard to understand. "I have no fear of your behavior at Skomar's castle, Macushla, for you are smart and strong, and quick beyond your years, and you will hold your own most of the time. It is no other who will be your real opponent, but yourself. The first task of a ruler is to win for her subjects, not for herself. When you gain honors, as I doubt not you will, don't accept them proudly and look about to see how the world thinks of Tara. When you learn new skills, be happy at what they can do for you, but do not think them prizes for your own pleasure, but rather tools for the better governing of Dyfed. If you do but remember this, I can want no more for you." She reached out her hand, and Tara felt a stab of foreboding to feel how thin and cold it had become. "So farewell, my dearest love. Jesu go with you, and the gods hold you safe. Now, I am very tired, and must rest a bit." She kissed Tara softly on the forehead, then turned away and closed her eyes.

When in the morn she came to see her Mama one last time, the woman said she slept and they fear'd to wake her. The King had bade her farewell in the nursery, but had to ride out to the assizes without waiting to see her off. Only Gruwent was there, and he had put his solemn expression back on—scant comfort, but better than if none saw her off.

The retinue was mounted and starting, and Tara's attention should have been on what lay ahead, but she could see only her mother's wasted body motionless in her vast bed up in the chill bedchamber. She is not asleep. I know she is not! They keep me out because she is ill, too ill to say goodbye. They do not tell me because they think to spare me. But they have no need to tell me. I know…I know!

As they set off down the cobbled road, Tara knew with a sudden dreadful clarity that a part of her life had ended, and never would she see her lovely Mama again.

CHAPTER 4

The anteroom at Aber Castle, where Tara sat with the captain of her escort group, was bleak and uncomfortable. She felt the sting of tears behind her eyes, and the same choking in her throat that had assailed her when she left home. The trip had been mercifully quick, stopping briefly at Saint David's priory for a meal, then hurrying north along the coast road so the escort might get back before dark. Tara was grateful that none sought to engage her in talk. The immensity of the Irish Sea overwhelmed her, but the emptiness of it underscored her loneliness on this foreign shore.

The troop reached Mathry in early afternoon, and Tara stared with deep misgivings at the massive stone watchtowers from which high stockades extended along the crest of the hill. The castle itself was a stark structure of dark stone, and from its peak flew a huge black pennon emblazoned with a great hovering bird. To her troubled mind its baleful eye seemed to glare at her. Then the great gate swung clear, and they rode up the rutted path and into the space between the walls, to compose themselves for such welcome as was offered.

The oaken door opened to admit a man-at-arms, who seemed to expect them for he spoke at once to the escort captain. "I am instructed to bring the new page to the Esquire Captain, Sir Knight. The Eorl recks you'll be on your way back without delay." And as quick as that it was done—the escort force gone, and she led out of the arras alone to the office of Sir Aelfgan.

"Od's blood—a lass in sooth," growled the old knight. "And I'm to make a fighting man of such as she?" He tugged angrily at his moustache. "I reckoned the Eorl jested when he told me." He snatched off her phrygian cap, and the braids Brigidea had tucked in fell down her back. With a grimace of disgust, he turned to a big heavy-browed lad who was the only other occupant of the chamber. "Ugri, get this lass proper garb and find her a place to bed down."

Ugri, making sure to tell her he was Head Squire, proceeded down the hall with strides so long she had to run to keep pace, and delivered her to the Steward's office, where she was slightly comforted to see what must be the other two new pages Gruwent had mentioned. She was issued skintight black hose, rough black undershirts, and a yellow tunic bearing the tower-and-hawk device she supposed marked her part of the Eorl's household. She scarce had time to don her new livery when Ugri hurried her up to the gallery, depositing her with a matronly person who turned out to be Madam Agrinore, the Chatelaine.

"Come in, child," said the latter, the warmth of her tone stamping her at once as an ally. "When we get over the shock of a lass in page's garb, the Eorl's daughters and I will bid you welcome. Come in and meet Ladies Algrain and Alteria, who will bed with you."

Two of the three pallets in the alcove where Tara was taken were occupied, but at their entrance two young girls sprang up and hastily wrapped garments about their nakedness. "Here are Algie and Altie," announced her hostess. "Girls, this handsome page is Princess Tara of Dyfed." The two girls stared in awed astonishment. The older was of a size with Tara, but slighter and with a pout marring her good looks, the younger a smaller version of her sister but with a more pleasing expression. When neither spoke, Tara decided they waited for the newcomer to break the silence. "Thank you for sharing your chamber with me, Miladies," she said, wondering if this strange new occupant would be welcomed by them or no.

Algie found her voice, her answer somewhat reassuring. "We are glad you bed with us. But pray, why do you wear boy's garb? And is your hair cropped short under your cap as well, to make you seem more a boy?"

Madam Agrinore broke in brusquely. "Time for all that in the morn. Tara wears livery because she is a page. Her sire is a King, and she must learn the duties and burdens of a prince. And her hair is as long and bountiful as your own, my young Lady Algrain. Now leave you off questioning your guest, and help her to get settled in!"

Tara was shocked to find how early her day started, when a rude pounding at the door before sunrise summoned her to the buttery for the early meal—rough-cut bread and a horn of small beer. In what seemed but a moment later she and her two new companions were dragged off to the Great Hall for serving instruction. The dour Butler drilled them with an impatience he was at no pains to hide, and Tara was outraged when her clumsiness brought a stinging cuff on her ear. About to turn on him in fury, she caught herself. He struck her only because she was a princess and he saw her thinking herself too highborn for such duties. He hoped she'd fail—belike would try to make her fail. But she'd not fail!

The detestable drill ended when the horn blew for fifth hour, and the household assembled for supper. Tara stared with fascination at the Eorl she'd never met and his haughty Countess, until a sharp prod from the Butler sent her hurrying up to serve the Eorl. She saw his sideways glance at her as she knelt to proffer the joint of ox roast, and a hot flush suffused her face at the shame of seeming little more than a lowly scullery maid. Then she was rushing to get the next course, and too preoccupied to dwell on it further.

The Eorl rose finally, and at the signal the entire company ceased eating and left the hall. She wondered how she would sup, until she saw the older pages tussle to sit at the seats with most leavings and quickly wolf down what was uneaten. She gagged with disgust at the sight, but a gnawing in her stomach overcame pride, and she did the same.

Eorl Skomer's household included 13 pages, 15 squires and eight thegns in various stages of training, but the group of three newcomers was on a shortened schedule imposed by the King. Belike Rhiall and Cadfan were included to cover over her special treatment, but it was unlike to fool anyone and sure to irritate the older pages. The abbreviated regimen consisted of instruction by the Countess, and by the priest in Priory school each morn, and martial arts each afternoon. Many times during the tempestuous years that followed, Tara would thank the gods that the Priory priest had taken orders at Colchester Abbey in Danish East Anglia and deemed teaching a thorough fluency in Danish more helpful to Britons than any continental tongue.

The first day of the week was horsemanship, the second swordsmanship, Wednesday hunting and hawking, Thursday tilting and jousting, Friday archery, and Saturday wrestling, cudgel and quarterstaff. This first day was Tuesday, and Tara was picking through the remnants on her plate when the Master of Pages yanked her from her bench along with Rhiall and Cadfan.

"Follow me, with no lagging," he said curtly. They stopped before a weapon rack in the Armory, and he bade them accoutre themselves. Tara watched the older pages already there, and tried to do as they did. She climbed awkwardly into heavy britches far too large for her, donned a byrnie of thick leather sewn with mail, and stuck her head in the clumsy open-face bascinet helmet she detested at once, unhappy that he'd left her no time to fetch her own helm. Thrusting her left arm into the straps of a leathern shield, she picked up an iron broadsword far heavier than the one she'd brought, and gripped it unsteadily in her right hand.

They were taken past the tilting court to the pels, six foot ash posts planted in the ground, and set to slashing and thrusting at them. At first it was easy, even fun, but the heavy armor made every move an effort, and soon her muscles ached cruelly. Then three older pages faced off against them in martial attitudes, and Tara wondered what would come next.

"New pages attack your opponent and seek to breach his defenses," shouted Ugri who had suddenly appeared. Tara snatched a look at the sturdy youth she faced, and her heart sank. He's near man's size, she thought. She knew he planned some trick, but was helpless to prevent it.

"Attackers ready! With backhand stroke, attack!"

Carefully, so as not to hurt her motionless adversary, she swung the heavy broadsword. With a mere flick of his wrist he turned it aside, and the heavy weapon pulled her off balance.

"What are ye doing, dancing the jig?" shouted Ugri. "Again, and this time try to look like men-at-arms. Attack!"

Irritated, she swung with all her strength, but a jarring blow knocked her sword away and simultaneously a dizzying thump on her helmet brought tears to her eyes with the pain. Her bascinet was knocked askew, and as she reached up it fell off and her shameful braids fell down.

Her adversary leaned on his sword, laughing, but his grin changed to a shocked look when he saw her hair, and he made as if to help her, but stopped and looked uncertainly at Ugri.

"And what is your problem, Crosbey?" he demanded. "Hast never seen a lass before? Belike you'd rather tread a minuet with her."

Tara clumsily replaced her helmet and swung again, alert to keep her shield up against an attack, but her opponent contented himself with carefully parrying her uncertain blows. After an interminable time the period ended, and pale with fatigue she trudged back to the Armory.

When she turned from the weapon rack and started out the Armory, Crosbey appeared at her side. She stared stonily ahead of her, waiting for his taunts. "Master of Pages bade us strike off your helms," he began hesitantly, "but had I known you a maid I'd not have struck you."

Tara looked at him then, moved by his expression of concern, taking in his erect carriage. She held her response until she'd overcome a surprising urge to give way to tears. "I am a page, Sir, before I am a lass. It recks not that I be a girl, for I must learn as if I were a boy."

The older page struck his forehead in dismay. "Od's blood—ye be the Princess of Dyfed! We heard you would come, but could not credit it. And I banged a royal princess on the pate!"

"Do not fault yourself, Sir. I am a page, and all must see me so. The King would fret if I got special treatment." She paused, but thought of more to say to him. "So would I."

Crosbey smiled. "Well said, page. I may have trouble forgetting you are a lass, but I vow to forget you are a princess."

At supper Tara was detailed to serve the Countess—doubtless, she concluded, so the lady could look her over—and received the same sharp scrutiny the Eorl had given her. Quickly she looked down, wishing no attention drawn to herself, and withdrew as soon as she could. When the diners departed and the pages scurried for seats, she was surprised and embarrassed to see Crosbey beckoning her to a seat beside him.

"We go hunting on the morrow," he said. "Have you ever hunted, Prin...er, Tara?"

"Yes, Sir. We hunted near every week back in Menevia."

"And you have your mount? And a longbow?"

"I have a pony only, but he is fast and able. And I have a bow of elm, though belike you'll laugh at its small size."

"Well, if it be too small, I can find you another from the Armourer's store. But you'll be comfortable with your own weapon, so better you stay with it for the nonce."

"What will we do on the hunt, Sir?"

"I know not for certain. But likely we will go south for grouse. If Squire Ugri does not interfere, I will show you the way. And have done with 'Sir'," he added. "I am a page, same's you."

South! Perhaps hard by the cromlech Atheurin mentioned, Carreg Samson cromlech with the six standing stones. Might it be she'd see Atheurin? No, he'd never be so far from home. Best not tease herself with the hope, she concluded despondently.

But she could not get the cromlech out of her mind. And when they did indeed head south as Crosbey had predicted, she had no ears for the young gamekeeper's instruction where she was to range. She found herself in a dense field of bracken at the foot of a craggy hill, and the image of the cromlech came upon her so strongly that, with no sense of how it came about, she was galloping headlong toward the rise. When she gained the top, she saw naught save great boulders scattered about, as if by careless gods at play. Undecided, she headed down the far side where a faint path seemed to beckon. Her mount's head went up and his nostrils flared, and she freed the reins to give him his head. They threaded rapidly between trees so close-set there was scarce room to pass. Then the way opened, and she caught her breath.

The six rough-hewn pillars, covered with gray lichen and towering high as if standing sentinel against intruders, stood before her. But Tara had no feeling of intruding. Dismounting, she entered the circle and ducked her head for the dark entrance she knew would be there. As in the old cromlech on Presceli Top, she felt she'd been here before. But the place was empty, with no whispered voices. Reluctantly she turned to go, and suddenly he was there.

Atheurin!

Her heart jumped as she caught sight of her beloved tutor, smiling at her in just the way she remembered. "So you come at last, my page," he said. "My compliments to you, child."

He calls me 'child', not princess as he ever did at home, she thought, and wondered why. And something different: he wore Eorl Skomer's livery, the same as hers.

"Why do you dress so?" she asked in confusion, then let it drop."But no mind that! I thought never to see you again."

"Never see me again? And when did I ever fail you? But as for the livery—the wearing of it will make me invisible to the Eorl's men."

"Then you will stay here?"

"Not stay, but I will return oft to the cromlech, and we will meet here."

"But how will I know when you're here?"

The Bard smiled again, making his face glow in the gloom. "You will know."

"And what will we do when you come?"

"It is high time you start your apprenticeship. You are called to be a Mabinog, Princess, and you must learn the old truths. The gods do you great honor to call so, and I know you'll be worthy. We have much to do."

Tara looked down in embarrassment. "I can but try," she said. But he made no answer, and she knew, even before she looked up, that he would be gone.

That night Algie and Altie tried to engage Tara in small talk, but she had little room in her thoughts for trivial matters, so filled were they of the meeting with Atheurin. So much was happening, and she doubted she could handle all the learning. She felt pressed by a sense of urgency. I am no prince, she realized with discouragement. I am but a muddled lass scarce nine years old.

I cannot satisfy the high aims of the gods; they expect too much of me!

At twelve, Tara was much taller, her body slim but strong withal, and assiduous practice had perfected her skills as a horseman. No longer did she strive to hide in braids the fiery gold-copper tresses that marked her as a girl, but wore it evenly parted to flow unabashedly down her back, with a metal circlet keeping it in place under her saucy Phrygian cap. The very sturdiness of her youthful build, fully the match of lads her own age, served only to enhance her feminine essence, and she was a constant object of furtive admiring glances from the older pages. Her self-confidence had surged in her three years at Aber Castle, as she had mastered the gruelling regimen imposed on the younger pages. Tara had become fully able to hold her own in the dueling ring or wrestling circle, and was able to meet the boys on their own terms in almost any physical challenge. And despite an inauspicious beginning to her page-ship, she had remained always cheerful and fair-minded to her fellows.

Whenever horsemanship practice was over, Tara had formed the practice of riding away unnoted, to meet with Atheurin in the cromlech, and today as she entered the old cave where Atheurin waited, her step was firm and she carried herself with inborn pride.

Crosbey, the page who befriended her in her first dreary days, had become her stalwart ally during those bleak times, and through her heartbreaking period of mourning when Gwenwed was laid to rest. Between his support at the Castle and Atheurin's clandestine presence, she had survived that interminable first year. And as time went on, she learned to find a modicum of pride and even pleasure in the hard life. Each year she fit in better, and gained more grudging respect, from her superiors no less than her peers.

From Atheurin she was learning the rich Celtic heritage of the Cymri nation, and the enduring influence of the Druids on its history. The Druids educated their young in the disciplines of the old gods— hearing grievances sympathetically, dispensing justice fairly in keeping with their traditions, and governing the transmigration of souls. Their religion was harsh, rife with human sacrifice to placate or supplicate the stern gods who controlled life and death, and the practice of dark pagan rites in deep groves and secret recesses. But they held the tribes together despite the endless battles and sieges, ever looking toward the future of Cymru.

As do I, Tara vowed, faithfully mindful of her mother's last solemn adjuration—that as one chosen by the gods she must strive always for the betterment of Dyfed Gwlad, and that she must dedicate her life to that goal.

Atheurin showed her that the Bardi were much more than poets and jongleurs. They did far more than write songs and ballads for kings and taeogion alike—they were soothsayers, and when the gods allowed it they could peer dimly into the uncertain future. As seers, they served as royal advisors, this function diminished no whit when their counsel was so cloaked in riddles at times that even the wisest kings oft found it difficult to reck the true course.

Atheurin, three years earlier, had ushered Tara into the study of Mabinogi, warning her of tales cloudy and dark, filled with fearsome beasts and supernatural events to affright her. But amongst them were found actions devoted to the honor of her people. The great vows of knighthood all were rooted in the Mabinogi principles. And as a Mabinog, Tara had pledged to honor Jesu and Mary, but to love the old Celti gods as well, and never to abandon her faith.

"The time is past due," announced Atheurin when they met, "that you become acquainted with your Lord the Eorl."

"What do you mean?" Tara asked with surprise. "I have been his page these three years past. Belike by now he knows well enow who I am."

"In one way, yes. He knows you are the young princess from Menevia, and I'm certain he holds you a right good page. But has he yet seen you as future Queen and his Liege Lord? Has he turned his mind to holding from you his lands in fee and fief? Does he understand he must swear fealty to you one day—and if so, how sets this with him and his Lady?"

"When I am but a page in his household, and a lass as well? How could he look on me so?" She almost laughed at the thought. "The Eorl sees me only as someone in his demesne, serving at his pleasure. You cannot think…"

"…that you could be so wrong?" Atheurin broke in. "Aye, that I can. Eorl Skomer would not have you suspect as much, but he and his Countess have watched you, and had you in their plottings, since first you came and e'en well before. He is schooled in court intrigues, and his schemes center on the state of affairs if King Llywarch dies." The Bard's face was solemn and his words confusing, making the inexperienced girl struggle to make sense of them.

"Are you saying the Eorl has thoughts of…of removing me?" she whispered in disbelief. "And he my guardian in Aber Castle. That's not possible!"

"Nay, Tara—very possible. And Skomer would be a most unusual uchelwr if he did not consider such plottings."

Tara forced herself to consider Atheurin's words. Certainly the Eorl would wonder how he might change the succession to his advantage— anyone could see that. Were I in his shoes, even I might do likewise, she saw—though not to the point of murder.

"But how could he remove me to his advantage?" she protested, after a time. "And why would his thoughts be such when Sire is healthy, belike even stronger than the Eorl?"

"King Llywarch strong and hale? Look inside you," Atheurin pressed, "and give me your solemn oath that you think as much."

The abrupt question shook her greatly, forcing her to probe her deepest thoughts of her dear Sire, not as she had enshrined him in her heart, but facing facts honestly. As she did, she knew with a stab of grief that the King was no longer the robust figure of yore, but a tired and aging man.

"No," she confessed in distress. "I cannot."

"Then, child, you must plan to win Skomer and his Countess to your cause. You are shrewd, and your Mabinog studies have matured you vastly, and you can have the Eorl seeing the future just as you wish, and his Lady, too—both of them thinking the plans are theirs."

"How may I do that? I do not understand."

"You do understand, at least in part. You must puzzle it for yourself. So go now, Tara, but make your plans with great care. Skomer is no fool, and his Lady is yet vastly wiser than he."

Riding back to the castle, Tara puzzled intensely over Atheurin's warning. She had known from early childhood about the derbfine of kingly succession, that although she was primary heir to her father's throne, all descendants of the King's great-grandfather were in his derbfine and eligible to succeed him. Thus if aught befell her, Eorl Skomer doubtless could prove such descent—particularly if he reinforced his proof with the chicanery in which he and his Lady would be vastly skilled, backed up with the considerable might of his fighting troops.

Suddenly she understood with stark clarity how exposed her position was. Thinking on it more deeply, she realized the Eorl's scribes and chaplains could have been combing baptismal records four generations back, cobbling up some sort of proof of an ancestral link. Records were locked in church vaults, but scarce secure from secret intruders and clever forgers—particularly when the very kingdom was the prize.

Whether in truth or by deception, if Eorl Skomer contrived a credible claim of being in her father's derbfine, then she, a young page named Tara, would become an inconvenient obstacle to any kingly ambitions he and his Countess might nourish.

She knew she should not share her heavy burden with anyone, but was bursting to speak of it with some other person who could provide a measure of wise counsel. Crosbey was a person of honor, who would hold her grim secret close, and he had proven himself a trusted friend—and of equal import, one whose counsel she sorely needed.

Crosbey, now in his fifteenth year, esquired to an impoverished country knight who held a farmsteading fee from the Eorl, was totally in thrall to the girl, and would come close to giving his very life for her. As the son of a grwda, he was but a low born squire and fortunate to have been chosen one at all, and would know he could never aspire to the hand of a princess. But he could not stifle his constant dreams, wherein he was defender and protector of her life and honor. Having attained almost his full height, though not yet fleshed out, Crosbey's build was sturdy and his bearing resolute. His hair always was neatly trimmed, his clothes ever carefully patched and brushed. Perceptive members of the Eorl's household had speculated on the possibility that Crosbey's escutcheon bore the imprint of some noble ancestor, but on the wrong side of the blanket. Tara was unaware that her mysterious summons had set his pulse pounding, but she could see that he had scrubbed up after the day's exertions and had donned fresh livery for their clandestine meeting in the dimly-lit chapel.

She wondered bleakly how to explain her ominous problem, and hesitated for such a spell that he was impelled to break the silence. "Is it trouble you are in, Tara? If so, you know without any saying that my sword is yours for the asking."

The concern and feeling she saw in his young face moved her deeply, and her spirits rose. "There's no trouble the way you mean it, Cross. That is, I cannot answer if the trouble is real, or just imaginings." She related Atheurin's warning, as if it came from her own thoughts, adding her suspicions about whether the Eorl qualified in truth for the derbfine of succession. "Could be it's but an oldwife's worry, and no cause for fretting, but if I read it aright I must be on guard for my life—knowing not where to watch, for danger could strike from anywhere." Her embarrassment was topped by relief at sharing her troubles with another, but she fear'd her truest friend might scoff at her concern.

As the significance of her words struck home, Crosbey sprang to his feet. "God's wounds, Tara, you stand in deadliest peril! You could be murthered anywhere, any time…a knife in your back…a potion in your ale…an arrow launched while you ride out…anything! There are an hundred ways to do away with you, and you can't guard against them all." Unconsciously his hand gripped the dagger at his belt. "What in Lug's name can we do to hold you safe?"

The 'we' warmed her heart. She cherished his willingness to spring to her defense, no less his instant acceptance of her tale. He's a ready friend and ally, she thought gratefully, and I was right to speak with him. "Mayhap the danger's not so close upon me as that, Cross," she said. "Whilst my Sire's good health holds, Eorl Skomer will forbear to take any action likely to bring down the King's inquisitors upon him. If Sire sickens, that's when the Eorl and his Lady must act, and that day is not yet."

"Aye, you make sense." The taut lines of his jaw relaxed, and he sat back more easily. "Belike he and the Countess will but watch and plan so long as the King is hale. There may not yet be real danger for you here."

"But what can I do now, while time is on our side? My father looks well enow to the cottagers, or when he rides out on the hunt, but inside he is not truly a well man. I beg you keep this privy, sharing it with none as you hold our friendship dear, for such news would cause grievous harm if it got about Cymru."

Miraculously, Crosbey lifted her hand and touched it to his lips. "I so swear! None shall hear it from me, by word or deed." But as he thought more on it, he could see that all might not be well at all. "If your Sire be as you say, the Eorl's spies could have noted it already. Your life stands in danger, Tara, e'en this very moment!"

"I think not yet. Eorl Skomer does not see the King close at hand, and my father is careful when others look on him. Though it may not be long, for the Eorl will have spies at Menevia. So betimes, what must I conjure up to change the Eorl's plans? How best may we use what time is left?"

Both fell silent, pondering how to counter the Eorl's deadly scheme, if such he had. On the walls outside the torches guttered and crackled, and they could hear muted talking in the guard chamber and the measured footfalls of watchmen on the tower stairway.

"I have a thought, Tara, though one that's chancy of success," said Crosbey after a space, so intent on his plan that unconsciously he grasped her hand. Not wishing to disturb his thought, she let it lay. "If it comes to worst, and the Eorl does you harm, and then produces records purporting to put him in the derbfine, I wat his claim will not be the only one. Have not other uchelwyr claims of their own?"

"Yes, there will be others. Belike Rhiall's sire can make claim as well, and the Lord of Llawhaden. And my mother has spoken of the Master of Saint Gofan's Head as kin. Mayhap four or so with as good a claim, as good a lineage as his."

"Then do you not see?" he demanded excitedly. "Let him do away with you, and there's still no surety he can claim the throne for himself. He must fight others as mighty as he, and no one can foretell who might prevail."

She still did not understand. "Cross, if be it the Eorl kills me, I will be as dead one way as another, no matter who wins out in the end."

"No, no! We won't let him slay you. That's to say, we must make you more useful to him alive than dead. You needs make them see you as a frightened lass with no stomach for the cares of a throne, anxious for staunch friends to take up your burthen. Play to them as if you hold them true friends. Make them think they know that on your succession the Eorl will stand behind you as Regent, guiding the hand of a simple maid, while meantime able to arrange affairs to profit themselves."

"Cross...of course! They will think to put themselves in the way to seize the throne one day, without calling down my father's vengeance, or risking loss to a stronger Eorl." She smiled at him, and his heart beat faster. "I vow, you are the smartest squire in Cymru, to find so neat a way to muzzle the Eorl's action against me. That's just what we must do."

She rose, squaring her shoulders in determination. "This will not be easy to bring off, but belike it's the only plan that offers, and I can do it. I can do it so well both Eorl and Countess will think it their idea. Now we must come away, Cross. We've been here overlong, and if any suspicion falls on us the plan will fail."

Still hand in hand, they slipped out of the Chapel, alert for the guards, and tiptoed to the stairwell. Close though they had been for three years, Tara had thought of Crosbey as just a comrade, but of a sudden she saw him in a new and unsettling light. He had offered far more than she had expected, all but proffering his very life to her service. It came to her that he saw her no longer as a comrade-in-arms, but as a maid. No, more than that—Crosbey actually loved her!

But such a relationship was impossible. Not only was the gulf in their social status a complete barrier, but her feeling for him, strong though she knew it to be, was as a beloved brother. Tara realized with a pang of regret that she'd never had occasion to learn of the feelings shared between man and woman. She stole a quick sideways glance at his strong young profile, and a hot flush suffused her cheeks.

Flustered by the disturbing stirrings within her, she felt her heart pounding so hard she fear'd he must hear it. Her hand, still in his tight grip, grew hot, and she felt apprehensive but at the same time secure in the warmth of his caring. The strongest urge came over her to abandon her lonely coping with problems grown near too heavy to bear, and to place herself completely under Crosbey's protection. A rush of feeling engulfed her, and under its spell she ached to take refuge within the encircling comfort of his strong arms.

But Crosbey, with no way of knowing aught of her intense longing, disappointingly made no move to fulfill her wish.

I must get this out of my mind, she decided at last, trying firmly to stifle her tremulous feelings and still her rapidly beating heart. This is no time to puzzle out my own confused emotions; vastly more important matters are clamoring for all my attention.

Tara reached the bower, hoping with all her heart that her chambermates would be asleep so she could reflect in privacy on the confused emotions Crosbey had stirred up, but Algie and Altie were sitting up in their pallets, ready to pounce on her with great news when she entered.

Algie had a suiter—a real champion to defend her honor and do her homage. Altie turned to Tara, her eyes alight. "You'll never guess who it is, not if you was to try all the night!"

Tara resigned herself to having no peace until all was told. "Since I have not all the night to try, Altie, you must tell me. Who might it be then?"

"The squire Grosseteste! Oh, he's a fine great brute of a fellow, and I vow he's strong as an ox. Can you imagine any finer knight to wear Algie's talisman and keep her from harm?"

Grosseteste! Of all the squires, or the older pages, he was near the only one who never had ceased baiting her, who continued to scorn her as a mere maid in a male domain. A great brute he was indeed, and that he could protect the Lady Algrain from many hazards she had little doubt, but who would protect her from him? But this was no time or place for such warnings. "That's a fine bit of news, Algie," she said. "He is in sooth a big brute of a fellow." She knew Algie would want more talk of her exciting news. "How did he pay you his court?"

Altie answered before her sister could reply. "We knew he had his eye on Algie, the way he helped her with her goshawk when we rode out hawking, and spoke with her in the courtyard whenever he saw her. But just today he bespoke her for a talisman to wear on his sleeve when he jousted, to show she was his lady fair and he sworn to defend her honor." Her face was all aglow with the thought. "Then we knew he was plighting his troth, sure!"

"That's wonderful tidings, Algie. I'm very happy for you. I'll watch for your token on his sleeve whenever I see him in the lists."

"And you?" Altie looked keenly into Tara's eyes, as if to probe her inmost feelings. "Do not you have a knight-errant as well?"

"I? Whatever do you mean, Altie?" Tara was furious at the flush of embarrassment she could feel on her cheek. "I'm a page, training to be a squire myself. What would I need of a squire playing at knight-errantry?"

Altie was having none of it. "You know who I mean—that handsome young Crosbey, who fair faints when he looks at you, and methinks you look back at him the same. Confess it now. Crosbey is your suitor, is he not?"

"What nonsense you talk, Altie. But I must be abed, for there's much brewing on the morrow, and I'll have need for all my strength. Congratulations to you, Algie, on your big and strong suitor." She turned away and sought out her pallet. There'd be an opportunity to start her campaign the next morn, and she'd best have all her wits about her.

The Eorl's habit was to rise from his pallet with two pages in attendance. One shaved him and dressed the hair of which he was inordinately proud, and the other helped him don attire suited to the weather and his day's happenings. When the Master of Pages detailed Tara and Rhiall to serve their turn, she realized she'd never have a better opportunity to converse with her Lord in private. At once she set about devising a plan to be alone with him.

Eorl Skomar slouched in his chair, scarce aware of the silent Tara busily dressing his shoulder-length hair and trimming the uneven wisps of his drooping moustache. She had never found anything to admire in her Lord, but now, pondering his devious schemings, she detested him. She ached to sink her scissors into the fleshy folds of his thick neck, but steeled herself instead to assume a soft and timid attitude.

"Milord," she said shyly. "Permission to have a word with you?"

"Eh? What?" He turned about to look at her, and she saw an expression flit momentarily across his face that sickened her even as it filled her with a vague disquiet. "Oh, Tara is it? Speak then. What would you say?"

Tara swallowed the nervousness that almost held her speechless. "I have been fretting on a matter, Milord. Someday, you know, I will inherit the throne, though many a year hence I'm sure. But the thought affrights me grievously."

She harked how his eyebrows lifted, and knew she had his full attention. Her heart pounding, she went on with the speech she'd so carefully composed. "I am not a man, Sire, and though I take instruction in your demesne, for which I owe you and the Countess deep thanks, still I am ill-equipped to rule the realm. Would you not agree, Milord?"

Her eyes were downcast as she spoke, but she lifted them momentarily to catch the quick flash of understanding as her words sank in. He was no stupid dullard, and she knew her choice of words needed exquisite care. "You're right, lass," he said, and the pompous tone in his voice told her he was well hooked so far. "The ruling of a kingdom is a parlous task even for an experienced man, one with the strength and knowledge to bang heads together when needed. A task well nigh impossible for a female, unschooled in court arts. I agree, of course. But what were you thinking? What would you ask of me?"

Rhiall entered the chamber at that moment, and her heart sank to be interrupted at this vital point, but the Eorl had no thought to terminate this fascinating exchange. "Hie to the buttery, lad, and fetch me a horn of ale. Bid the butler heat some honey with it. Begone with you."

"Now," he said as Rhiall scurried out. "Continue."

"What was in my mind, Milord, was if you and your Countess would be of a mind to help me with the duties of the kingdom. I'm asking much, and I know you'd fret at the time away from Aber Castle, but my mind would be much easier to know you'd be there to manage affairs and take the heavy load from my shoulders. Belike there would be some benefit for your fortunes in the doing of it, though I am too unskilled in matters of the realm to know what they would be." Now, I've said it, and I must wait to see if he takes the bait.

"You have spoken well, Princess," he answered, and reached back to give her hand a pat of reassurance. "Sorry though we'd be for any time away from our lands, we cannot refuse if the kingdom needs us. You need have no worry on this further...the Countess and I will give you aid in full measure when that sad day comes."

"I cannot know how to thank you, Milord. It's a heavy load off my shoulders." And another heavy load will be off my shoulders as well if you and your Lady credit my plea without raising suspicions, she thought earnestly. But she had not failed to note that the Eorl, for the first time, addressed her as 'Princess'. Mayhap my speech has moved me to a higher station in his schemes, she thought, and Lug grant that meant he was crediting her plea. Whether his Countess would see through her words, where he had not, was yet to be seen.

The Eorl wasted no time conferring with his Lady, for that very afternoon a handmaiden fluttered out to the quarterstaff yard and summoned Tara to see the Countess. When she asked Ugri permission to leave, he demanded to know what trouble she'd been in now. "Doubtless summat about you and your trained cur, Crosbey," he growled. "All have noted the two of you stealing out to your hideaways—you be the gossip of the castle. I knew the Countess would hear of it soon. You're for it now, my gel!"

What have they heard, wondered Tara in alarm, as she hurried along. She thought back frantically to their meetings, but was sure they had taken ample precautions against being overheard. It was with more than a little apprehension that she knocked at the solar door.

The Countess herself came to the door, and courteously bade her enter. "Do come in, Tara," she said in friendly tones. "Now sit here beside me and let us talk. For many weeks I've wished you to call upon me, but the management of a large castle leaves little time for pleasures. No matter—you are here now." She cleared a space at her side, and Tara sat stiffly erect, all her senses on the alert.

"Tell me, little Princess, how do you enjoy your training here? Is all as you hoped to find?"

"Your training is very instructive, Milady. I'd no idea how little I knew, or how much there was to learn."

"Ah. Then you did not learn such things at home, from the time you were out of your cradle? The King did not have you taught in matters of state?"

"No, Milady. We had few pages or squires at the castle, and none in training, and I was not taught the warlike arts nor how to manage. I fear I was but a playing child at Menevia Castle."

"Of course. Tell me now, Tara—think you the Lady Agrinore and Sir Aelfgan teach you what you will need if you are to rule Dyfed some day?"

Here it is, thought Tara anxiously. Careful…she will seek to trip me, and decide if the Eorl was deceived. I cannot play the timid lass with her as I did with him, for she will not be fooled an instant. Tara regretted that the summons had caught her before she'd rehearsed her replies, then decided that the closer she stayed to the truth the more chance of convincing this shrewd lady.

"Aye, Milady, I wat your schooling is in the right direction. All we are taught are matters that must be learned by highborn children who aspire to titles. I know the duties that will be mine one day, and they do not affright me…"

"But did you not tell the Eorl a somewhat different tale?" interrupted the Countess. "Did you not say the very thought of ruling affrighted you grievously?"

Here was the critical point, where if she could convince the skeptical Countess of her supposed feelings in the matter, the battle was half won. "I fear'd to speak up strongly before his Lordship, Milady, for men are like to take it unseemly when lasses are too bold." She saw the flicker of a wry smile touch the Countess's face and disappear as quickly as it had come. "We are both women, Milady, if you permit me to speak so, and women may not make so bold as to show any manly traits. No, Milady, it is not fright that afflicts me, but a sensible worry as to what awaits me. The way I spoke to the Eorl was part make-believe, but the problem I presented to him was real."

"Go on."

"I am neither affrighted nor stupid. I know many a year must pass before I have the experience to judge the weighty matters that press in on the Crown. I know great lords will find it mightily distasteful to submit to a lass, no matter that she calls herself Queen. I know I need help in this for a time, Milady, and I had thought to turn to the Eorl and yourself because you have my respect—and because in this matter you are the only friends I have."

She stopped and sat silent. She'd done her best, and she could but hope it sounded convincing.

The Countess rose slowly to her feet, walked to the balcony overlooking the Great Hall, and stood there for a time staring down with unseeing eyes at the activity below, then turned back and stood directly in front of Tara. "Look at me, child," she commanded.

Tara looked, and for an instant could imagine she detected a suspicious moisture in the Countess's eyes. "Yes, Milady," she said, rising and standing stiffly erect.

"You did right, child. I am…we are your friends. You can count on us to advise you when such occasions arise. But the succession may not be for many years, so we'll speak no more of it. Now let us sit again, and speak of more immediate affairs. I am anxious to hear how you pass your time. And mayhap you can tell me something of the lovesick lad who follows you about."

The Countess kept her in conversation half an hour more, but Tara knew the substance of the interview was completed. Whether she fooled her mistress she knew not. She returned to the quarterstaff court restless and ill at ease.

The news of her summons to the solar had spread widely, and Crosbey was at her side as they lined up for the supper horn, anxious to speak with her. She turned away abruptly, distressed at the thought of hurting him but fearing to be seen deep in conversation with him just now, so soon after the interview. I know they spy on me, she thought, and I must do naught to fan their suspicions.

It seemed an eternity before the pages next were exercised at Hunting and Hawking, when Tara could steal away to the cromlech and tell Atheurin what had transpired. Events then seemed to favor her, for her group ranged southward after deer. They were on reconnaissance only, with strict orders not to draw bow but to mark the location of deer for the Eorl's pleasure. She found it easy to steal off and ride to the cromlech.

Atheurin stood outside the cromlech, and she started to go in but his hand barred her way. "Will we not meet inside today?" she asked. "Is it not safer so, lest we be seen?"

"No," he said, then answered her question oddly. "Today you will be safer outside."

She did not understand, but often she failed to grasp the meaning of his remarks, and thought no more about it in her impatience to relate the happenings at the castle.

"And you think you deceived the Countess?" he asked when she had finished. "You saw no suspicion in her eyes?"

"Not suspicion—at least, I think not. But I may have seen a tear, though only for an instant, and I could not be sure."

"When was it? What was being said?"

"When I said she and the Eorl were the only friends I have in this matter."

"Yes, that would have been the time. She is a complex spirit, your Countess. Many things struggle within her, and the gods alone can tell which will triumph. But don't be fooled. You must be very sure never to let down your guard when you are with her. No matter how kind she is to you, how warm you feel in the glow of her affection, you must never trust her. Never!"

She started to reassure him, but was interrupted by a sound behind her, and turned to see the Eorl on his black stallion break through the ring of trees.

"And what is this, girl?" he demanded, his face dark with suspicion. "What is your business away out here? What mischief are you plotting? Tell me at once, my gel!"

She could not find her voice. He had caught them whispering together in this secluded rendezvous. All she could do was stand dumbly before him. All was lost!

"Ugri was right, then! You sneak off here to meet someone, to scheme against us? I ask you once more, and I demand answer! What is your business here? What is hid in the cave?"

Suddenly she realized that he did not see Atheurin. He thought to find someone in the cromlech, but he would not. She breathed a bit easier, and found voice to answer. "A hind, Milord—a wondrous beast! I tracked a black hind to this spot, and dismounted to search. I have only just lost him, but I vow he is hiding near."

His eyes darkened in disbelief. "You lie!" he thundered. "Never has a black hind been seen in these woods, and you saw none today. We will see who is skulking away in the cave!"

There was a dull thump, then another, and out of the dark entrance sprang a slender hind, its sleek hide gleaming in the slanting rays of the sun. Its coat was a glossy black, relieved only by a silver blaze on its brow. It stood motionless, looking at them unafraid, its eyes gleaming with a human intelligence, then turned to bound through the trees out of sight.

No one moved. Tara stole a quick sideways glance at the Eorl. He was staring slackjawed at the spot where the animal had been, stunned surprise mingled with awe on his bloated face. She realized that her own amazement was no whit less than his.

Atheurin! She breathed the name in silent wonder.

CHAPTER 5

There was to be a jousting tournament, by squires who had gained the most proficiency in the lists, demonstrating the techniques of the course which all knights of the realm rated the highest of all forms of chivalric combat. Tara was proud to have been included in the group receiving instruction in tilting with the lance, recognition that she had become adept in the martial arts.

Two squires, selected as most promising contenders and honored to be so chosen, entered in full jousting regalia, and with a rush of excitement Tara recognized one as Crosbey. The other was Lady Algrain's new champion, the burly, pockmarked Grosseteste, whose bullying and boorish behavior made her hope to see him roundly defeated in the lists. Ugri, Master of Pages and charged with keeping order, gruffly demanded strict decorum of the pages, for the drill would be conducted with all the pageantry of a formal tournament. Then the horn sounded for silence, and Sir Aelfgan stepped forward. "Knights champion," he called out, "Go thee amongst the pages and select squires for the tourney!"

The contestants approached the group of pages, carrying crested helms of a design Tara had never seen in training, and she could see Crosbey's eyes casting about. Might he be seeking me out, she wondered, her heartbeat quickening, and in the next moment he stood before her. "Wouldst do me the honor to serve as mine own esquire and equerry, Tara?" he asked most formally, and without awaiting reply tendered her the ornate helmet with its soaring white plumes.

The course, sixty paces long, was divided by a stake barrier defining the two runways, and they walked together to the end of one run, Tara nervously feeling all eyes upon her. She took Crosbey's brightly caparisoned war horse from the groom, and helped him mount. A servitor brought the practice lance, and she assisted him to socket it, trying to control the shaking of her hands. Then, as she'd been trained, she stood erect at his left side and cradled the heavy helm proudly in her arm. Would that Sire might see me now, she thought proudly. The buzz of talk in the gallery died out, as Sir Aelfgan mounted to the Marshal's chair and gave the order to don helms.

Tara handed up the heavy cylindrical tilting helm for Crosbey to don, and he adjusted the occularium to clear his view. The Marshal's call rang out, "Herald, read thou the challenge!" Ugri stepped forward and read from a scroll the contestants' names, and the gage was thrown down and accepted. Then the Marshal called out those momentous words, "Art ready?"

"A moment, Sir Knight," called out Crosbey unexpectedly. He bent down and handed Tara a pouch. "Do you take from the pouch the scarf within," he bade her in a firm and confident voice. Confused, she pulled out what was inside with fumbling fingers, and her face crimsoned. It was her own scarf, worn on her trip from Menevia Castle, but tucked away since beneath her pallet. How could he have found it?

"Tie it on my arm," he commanded, and she hastened to do his bidding, her mind in a whirl. He wears my scarf as his talisman, she marvelled, as if…as if I were his lady fair! But I am no puling maiden, she told herself, languishing in a tower whilst knights-at-arms battle for my favor—I am of the company of knights-at-arms myself! Would it appear as if he belittled her, wearing her favor as though she were but a maid? Not so—he chose her his Equerry, and many would envy her that honor. They were comrades-at-arms, but there was something more between them withal—and that something was what quickened her pulse and made her cheeks flush hotly.

Hurrying, all fingers, she managed to knot the bit of silk on his lance arm, and rigidly resumed her post. Only then did Crosbey salute the Marshal and call out, "I am ready, Sire!"

Instead of a regular tournament of three broken lances, there would be but a single course, with the first unhorsed the loser. Contestants were permitted to strike no higher than the shield, and both well knew that though a fair blow centered on the shield was the best attack, usually unhorsing the opponent at once, a miss left the attacker vulnerable to being swept from his saddle with a sidewise swing of his opponent's lance. Experienced jousters usually essayed the direct blow, but Tara knew novices would scarce be so rash as to risk it.

The Marshal raised his baton, and the horn sounded. The two spurred their mounts, and thundered down the course with lances elevated, and Tara's heart was in her throat.

Both contestants held their lances dead ahead, indicating that each planned a sideways sweep, but in the instant before they met Crosbey suddenly shifted aim, and the padded point of his lance crashed into Grosseteste's shield—nearly centered, but slightly to the far side. Its force twisted the other violently about in his saddle and smothered the sideways sweep of his own weapon. He swayed precariously over, and for a long instant appeared to be falling, but with a prodigious effort clawed his way back into the saddle—badly shaken but not quite unhorsed. The bout, under the artificial rules of the practice tourney, had to be ruled a draw.

Crosbey would be keenly disappointed, Tara knew, e'en though all would see his jousting far superior. At supper she tried to tell him as much, but he was inconsolable. "Such a miss in battle would be fatal," he fretted. "I thought to take him on the umbo of his shield, but my aim was abominable! I'm only sorry you had to see it."

"I'm not sorry at all," she said hotly. "Had it been a fight to the finish, he was so unbalanced you'd have had him in another instant. I was proud to be your Equerry, and I do but wonder that you did me the honor."

Her words reminded her of the other matter. "Cross," she demanded indignantly, "how did you get my scarf?"

He laughed, cheered up a bit. "I had help from a fair maiden who cherishes the chivalric customs," he said.

"It had to be Altie, I vow. Not Algie, because Grosseteste was her champion. Tell me, was it not Altie?"

"I may never tell. A knight is sworn to secrecy about a lady's affairs. But the charm didn't quite bring me the victory, did it? Mayhap that's my penalty for stealing it instead of asking it of you direct."

"True enow, you did steal it. Next time ask me for it direct."

"And if I do, will you give it to me?"

Of a sudden, their talk had turned serious, and she could feel herself reddening hotly at his pointed question. She averted her face in confusion, but not fast enough to keep him from seeing. Emboldened, he grasped her firmly by the shoulders, and turned her face to face with him.

"Will you give me your favor if I ask, Tara?"

She found herself oddly mute, unable to respond, but belike the shy pleasure on her face betrayed her true feelings. They stared at each other, pulses quickening, savoring the moment.

The poignant moment reminded Crosbey of another matter, and his heart caught with sudden alarm. "Have you aught to tell of your converse with the Eorl? What portends there?"

Speaking soft, lest she be overheard, Tara told him she had met with both the Eorl and his Lady. I cannot speak to him of Atheurin, she told herself, and he'll scarce believe the tale of a magical black hind. But her joyous mood remained, and again she felt a longing, not only to share her troubles with Crosbey, but to put herself in his care. At last she told him all, except any mention of the Bard, saying only that it was a sacred place where she sought the old gods.

"What frets me, Cross," she said, "Is why the Eorl followed me. He said Ugri told him, or the like. Could he think I meet with his enemies, to scheme against him? And if that be so, must he not then disbelieve the tale you had me tell him of needing his help in reigning?"

"You've caught up a tangled skein for sure. But he must believe your account of the hind, since his own eyes confirmed it. You say he searched the cromlech later?"

"Aye, from tip to tip. And found naught."

"Then you can make your mind easy. Belike Ugri told him a tale of you stealing off from the hunt, and there's no surprise he did, for we all noted your visits to the southern forest, and many wondered about it. Mayhap being found out this way is best, as you've put it in the open now that you visited Carreg Samson to call on the gods, and who could question that?"

"Think you the Eorl will see it so? And his Countess? Will that tale quiet her suspicions?"

"Aye, I'm sure on't. If the Eorl had reason to question your faithfulness, I wat he does so no longer. Go you to your bower with a clear heart, Tara. Mayhap Altie will seek to know if your favor won the joust for me, and you can puzzle out how to answer."

Friday was Tara's favorite day, for the afternoons were devoted to archery instruction. The range, fifty paces long, had straw targets at each end. The pages shot in turn, first from one end then running to score their points and fire back from the other end. Tara still used the bow Sire had given her; it was growing small for her taut-muscled, rangy frame, and lacked penetrating power for large game, but its careful workmanship effected a precise accuracy few other pages could surpass. Next year, she thought, I will discard it, but not yet.

The competition was keen; four pages matched with her in the lead, onlookers shouting bets on the outcome. Tara looked up, and caught her breath—the Eorl watched. She hadn't seen him come, and disconcerted by his scrutiny she lost concentration. Her final shot went wide of the circle, to drop her out of the competition.

So much for my skill when the Lord watches, she thought in disgust. Was he seeking her? If so, could it bear on their unhappy encounter at the cromlech? Fervently she hoped not.

That hope was to be dashed, for the next moment the Eorl strolled casually over to Tara and bade her step apart with him. "I have been thinking on that affair in the south woods yesterday, lass," he said. "I'm told you've ridden there more than once, and it frets me."

"Oh, Milord," she said hurriedly, "I do ride to the sacred mound sometimes, when our path takes us near, but only to pray to the gods as my father instructed. I meant no harm." Will this content him, she wondered prayerfully.

"I hold it no fault to show respect for the gods," he stated. "Though you did wrong to steal there in secret, telling none where you went."

"I see that now, Milord, and pray your forgiveness for my errant behavior."

He waved her apology away impatiently. "You've committed no great sin. We put it down to your youth, and mayhap our failure to teach you the close rules that govern a page's behavior. I will speak to the Countess, that you be instructed more closely in these things. But that is not what disturbs me."

She looked up in alarm. Did he have some notion she was meeting Atheurin there? He had been furious with suspicion when he surprised her at the cromlech. Was he suspicious still?

"I understand now that your motive was innocent enow," he said in buttery tones. "But what you have been doing is most dangerous for you."

"Dangerous, Milord?" Alarm knotted her stomach. "How so?"

"Outlaws. We patrol our lands as best we can, but my holdings are too vast to chase off all varlots who hunger for deer. I have a sacred trust from the King, and if I allow you to be set on by lawless churls, he'd hold me responsible. I must forbid you to ride that way again. Dost understand?"

"Aye, Milord. I'll not let it happen again." She could scarce hold back the tears, of anger as much as sorrow. This meant the end of her meetings with Atheurin, of the link with home that kept fresh her memory and made bearable her absence from Dyfed and all she loved there. His casual command was the cruelest of punishments! But she could do naught but obey.

As the days passed, one on another, she made sure to behave normally, so none would know the shattering blow the Eorl had dealt. Crosbey seemed puzzled by her unusual quiet, and she came very close to pouring out all her worries to him, but she could not explain about Atheurin, and he'd be fretted needlessly. To ease his mind, she made him believe she was showing a pretense to the Lord and Lady. As the days stretched into weeks, the ache in her heart gradually dulled, but never entirely left.

Part of a page's instruction involved managing the Eorl's income-producing properties: the land and its bounty. The Reeve was a crusty commoner, whose whole life revolved around farm crops, both land and animal. It was he who parceled the Eorl's holdings into furlongs and selions, oversaw fishponds and dovecotes, breeding pens and pigeon lofts, operated the mill and looms, kept the storehouses filled, and husbanded cattle, sheep and swine. He saw to making the butter, cheese and curd, scheduled planting, cultivating and harvesting, supervised wagoners, swineherds, ploughmen, shepherds, haywards and dairymaids. He oversaw the workshops of wheelwrights, smiths, carpenters, potters, tanners, masons and dyers. He did all this to keep the manor population fed, clothed and sheltered, for near all being used or consumed in the Eorl's demesne was grown or made on his holdings.

In a small chamber off the Solar, Tara and her two fellows were drilled in the customs and management of the manor, either by Lady Agrinore or by the Steward, Sir Elwain. Their speeded-up program joined them with the older pages at the barns and shops clustered in the far bailey, to lay hands on the work in process. Mindful of her father's dream of improving his subjects' lot by increasing the land's bounty, Tara was determined to fulfill his hopes better than any prince could have done. But she knew she must attend closely to all she saw, for if she would show how things might be improved she should first learn how they were done now.

When the Reeve took them about the area, Tara marvelled to see heavy ingots of glowing metal beat skillfully into tools and implements. She watched sadlers scrape and grease bloody hides to stitch into pillions and saddles. She marveled at the flashing fingers of the willow and wattle workers, weaving panniers, store baskets, creels, cart sides and willow kiddles for storing fish. How anyone could fashion these things faster or better she could not conceive.

Her head was spinning when the tour ended. It explained Sire's frustration, trying to better the work processes of such skilled artisans. How could she hope to improve on workmen who devoted their lives to these difficult tasks?

When their tour was done, the Reeve dispatched the three new pages to assist at the mill. They were done with watching, and now was the time for working. Tara had seen the great Mathry water mill in the distance, when they hunted or hawked outside the tref, but had paid it no heed. The clear brisk air of the autumn morn, the riot of bright fall colors, gave her a feeling of freedom and release so poignant her heart sang with its wonder, and she was sorry when their ride ended and they reached the mill.

She was sorrier yet when they crossed the spillway, tethered their horses and entered the mill—to see the fat squire who had opposed Crosbey in the joust. Grosseteste's eternal ill temper was a source of constant unpleasantness, and she knew instantly that he'd find a way to make her work here a misery.

Most of the fall corn harvest brought in from the sickle reaping was piled in the wains for threshing and winnowing during winter, and was kept stored in oak chests to mill as needed. It arrived at the mill in large transport baskets, needing two men to handle. It was to this arduous task that Grosseteste set the slight pages, scorning to help with their heavy load but rather laughing as they staggered under its weight. Tara gritted her teeth, and strained mightily to handle her end. He'll not hear me crying for help, she vowed!

When the baskets were inside, the pages sprawled exhausted on the straw-strewn floor to await the Miller's return, but the ill-tempered squire had other plans. "Come, my lovelies," he ordered. "Thou'rt not done. The corn must go into the hopper. On your feet, and step lively!"

He was exceeding his authority, Tara was sure. The Reeve had warned him explicitly to wait for the Miller. But Grosseteste was in charge, and she could not question his orders. They rose wearily, and she and Cadfan dragged the first basket to the hopper.

Grosseteste shouted impatiently at them over the millstone's rumbling, holding the bolting cloth open and ordering them to dump the heavy loads into the hopper. "Are ye babies, then?" he taunted. "Is the load too much for you? Shall I call your mothers, then?"

Seething, Tara signaled Cadfan to take one end, and they gasped and grunted, struggling to lift the basket high for dumping. Rhiall crawled beneath to add his strength, and finally it was balanced precariously on the hopper's edge.

"Quick!" Tara shouted for them to dump it, but it overbalanced and the load filled the hopper and overflowed onto the floor.

"What have ye done?" screamed Grosseteste in fury and some alarm. "Ye have jammed the hopper! Stupid whelps!"

"What shall we do?" cried Tara, upset by his shouting.

"Do? Do? Get in there and clear it!" She only half understood his screamed order, but realized the hopper somehow must be opened to free the flow of corn. Unclear how to respond, but reacting to his urgent commands, she clambered up on the edge and plunged her hands deep in the corn, but could not find where it was jammed. As she groped more deeply, her sleeve was seized as if by a giant hand, and she screamed to feel her arm being pulled into the maw. Her efforts to resist were useless; inexorably the pulling continued, until her head was submerged in the swirling grain. Rhiall and Cadfal screamed in panic, and tugged ineffectually at her feet. She thought to hear another's voice through the hubbub, but the corn closed suffocatingly about her face, and mercifully she fainted.

Slowly she struggled back to consciousness, to find an unfamiliar face above her, its deep worry lines relaxing as her eyes opened. "Art a'right, lass?" a voice asked, and she bethought who it might be.

"Are you the miller, Sir?" she croaked, hoarse from the choking dust in her throat and lungs.

"Aye, lass. And 'twas in t'nick of time I was, or ye'd be that crushed, 'n' dead. Ye were cot in t'wheel. When I throwed t'brake ye was nigh gone. Art a'right?"

"I'm all right," she replied shakily, trying to ignore her burning throat, the pain wracking her back, and the whole terrible nightmare. Hands were laid on her, carrying her up to the castle, where the Lady Agrinore thrust her at once into bed, and set a handmaiden to rubbing an embrocation of horseradish and goose grease on the angry bruises and torn skin. "We've witnessed a saintly miracle, lass!" she said with relief, ignoring the fact that she'd seen naught. "Sure the gods were perched on your shoulder, or we'd now be lighting candles to your everlasting soul, instead of tending your poor tortured arm." She felt carefully of Tara's cuts and gouges, and searched expertly through her medicine chest. "Here's an ointment of yellow broom bud, lass," she announced, applying it lightly as she spoke. "Shepherds rub it on the beasties, whenever they shear too close, and we'll hope it works its magic on you as well. Now, just close those pretty eyes for me, and have a lovely sleep."

A worried Crosbey was waiting impatiently, when hunger pangs at last forced her down to the scullery. He'd heard at once, he told her, his face troubled with concern. "But you were whisked off to the bower, with none able to see you, e'en before I got there. Are you all right?"

"I think so. Some bruises, and some skin gone, but they say naught that won't heal." She sensed his anguish, and was grateful for it. "And how of you, Cross? Are you all right?"

He ignored the question. "That ape Grosseteste bears the blame, does he not? Sure, it was his doing!"

Tara kept silent, unwilling to inflame him more.

"You need not say so, Tara. Rhiall gave me the right of it. But the Reeve never did hear what in truth took place, and that fat beast Grosseteste seems to have got off light. But not with me, he won't," added Crosbey grimly.

"No, Cross, I want no fighting. Promise me you'll say naught to him, now or ever." But she gloried in his quickness to spring to her defense.

"But why? If we don't stop him now, he'll be after you all the worse next time. Don't you see?"

"No. This is my problem, and I can't have another taking up my fights, if I expect to be a squire and a very perfect knight some day. And anyway," she added, "belike he'll be very happy to stay well away from me, hoping all will be forgot."

"Mayhap," he said doubtfully. "But whether he does or no, I will abide by your wishes. I still wish he could be made to pay, risking your life and near killing you."

"Don't fret, Cross," she said levelly. "He will be."

It was just a week later, with her injuries fast healing, that the Captain of Esquires sent for her, to announce that her father was coming to inspect her progress. "We'll have a tournament in his honor," he annnounced. "The Eorl looks to you to do well. If you fall short, Tara, you will dishonor him—and me as well, for your training has been in my hands."

She looked at him, astonished, her heart pounding with excitement. "My father coming here, Sire? I did not know." She had been home for infrequent brief visits, but never had Sire come there. It must be a very special occasion, to bring the Court to Aber Castle. "When will he come, Sir Aelfgan?" she asked.

"Very soon, mayhap within the month. We had little notice. Will you be ready?"

A month, maybe less! So little time to practice all the drills she must show him! So much to learn! But I can be ready, she told herself. I must be!

"I will be, Sire," she said simply.

At news of the royal visit, training intensified markedly. Each day was devoted to endless drilling, with broadsword and rapier, in horsemanship, at the tilts, on the archery range, and with quarterstaff, until pages and squires alike were groaning in weariness. The King was coming to inspect them, and their reputation and honor were at stake.

The tournament would take the entire day, as every contest that could be squeezed in was added to the schedule. Most of the events featured squires, as they were closer to man's estate and possessed higher skills to show the King, but the senior pages would demonstrate in archery, horsemanship, and dueling with the small sword, in all of which size counted for less than skill and practice. As a senior page, Tara was drilled interminably in all three.

One more event, so novel and extraordinary that it did not have the Captain of Esquires' approval until the last minute, was a quarterstaff competition between pages and squires, each bout matching one squire against two pages. None knew where the idea originated (though Crosbey had his suspicions), but it generated enormous enthusiasm, even the Master of Pages advocating it to Sir Aelfgan, arguing its inclusion as an equal contest and a novelty for the King. Privately, Ugri no doubt reckoned any victory by pages would redound to his credit.

The King was taking advantage of his trip to inspect his northern holdings up as far as Ceredigion, and two days before the tourney there still was no word of him. Sir Aelfgan was grumbling dourly of cancellation, when a dispatch rider came pounding down the old Roman way from Pwll Deri, to report that the King's party would arrive during the night.

Tara, breathlessly impatient to see her father, was leaving the buttery next morn when a harried messenger rushed her to the Eorl's gallery, where the King awaited her. She knelt before him respectfully, as befitted a page to her monarch, then flew into his arms. "Oh, Sire," she cried. "You are come so late! I fear'd you'd not come at all."

"There was so much to do, lass," he said in his dearly remembered deep voice. "We came as swift as could be. But no matter. We're here now, and all's well." He held her at arm's length to see her better, and she studied him closely at the same time.

In many ways he was unchanged. He still held his large frame erect and proud, as she remembered from her childhood. But when he dropped wearily into his chair with a grunt, he seemed somehow diminished, and his cheeks, lacking their former color, seemed to have lost something of their firmness as well. He had faded even since her last visit home, scarce half a year back, and the vitality of his once commanding presence was little in evidence. Tara knew he still could strike fear into anyone who played him false, but unmistakable signs of aging were there to one who knew him well, and she felt keen distress.

"I wat you grow more sturdy by the day, lass," he said, clapping her on the back with a semblance of his former heartiness. "Your Lord tells me you're the full equal of any page in the exercise of arms. In that livery and cap, did I not know better, I'd take you to be a sturdy young prince of the blood. Tell me, then, is it all to your liking?"

"Oh, it is, Sire," she said, responding more to his underlying meaning than the exact words: did she take herself the equal of a prince in the martial arts? Could she perform better than a lass had any right to do? As well as the wee prince, had he lived? "I am become full as skilled as the other pages. I have learned…but you'll see me, Sire, in the tourney."

"I make no doubt of it, Tara." He grasped her two arms tight, and his expression held some of the old fire. "And it is high time I tell you, lass, that I hold you the equal of any prince who might have lived to inherit the throne. You are my rightful heir, and I have no doubts of you. You've done what no other lass could equal, here at Aber Castle, and I'm right proud to proclaim you my successor. You have earned the right, and you'll do well." He paused to look her over. "I may have thought different once, my Princess, but I was wrong."

Tara was speechless, knowing not how to respond. Never before had he accorded her full acceptance thus. Observing her confusion, he hastened to pass the moment by. "I'll visit your Eorl anon, so you'd best go to your drills now. Know that I have high hopes for you, lass, and will be watching with a keen eye and a proud heart."

A formal dinner was served in the Great Hall, the vast company leaving no room for pages to be in attendance. As they had for the preceding two weeks, Tara and Rhiall met secretly with Crosbey to exercise at the quarterstaff until nightfall, and they were bone-weary. I'm as ready as I'm likely to be, she thought, as she waited for sleep. Only Lug can know what the morrow holds. And perchance Atheurin.

The whole of the tourney passed in a blur for Tara. She knew she had done well at archery, though she still could not best the oldest pages. The lightweight broadsword the armourer had made for her proved successful, and she finished a respectable third in the swordsmanship duels. Horsemanship was a team drill, but her own performance was more than adequate. Sure Sire could not have expected more had she been the wee prince. But her real attention focused on the day's final event.

Scheduled were three sets of quarterstaff bouts, each pitting a senior squire against two of the older pages, for the best of three turns. The contestants wore heavily padded jerseys and trousers, with quilted helms to prevent more injury than a painful headache, and the first side to land two proper blows would be adjudged winner. Tara and Rhiall, waiting their turn behind the stands, could not see the first two bouts, but the grunts of the contestants and excited cries from the crowd told them the affair was a vigorous one, and she was half crazed with the suspense. Then it was time, and Ugri came to open their tent flap.

"Good cess to you both," he said gruffly, and Tara sensed a hitherto unseen depth of feeling. "Squires won the first bout, but we the second, so we be all even up to now. This puts the outcome square up to you two. But win or lose, I'll be proud on't. Go you out there, and give your best." He turned abruptly on his heel, as if ashamed of his display of sentiment, and silently the pages followed. Could be he really cares after all, thought Tara in amazement. He really does care!

As Rhiall and Tara walked out before the pavilion, she was not surprised to see Grosseteste waiting in the lists—with much cajoling she had persuaded Crosbey to arrange it. He had thought her daft to go up against the powerful and experienced squire, but failed to break her resolution. She scarce heard the head judge's instructions, so intent was she on reviewing her plans for the bout. At last the horn blew for the start, and the waiting was over.

The first two turns passed quickly. After Grosseteste's initial surprise at seeing who faced him, his face broke into an ugly grin, and Tara knew he was remembering the censure he reaped after the episode in the mill. That grin was an evil omen, for her strategy depended heavily on getting him angry, which could make him act on furious impulse, and become careless. Something of this could be happening already, for in the first turn he was so eager to deal her a telling stroke that he overlooked Rhiall completely. Given such an opening, the young page seized the chance to thwack him smartly on the helm and gain the first point. The squire changed his tactics for the second turn, however, and quickly managed to land a stinging blow across Tara's leg to even the match.

Sir Aelfgan sensed something significant taking place down on the field, but naught he could put a finger on. Caught up by the drama of the occasion, however, he halted the bout long enough to announce that the quarterstaff event being even to that point, the next turn would decide the match. He signalled the herald to sound the horn, and the final turn began.

As the contestants advanced, the crowd was dumbfounded to see Rhiall toss down his staff and stand aside with folded arms. A slow murmur of appreciation welled up from the assemblage, and their level of attention heightened to a knife's edge, as they realized one slight lass would go against the burly squire.

The astonished Captain of Esquires would have stopped the turn had time offered—and had he been able to muster up the courage to confront the clear wishes of the aroused audience—but the instant Grosseteste saw how the wind blew he sprang forward and launched a fearsome sweep at Tara's legs. Though she was prepared for such a move, its very suddenness was unexpected, and she barely leaped back in time to avoid the heavy shaft whizzing by. Grosseteste was so unbalanced by his furious attack, and so ready to believe that it would end the bout then and there, that his backhanded follow-up was so indifferently executed that she parried it harmlessly aside.

"Counter!" cried Crosbey, unable to restrain himself. "He was fair open then. You could have had him!" Why did she not counter to the helm as they had practiced? She could have ended the bout right there!

Tara knew she could have countered while her opponent was off balance, simply by bringing her staff around to tap his helm, but a light tap was not her plan. She had something more in mind.

The furious Grosseteste knew he'd left himself open to the riposte, and counted himself fortunate that the stupid wench had not seized her chance. He backed off momentarily to rethink his strategy, for it was clear a great sidearm swipe not only would fail to strike his nimble opponent, but would hand her a second opening, and he was sure Crosbey's shouted advice would make her ready next time.

He backed off, but disconcertingly the hateful Tara pursued him, prodding at him with her staff, forcing him to give ground awkwardly as he made shift to parry her light thrusts. His heel caught the uneven turf and he tripped. In a frenzy he struggled to regain his footing, and saw that the insufferable gel was playing to the grandstand, standing back and making no move to capitalize on his misstep.

The spectators cheered lustily at her knightly gesture. This applause at his expense, coupled with what he read as Tara's taunting look, enraged Grosseteste. Forgetting strategy, he charged the girl, and brought his quarterstaff around in a furious swing, straight at her ill-protected head. He wanted nothing less than to kill her!

Tara's heart pounded, and her throat was dry with real terror at the vicious assault, but she managed to keep her mind on the problem at hand. She had read Grosseteste aright and was expecting just such an assault. Her reflexes lightning quick, she dropped to a deep crouch and tensed her muscles. It barely sufficed, and she felt the wind from his sweep ruffle her hair hanging down below the helm as it whistled menacingly past. Still crouching, and with a sudden thrust carrying all her lithe strength behind it, reinforced and doubled by her hatred for his treacherous behavior back in the mill, she drove the shank of her stout hickory shaft as if it were a spear, deeply—and painfully, she knew—into the heavy bulge of his stomach.

The exultant pages broke from their ranks and overflowed the field, roaring their victory, crowding about Tara to sweep her up on their shoulders, and bore her triumphantly to the pavilion where the Marshal waited. Behind Sir Aelfgan, who completely failed to suppress the broad grin spreading across his seamed countenance, she saw the face of Sire, lighted with a fierce and loving pride in his daughter. Pride in his heir!

CHAPTER 6

After Tara bathed, Altie helped shampoo and brush her long hair dry, until it shone like burnished copper and gleaming gold in the bower's warm candlelight. Then came her fresh white undergarments, and the luxurious red robe Sir Elwain had provided for the ceremonies. When all was ready, two solemn squires escorted her to the Chapel, each bearing a lighted taper up to the altar where the Chaplain waited. He drew the sign of the cross on her forehead, and she handed him the heavily ornamented sword Sire had sent, with the holy relic inset in its golden pommel. The venerable weapon was placed on the altar of the darkened Chapel. There Tara knelt alone through the long night, to pray for the purification of her soul. At first light of dawn, the Chaplain was to hear her confession and celebrate Mass, and her lonely vigil would be rewarded with a hearty breakfast at the high table with the Eorl's nobles, followed by the hoary chivalric ritual of her investiture as esquire.

The guard chamber outside had been vacated for the nonce, and that part of the castle empty save for her, that she might contemplate her sins and purify herself in complete solitude. Since all the prayers she could summon up had been recited thrice or more, she was left with naught to pass the lonely hours save her thoughts.

She had survived the past two years without the comforting presence of Atheurin. She had not seen him since the Eorl prohibited further visits to the cromlech. Her initial impulse had been to defy his order, but realizing she could not conceal her movements indefinitely from the hateful

Grosseteste, she had put the idea aside reluctantly. Her growing skills and elevated rank had kept his envy alive, and belike he and his cronies watched her movements keenly for any hint of untoward actions.

She had not forgot the Bard's appearance. His features were etched on her brain, and she could see him in her mind as if he stood before her. Would I please him, she wondered. Would he take pride in all I've learned, all the skills I've mastered? Have I fulfilled his hopes, and those of the gods he serves? Would he think me suited to become a gallant Queen, like Elen Luyddog, or find me still a callow lass, sorely lacking in the merit demanded by the gods?

Tara, at age fourteen, was far from being a callow lass. She cut an impressive figure, long-limbed and well-muscled, endowed with her father's sturdy shoulders, but with the sinuous grace of a leopard rather than the ponderous strength of a bull. Her complexion glowed with an inner vitality. The stunning elegance of her posture bespoke a firmness of character that actually enhanced her unabashed femininity, without in the least detracting from her aggressive spirit. At first glance, she would be taken for a fit and well-proportioned young man, until closer scrutiny disclosed soft facial features and a spectacular diadem of splendid coppery-gold hair falling nearly to her waist. In pure white undergarments and scarlet robe, with a slim dagger in its jeweled scabbard at her belt, along with her clear countenance and delicate coloring, she was the very model of a pure and perfect knight without sin or stain.

The passage of time had wrought many changes. Tara's implacable nemesis, the brutish Grosseteste, had left for service in Lleyn far to the north. Ugri, the former Master of Pages, had become, if not her friend, at least her supporter and ally. Her warm friendliness and martial skills served to put her on a pedestal of near-goddess stature among the younger pages. The jealousy and resentment of the older squires had been transformed into the friendship due a respected and well liked comrade-at-arms. Algie and Altie, awed by her mastery of manly pursuits, reveled in her company whenever her schedule permitted.

Relaxing with them in the privacy of the bower was for Tara a welcome interlude of luxuriating in the pleasure of her maidenhood. Crosbey, while often away attending his master, remained a devoted admirer, and a rock of stability on whom she could lean. On the whole, there appeared little Tara could find wanting in her service to Eorl Skomer.

Little, that is, except the Eorl himself.

Tara had begun to recognize a vastly different regard in his glances. He took great pains to pay her flowery compliments, and to give her special attentions that she found unpleasant. But she was powerless to disobey when he selected her as his own personal Esquire. Though she was the undisguised envy of her mates, she would have been happy to forego that honor. She was required to attend him frequently when not at drills, and was mandated to accompany him whenever he fancied to ride out hunting or hawking. She told herself firmly not to brood, but to keep reminding herself of the good side to his favor—that he must be accepting the fact that his best interest lay in supporting her claim to the throne, rather than doing away with her. If she could but keep his unwanted attentions from her in the meantime…

While the Eorl's behavior was a constant nagging worry, most of her concern was concentrated on the great event coming up. She could not have imagined, as a terrified young lass arriving at Aber Castle, that in a few short years she could achieve so much in a man's world. Looking at her achievements impersonally, she knew her performance would have done credit to any male candidate, however endowed with physical prowess. The pages and squires accepted her without reserve as one of them, and she now knew they would accept her one day as their Queen and Liege Lord. Did Sire have this in mind, she wondered? Did he know she'd need to build supporters against the day she pressed her claim to the throne? She had never credited him with so shrewd a plan, but thinking on it now it seemed this must have been his purpose. Why else send off a Queen to learn martial arts that belike she'd never need or use? He is a rare good father to me, she mused, probably better by far than I merit. I pray I have the chance to tell him as much one day.

She thought of Crosbey, her closest companion and dearest friend. Was he more than a friend? The thought was unsettling. That he was hopelessly in love with her she had little doubt, asking no more of life than to serve her always. As for herself, she was never happier than when in his company, warmed unaccountably by the glow of his devotion. But was it love she felt for him? Putting aside the knotty bar of his inferior social status, which made their union all but unthinkable, would she wish him for a husband?

She tried to imagine being Queen at Menevia Castle, with him beside her as Prince Consort. She pictured the two of them together, discussing problems of the realm, dealing with crimes, bringing to fruition Sire's great dreams for Dyfed. That they would make a wonderful team she never doubted. But as to the other side of their imagined life, in the boudoir, she was thoroughly confused. Still virginal and immature despite the martial skills that made her seem almost an adult, her demanding regimen and special status had left little opportunity for romantic musings. She had attained budding womanhood without ever being exposed to maidenly whisperings of forbidden pleasures, or light-hearted dalliance with amorous youths, or advice on matters of the heart from a mother or chatelaine. She was appallingly ignorant of what went on between lovers, or husband and wife, and thus was ill equipped to judge whether she was drawn to Crosbey or not. Despite unsettling stirrings she could not analyze, she simply could not think of Crosbey in that way.

She liked him, admired him, respected and trusted him, wanted him always at her side—but could she be in love with him? As she knelt in the still darkness, trying to work out her feelings for Crosbey, she found no answer.

She had been determined to remain awake and alert throughout the night's vigil, as was expected of a squire novitiate, but awoke with a sudden shock at the sound of the Chaplain's entrance. Hurriedly she brushed the sleep from her eyes, and groped forward through the early morning chill to kneel before him and make a confession of sorts.

Breakfast over, the assemblage gathered in the pavilion to witness her investiture. Tara stood erect and motionless, her mind on her mother's last words of advice. 'When you gain honors, you must not accept them proudly for yourself, casting about you for admiring looks. You must think of them as tools for the better governing of Dyfed.' And I will, Mama, she thought with a rush of emotion. Then the minstrels were playing, and the tutelary knights went through the hoary ceremony of attiring her in helmet and armor. Somehow she found herself kneeling on a silken cushion, bending her head to kiss the hilt of her newly consecrated sword.

The Eorl Skomar stood above her, and as he spoke she lifted her head to look him square in the face. "If it please my lords here assembled," he intoned, "I beg leave to select the Princess Tara map Llywarch ap Ceorle ap Frych ap Cadwallan, and descendant in direct line from Maelgwn Gwynedd himself, to become and be my trusted squire."

He beckoned, and Sir Aelfgan, Master of Squires, stepped forward, his craggy face glowing with pleasure, and Tara remembered with satisfaction his disgust at their initial meeting when he struck off her cap to see her naught but a lass. He has changed his opinion of me, she recognized with quiet pride. And I of him. He is gruff and severe, but a fair and honorable knight who has taught me much. I owe him a heavy debt of gratitude.

"I shall stand sponsor for you, Princess Tara," he said with unaccustomed warmth. "I present your sword. Take it, sheathe it, and wear it in honor and pride." As she stood stiffly at attention, he buckled her sword belt about her, raised the sword smartly to touch the hilt with his lips, and snapped it forward in salute. Then he reversed the shining blade and laid it athwart his left arm so the hilt was presented for her grasp.

He waited, solemnly erect, as she slipped it into her scabbard, then turned smartly away and stepped back from the dias.

The Eorl stood before her, his own ceremonial sword drawn, and she knelt before him with head lowered, whereupon he tapped her lightly on the shoulder. "I dub thee Esquire in my service, and charge thee to perform thy chivalric duties with honor and fealty to thy Lord."

Then it was over, and pages and squires clustered about, among whose number she spied a few of the Eorl's knights. She took their hands one by one, reveling in their pleasure and the sincerity of their praise. Her eyes roved over the group, searching in vain for Crosbey. How could he not be here, to see me invested? Could he be jealous of me? She put the idea from her the moment she thought it, knowing it unworthy.

As the well wishers moved away, she caught sight of him, standing well apart and half hid behind the pavilion. She felt a quick jealousy as she saw Algie and Altie by his side. The girls waved enthusiastically at her, and she waited for them to come over, but they made no move to approach. She concluded her conversation with the few remaining pages, and quelling her irritation she went over to join them.

The Eorl's daughters were prettied up in their morning finery, long-skirted smocks of fine linen, with delicately embroidered kirtles, and their best golden circlets on their heads. Crosbey was dressed in regular livery, looking as dour as the maids did joyful.

"Oh, Tara, I vow you looked full as fine as a knight-errant!" bubbled Altie. "None could have thought you a lass in such elegant garb! And to think, such a brave esquire sleeps with us, in our very bower!" She giggled at the wickedness of the notion.

"Altie!" snapped her sister. "Do hold your tongue. Anyone would take it we really do share our bower with a squire. The very thought!" She turned to Tara. "But we are most pleased for you, and so glad we were allowed to see it."

"I'm so happy you could, Algie. I did not look to see you, for the ceremony is privy to men." Nor did I expect to see Crosbey escorting you hither, she thought tartly.

"It is privy, but our Lady Agrinore pressed the Steward, saying if the ceremony honored a maid, sure other maids might watch. He liked it not, fearing to be upbraided by the Eorl, but when she threatened to go straight to the Countess, he said we might come." She laughed. "He fears my mother more than my father, is the truth of it."

"That's why Crosbey is with us," added Altie. "We are not stealing him from you, but Sir Elwain allowed our attendance only if Crosbey escorted, and we stayed behind the pavilion."

Tara's heart sang at the simple explanation, and she looked at Crosbey to see a sheepish grin. "So that's why you bade me no good fortune, Cross. I thought you'd forgot. Art sure you did not?"

"Yes," he said, with a meaningful look. "I'm sure. I'd have given my soul to Bodb to be there. That is…" He stopped, dismayed at how the girls would take his remark. "I was much honored to escort you of course, Miladies…"

"That's all right, Crosbey," giggled Altie. "We understand very well."

After the girls had been returned to the Chatelaine and Tara's sword put away, she confided her vexation to Crosbey. "I just know not how to handle it, Cross. How may I attend the Eorl whenever he summons me out, yet keep distance from him as a proper squire?"

"But he does you great honor, picking you above all squires as his Equerry. Can you not look on it so, and forget the other?"

"He never lets me forget! He sees me not as a squire, but only as a maid. He thinks to have sport with me when we ride out, with his Countess at home. It shows plain in his manner, and I know not how to deal with it."

"Would it help if I were to slash his throat?"

She looked at him aghast, until the corners of his mouth turned up in a grin. "I do but half jest, Tara. If he molests you, by the rood I'll do just that, and a pox on the consequences."

"And I'll help steer your poinard." Involuntarily she gave his hand a squeeze. "I'll try to handle our Lord carefully enow to keep it from that. At least I'll hope to. If only we could conjure up a way."

"Could you arrange for some whispers to reach his Lady's ear? I wat she'd tame him."

"That's a happy thought, Cross. You always find a way out. Now I'll try to think how."

The problem was left there, half solved. Belike the Countess would cool her Lord's passion if she got word of it, but try as she might Tara could think of no prudent way to inform her.

Scarce a week later, Sir Aelfgan sent word that the Eorl wished to go hawking in the North Wood, to test his new Icelandic peregrine falcon, and Tara was called to attend him. She went with the Head Falconer to the mews, and waited while the austringer fetched the bird. Its jess was of new white leather, and its silvered vervel shown in the sunlight. Though still hooded, it moved restlessly on its frame, and Tara hoped they'd not keep this untried bird in the field too long.

"T'bird's just been unsealed," grumbled the Head Falconer. "I tole t'Eorl it be too soon by a fortnight to risk him in t'field. Best take a brace of tethered doves, case she won't come to t'lure."

"Why does not the Eorl take an older bird?" asked Tara. "Does he know she's not ready?"

"Aye, he rightly knows. He be telled time enuf. Aweel, 'tis his bird, and he be t'laird." He turned sourly away, leaving her to accompany the austringer to the byrne where the horses awaited.

Tara chanced sideways glances at the Eorl for any sign of unwanted attention, but he rode in silence, and she hoped earnestly that her suspicions were unwarranted. The dog boy had brought alaunts and short-legged brachells, with an ancient spaniel to calm them, and the beaters trotted ahead of the horses, with the young dogs tugging excitedly at their leashes. The sky was bright and cloudless, bird songs filled the air, and a light wind rustled the grass tops like waves on a gentle sea. Tara's mount was quick to respond, and she allowed herself a measure of enjoyment at the outing.

Suddenly the old spaniel halted, one paw raised, and the beaters quickly pulled in the hounds, alert to see what would be flushed. The austringer held the peregrine's hood ready to pull off at the Eorl's command. Suddenly a lone pigeon rose from the heath and flew low toward the woods.

"Hold!" called the Eorl. "We'll not waste the bird on that one. On we go, and flush me a woodcock this time."

But there were no woodcocks. They put up a pair of doves, a trio of cawing crows, and twice a single pigeon. The Eorl's temper grew shorter as the morning wore on, and finally he called a halt. "Have done," he said. "Naught's abroad today. Take the hounds home." The beaters looked at him in bewilderment, but he gave a peremptory wave and they scurried off with the dogs.

"Will we return as well, Sire?" asked Tara, dreading his reply.

"Nay, lass. We have a fine day, and we'll ride on for a bit. I wat you'd like a little holiday well enow, would you not?"

She hesitated, but he was waiting. "Yes, Sire, a holiday would be fine." It would be fine if his mount stepped in a gopher hole, but no such fortune was like to come her way. "Will we keep the hawk, Sire? Mayhap we'll stumble on a bevy of quail in the long grass, where we'll have no need for hounds." If the austringer stayed, the Eorl would hardly make advances on her.

Her strategy worked, but not as planned. "Perchance you're right, lass. I'll take the bird myself." He donned the leathern glove and took the falcon, then to her distress bade the austringer go, and the man took off at a run. Her worst fears were realized: alone with the Eorl!

"Now, lass, time we enjoy ourselves. We've never had the pleasure of riding out together, just the two of us. May today be the first of many pleasurable outings, aye lass?" Her silence at his question disconcerted him, and he looked at her sharply. "Are you not happy to be riding out on this fair morn, girl? Wouldst rather be back huddled over the Prior's books?"

"Nay, Sire," she said cautiously. "It is a bonny day for a ride."

"And that's more like it. Come up alongside, lass, and we'll have a chance to talk."

She spurred her horse to pull abreast of him, wondering how to deal with the situation. I'll not allow him to lay hand on me, she vowed.

She was relieved of the need to face that problem for the moment. A fat mallard hen sprang up under the horses' hooves, followed by two drakes. They shot across the field toward a distant pond, necks out-thrust, their swift wingbeats pounding the still morning air. With a hoarse cry of excitement, the Eorl snatched the hood from his falcon and flung it into the air. "Go!" he cried. "After them!"

For a brief time the falcon circled about their heads, confused, while the enraged Eorl cursed at it. Then it mounted swiftly into the sky. "Aha!" shouted the Eorl. "She has the gage now. In a moment she'll spot them, and drop like a stone on one of those fat drakes. You watch, you'll see."

But the bird of prey did not do as the Eorl predicted. Instead of pursuing the ducks, she flew uncertainly toward the trees.

"God's wounds!" roared the Eorl. "What's got into the accursed bird? Has she no training? Where's she bound?"

"The Head Falconer said she might not be ready yet, Sire," offered Tara uncertainly. "She's had her eyelids unsewed only this morning. Mayhap she's not yet certain what she sees."

"Nonsense! He's had two full months to train the bird. Come! After her!" He dug in his spurs and galloped across toward the woods, Tara close behind.

When they reached the wood, the falcon was perched on the topmost branch of a dead oak. Skomer pulled up and dismounted, Tara following suit. "The lure! Let me have the lure. We must retrieve her at once! Let her get into the trees and she's lost." He snatched the feathered lure from Tara and waved it impatiently about his head, but the peregrine turned away, and shifted restlessly on its perch.

"Shall I use the live lure, Sire?" she asked.

"What? What's that?" He looked back impatiently, and saw her lift the tethered dove from the basket she carried. "You've brought a live bird! Good. Then use it! Toss it out!"

She released the dove, which darted out until the tether brought it up short. The falcon turned its head down and left the branch, as if it might take the lure, but instead flew to another tree deeper in the dark forest. They could still see it as it landed, moving restlessly from one foot to another.

"After it!" shouted the Eorl excitedly. "Keep after it! Don't let it out of your sight, girl. Don't come back without it!"

At the base of the tree now occupied by the falcon, Tara tossed up the dove once more, and again the raptor looked down, but perversely flew deeper into the trees. It was hard to keep her quarry in focus, and Tara lost sight of it. She ran on in the same direction, hoping against hope that the bird would maintain its same course.

She spied it again, perched high in a dead tree, where the lack of foliage gave her a clearer view. When it took off again through the branches she pursued as best she could guess its path. Another momentary view as it crossed a clearing heartened her briefly, but the moment she released the dove, the peregrine again headed deeper into the woods.

She held to her course, with little hope of seeing aught through the dense thicket of branches, knowing the Eorl was left far behind. If she went much farther she would be lost, but his orders were not to return without the falcon, so she must continue the fruitless search.

"Good morrow to you, Squire."

Tara whirled at the sound of the voice, but found nobody. She scanned the woods carefully, but without success.

"Come, child, have you lost your forest eyesight? Look more carefully."

Her heart pounding, she painstakingly searched the undergrowth, staring intently at each bush and clump of grass.

Then she saw him, the tan of his jerkin blending so naturally with the dried grass that she had to look twice to be sure.

Atheurin!

"It can't be!" she cried excitedly. "I had given up all thought of seeing you again! I was sure you'd forgot me."

"You thought I recked it time to leave you on your own, did you?" he asked with a smile. "That the time had come for your testing?"

"I suppose I did. I don't know. But oh, how I've missed you, and wished I could see you and talk with you, and tell you…" She fell speechless, spreading her hands in mute declaration of her feelings.

He made as if to take her hands, but did not. Never has he touched me, she realized suddenly. Perhaps he has no substance. Perhaps he is naught but a spirit, that I see but no others do. No, that could not be, she realized, for they'd all seen him at Menevia Castle. But when the Eorl surprised them at the cromlech, he did not see Atheurin. Aching for some sort of closer contact, she tried to take his hands so near to hers, but felt strangely powerless to move.

"You've done well, child. Or must I use your rightful title of Esquire? And you need not fear that the gods find you wanting. They are well pleased with you, and even now they wait to see you in the cromlech."

The cromlech! But that is away over to the south…" She stopped in confusion. They were to the south. Then they must be very close to the cromlech! She looked up and about, as if she expected to see it before her eyes.

"Not quite so close as that, Tara. But its spell is on you as you stand, and soon you must come to it again, and make your initiation before the old gods, that they may dedicate you to the course you follow."

The sense of his words was lost as her mind suddenly reverted to her problem. "The falcon!" she exclaimed. "The Eorl commanded me to find it, and I cannot. And the Eorl himself—he awaits me on the edge of the wood. I must be away!"

"Do not distress yourself, Princess. The Eorl rides back to the castle even now, and belike he's forgot the lost falcon, his errant squire, and even why he rode out. When he gets back to the byrne, his head will be spinning with a great wonder of where he's been."

"But the hawk?" Tara gasped, astounded. "I was commanded to find her and bring her back."

"Do you mean Anitra, the peregrine falcon? She is here."

Atheurin rose, allowing her to see him better. On his shoulder perched the lost bird, her great talons gripping his jerkin. He must have summoned up a miracle!

"No, Tara, there was no miracle," said the Bard, as if responding to her thought. "If you live in the wood and can list to its messages, you learn the language of the wild. This bird came to me because she was affrighted, and heard my call as from a friend in the wilderness. She will go quietly with you now, without need for hoods or jesses. And I will call you soon, to come to the cromlech where the gods await you. Now, take the bird."

At his words, the falcon flew from his shoulder to Tara's. Its grip was firm, but she felt no pain. Its eye was fixed intently on hers, and she knew it would not fly off again. She looked back to bid farewell to Atheurin, knowing even as she turned that he would not be there.

"Can you tell me again how you caught the falcon?" asked Crosbey as they sat at supper that night. "You speak in riddles, and I cannot make out the sense of it. You say she landed on your shoulder, but what did you do to make her come? Hawks do not fly to an uncovered shoulder, and to one who is not e'en a falconer."

"I cannot tell you any more, Cross. She came to me, that's all. Mayhap I'm bewitched," she added, smiling to make light of it.

"Mayhap you are, girl," he said solemnly, and he did not smile.

It was impossible for her to keep attentive to her religious studies, and Father Eliswen had to call her to account repeatedly. "Thou'rt bemused somehow," he said gravely. "Some spirit holds you in thrall, and I must find what it is, that we may exorcise it." He questioned her closely about her experience in the woods, and was much disturbed at her evasive replies.

He dismissed her, deciding it was something more portentous than his experience could encompass, and resolved to bring the problem before the Bishop at Saint David's. Doubtless the stern prelate would ridicule him, and admonish him to cease these absurd notions and get on with the Lord's work. Nevertheless, Father Eliswan doggedly saw where his duty lay.

The Eorl's outing had afflicted him with an attack of the vapours, and his Countess kept him abed for a space, leaving Tara some glorious freedom for seeing to her own affairs. She took advantage of this brief release to ride out with Crosbey after rabbits, whereupon without knowing why she felt a strong impulse to head for the same southern woods where she had encountered Atheurin. She wondered if it were wise to take her friend and confidante along, but had heard naught from the Bard, so belike her summons to the gods was not imminent.

"I wish you'd see it clear to share your worries with me, Tara," said Crosbey as they rode the same course she and the Eorl had traversed. "I know summat frets you. But it can't leave unless we talk it out. Canst not bear to trust me?"

She longed to tell him all, but some inner caution warned the time was not yet. "You are no fool, Cross," she told him. "There are matters of import on my mind, and I'd like more than I can tell to share them with you. But I may not do so yet. You must take my word for it now, my dearest friend, and not press me. When the time is right, I will speak, but for now I must not."

And with that he had to be content. But his brow was furrowed as they continued on, and she knew her silence troubled him beyond measure.

The moment they reached the wood, she felt a call emanating from it, so powerful she could scarce resist spurring her mount that instant and galloping into its deep shadows. But it would not do to take Crosbey, so she suppressed the impulse for an instant, and spoke with him.

"Now, Cross," she said. "I must ask you to do as I tell without questioning me on't. I must go on by myself now. One day you'll know and understand. So please leave me and turn home. Have no fear for my safety, Cross; no dangers await me today."

His expression was unreadable, but resignedly he wheeled his horse and cantered off without a word, not looking back.

She had almost forgot the way, but as she rode on it came back to her as if she'd visited the cromlech yesterday. Again she heard the muted whisperings in the old tongue, and felt the friendly presence of unseen spirits about her.

But something this time was different. The altar was surrounded by a circle of smooth stones that she'd not seen before. As she marvelled at the sight, she saw something else. Atop the altar stone, which was bathed in a ghostly light, lay a robe of shimmering purple edged in purest white fur. She put it on, knowing not why she did, and felt warmth from its folds. Beneath it lay a sword of stone, yet it glistened in the dim light as if fashioned of polished crystal. She grasped it and held it aloft, and heard herself say 'The Gorsedd Sword', marveling that she could know.

She looked down to find a pillow on the packed earth, where none had been an instant before, and she knelt and spoke to the gods. She knew not the words, yet they came to her. She called to Gwdion ap Don, the deity who created the maiden Flower-aspect from the rose and the broom and the anemone. She called to Elen, goddess of marching armies. And she made supplication to Ceridwen, goddess of wisdom and knowledge, seeking to be endowed with the understanding she would need in a life of service to the gods and to Cymru. She knelt silent a long time, letting the whispered messages and blessings of her special deities sink into her spirit.

At last the voices stilled and the spirits withdrew, and she was left alone. Slowly, as in a dream, she rose and turned to go.

"Aha!"

With a frightened start at the angry cry, she looked to the entrance. Father Eliswen was there, his face contorted with horror. But her eyes were not on him. Beside him towered a fierce accusatory figure, red robes gathered about it, and lifted from the ground as she watched, as though to avoid contamination. The face was in shadow, but she could see fierce staring eyes above the beaked nose and thin lips. The dread figure lifted a bony hand, and one finger, curved like a claw, pointed accusingly at her.

"Apostasy! The creature is bewitched! She must be exorcised of her pagan filth, and at once! Seize her!"

Father Eliswen made shift to grasp her shoulder, and though she could easily have thrown the slight cleric aside with her superior strength, she did not. Speechlessly she went along with him, her mind in shock.

A guard released her from the locked cell, and she was prodded up to the Eorl's chamber. The Eorl was there, but standing, and Tara was filled with unease to see the gaunt figure of the Bishop seated in the Eorl's great chair. She knew her fate was no longer in her Lord's hands, but in those of the fanatical prelate who sat so still and so grim.

The Eorl spoke first. "You have committed a grave sin," he said somberly, his voice quavering as if somehow he shared her blame. "You have blasphemed in the eyes of the Church. You must be purified, lest you burn in the eternal fires of Hell!"

What will become of me, she thought in horror. Will I be bound to the stake and burned? Is my very life to end this way? Where are the gods that protect me? Is their power helpless before this holy man?

The Bishop rose, and gestured imperiously. "Down on your knees, heretic!" he intoned in sepulchral voice. She stumbled down in obedience. "You have committed a mortal sin by consorting with pagan gods, by turning your back on the True Faith! You are strayed from the ways of righteousness! You must be saved, and at once!"

She kept silent, not knowing what answer was expected of her.

"You will be sent this very night to the Convent of Dewi Sant. There you will be delivered to the Prioress as a novice, and it will be her sacred duty to purge you of these false notions that contaminate you. She will strive to save you from Hell's fires, and redeem you for the service of the one true God!

He sat down, folded his hands, and gestured to the Eorl to speak.

"Go to your bower and prepare," said Eorl Skomer. "Take only the clothes on your back. You leave for the convent this night!"

CHAPTER 7

Sister Melangell forced her eyes open, to stare at the stark walls of her rude cell, indistinct in the half-light of dawn. The rising bell still clanging in her head, she slipped her icy feet into the stiff leather alpergatas, and wrapped a torque about her bare head, as she rose from her cot. Shivering in the cold, she drew a linen underslip over her head, donned her bulky black habit, and struggled into the stiff wimple that forced her cheeks into a perpetual pout. Then snatching up her bodice and scapular, she hurried out to matins. Other nuns materialized along the dark passage, hurrying without a sound, obeying the rule of silence. Stumbling sleepily down the stone stairs into the antechoir alcove, Sister Melangell tiptoed across the wooden boards to her seat on the plain wooden bench against the wall.

Mother Prioress and Mother Sub-prioress, stiffly erect in their highbacked chairs, began the early hour of prayer and meditation. Through the confessional grille, the great Caldey Island candle in its ornate copper holder shed a flickering light, too faint to dispel the gloom. Despite the chill pervading the chamber, Sister Melangell welcomed the quiet that matins with lauds provided her, as a time to dream of the day the Bishop would remit her sentence to this awful prison. Too tired to exert the mental discipline of shutting out the memory, she let her thoughts slide back to those first dreadful days in the convent…

Before first light, she had been attached to the Bishop's party and escorted under guard to the Saint David's Ecclesia, and it was still daylight when the party arrived at the Convent of Dewi Sant. She was hustled into the chapter house, and commanded not to stir. Sire will have me out as soon as he hears of this, she told herself. But will he hear? And if he does, has he the power, or even the will, to stand before the dreadful Bishop with all the might of Rome behind him? Tara had hid her study of the old gods, and if he heard of it from the prelate in its worst light, could he oppose a brief period of study in the Convent, to purge her of paganism?

She was snatched from her reverie by the entry of a black-garbed nun, who seated herself on a facing bench. The nun's angular face was seamed and reddened, as if it must have endured pitiless scouring to cleanse it of all vestiges of human frailty.

"I am Sister Garbildi, the Mistress of Novices," she announced in precisely enunciated syllables. "Our Bishop has decreed that you will join our Community." Her eyes were devoid of expression. "I am most happy for you that Mother Prioress will admit you. I come to teach you your responses for the ceremony of admission tonight, and you must learn them without error, lest Mother Prioress be displeased." She paused to let her words sink in. "You must strive to please Mother Prioress, for only thus may you avoid punishment and live among us in blessed peace."

After a painful hour of instruction, each of Tara's mistakes greeted with the same patient thin-lipped and empty smile, Sister Garbildi pronounced her ready. "Come along, my child," she commanded brusquely, and without further preamble she grasped Tara's hand and led her out and across the courtyard. They stopped before a huge oaken door, and the Novice Mistress said, "Now I deliver thee, at the entry to thy new life of glory. Knock thrice to be admitted."

Tara's impulse was to turn and run, but where could she go? Summoning up the shreds of her waning courage, she struck the great iron knocker, and as the door opened her heart fell. Two silent rows of black-garbed nuns lined the hallway within. Forgetting her instructions, she stood motionless, irresolute. Then she saw the Mother Prioress walking toward her.

The Mother Prioress stopped a pace away, holding Tara with her deep-sunk eyes. She was very tall, with a grim bloodless countenance. A massive crucifix dangled from her neck, and a great bundle of keys hung at her waist as if symbolizing her badge of office. Her eyes, bare of any hint of human emotion, bored into Tara's with fanatical fire, Aghast, Tara knew beyond questioning that this gaunt creature would brook no opposition, and that her survival in the convent would hinge on full and instant obedience. This is my 'blessed peace', she thought bitterly.

"Dear Sister," began her inquisitor, her harsh voice mocking the gentleness of her words, "we welcome you to the Community and beloved Convent at Dewi Sant. What ask you of us?"

Transfixed, Tara stood mute for an interminable moment, then with an effort recalled the response so recently learned. "Drawn by God's merciful grace, I ask that you instruct me to follow Christ the Good Shepherd, and to live in poverty, chastity and obedience, and ask to be allowed to learn the rule."

"May the merciful God nourish you with His grace, and may Christ our divine teacher grant you His light. Kneel with me now, to be presented to the Lord."

Tara knelt beside the grim Prioress on the steps facing the unlighted Sanctuary, and for the first time was presented to the Lord, but so little attention did she pay to the ceremony that she remembered almost nothing of it. Then the Mistress of Novices bade her genuflect before the burning lamp set on the altar, and before every grim member of the Community to receive the kiss of peace. In the Chapter House, she was given her new name in religion, and surrendered her old. When all was done, at what seemed a furious pace, she was pushed into a small office and the door closed behind her.

She looked up to see the Prioress attending to some papers on the table before her. After a brief time she rose. "Remove your lay garments, to be clothed in postulant's garb." Tara hastened to comply, and when she stood naked and ashamed she was handed a coarse linen underslip, double wool bodice, long black woolen robe, and the clumsy alpergates with leather tops and hemp soles that would be her only footwear henceforth.

The Prioress bade her sit on a low stool, snatched off her circlet and bound a coarse black torque about her head, and whipped out a pair of shears. Giving Tara no time to protest, she began to crop off every strand of the long tresses that showed below the torque. When she was finished, she gathered up the thick pile of shorn hair, tossed it into a rush basket, and curtly commanded that Tara clothe herself with her drab new garments.

"Now you are a proper postulant. We will dispose of your secular clothing. You have no further use for them. Your new name in Christ is 'Melangell'. Go now, Melangell. Sister Garbildi will show you to your cell. It will strengthen your Christian resolve to eschew food until morning."

The tiny cell was bare save for a cot with a lumpy straw mattress, and a rough wood table on which stood a stub of candle in a votive glass. Before she had a chance to bid her guide good night, the door closed, and she heard the sliding bolt telling her she was locked in.

For the first time in her young life she felt completely abandoned, her self-confidence earned so tortuously at Aber Castle shattered by this bitter exile. Distraught, she longed desperately to reach out to someone, to anyone. Imprisoned in a bleak cell in this cheerless place, everyone she cared about far off and powerless to help, she realized what it meant to be truly alone.

She endured the ordeal of scrubbing in the chill lavatorium under the watchful eyes of Sister Garbildi. She sat through the silent and cheerless breakfast governed by 'custody of eyes' where ritual gestures sufficed to request food, and kissing the floor served as penance for breaking silence by so minor a sin as dropping a spoon. And she was one of those figures shuffling along the stone-flagged corridor to the chapel for matins, lauds, prime, terce, sext, none, vespers, and finally compline.

"You have much to learn, my child," the Prioress began in her first long session with Melangell. "Your sins are most grievous, but Reverend Bishop's tender charity gives you this opportunity to expiate them and come to grace. This is not our season for admitting novices, so you are the sole entrant, which gives Sister Garbildi and myself the time to guide you closely, and chastise you when you err. Let me warn against fruitless weeping or melancholy, for these are enemies of the soul, and we have medicines to cure such peccant humours." Numb and resigned, she listened silently to the rest of the peroration. She would cultivate humble and blind obedience. The slightest disobedience would bring a whipping in the Chapter House, or confinement in the dank cell beneath the dormitory. Penance was each Friday, when she must flagellate herself with a thrashing cord, for her sins and those of the world. Sunday, after compline, she would kiss the feet of the entire Community to show humility. Mother Prioress would be addressed as 'Blessed Mother', but before speaking Melangell must kneel and entreat with 'Benedicite', and unless the response was 'Dominus' she might not speak.

But the last was shattering in its import. If her conduct as a postulent were satisfactory, she would be admitted to orders in three months. Thereafter, leaving the convent without authority was a mortal sin punishable by excommunication. The Holy Father commanded that all nuns remain in the convent in perpetual enclosure. Melangell's life hereafter would be at Dewi Sant!

Tara could not restrain her shock and outrage, but was sternly commanded to cease her protesting at once, and as punishment for her insubordinate speech would wear the hair shirt and loin belt, that these might help her cultivate the virtues of obedience and silence.

Surely the Mother Prioress misunderstood the terms of her stay! Surely Sire never would allow such a thing! Had he not said that she was his heir? Surely she must return to Menevia soon, to take up the duties falling to successor to the throne. This was all a terrible mistake!

But how to explain, how to protest, when none would listen?

The cure for her accidie, said Sister Garbildi primly, was hard work, but before being taken to her work assignment she must be put in the hair shirt and girdled with the loin belt as Blessed Mother decreed. She looked thoughtfully at Melangell. "I advise you most seriously never again to make the slightest protest to Mother Prioress, or fail to render instant and complete obedience." It must be understood, she went on, that for the transgressor life would not be worth living, for within the convent Mother Prioress exercised absolute power.

The hair shirt was of horsehair, roughly knotted with uneven loose ends to insure that the wearer could find no comfort. The loin belt, of similar construction, was laced tightly about the hips. They were put on Melangell beneath her underslip, and with her first step she felt nigh unbearable itching and chafing from the penitential garments. Never, she vowed to herself, would she give the hateful Prioress excuse to punish her again.

Thus garbed, Melangell was escorted past the cooking office where flour-coated nuns pressed out altar wafers, past the buttery's fragrant odors of baking wastel bread, to the whitewashed courtyard where a sturdy nun with sleeves pulled up rose from her kneeling among the flowers to greet them cheerily.

"Good morning, Sister," she hailed the Mistress of Novices. "May I hope this is your sole new postulant, come to make my life easier?" She wiped a grubby hand vigorously against her dirt-stained habit, and extended it. "You must be Melangell. A lovely name! I suppose you know she's the patron saint of hares. Mayhap you can help me rid the garden of them, for they gobble up everything I grow."

"Good morning, Sister," said Sister Garbildi in an unctuous tone. "Melangell, this is Sister Pebligia, who tends our gardens and supplies us with vegetables. Mother Prioress has placed you under her direction.

She will assign you duties and grade your performance. See you give her no reason to fault your work!"

"Gracious!" exclaimed Sister Pebligia when the Mistress of Novices had left. "How could a sturdy young thing like you possibly give reason to find fault?" She took Melangell under her wing, asked innumerable questions, and in short order had won her trust sufficiently to be given the whole story, omitting only reference to Atheurin or her noble birth. Pebligia exuded amiability, and was so reassuring she soon had the postulant answering to her unfamiliar new convent name, Melangell.

Melangell's brain knew her problems still remained, and naught had changed, but the cheerful attitude of her new supervisor gave her hope that somehow all might work out. I've given up without a fight, she realized reproachfully. Her new confidante was right; she must ignore her difficulties, and rebuild her strength to deal with them when opportunity offered.

From Sister Pebligia she learned that the Mother Prioress was not a cold-hearted creature, but truly cared for all her flock. Bitterly unhappy herself when she first took vows, she did not give in to despair but tortured herself unmercifully—with scourgings, bleedings, the studded cross lashed against her back, fasting, standing with arms outstretched in the shape of the cross all night. At last she overcame her weakness, if weakness it was, and became the stronger for it. Miserably unhappy at first, she found happiness in complete submission to God's will.

"But she does not look a happy person," said Melangell, unable to picture the grim-faced prioress so. "She looks angry at the whole world. Certainly she is angry at me."

"That she is not, Melangell. She conquered her own great despair by dedicating herself in all things to serving our blessed Savior, and turning her strong will to the thousand small tasks of running a convent. She truly thinks this way will bring happiness, or at least contentment and peace, to all who find their way inside these walls. She takes stern measures with you now, as she did to all of us…" She smiled ruefully at the recollection. "Myself, I held some most unchristian thoughts about Reverend Mother when I first entered. She takes strong measures to make a clean break with your past, and shocks you to find something to ease your despair. I'm not surprised she thrust you into the hair shirt your first day, for she does the same to all. Even had you behaved like an Angel of God, she would have found a reason."

She smiled gently, and took Melangell's hand in hers. "I pray you to believe, hard though you find it just now, that in her strange way Mother Prioress truly cares for you, and seeks your happiness. Underneath her stern shell, she is a good person—you will see."

"Never will I be content here!" cried Melangell. "I have plans to which my whole life has been directed, and a nunnery is no part of them! I was dragged here with no asking what I wished. Mayhap it brings happiness to the Mother Prioress, who belike found no pleasure in her other life, but I vow to you there'll be no happiness here for me." She fought to keep tears from springing to her eyes.

Her new friend, a frown on her bright face, rose briskly to her feet. "Don't fight the future, Melangell," she said quietly. "God has his way of solving our problems for us."

After Melangell learned her way, she was given responsibility for the chicken yard, which meant the small enjoyment of scattering corn to hungry fowl, and collecting the bounty of warm brown eggs, but also the itchy chore of scraping up manure to compost with grass cuttings. After a time, she began to concentrate on how such tasks could be made more efficient, as a start on furthering Sire's dream of bettering the life of his subjects, and this brought a small measure of contentment to moderate her gloomy thoughts. Now Melangell met with Sister Garbildi each evening, drilling in the ceremony of taking vows. Though she swore she'd not enter the order, no feasible way to escape came to her mind. Despite recognizing its inevitability, the shock was none the less when the Novice Mistress advised her that her vows would be said in Chapel the next Sunday. On the eve of that fateful day, she cast about in vain for a way out, and the Sabbath morn saw her garbed in white bridal dress, kneeling before the detestable Bishop.

Almost in a whisper, she voiced the ritual request to enter the Community, and awaited the Bishop's response.

"Dost thou promise to remain in the holy estate of chastity?" he demanded.

"God being my Helper, I do so promise," she heard herself respond, but with complete detachment, as though she heard incomprehensible words from some far-off place.

"Dost thou promise to remain in a state of poverty?"

"God being my Helper, I do so promise."

"Dost thou promise to remain obedient to the laws of God and the Catholic Church?"

"God being my Helper, I do so promise."

"Ask thee the mercy of God and the Grace of the Holy Habit with thy whole heart?"

"Yes, my Lord, I do."

"God grant you perseverance, my daughter." At these final words, the choir began the chant of Veni Creator Spiritus, and the Mother Prioress escorted her to a small room adjoining the Sanctuary, where she stood as if under a spell while two sisters removed her headdress, veil and bridal costume, and clothed her in the long black habit, cap and wimple. Returned again to the Sanctuary, she stood dumbly as the detested Bishop buckled a leathern girdle about her waist and dropped the floor-length black scapular over her head.

"May the Lord gird you with justice and charity as you approach the divine bridal chamber, and may you be worthy to receive the yoke of the Lord which is sweet and light." She knelt on the prie-dieu and reached for his clawlike hand; nearly gagging, she forced herself to kiss it, then rose and went to the door of the enclosure.

"Open to me the gates of deliverance," she requested in the old ritual, and from inside heard the response. "This is the gate of the Lord.

Only the Just may enter." She knelt on the threshold of the open door and forced herself to utter the dread words. "This is my last resting place forever." She rose dispiritedly, holding her mind empty, and the doors closed and locked behind her.

As the months passed, Sister Melangell began to despair of ever escaping from the convent and the order, and sank into a passivity serving to shelter her from the reality of her nigh hopeless situation. Sister Pebligia continued to greet her cheerily and praise her work, as if oblivious to her preoccupation and gloomy air.

"I have a warlike task you should enjoy, with your knightly training," the older nun said one morn, trying to lift Melangell's spirits. She beckoned her to the implement shed. "The weeds in the far field seem tainted by the Satan, sorely in need of whacking down with the billhook, and it's far too much for my feeble muscles to wield so monstrous a weapon. Here, you try it."

Melangell doubted if any manual task would be too much for the sturdy Pebligia, but accepted the assignment willingly. It offered a chance for stretching her muscles, imagining she was back in the jousting lists. The pruning tool was heavy, and its menacing hook made it serve proxy for the sword she no longer used. She flailed angrily at the weeds, but the hook kept catching on her billowing habit. Dare she remove it? The garden wall concealed her from view, so she took courage, stripped off the heavy robe, and set back to work on the weeds.

So engrossed was she that she neglected to keep watch. It was with confusion and dreadful shock that she suddenly saw the grim figure of the Mother Prioress, standing ominously at the gate. Looking into those pitiless eyes, she knew she was undone.

"Come with me, Sister," commanded the Prioress. "No, do not stop to don your habit! Come just as I find you." She marched Melangell through the inner garden and along the corridor to the community room, where she turned. "You will be whipped for your scandalous conduct, and in the sight of the entire Community. Wait here, and ask pardon of the Blessed Virgin for your sins, until the Community assembles and I return."

Silently the nuns filtered in, and lined up around the walls like so many faceless puppets. When all were foregathered the Prioress was sent for. "Unclothe yourself," she ordered, "and kneel with bowed head to beg your penance."

Melangell recoiled in shock at the outrageous command. Strip herself before the entire Community? Slowly, her face burning with rage and embarrassment, she pulled her underslip over her head, and knelt naked before the Prioress, head down, eyes closed, waiting for the blow to come.

There was a sibilant swishing, and she started involuntarily at the stinging pain on her bared back. Again she felt the lash, and again. Summoning all her will, using her rage as a tool, she forced back the scream boiling up in her throat, and waited, with no movement that could give the hateful Prioress satisfaction, for the degrading punishment to end.

"Rise, and look at me!" Melangell rose stiffly. The nuns were gone, and only the Prioress stood before her. "You will thank me for this whipping, to teach you obedience." Her face was flushed with fanatical fervor, and deep within her hooded eyes there burned a darker emotion, one that was strange and unsettling.

Mumbling ritual thanks, Melangell stumbled out, and found her way back to the field, seething with resentment, scalding shame welling up inside her. Her trembling fingers made shift to refasten the awkward habit about her. I will kill her, she swore! I will! Never again will she take the lash to me! I leave this accursed place this very day! I will go, no matter where, and return only to thrust my blade into the stone she calls her heart!

She brushed past Sister Pebligia, angrily spurning her compassion, seized the billhook without knowing what she did, and clambered up into the darkness of the hayrick to be alone with her furious emotions.

She thought to plan how she might escape, but could think of naught save the shameful humiliation of her ordeal.

She sat thus for near an hour, when her troubled thoughts were interrupted by the murmur of muted voices on the floor below. Thinking she must be imagining it, she eased her body cautiously to the opening and looked down.

She was not imagining. Two rudely garbed men stood below, peering out through cracks in the byrne at the Convent. Their garb, and the swords at their sides, marked them as deserters from some lord's levy. At the menace of their presence Melangell froze, lest a sound alert them. She sought to assuage her fears by deciding they were half-starved fugitives looking to snatch a fat cockerel, and earnestly hoped they'd take one and begone.

But their words disclosed that they sought more than food. "T'scullery gel said they'd all be in t'chapel, soon's t'bell tolls," said the shorter of the two, a thickset man with a flaming scar running down his cheek and into his chin, and an empty socket where an eye had been. "Soon's ye hears it ring, be off to t'chamber t'way she told, and fill sack wiv t'plate. I'll bide here 'n' keep watch for t'guard." An ugly grin spread across his pock-marked face. "An' 'twill be t'last trip for that'n be it he comes on me."

The plate! Horrified, Melangell forgot her humiliation in the greater shock of what they were scheming to do. The Sacristy with its priceless holy service stood unguarded when the Community was sequestered in Chapel, and a bold thief could enter unchecked. A low whinny told her they had mounts tethered beyond the wall, and she realized that naught could prevent their unthinkable sacrilege—stealing the relics and fleeing whilst all were at prayer!

All were at prayer except herself!

The bell tolled, and she thought furiously what she might do to prevent this unspeakable act. The man with the sack left the byrne as planned, leaving his mate peering through the open door after him. He watches for the guard, she thought, and shuddered to think of what would happen to doddering old Gamber, if he chanced to hobble into the byrne on his rounds.

She must act!

Her knuckles white from gripping the billhook she'd retained so fortuitously, her muscles tensed for action, she dropped lightly to the floor behind the watching man. He whirled about, his alarm turned to anger, and grabbed for his sword. The heavy billhook crashed down on his pate, a gout of blood oozed through his unkempt hair, and he collapsed on the hay-strewn floor. The great bull penned in his stall stirred at the scent of blood and surged against the bars, hooves restlessly furrowing the dirt. The beast is as wrought up as I, thought Melangell.

She stood uncertain for a moment. Incongruously, she marked the hay clinging to his hair, and wondered that he'd fallen so easily. Snatched from her reverie by the realization that she must find a way to truss him up before his senses returned, she fumbled hastily through the boxes and hooks until her hands fell on the remnants of an old halter line. Commanding her trembling hands to be still, she tied his wrists and ankles securely behind him, wetting the knots from the water barrel so they would not come loose, and turned him so she could draw his sword.

Encumbered by her habit, she stripped off scapular and wimple, thinking how shocked Mother Prioress would be. On impulse, she unwound her torque and freed her cropped hair, realizing it had not felt open air for a year. She hefted the sword, glad to find it a sturdy one, and taking pleasure in the familiar feel. But she knew her skills and muscles were woefully rusty for the frightening encounter that lay ahead.

The outlaw groaned, and shifted about. Gritting her teeth, she struck him smartly across the back of the head, and watched with satisfaction as he slumped into inactivity again. She could not let him shout a warning; she sorely needed the help of surprise to cope with the other one.

But the surprise she planned was not to be. Though she peered intently through the half open door for the thief's return, he entered unseen. Alerted by a muffled curse, she spun around to face him. He stood in the back door of the byrne. Bitterly regretting her carelessness, she brought her sword up to the ready and tried to summon up her waning courage.

The fear and anger on his face became a derisive grin to see a half-clad nun facing him. "Yer God's done ye no good, little Sister," he said with mock sadness. "Ye should a'bin wif t'others. No mind, ye'll be wiv yer God soon enuf." He drew his sword back for a thrust, and asked scornfully, "'n" wat'll ye do wiv t'sword, then, me pretty?"

"This!" snapped Melangell, feinting at his face, but shifting to rake the point across his near shoulder. The quick welling of blood through his slashed tunic told her he was wounded, but scarce enough to disable his sword-arm.

He pulled back, grimacing with pain, jaw-fallen surprise on his face. "She-devil! What manner of nun be ye?" he croaked. His expression turned from surprise to a sly caution, and Melangell knew he'd now be doubly dangerous. Blood pounding in her temples, she knew she was, for the first time in her short existence, fighting for her very life.

Surprisingly, he fell to his knee, one hand leaning on the dirt floor as if for support. Could her blow have disabled him so, she wondered. Incredulous, she lowered her blade without thinking, momentarily off guard. The outlaw quickly scooped up a handful of dirt and threw it in her face. She backed away, momentarily blinded, blinking furiously to clear her eyes, and her hand felt a frightening shock as her weapon spun from her hand.

She froze as the outlaw slowly got to his feet, and with her clearing vision could see his eyes gleaming in anticipation. The blood coursed to her brain, and her mind grew clearer. Swiftly she jumped right and, as he moved to block her, darted left to the door of the bullpen. His momentary hesitation gave her an instant to pull the latch pin and open the stall door.

The sight of the huge animal, unpenned and directly in front of him, disconcerted the outlaw. His jaw working, fear palpable in his face, he backed away. But the bull did not follow as she'd hoped. Oh Lug, she breathed, give him no chance to pen the beast! The same thought reached the outlaw's mind, and he began inching cautiously forward to resecure the gate. Disturbed by the movement, the great beast snorted, and shook his mighty head in irritation, and his foreleg angrily pawed the turf. The outlaw's courage suddenly dissolved, and he whirled about and rushed out the door. Aroused even more by this activity, the bull lumbered after him.

Gasping thanks to the gods for her reprieve, Melangell scrambled to regain her weapon, and her spirits lifted as the hilt nestled reassuringly in her hand. She knew her opponent would evade the witless animal in short order, and return to silence her, but the knowledge served only to lift her spirits to meet the challenge. He'd not succeed! Her panic was gone, her senses keenly alive.

And in a moment he was back in the byrne, closing the door behind him. His eyes narrowed as he marked the sword in her hand. Slowly he came forward, his sword held wide to the right, his chest seemingly unprotected. Tensing her muscles, Melangell lunged, but her thrust was skillfully deflected and countered with a savage uppercut that came within a hairsbreadth of gutting her. She leaped violently aside, and his blade caught a fold of her underslip, ripping it free. This was no clumsy churl, but a seasoned fighter with a score of tricks, and she was not back on the sward at Aber Castle, but in a rude little byrne fighting for her life. She was assailed by a dreadful doubt of her ability to cope with so skilled a foe.

Had she but known it, she was not alone in having second thoughts. Her opponent had scoffed to cross swords with a woman—and a nun!—but found himself fighting in deadly earnest, his attention focused grimly on the bout, aware that he faced an experienced foe.

Drawing on her skills learned back at the castle, Melangell kept parrying his tentative attacks, while furiously seeking to decipher his fighting style and find his vulnerability, as Sir Aelfgan had taught. "Ye must turn your opponent's attack back on him," he had counselled. "Look for any excess, any overreaching, and make him pay for it. When he lunges too far, he makes you a gift. Accept it!"

She searched intently for an opening, but his defense seemed solid. When he drove for her sword side, his thrust was deep, as if to smother any riposte with the force of his attack, to drive her out of position for a counter-thrust. But mayhap this very power of his drive was an opening. The risk of acting on her thought was great, belike the chance of success slim, but she must act while her rusty muscles still had the strength for the delicate maneuver.

He lowered his blade slightly, his eyes hardening in preparation. Now! she thought. With a vicious lunge, his weapon flashed toward her right shoulder, his body driving forward to add power to his attack. Instead of giving way as she had previously, she twisted left and forward, and tossed her weapon to her left hand. For an awful instant she thought she'd fumble it, but recovered, and felt the hilt seat firmly in her hand. The delay bore a heavy cost, for a searing pain in her shoulder told that his attack had struck partially home. Then her blade found the soft spot beneath his rib cage, and she thrust with all her remaining strength, feeling his muscles tear as her blade penetrated the hard tissue and slipped cleanly into his stomach cavity.

He appeared not to have been hurt, and an unreasoning instant of fear assailed her that she had misread the feel of her thrust. But an expression of bewilderment spread over his face, followed by a sighing moan, and he fell to his knees and pitched face down onto the earth.

Stomach heaving from her unaccustomed exertions, heart pounding with a mix of horror and exultation, Melangell let her thoughts run unchecked. I have killed a man! I am a nun, whether by my choice or no, and I have taken my solemn oath to live in peace—but I have killed by the sword!

But had I not, he would have killed me! A dizziness from these heavy thoughts assailed her, and she had to sit down lest she faint. She felt the trickle of blood, and looked down, fearing what she would see. Her whole upper arm had been cleft open, and from the bottom of the deep angry wound her blood was welling forth. If she didn't take quick action to stem the flow, she would die right here in the byrne, and all her dreams would die with her.

Exerting a strength of will she didn't know was there, she roused herself to the urgency of her need. With her teeth and good hand she tore her underslip into strips, and tied them about the ugly slash as tightly as she could. She was forced to stop frequently to clear her head, but at last she managed to staunch the bulk of her hemorrhaging, leaving but a slow oozing that she disregarded. She sat back, collecting her thoughts, forcing her brain to tell her what to do.

She was a nun, and nothing could put right what she had done to one of God's creatures. She must flee—but not in the habit! She started stripping his garments from the dead man, suppressing a reluctance to touch them, and gagging at the sight of the ugly wound in his abdomen. With great difficulty, she turned and tugged at the body until his britches and tunic were free, then awkwardly, because of her injured left arm, contrived to get into them. She went back to the corpse to unbuckle his sword belt, and strapped that about her waist. All this while the trussed-up outlaw did not move, but his labored breathing told that he still lived.

Surely they would think her dead. After she was gone, and the dead man with her, then when they questioned this one they might learn he had a companion. But he'd not seen the fight—or the manner of their leaving. They'd reck her absence meant she'd been abducted or worse, and assign no culpability to her. They must not learn of her mortal sin!

Now to remove that terrible limp creature from the byrne, and quit this dreadful place for all time. Shivering uncontrollably, she rolled the body face up and dragged it by the heels out the rear door. She had no thought how to haul it away, or to escape herself, until she spied the pruning ladder against the wall. With fingers that scarce did her bidding, she ran the remains of the halter line under the corpse's arms and secured it behind his back, then with the free end in her mouth struggled up the ladder to pass the line over the top rung and down again.

She had to rest for a bit, but knew this was no time for weakness, so she wrestled the body upright against the rungs, and thrust her head between its legs. By heaving up with all her waning strength, and pulling on the rope with her good arm between steps, she inched it laboriously up. Hampered by her injury, she lost her grip and fell beneath the limp corpse, and was sorely tempted to abandon her efforts—but knew she must not. She persevered, despite the macabre sensation that near undid her resolution, until at last the body was at the top, and she was able to lever it over the wall and dump it to the ground outside.

The mounts looked to be emaciated farm animals, ill-suited for any long trip, but they'd be used to the scent of barnyard blood, and appeared scarce to have spirit to be affrighted. Thinking how to manage, knowing she had no strength left to wrestle the corpse over a horse's back, she secured the halter end to the pillion of the stronger horse for dragging the corpse, and tucked its reins into her belt, then painfully hoisted herself astride the other mount.

As she started, the draft horse dragging its grisly burden, she thought to hear voices behind, and pictured their reaction when they reached the scene. Then, grateful to be abandoning the hateful soubriquet of Melangell, she dug her albergates into her mount's flank, ignoring the throbbing pain in her arm, and turned his head eastward, toward Menevia Castle and home.

CHAPTER 8

Tara looked about in confusion, not knowing where she was. The surroundings were strange, and she seemed to be lying on lumpy straw. Could it be her convent mattress? She saw whited clay walls, and a ragged thatch roof supported by rough timber crucks. A smoke hole over the stone hearth admitted the only light, but there was no fire against the chill, and a rusted iron pot with trivet and chain hung empty in the penetrating cold. The rude hut boasted naught save a chipped platter and a pair of horn mugs. Nausea rose in her throat, and she retched violently, perspiration beading her brow. She sank back, hugging the thin mantle, shivering from cold and the shock of blood loss.

She realized after a time that she was not alone. A barefoot peasant woman, her hair bundled up under a tattered kerchief, was sweeping the dirt floor. Seeing Tara awake, she sat on the floor by the rude pallet without speaking, showing little expression but no hostility.

"Where am I, goodwife?" asked Tara weakly. "How do I come to be here? Did I perchance knock at your door in the night?"

"Nay, miss," answered the woman, and Tara was surprised at how young she was, scarce older than herself. She related that her man, out tending his snares, had come upon what he took as a dead body on the nearby sward, and was turning to run lest he be held for the death, when her moans brought him back. He'd fetched her to the hut, and she'd lain unconscious for two days, mumbling betimes but saying naught of any sense. Her arm was swollen and feverish, and the man thought they'd best get her to the Abbey at Roch Dinas.

Gingerly, Tara examined her arm, noting a crude dressing covering the wound. Mayhap the injury was not as serious as she feared, but at her touch the pain was as sharp as a knife thrust. "You are right," she told the girl with the anxious young-old face. "Best I go as fast as your man can take me."

There was more, the girl whispered, and hesitantly told Tara what else he'd seen. There was a horse, with a dead body roped behind. He put her on the horse, and pushed the corpse into the rushes. Tara understood the girl's worry, but hadn't the strength for the long and complicated tale of how she came to be riding it, and there was no reason for these simple taeogion to be confused by so tortuous a story in any case. She did admit that it was her horse, with no explanation of how she happened to ride this way or whence had come her wound, but thought it best to disclaim any knowledge of a body. In recompense for their kindness, she said they might have the horse. Best not mention the dead body to anyone, however, she warned.

When the husband returned, and bundled Tara carefully into the saddle for the arduous trip to the Abbey, she thanked the woman again.

"Oh, no, Lady," the girl said firmly, shaking her head. "Ye've giv us a good horse, Miss, wot we niver had afore, 'n' a good strong horse for the plough is thanks enuf for wot we done. Best ye go quick, now, to see to yer pore arm. T'lord be wiv ye." Impulsively she took Tara's hand, only to drop it with a quick look of alarm. "But us daren't keep t'horse, Lady," she protested. "T'bailiff'll wat us stole him, 'n' levy a dirwy on us, 'n' Thom'll lose his ox!" She dropped her hands, the picture of despair.

"You may keep the horse, and the bailiff will do naught to you or your man," Tara said firmly. "Tell him the horse was a gift, from me."

"From you, Lady? Yer horse?" A flicker of hope lighted her countenance, and Tara thought how pretty she could be. "But who may ye be, Lady?"

Tara hesitated to disclose any more about her identity, but could see no choice. "Tell your bailiff the gift was from Princess Tara of Dyfed. Tell him the Captain of the King's Guard rides this way a fortnight hence, and your bailiff will answer to the King if aught befalls you."

She asked Thom to be on their way, suddenly unable to look longer at the wonder and hope that illuminated the girl's face. With a lump in her throat—and a firm resolve to look into the practices of this bailiff—she turned her face east and they set out.

At Roch Dinas, the Abbott was suspicious of this unusual petitioner, a lass in a man's rough garb, wearing a man's sword but with a nun's cropped hair and a woman's feminine features. Too many conflicting signs, the Abbott thought, and kept her waiting in the anteroom while he pondered on the matter. If the problem was an injured arm, what lawless act had earned the wound? And why was there a bloody tear in the tunic, with no injury to be seen beneath? Why was the girl's hair cropped like a nun's? Just who was this supplicant, to demand succor so boldly, yet ride in so poorly horsed and with so mean an attendant? He reentered the anteroom and began to question her further, his manner bespeaking his stern disapproval.

Perilously near fainting, Tara mustered her rapidly ebbing strength to stem this pompous pettifogging. "I am heir to the throne of Dyfed," she announced imperiously. "Replies to your questions will wait, but my arm will not. I pray that you will see to it at once!" And none too soon, she knew.

All questioning ceased immediately. She was rushed to a commodious bed in the chamber reserved for the Bishop, the healing friar scuttled in with fresh wrappings and unguents, and the cleaning and dressing of her throbbing arm began. The following morn, a dispatch rider left the Abbey at first light, in furious haste, for Menevia Castle.

Sir Gruwent rode in with the party, striding stiffly into her chamber as she picked at her meal, and the sight of his familiar face brought unabashed tears to her eyes. He strove to hold his dignity, but his eyes glowed with joy and relief. "We thought you dead, Princess," he said in his well-remembered gruff voice. "The Bishop rushed word to us of the affair at Dewi Sant, but with your bloodied robe in the byrne, they made sure you were taken, and belike killed. The gods be praised they were wrong!"

"Oh, Sir Gruwent, what a handsome sight you are," she cried, her overflowing joy stemming for the moment the pain in her arm. "There were time I thought you'd all forgot me, and I'd not see any of you again. And my father...?"

"Off on a court trip, Princess, and knows naught yet of this affair. He had left when we got the grievous tidings of your abduction from the convent."

"Oh. When does he come home?"

"Not for a week yet, Milady. But just as well he is away now. That is...the Abbott says...well, you may not be fit to ride soon. Mayhap a litter..." He seemed unable to find words. Poor old man, she thought, he looks as if he sees a ghost. He is too old for such strains.

"Have you strength to tell what befell you after your abduction, Princess?" he asked, his voice under control again. "How you contrived to escape from the outlaw...?"

"Nay, Sir Gruwent, I was not abducted. You see, I abducted him." She told him the whole story, noting with quiet satisfaction how his jaw dropped. She thought to speak only of the encounter with the outlaws, but without really planning so she found herself telling of her arrival at the convent, and the Prioress's words about her perpetual enclosure.

Now that it was brought up, she might as well have done with it all. She made it clear to Sir Gruwent, her voice charged with determination, and outrage at the memory of her treatment, that she would never return to the nunnery. Sire could not possibly want her life wasted in the cloister! But she warned that the stubborn Bishop would take much urging to grant a rescript of release, for under unremitting duress she'd been forced into seeming to request final vows.

As she studied the look on the old Seneschal's face when he learned she'd actually been taken into the order, she began to understand, dismayed, that not even here had she escaped the long reach of the Prioress.

But of more immediate urgency was the condition of her arm. The constant ministrations of the friars had failed to stem the infection, despite the most careful cleaning and repeated application of various healing unguents. Ugly reddened streaks crept down to her fingertips, and an ominous stench of putrefaction began to pervade the chamber. Her body began to burn with fever, and at times she fell semi-conscious, tossing restlessly and mumbling words none could decipher.

The day came, inevitably, that the healing brother spoke with Sir Gruwent about severing her arm. "It must come off, Milord," he announced grimly. "The miasmal fluids creep into her body as we speak, and we must excise the putrid flesh less it destroy healthy tissue, and in the end, herself. I have done all I know to do. I pray nightly for her recovery, as do we all, but to no avail."

"Can we not wait but a day or two longer?" implored Gruwent miserably. "The King cannot be delayed much longer in his arrival."

"I fear to do so, Milord. It is woefully late already. If we hold e'en one day more, I fear the Princess may die. I cannot be responsible."

The aging Seneschal stood irresolute, his wrinkled face an agony of indecision. His fists clenched until the knuckles showed white, as if he would squeeze the foul humors out with his bare hands. For a long space he was lost in some far off reverie, perhaps seeking advice from the gods. Collecting himself, he turned to the waiting friar. "Prepare at once, then, since you offer no choice, and I can think of none. Cut off the arm."

The conversation was taking place in Tara's chamber, but she was beyond understanding, or even hearing, their discussion. But she rose to semi-consciousness enough to hear Gruwent's last words as if from far away, and slowly was able to decipher them. Struggling desperately to escape the lassitude that engulfed her, she clawed her way through the thick mists, and her eyes opened wide.

"No!"

She looked wildly about the empty room. They had gone, Gruwent to speak with such gods as would hear, the friar to prepare, and she realized in horror that there was no one to tell. If she lost consciousness, they would take her arm, whilst she lay helpless to gainsay them. What could she do? How could she save her arm? "Help me!" she cried, but her voice was only a whisper on the wind. An image from the past flashed before her, and she called out weakly once more. "Atheurin! Help me!"

She fainted then, and in her troubled dream she was in a forest glade, her bed a soft canopy of rushes. Her eyes were open, but she could not speak. Even as she tried to call out, she felt a gentle touch on her swollen arm, and the throbbing pain lessened.

Then, soft and soothing, came the voice she had not heard for so long, its reassuring tones seeming to recharge her waning strength.

"The fever subsides, Princess. The life-force is driving out the noxious humors that beset you, and reawakening the healthy tissues." A pause, then the voice again. "List to it flow."

She listened, and finding its way to her inner ear was the veriest whisper of sound, sensed rather than heard, but strangely reassuring for all that. In the dream, her open eyes closed, her feverish body cooled, and she slept.

The friar's excited voice woke her. He was speaking to the Seneschal. "I have witnessed a miracle, Milord! The swelling is down. The arm is cool to my touch—feel for yourself. I had hoped such would come to pass, but I allowed myself to fall prey to despair. I had too little faith. Her healthy tissue conquered the poison, in the Blessed Lord's good time."

The arm would heal, he told Gruwent, not because of any poor skills he had, but because of her youth and strength. "That," he added devoutly, "and the blessed intercession of our Lord God and Creator, who watches over all creatures high and low." The friar crossed himself, and dropped to his knees.

Gruwent was about to comment, but instead he dropped stiffly to his knees as well, and joined the friar in prayer.

Those of the Abbey of Roch Dinas knew, that sunny morning as they left their many works to watch the Princess depart, her arm healing and sound, that a miracle had touched their lives.

"I still find it devilish hard to credit your account," King Llywarch told the convalescing Tara. "The Bishop convinced me a brief sojourn in the Convent as a claustral sister would clear your mind, and cleanse you in the eyes of Rome and in the sight of God. He said naught of any perpetual enclosure!"

Tara's return to Menevia Castle had been triumphant, and she basked in the joyful glow that pervaded the Court. Exercises the solicitous friar had pressed on her were restoring vigor to her arm, and revitalizing the atrophied muscles. But this topic about which they spoke now was a constant and disturbing irritant, and she wanted it settled as fast as possible. "The Bishop may have told you that," she said evenly, "but at Dewi Sant I heard a far different tale. Mother Prioress told me I would never leave its walls, and the Bishop himself swore me into the order. His words to you were false. He is no man of God!"

"Mayhap not false at the time he uttered them," the King conjectured. "He came to me hard after your departure from Aber Castle, and at that time mayhap he harbored no thoughts of aught more than a curative stay in the Convent."

"Certain the Prioress did, for she said as much the very eve of my arrival." Her look turned bitter at the memory. "She had ever in her mind that I must stay in Dewi Sant all my days, and belike she brought the Bishop around to her thinking."

Llywarch looked his disbelief. "Be sure a Prioress could not make shift to control the Bishop of Cymru."

"This Prioress could, Sire. You do not know her."

The worried monarch strode up and down the chamber, as was his way when puzzling out a difficult problem. Finally his decision was made, and his pacing ceased. "We will ride to Saint David's, you and I, and see the Bishop with your Mother Prioress present. I would meet this fearsome creature. Our Bishop may be a bold man, drawing strength from his steadfast faith, but I misdoubt he's quite bold enow to stand against his King in this matter. If he proves stubborn, I will cast him out from the Cathedral, and face down the Roman Prelate in his wrath." If the King harbored any doubts of his ability to intercede for Tara so, he showed no sign of it. More than a King pitting his authority against the Church, he was a father fighting for his child.

Tara was vastly impressed with the grandeur of Saint David's graceful arcade, its circular arches soaring on pillarets of white and purple stone atop alternate octagonal and round columns, and marvelled that intrigue and deceit could exist in so inspiring a setting. Even now, as its vast expanse opened before their approaching troop, she still found much to admire in its architecture, and hoped the beauty of its structure would be matched by the grace of their reception. A welcoming party escorted them into the broad nave, where the Bishop awaited them with eyes only for the King. As they entered the Presbytery, Tara saw the Mother Prioress, expressionless, standing stiffly in the back.

The King made plain his irritation at the necessity for his visit. When he had finished his litany of complaints, he fired the key question at the silent Bishop. "How could it be, Grace, that you told me clear the Princess was at the Convent as a claustral sister only, when the Prioress made plain to her at the moment of her arrival that the lass was fated to reside there in perpetual enclosure?"

If the Bishop was flustered, he gave no sign. "So I intended, Your Majesty, but Mother Prioress saw it differently."

"By whose authority, pray?"

"By the authority of the Catholic Church and the Blessed Savior." The Bishop's tone was unctuous, his lips firmly compressed after he spoke.

"An authority the Savior saw no necessity for transmitting through you, since apparently you knew nothing about it! Who runs Saint David's, Father—you or the Prioress?"

"The Lord moves in a mysterious way…" began the Bishop, but the King interrupted.

"As do you, Bishop, since you administered the vows to the Princess with no word to me, then or since. Why was I not advised of your intentions, before you took this serious step?"

"There was no need to do so, Your Majesty, since the postulant herself requested admission to the Order. This was a matter between the postulant and God. It would have been blasphemy for another to have obstructed this clear desire, Sire—even yourself."

"You are a bold man, Bishop," seethed the King. "I had not thought you quite this bold. In your best interests, I shall consider that a serious mistake has been made. I shall expect you to issue a rescript releasing the Princess from her vows, ready for our departure this day—if you value your post here in my demesne!"

The Bishop rose, his thin face bloodless and his hands trembling, but his dark eyes gleaming with the light of fanaticism. His demeanor spoke that he stood ready to sacrifice his present high stature for some forlorn hope of future beatification. "In the sight of God," he intoned, "I must refuse to…"

"Wait!"

All eyes turned to the back of the room. The Prioress had risen, and was striding toward them. "The King is right, your Grace," she said. "A serious mistake has been made."

"What are you saying, Reverend Mother?" demanded the astounded Bishop. His voice was steady, but his upraised hand was trembling.

"We did make a mistake in expecting the Princess could be a sister in our Order. When she came, I saw rebellion and deep distress, which I thought the peace and order of the Convent would cure, as it has so many others. I was wrong."

"How can you know that?" The Bishop had regained control of himself, and his tones were icy. "Might you not as well be wrong now?"

"I think not, your Grace. When I read the scene at the byrne, I knew at once what had taken place, and realized we had miserably failed this child."

"And what did you read there? You have never told me aught of such a notion."

"No, your Grace, for until now there was no need. What I saw was a selfless act by Sister Melangell, to save our priceless relics from theft and profanation, at the serious risk of her life. I was not deceived by the signs she left there. I was convinced that she killed the missing outlaw, just as the signs spoke plain she subdued the one we found trussed up in the byrne. And when my emissaries returned from Newgate Glan, with tidings of a dead man in the surf, conviction became certainty. I knew then that I had sought to imprison a spirit whose destiny was on the field of battle, and not in the cloister. I allowed my foolish pride to overcome my Christian charity. And I was very wrong, Your Grace, as were you when you acquiesced in my program. You must grant her the rescript; to do otherwise would be to sin in the sight of God."

She dropped to her knees. "And I ask you now to join me in prayer to our Blessed Savior, that He may forgive our misguided efforts to lead her astray from the larger mission He holds for her. And to pray further that in His eyes our poor ministry may have served in some small measure to guide and consecrate her for the solemn duties to which her life seems to have been dedicated."

She threw back her strong head. Her level gaze caught and held Tara's, as if an unspoken message of strength and faith passed from one woman to the other. Unexpected tears sprang to Tara's eyes, relief and gratitude washing away the bitterness she had held toward the Prioress.

The Bishop stood frozen, his lips working soundlessly. He raised one arm, as if to contest the expression of faith all had heard, but without speaking let it fall limp to his side. He turned to stare silently at the King, his tortured face showing the marks of competing emotions struggling for mastery. Slowly his cadaverous frame hunched forward, and he sank to his knees beside the Prioress, his thin shoulders bowed in defeat.

Her arm healed, Tara enthusiastically took up her duties as heir to the throne of Dyfed Gwlad, visiting the sick in their rude huts, her inquiring eyes everywhere. She noted the meanness of their lives, and their oft callous treatment by the King's bailiffs. She rode out with the tax collectors, marking for later attention the inequities in their assessment of levies. She accompanied her father or his stewards on inspection trips, across the harsh lands from which the taeogion strove to eke out bare livelihoods. She was unwilling witness to punishment of convicted criminals—confiscation of oft ill-got property for minor thefts, shaming in stocks or ducking stools, mutilation, hanging—e'en, if deemed warranted, drawing and quartering. She stood in for the monarch at cantref fairs, bestowed prizes at sporting bouts, and presided at tournaments and performances. Her martial instruction continued apace, expertly tutored by Tellicho or his deputy, and assisted by the young knights, who eagerly essayed amorous dalliance with the stunning young amazon, only to be halted by a smile of perfect good humor and a glance as firm as iron. Perhaps also to be pounded painfully on the helm with the broadsword, if such stirrings in their blood proved a distraction to timely handling of the buckler. And all the while, she was maturing, observing, querying, and forming opinions on how she'd govern the realm when it devolved upon her.

The King reluctantly permitted Tara to join patrols searching the deep forests for bandits and outlaws, issuing strict orders that she remain in the rear if danger threatened—though Tara privately vowed she'd not shrink from risk if it offered. Her severely cropped hair had grown out somewhat, its brilliant mass caught back with a ribbon. Her cheeks were flushed with enjoyment, and her eyes sparkled in anticipation of adventure.

Sir Rhydder, the young knight who six years earlier had escorted her on the gloomy trip to Aber Castle, invited her along on a patrol to flush out a band of Cymri mountain men who preyed on small caravans. When she joined the force, a strange tableau met her eyes. Five of the troopers wore nuns' habits, mightily incongruous on their sturdy frames but looking nowise unusual at a distance, and a sixth the robes of a holy man. The outlaws would think it a caravan to Priory, with some modest treasure or at least horses to steal. The balance of the force would trail behind, listing for the warning horn if a raid materialized. Sir Rhydder shrewdly baited the trap thus, to see what nibbled.

When they approached the suspected danger point, Tara dismounted to remain in the rear in obedience to the King's order, tended by a foot soldier as protection against mischance. She doubted the disguises would cozen bandits who knew the area well, but she was wrong. Scarce an hour after the mummers in clerical garb had set forth, the signal trumpeted out. The following force deployed wide through the wood to intercept the raiders, leaving her behind with her guard.

She was annoyed that, despite hoarse shouts and the clash of weapons, she could see naught. The trooper, equally curious, had moved up the trail nearer the scene, when with a crackling of underbrush two armed men burst from the trees ahead. Catching sight of the lone trooper, they drew swords and edged cautiously toward him.

They would slaughter him for his weapons, Tara realized. They'd not spied her down the trail, and recked two on one an easy victory. Belike the trooper is better skilled than they, she thought, but they'd beset him from both flanks. His need to protect her would encumber him further, and she doubted he could prevail. Forgive me, Sire, she whispered under her breath. I must join in, and were you here you would agree.

She whipped her sword from its scabbard, keenly grateful to the gods for her restored strength and burnished skills, and ran headlong toward them. The two wheeled about at the sound, and their hasty conferring whether to fight or flee was settled almost at once as one broke off from engaging the trooper to meet her charge. In the corner of her eye, she glimpsed the trooper's agonized face as she joined the fray, and felt sorrow for the turmoil that must be churning within him.

Her opponent was stocky and heavy-muscled, and circled her with caution. He peered at her closely, noted her flowing locks, and drew up short with a muttered oath. He recognizes me as a woman, she knew, and heard the expected snort of contempt as he charged at her, his sword swinging in a great arc at her head. She parried the clumsy blow easily, and her riposte bit into his shoulder. He stumbled, and she closed in, but he scrambled backwards, bewildered.

There went my surprise, she thought ruefully. He knows now that he faces a swordsman, not a hapless maid. In the brief respite, she took stock of her feelings. She was more than a little affrighted, yes, but accompanying that emotion was an exhilaration that overrode her fears, a joyous release of tension that dismissed doubts and sharpened her senses. She thought for an instant of Queen Elen Luyddog, and in her imagination the warrior queen stood resolute at her side. With a triumphant shout she scarce recognized as her own, she tossed her head and faced her opponent unafraid.

He behaved with new-found caution, his glance darting from face to sword to stance. Mayhap his shifting eyes would betray his strike plan. As she watched closely, his eyes focussed on her left shoulder. She shifted her blade slightly, opening her defense that his target would seem more inviting. His legs stiffened. Now it comes, she knew. Pray Lug he plays no double game. But a voice within her told that she would not fail.

He lunged viciously forward, his blade lashing down at her shoulder swift as a striking snake. She twisted slightly away, and as his laggard blade swished harmlessly past her own sword drove for his now unprotected neck. She could feel her blade slice into his spine, and be twisted from her grasp as the momentum of his plunge hurled him across the road into the grass. She was weaponless, but she knew it mattered not, for he was beyond fighting. She stood motionless, exulting at her quick victory, her stunning head erect, her eyes aglow.

"By the Rood, Princess," marveled Rhydder when he rode back with his begrimed and blood-flecked group. Pride and astonishment competed for mastery in his face. "I've heard the tales of your soldierly prowess with the blade, and found such accounts hard to credit. But I'll disbelieve no longer! You've dispatched this varlot like a veteran." He looked about him as his troopers foregathered to witness the scene. "Hast seen aught like this from a maid before, soldiers?" There was laughing and murmuring, and more than one crossed himself, or made the old sign against a presence beyond comprehending.

Reveling in the knight's praise, she was as well stirred by his proximity and the male odor of him, but her efforts to deal with this foreign feeling were interrupted by his next remark. "S'wounds!" His face suddenly fell as he bethought himself of what his monarch would say of risking his heir's life so. "How will we tell the King we put you into the thick of a fight, and risked your neck so greatly for naught? Sure and he'll have my head for this!"

"Nay, Sir Rhydder," she answered happily, the thought erasing her previous emotion. "He need hear naught of my engagement today— unless you run to tell him of the matter."

The knight shook his head ruefully, then joined in her laughter. "I'm far from likely to do that, Princess. My thanks to you, then." He bowed his head formally, but with a twinkle in his eye. "And I speak for all my troop," he added. "With high pride, we salute our fighting Princess!"

CHAPTER 9

"Tara, such a parlous risk must never be allowed again! You put yourself in grievous danger of death, and in the very teeth of my firm command that you be exposed to no peril! I find it devilish hard to understand how you could have taken such a risk, in the face of my clear orders that you avoid any such situation that could lead to any chance of armed conflict involving your safety. I blame that young Sir Rhydder for risking your life so carelessly, but blame you as well!" Never had she seen Sire so disturbed. He was livid with anger, but beneath it she could read real concern, and knew how severely the discovery of her adventure must have shaken him.

For discover it he had. Neither she nor the knight had spoken of the encounter, but the tale of the Princess's gallant feat of arms was too exciting and known to too many. From stable to guardroom it was noised about, until inevitably it reached the Great Hall and the King's ears. He was in a towering rage, with scant patience for her plea that the sudden attack had allowed her little choice.

"Would you have your heir stand cravenly aside while two outlaws killed your guard?" she demanded. "Am I not descended from the gallant King Ceorle? Am I not your very daughter, Sire? Were I the Prince Royal, wouldst have me shun combat when a comrade-in-arms is sore beleaguered?"

He waved her words angrily aside, not deigning to dignify her arguments with a reply, and stormed out of the room. At eventide, however, he came quietly into the bower where she waited to speak further with him, and dropped heavily into the chair he had used when talking over matters with his Queen. Realizing that he was ready to talk, Tara settled on a bench and waited in silence. I must wait him out, she thought, for this is a serious matter he worries over in his mind, and the words do not come easily.

At last the King cleared his throat and spoke, visibly striving for composure. "I agree, when you put it so, that you acted in the best tradition of the Royal House and our lineage. I know full well that I've designated you as heir to the throne, with all the heavy responsibilities that entails. But by the gods above us, lass!" He rose and paced restlessly for a space. "I have lost my lovely Queen. Must I lose my lovely Princess as well, stabbed to her death in some useless foray into the wood, by some nameless wretch who'd know not e'en who he'd slaughtered? Where is the high purpose in such an end? Is that what you think the gods ask of us?" He stopped directly in front of her to stare down into her eyes, his own full of torment.

Mayhap he's right, she thought. Even were I the Prince, he'd think the same. He's saying the succession to the throne is too important to be imperiled by a chance thrust from an outlaw sword—not a question of honor but of simple prudence. "No, Sire," she answered soberly, her clear eyes meeting her father's troubled ones. "The gods have more in mind for us than that."

She heard the soft sigh of relief escape him, and his face cleared. "I am mightily glad you see it so. You cannot flee like a craven when danger threatens, nor may you hazard your life for no good cause. I will see that you never face so unhappy a choice again. There will be no more outlaw patrols! There still is much to learn here at the castle, if you are to sit the throne one day." He paused, thinking. "I have a court trip in the offing; you can accompany me, and mayhap even preside when the matter is a simple one."

She nodded, acquiescing, but her heart was heavy with unease. *I cannot leave it so*, she knew. *A King's heir cannot be coddled like delicate sculpting. Sire must understand what it is to be future ruler. If wars threaten—as when do they not—I may command Dyfed's forces.* She recalled her feelings on facing the outlaw, how much more confidence she brought to the affray than to her fight in the convent byrne. But in truth she needed far more experience to mature as a duelist. Both adversaries had been clumsy swordsmen, neither as well trained as she, yet in each engagement she had been at risk. Had she faced a seasoned fighter, the tussle might have had a different ending. *How could she make him understand that shielding her denied her the training that could some day save her life?*

But the matter was more than that. Flushing outlaws from the forest could teach her little of the larger aspects of combat. Crosbey had been right to say the fate of Cymru would be settled on the border with West Saxony. Thus her very future and that of Dyfed were hostage to the actions of King Alfred. It was from patrols against the Saxon King, not brief forays against minor bandits, that she would learn vital lessons about combat, and about protecting the realm.

She would obey Sire not to patrol the local woods hard by Menevia Castle, but how could she win him over to the far more hazardous course of action she had in mind?

Mama deferred to Sire on minor things, but she always was able to bring the stubborn King around to her thinking, when the issue was important. Queen Gwenwed never had argued or raised her voice against her master, but had sought to comfort the King, to assuage his worries with her gentle words and deep understanding. Only after his mood was tranquil did she hint at her concerns, but in such a way that he believed her idea had come from within himself. *Such maneuvering is scarce my way*, Tara knew, aware that near half her scant 15 years had been in man's pursuits, which gave her little or no experience in feminine wiles. *But mayhap Mama's way was the only one that would work.*

The King, thinking to have settled the matter, relaxed in his chair and sighed deeply, lifting his feet to the stool. Tara dropped to her knees and removed his heavy boots, then began to knead the soles of his feet with her strong fingers. He looked quizzically at her, and she feared he was wise to her trickery, but his face softened and he closed his eyes. Daylight was fading, the bower was quiet, and the walls took on a soft rose-colored hue from the dying rays of the sun. Tara continued her ministrations in the peaceful atmosphere, wondering if he slept.

Finally he spoke, with a sadness in his voice that tempered his contentment. "Tara, there is no way you could have known, but your mother did thus every time we met here, at day's end. Knew I not who it was, I could believe my Queen was here, speaking of the day's frettings and problems." He opened his eyes and turned them on her. "You could not have known."

Poor Sire, she thought. Of course I knew. How often her Mama had told her of those times, when Sire needed to shed some of his cares, and occasionally to be cajoled carefully into a decision he never would have come to himself. Sire is so grateful to me, she thought with a pang of guilt, when I have just such cajolery in mind.

She rose quietly and went behind his chair, to start massaging his shoulders. She kept at it diligently, feeling his tired body luxuriate under her deft touch. Then she spoke softly, careful not to disturb the relaxed mood that had settled over the bower. "When were you last at the High Court, Sire? Do you ever travel that way on your court trips?"

"What way?" His voice was heavy, and she knew he'd been close to sleep. Best not to waken him too far.

"Toward Brecon, Sire. But no matter; I spoke idly. It can wait."

"Brecon? No. That is…yes, I was at Llanddowror on the last trip, which is as close to the High Court as we can come in our gwlad. But that's two days from Brecon. Why?"

"It crossed my mind to wonder when you were last there. I thought to ask of King Cadell—how well he rules Cymru, how much he calls upon his kings such as you. Things like that, Sire." And other things, like sending me there to gain field experience against the Saxon.

"Indeed, that must have been before you were sent to Dewi Sant," answered Llywarch idly. "I find little to draw me there these days." Tara felt a sudden tension in him, marked by the hardening of his shoulder muscles under her hands. "The wider berth you give Brecon the better, Princess!" He rose abruptly to his feet, shattering the mood she had created so painstakingly, and left the room without another word. Why, she wondered. What unhappy recollection had intruded on their peaceful interlude? What was the King so loath to tell?

He summoned her to join him next evening, collapsing into his great chair as she took her place on the bench. She could see some portentous matter burdened his mind, but he was finding words difficult. She'd best draw his mind from what fretted him, and took her place again behind his chair, kneading the tense neck and back muscles as before. He relaxed in silence, his eyes closed. The atmosphere in the bower was soothing, and even her own eyelids grew heavy. His regular breathing told her his tension was abating. He was close to dozing.

Before he could fall asleep, she spoke in a gentle tone, not to disrupt the spell of the occasion. "You spoke of the High Court, Sire? You were telling why I must not go there."

"Nay, Tara," he said. "You did not understand me aright. I tell you rather why you must go there."

Must go to the High Court? What could he mean? Was Sire recognizing at last that she lacked instruction in what Mathry, Aber and Menevia could not teach—mayhap use of the mangonels and great siege engines found only in the armament of the High King? He could scarce mean she was to patrol along the Saxon border, for he'd reckon that far too risky. She ached to ask what he had in mind, but knew silence was more effective, so quelled her intense impatience and waited with what little equanimity she could muster for any explanation.

The King's voice was husky, and he spoke as if consciously holding himself in check. "I've not told you of an old compact I made with King Cadell, child, for it lay far in the future and I recked the gods would intervene ere the appointed time. But they've not spoken, and the time is near upon us, and you must be told of it." He raised himself and turned to face her. "How old are you now?"

What a strange question, she thought. Sure he knows my age. "I am a half and fifteen, Sire," she replied. "In six more months, I'll be full grown." To emphasize her maturity, she added, "the coming year will find me sixteen years of age, Sire; a year of great interest to me."

"Aye, lass," he said gravely. "Mayhap greater impact than you reck. I shall tell you this: my compact with King Cadell provides that before your sixteenth year be out, you shall become the bride of his son, Crown Prince Clydog."

Tara's brain refused for the moment to register his words. She the bride of Clydog! She could not have heard aright! Through her confusion, she realized Sire was explaining the why of the agreement, but made no sense of it. Bride to that disgusting creature, whose behavior made him the shame of the realm? Cloistered in the women's bower at Glamorgan Castle, like some sow penned up for the slaughter? Barred from achieving the destiny guiding all her training and aspirations? She would not credit it! Sire must be jesting.

But his glum tone told her, with all too painful clarity, that he did not jest.

She forced herself to listen, to understand the catastrophic news that had reduced her plans to rubble. "I did not speak of it ere this," he was saying, "for I made certain I'd not let it come to pass. I vowed to find a way to thwart such a dreadful alliance, lass. And I vow so still." He clenched his great fists until the knuckles shone white. As the years passed, he said, he had kept hoping fate would show a way out of the compact, but with time growing short and no solution in sight, he even contemplated having Clydog strangled as he slept—and swore if no other way offered he'd do the deed himself.

Tara scarce closed her eyes that night, so stunned was she by her father's news, and so little able to understand what had made such a dreadful compact necessary. At dawn she sought out Sir Gruwent, waiting with ill-controlled impatience until he awakened, to ask if he could shed light on the matter, and he referred her to Tellicho, who was there when the agreement had been consummated.

"My duty is not to explain the King's business, Milady," said the stocky Captain. "Or to question what he does. Best you ask your father direct." But Tara refused to accept so evasive a response.

"You were there, Captain Tellicho. Something forced the King to ally me with so misbegotten a wretch. You know what transpired there, when I was but four years of age, and you must tell me. In his present unease of spirit, it might pain my father were I to press him on't. If you would spare him this, I beg you tell me what you remember."

Thus pressed, the reluctant Guard Captain disclosed enough to explain the agonizing dilemma Sire had faced, and to help her understand why he acted as he had. She thanked Tellicho, and shortly after the fifth hour, when the court repaired to the dining table, saddled her bay mare and rode out into the deep woods to be alone with her tumultuous thoughts.

She had no conscious destination, but rode toward the clearing where she first had learned from the Bard that she was a child of destiny. And is this now to be my destiny, she wondered bitterly. She found the old smoothed log, and forlornly hoped he'd materialize to show her a way out, but knew he would not. She was a child no longer, and must meet problems with her own strengths. He'd expect her to resolve things by her own wits. And so I will, she vowed, but the courage and spirit which served her so well in combat rang hollow. What weapons had she to free herself from this hateful pact?

She sat motionless on the log all afternoon, furiously wracking her brain for a plan to avert the disaster facing her, without staining her father's honor or risking his neck. The night birds were calling when she rode back to the castle, discouraged, her problem still unresolved.

She was stripping off the saddle when a makeshift excuse for a plan came to her. As bride, she could choose her wedding date, up to the very last day of her sixteenth year. She had a year and a half to learn more of her betrothed by visiting Glamorgan Castle, where she could join the High King's patrols and hone her skills whilst seeking for a way out of a marriage she was determined must never happen. The plan would be a starting point for cobbling up a strategy.

Within the month, the royal party from Menevia Castle galloped under Glamorgan's old tri-decked gate. Her father, a glum companion on the march, had never truly accepted the prospect of such a marriage, and with its imminence was too depressed to think of aught else. Tara, suppressing her own gloomy forebodings, sought to cheer him up.

"Be not so downcast, Sire," she implored him. "You had no choice but to acquiesce in King Cadell's proposal. Have no fear. We will find a way out."

"How, child? Time grows devilish short for any plan, with scarce a year until you are to be wed. My burden it is to solve, and by Lug I will solve it, and in a way none can gainsay!"

"And get yourself hanged for your pains!" She understood all too well what he meant, and she vowed never to permit it. Desperately she sought to divert him from so calamitous a course. "Nay, Sire. We need no star-crossed action. I have a plan." *If only I did,* she thought.

"And what is that?" he asked, his countenance lightening somewhat with a flicker of hope.

Even as she began to stammer, the essence of a thought struck her. "I'll act so perversely before him, Sire, so addle-pated, he'll run from marriage to so shrewish a bride!" Belike the dullard Clydog would be so centered on his own voice he'd scarce note any such behavior. Her only goal in saying it was to flush these reckless ideas from Sire's troubled mind.

He considered her words a moment, then brightened. "By the rood, lass, it might work!" he exulted, taking the bait. "The dolt thinks to win a sweet submissive baggage. Let him see you more a viper than a soft, simpering maid, and he'll have no more stomach for the match." He was measurably cheered by the slender reed of hope she dangled before him.

By their arrival at Brecon, the King's mood was positively buoyant, and oddly enough, in view of the real purpose of her words, she was starting to lend the plan some credence as well.

"What a bonny princess thou're become, Milady," said King Cadell gallantly when they foregathered in his chambers. Since leaving the convent, it had been Tara's custom to appear in man's attire, with scarce any feminine adornments with which most well-born women bedecked their persons, but her dark-fringed gray-green eyes and full red lips left little doubt of her sex. "The account of your esquiring has reached us, but I took it as mere barracks talk. But by Lug," he said, with open admiration, "your posture is that of a fighting man. My Clydog will find it hard to credit."

"You are very kind, your Majesty," murmured Tara. Would that Prince Clydog finds much more in me hard to credit, she hoped.

"Tara has trained as a Prince and my heir," broke in Llywarch proudly. "Her sword bears two notches already, outlaws thinking to cut her down who now reside in the Otherworld."

A look of surprise broke through Cadell's courtly demeanor. "By the gods, Llywarch, you can't be serious! A trooper's skill at arms, and wondrous fair betimes! Did I not know you so well, I'd take your words as fatherly puffing. Clydog may come to fear he nurses a viper to his bosom."

Father and daughter exchanged surreptitious glances. Was it an omen, Cadell's father using their very term, viper?

Somewhat cheerful, not allowing herself too much hope, Tara dressed for supper. Though she had brought along a gown, she deliberately donned uchelwr's attire, that Clydog might have no illusions as to her martial bent. But sadly, the break in her gloom lasted only until she entered the Great Hall to join the group savoring the roaring fire.

The years had not dealt kindly with Prince Clydog. Though fullgrown, and heir apparent to the throne, he was but a pale imitation of his sire. His childish fat had solidified into corpulence, and though large of frame and with the potential to be well muscled, he had chosen the path of indolent dissipation. Fencing masters and archery instructors had labored to develop any latent ability, but his lack of industry left him an indifferent warrior. Capable of a veneer of charm when he chose, his uncontrolled rages made his associates defer to him in all encounters rather than face his temper. He avoided his father, unwilling to face up to the King's evident disappointment at what his son had become. Though his princely duties took him nominally on patrols against Saxon infiltrators, he went only to the safer regions, and even there seconded by a seasoned lieutenant in effective command. His dubious mettle never had been tested against a hostile blade.

It was this brave cavalier to whom Tara was reintroduced at supper. The high table was set for six, but only three people awaited at the hearth as she and her Sire arrived. Cadell himself came forward to greet them.

"We hold a family party this eve," he said, welcoming them and taking Tara's hand to draw her toward the others. "I misdoubt not you remember my hostess, Princess Meuriga, who took you under her wing when you visited us as a babe."

Princess Meuriga was twenty, Tara calculated, but in her youthful kirtle and unbound dark locks looked scarce older than Altie, and seemed agonizingly shy. Tara impulsively hugged her, and could feel the slight maiden tremble in her strong grip. Why do I affright her, she wondered, and tried to see herself through the other's eyes—mayhap an alarming figure indeed in her campaign attire. Silently she thanked her father, for freeing her from the sheltered existence of this timid miss standing so shyly before her, unable to find her voice.

The High King, sensing something of their tension, drew Tara away. "My second son, Prince Hywel, is delayed," he said, "but here's the one you came to see. Princess Tara of Dyfed meet Crown Prince Clydog, after a long eleven years." Here it was at last, she realized. She had kept her eyes averted from him, but at the introduction she looked straight at her betrothed.

To her surprise the Prince, while undeniably overfed, was sturdy of build, with features not as unpleasing as she had imagined. Recalling Grosseteste, she had to admit that Clydog benefited from comparison. The comparison was of small moment, however, since she vowed they'd never be wed, but their visit would be more bearable if the years had honed off his rough edges somewhat. Not knowing how to greet a crown prince, she decided to err on the side of formality, so dropped to one knee, raised his hand to her lips, then quickly rose. "I beg leave to pay my respects, Prince Clydog," she said courteously.

"I grant you leave," he responded mockingly, then spoke more abruptly. "This meeting has been overlong in coming. It seems you dis-remember that I will be your Lord." His scarce veiled rudeness was masked by an affable manner, belike designed only to mislead any casual observer, but making no secret of his true feelings.

Uncertain how to respond to his boorish greeting, Tara contented herself with a quiet answer. "I have not forgot, my Lord." She turned away in confusion and disgust, wishing herself anywhere but here.

King Cadell sought to defuse the situation by directing the diners to seats, putting Tara on a place of honor to his left, but as protocol required that Llywarch be to his right he had no choice but to put Clydog next to Tara on her left. She stared straight ahead, holding her temper, determined to speak only when required. But Clydog would not permit her refuge into silence.

"I find myself caught by your bizarre garb, wench," he began crudely. "Did I not know better, I would take you to be a trooper. What fancy impels you to such an affectation?"

"I dress so because I am heir to Dyfed's throne," she began stiffly. "And I believe it to be unseemly for the heir to be cumbered by a woman's gown." She decided to have it out with him directly. "And I am no 'wench', Prince Clydog. I am the Princess Tara!"

He flushed hotly at her words. "Heir you may be for the nonce, my gel, but you will be so little longer, for the bride of the Crown Prince should presume to no ambition save that. It is unseemly for my betrothed to be garbed so. I desire that you hie to the woman's bower early on the morrow, and bid Princess Meuriga clothe you in proper maidenly style from her wardrobe."

"No!" Tara could stand no more temporizing on this critical matter. She was determined to make her feelings and her position clear immediately.

Clydog's shock at her perceived affrontery turned quickly to fury, but before he could speak further she rose from her seat and turned to the High King. "I ask your pardon, Your Majesty, but I am afflicted with a sudden ague. I respectfully request leave to retire."

Cadell, deep in conversation with Llywarch, had not paid attention to the angry exchange, and was taken aback by her request. He looked quickly at Clydog, noticing the angry flush on his son's face, and his lips compressed. "We are sorry to hear of your indisposition," he said to Tara. Even as he spoke, he darted a momentary look of annoyance at Clydog, then turned back to her. "Indeed you have my permission, and we all trust the morn finds you quite recovered."

She bowed and hurried away, quickly mounting the stair to her chamber and throwing herself face down on her pallet. Things hardly could have started worse between Clydog and herself, but at least the gauntlet was thrown down and all knew where she stood. She would refuse to garb herself in woman's clothing, regardless of his petulance.

She began to take a more sanguine view of the situation. Mayhap the imaginary scenario she had sketched out to Sire on the trip—making herself seem such a viperish marriage prospect that Clydog would discard her forthwith—began to look more plausible. A showdown might come sooner than she or Sire could have hoped for.

After breakfasting in her chamber, and donning her field dress, Tara happened upon Clydog in the Great Hall, and stiffened herself for another outbreak over her garb. But he paid her little heed, and she soon learned the reason. He was preoccupied with preparations for an unexpected patrol foray into the Black Mountains, and she looked on quizzically as he rushed from one group to another, with a confusion of orders that seemed to her not only disorganized but conflicting. Llywarch and Cadell had breakfasted and gone, and when Tara moved to the breakfast board she found herself in the company of three young knights conversing together. At her appearance they ceased talking and addressed her.

"You must be the gallant Princess Tara," said one who looked a bit more mature than the others. "I am Sir Pumphrey, Milady, at your service. These two churls are Sirs Medweg and Calavie, knights of the realm, though you'd take them as pages from their downy cheeks."

"Good morrow, Sir Pumphrey, and to you two Sirs," she said, happy to find congenial company as a counter to Clydog's rudeness. "Both of you look fierce enow that I'd take you for squires at least." Enough bandinage, she decided. This was an opportunity to find out what was happening. "Do the three of you accompany Prince Clydog on patrol, Sir Pumphrey?"

"Aye, Milady, we have that good fortune," said Pumphrey gravely, but she thought sarcasm could be detected in his tone. "Wouldst accompany us? You would honor us all greatly."

She knew he offered in jest, but he'd given her an opening he'd be hard put to withdraw. "I thank you, Sir Knight," she answered serenely. "I accept with pleasure, and choose to be the fourth member of your noble group. Pray have my bay saddled and accoutred, whilst I fetch my weapons." Ignoring the ludicrous dismay on his face, she left the room.

She could see that Clydog had not noted the exchange, and he must not be allowed to notice her presence on the patrol until they were well away. She buckled on her sword, and on impulse strapped her dagger in its sheath inside her thigh, as Sir Aelfgan had taught her. Thus armed, she hurried to the stable.

The patrol was dispersed so widely that she had no difficulty keeping out of Clydog's sight. Pumphrey, recovering swiftly from his discomfiture, briefed her in his jocular way on the purpose of the exercise.

"I will not presume to hide from you, Milady, that we expect no dangerous quarry today. This is more a practice foray than a serious thrust, for Saxons are unlike to venture so far west. In honesty, the whole patrol is but..." He broke off, realizing he was close to being indiscreet.

"Pray continue being honest, Sir Pumphrey," said Tara, a twinkle in her eye. "What more would you say?"

"Nay, Milady, I've no wish to say aught more."

"Come, come, Sir Knight. I took your word to be more trusted than that. Were you on the verge of admitting it's but a bit of playacting, with the Prince in the leading role?"

"I plead your pity, Milady," he said, with a hint of apprehension. "Those are your words, not mine. I be but an humble knight, going where my betters direct. If they say Saxons lie ahead, then ahead they lie, and I'll hunt them down with a sharp lance and a right good will."

"Of course. But answer me the one question, Sir, and I'll fret you no more. Can we expect Saxons in these woods?"

Unsmiling, he made answer. "No, Milady."

"Then I will keep a close watch for them," she said, her eyes smiling.

"And I too, Princess," he agreed.

The sun was at its zenith, the troops bivouacked for lunch, when Tara's efforts to remain undetected proved a failure. From a distance, she could see Clydog staring in her direction, and soon a messenger rode up to say the Prince desired her presence. She made ready to follow, but he stood irresolute.

"Your pardon, Milady. The Prince directed particularly that you be disarmed ere you attend him."

Reluctantly she unbuckled her sword, and tendered it to Sir Pumphrey for safekeeping. I will not remove my dagger, she told herself. Who knows but I may have need for it. The messenger led her directly to a field tent where the Prince's mount was tendered, lifted the flap, and stood aside for her to enter.

The Prince sat on a folding stool, legs planted apart, countenance black as thunder. He made no move to rise at her entrance. "Pray tell me why you are here without my permission," he demanded. "Do you not know that these be men's affairs, and we want no women along?"

"I was invited, my Lord," she answered stiffly.

"Indeed! And who invited you?"

"One or another of the knights. I disremember his name, but he said I might come if I insisted."

"And belike the young Princess who thinks herself a man gave him little choice but to invite you, is that it?"

"It is, my Lord."

His anger was changing into something she did not like. "Very well," he said. "You are here, and here you stay. But I am in command, and you obey my orders. Do you understand?"

"Of course, my Lord," she said uneasily, wondering what he had in mind.

She had not long to wonder, for soon came the sounds of breaking the temporary camp, and the muted commands as the troop set out, but the Prince made no move to join them.

"Should we not be starting, my Lord?" she asked nervously. "Might they not be out of earshot if we tarry?"

"That is my purpose, wench," rasped Clydog, his disturbing look rekindling an unsavory recollection of Squire Grosseteste, laughing as she stood at his mercy in Mathry mill. "We have no need to catch them. I have other plans, far more titillating than soldiering. Sit you down on yon stool, and try to hold your tongue for the nonce."

She started to speak, but he silenced her with a gesture. They waited, not talking, until all sounds of the departing troop had died out. He rose, and lifted the tent flap to peer out—and let it fall suddenly down, his pudgy face turned ashen with terror.

"Saxons!" She could scarce understand, so quietly did he breathe the word. His eyes darted frantically around the tent walls. "We must escape, at once!" But instead of putting his words into action, he stiffened into immobility, as if frozen by fear.

Despite her panic as she heard the dread word, Tara fought to keep her head and arouse the terrified Clydog from his catatonic state. "We must act! Hurry, my Lord," she whispered. "Make haste—we can crawl under the tent wall whilst it still hides us from view, but we must be quick! My Lord, list to me! Hasten!"

Her urgency broke his trance. Dropping to his knees he scrabbled at the bottom of the tent and jerked a section free. She thought he lifted it for her, but he thrust her back so roughly that she lost her footing, and scrambled out the opening himself. Even as she arose, she heard the slap of his legs against the saddle, and the crackle of twigs as he fled. In a panic now, she scrambled through after him, but immediately heard the sounds of men coming around the tent, and knew she was too late.

"God's wounds! I thought all had left. The varlot will spread the alarm! After him, as you love your life!" Their horses were tethered in the woods, for she heard the sound of running feet, and an instant later the pounding of hooves hard on Clydog's trail. With a rush of relief that they'd not discovered her, she hurried around the tent—to collide heavily with an armed Saxon trooper!

She tumbled to the ground, breath knocked out of her. Recovering quickly, she sprang to her feet, but before she could flee, a steely grip closed about her wrist.

"Od's blood! What have we here?"

For the first time, she got a clear look at her captor. Though in campaign attire, his stance and the cut of his beard told her this was no common soldier, but a person of consequence. But he was a Saxon! Despite her fright, she felt an odd exhilaration that at last she was seeing the enemy. Oddly, he had no fangs or evil countenance, but a stalwart look and a sturdy frame. Under kinder circumstances, she might have thought him quite well favored. But for the nonce he was an implacable enemy—and she his prisoner.

His stern features relaxed into a grin. "A wench! And out in the Black Mountains with a patrol party no less. What was it, then? Were you packed in with the supplies for the pleasuring of your commander?" He laughed outright, his tone almost friendly, but made no move to release her. "A sad mischance we interrupted your fun."

He studied her speculatively. "Mayhap I can make it up to you, lass. You'll find me a more gallant lover than the craven who abandoned so tasty a baggage. You need not mourn his loss."

His meaning was unmistakable, and she struggled furiously to free herself, but his grip was too firm. "Come, my lovely," he said cajolingly. "Cease thy maidenly fluttering. I am a better man than you deserve. Come in the tent, and I'll let you show me your charms at closer hand." His free arm swept under her knees, and she was lifted high in his strong arms and carried back into the tent, to be dumped ceremoniously on the ground.

Her brain worked frantically as he stripped off his tunic and with deliberate slowness stepped out of his pantalons. "Now, wench," he said. "High time you shed those trooper clothes. They hide your charms too well." Naked except for boots, he stepped toward her, his hands groping to disengage her belt.

No! He'd strip off her clothes and find the dagger, her sole defense now against assault. "Nay, Sire," she breathed, feigning a coquetry she was far from feeling. "'Twill disengage me if you disrobe me. Pray turn your back, Sir, whilst I disrobe for myself."

He looked suspicious, as if he read her mind, and she feared he would ignore her plea. Then he laughed, casually turning his back. "Perhaps your way is best after all. But make haste, wench; I have not all the day, for your gallant may return in better fettle, with his troops behind him. I must taste of your delights quickly and begone."

With frantic hands she untied her garment and groped for the dagger, breathing a sigh of relief at the feel of it in her hand. She redid her clothes, secreting the weapon in its folds. Scarce had she done so when he turned impatiently back, frowning to see her still clothed. "What's this? Do you not strip down as I command? Do you trifle with me, gel?"

"Oh no, Milord." She tried to essay a teasing smile, sure it would not deceive him. "I'd be feared to trifle with so grand a cavalier. Best you do the unclothing, for belike you have much experience with such dalliance."

His suspicions swept aside, he guffawed in high good humor. "You read me too well, wench. In sooth, I have had some small experience so." The hot male smell of him was suffocatingly strong in her nostrils, as he grasped her tunic and began to drag it over her head.

Of a sudden strangely reluctant to harm his strong young body, she could scarce bear to use her weapon, but knew it was then or never. Summoning all her will to stifle the strange sensation, she thrust the blade hard through the smooth naked flesh, and into his unprotected side. His face, so close to hers, stiffened in agony and shock, and she felt his searing pain as if in her own body. He twisted violently, his involuntary move wresting the slim dagger from her unnerved fingers to fall to the ground, and pressed his hand convulsively over the wound, and the blood welled out between his spread fingers.

"She devil!" he hissed, grasping at her throat, the assault spattering her with his blood. Then he staggered, his hands clutched at his side, and dropped heavily to his knees.

Sobbing with fright mixed with regret at what she had done, she grabbed the dagger and burst out of the tent, looking wildly about for the horse that must be tethered there. She cast about her erratically, not seeing it, frantic lest her assailant burst forth to frustrate her escape. She was at the point of dashing aimlessly into the protection of the trees, when by chance she stumbled into a copse and collided head-on with a great black stallion. The aroused beast, belike scenting the blood, was straining powerfully against a tether drawn tight as a bowstring. With fingers trembling so hard they'd scarce do her bidding, she labored to loose the iron-hard knot that refused to give. She bit down on a loop with her teeth and tugged with all her strength to break the under strand free. Alternately biting and tugging furiously, she felt the stubborn knot give, grab, and give again, until at last it came free in her hands. Not stopping to secure the dangling tether, she hurled herself desperately into the saddle, and thundered off into the wood, heedless of direction, seeking only to put the accursed place behind her.

Chapter 10

She did not really expect pursuit, for the wounded Saxon scarce would be in condition to give chase, even had she not taken his mount. But his fellows could be hot after her soon, thirsting to avenge their leader. Tara was familiar enough with forest signs to know any woodsmen could follow her track, but they'd make slow going, and her mount could outpace any such hampered pursuers, so she set out for where she judged the setting sun would meet the horizon. There, she fervently hoped, lay the Black Mountains and Glamorgan Castle to the west.

A far more pressing worry was the situation awaiting her at the High Court. The Saxons could have foiled Clydog's escape and taken him, but Tara doubted that. Clydog's knowledge of the area was superior, he had fled early on, and his troop must be nearby. No, doubtless he had rejoined his force, and concocted a story placing him in a favorable light, though greatly at variance with the facts. His account would have to be shrewd beyond what she judged to be his mental powers, to explain away his cowardly escape while leaving her a prisoner. No, whatever he told could scarce help discrediting him, when all the facts were in.

She had thought to find it a quick matter to make her way, but when she broke clear of the wood she was in totally unfamiliar terrain. She came to an uncertain halt, scanning the horizon, puzzling out her best course of action. Surely Brecon lay to the west, and she must keep on the move to keep ahead of any pursuit, so she turned her horse toward what she took as westward. As afternoon drew on, with little danger now from the Saxon party, she slowed to spare her mount, but the mighty stallion's even breathing signaled ample reserves of energy for flight in the event of any hostile encounter. Pray Lug there would be none.

The sun had almost set when she discerned a great mass highlighted by the ruddy horizon. She was sure it must be the rugged Brecon Beacons, looming huge against the evening sky. Every Cymri child had heard of the great cliffs which lay scarce an hour's ride due south of Brecon. Whispering a prayer of thanks to the gods, she turned her mount's head northward.

The stallion, even with his vast reserves of strength, was covered with sweat and starting to stumble, when they crossed over the oaken draw-bridge into the keep—to come upon a scene of frenzied activity. She and her father spotted one another in the same instant, and with a hoarse cry of welcome and relief he ran to lift her down.

"Tara! Tara, lass, is it truly you?" he choked out, pressing her hard to him, and she thought to detect a slight moisture in his eyes.

"Aye, Sire, truly I. It was quite a parlous adventure, but all is over and I'm back safe now."

"We were readying a party to search the Black Mountains." He released her, but continued to stare at her as if assuring himself she was real. "Tell us what happened, how you broke free. And how came you with the stallion? When we heard Clydog's tale…"

Yes, she thought wryly. Clydog's tale. What had he conjured up as excuse for his base cowardice? "Sire, I'm sorely wearied," she interrupted. "I'll tell my story when my strength is recovered."

"Of course, child," he said, all solicitude, and took her arm at once to escort her to her chamber, where he closeted himself with her.

Her strength was ebbing, but she could not postpone the matter. "Sire," she said wearily, "my aim was to tell you in privy what took place today." She told him all, making no effort to hide her bitterness at the craven Clydog's unspeakable conduct.

Llywarch's anger rose as she spoke, and when her tale was done he was livid with rage. "The despicable hound…the coward…abandoning you thus, to save his own worthless neck! Crown Prince or no, I'll call him out. He'll feel my blade in his entrails before the morrow is done!" He sprang up, and she laid urgent hands on him, to restrain him from rushing forth.

"Nay, Sire. At all odds, you must not react so! It would spoil our careful plan—but much more, would drive a wedge of hatred between your court and the High King that no future suit of ours could discharge. Can you not see how his behavior plays straight into our hands?"

Gradually, continuing to speak in this vein as earnestly as she could, she calmed him. She pointed out that the episode would make Clydog detest her—and more, fear her lest she speak out before all, relating the true story of his craven desertion of his betrothed. Indeed, she said, this could force him to end their betrothal. When finally her eloquence brought him around to her viewpoint, he laughed, albeit hollowly, at the opportunity the gods had presented them.

Then he told her Clydog's tale.

The Prince had been talking with Tara in the quiet of the tent, so went his tale. He had just handed her into the saddle to join the patrol, when he was struck from behind and rendered unconscious. Sometime later, he regained consciousness to find himself alone. He searched the area frantically, finding his horse wandering untethered nearby. He mounted, and combed the woods near where had been struck, but with no success. Concluding that his attackers had made off with Tara, and further search would be fruitless, he decided to ride ahead and catch up with the patrol. As for his attackers, he guessed they were outlaws thinking to hold the Princess for ransom, and assumed they'd make their terms known at the Court soon. Cadell then asked him why the outlaws would abduct the Princess but leave him, when he could bring an even greater ransom, at which point the Prince retreated into sullen silence, and would say no more.

"You can see the right of it, Sire," said Tara angrily. "He knew the Saxons could not release me to give the alarm, so thought I'd never return to throw his tale in his teeth."

"Aye. Now he dies a thousand deaths, fearing you are ready to give him the lie before all the Court."

"And what pleasure it would bring me to tell it true! But we must go along with Clydog, for our own aims. I pray you escort me to the High King, Sire, to have done with the unpleasant task, and leave me to seek out my lovely pallet."

They were met in the Great Hall by King Cadell, his expression unexpectedly bright. He showed them the reason for his pleasure: the stallion carried a saddlebag crammed with Saxon sketches of Cymru terrain, indicating clearly that the small force had been a Saxon advance guard, and their documents provided intriguing clues to Alfred's probably intentions.

Llywarch had known from Tara's account that her assailants were Saxons, but the saddlebag was an unexpected plum, and the need to study and ponder its contents would put by any attention to Clydog's confused account. Privately Cadell had taken a sceptical view of his son's story, but this clear proof that they were indeed Saxons put a more believable face on it.

"We've had a tremendous stroke of luck, Sire," said Llywarch with satisfaction. "Of course my lass could not have known the contents of the saddlebags, or e'en the identity of her captors—though her private words to me made clear she thought her assailants Saxons—I confess pride in her stout conduct and bold escape." In which appraisal Cadell was quick to concur.

Spying Clydog huddled broodingly beside the hearth, Tara thought it was time to put a good face on the parlous episode. "I was most fortunate, Your Majesty," she broke in, hoping the gods would forgive her fabrications. "When the Saxons struck Prince Clydog down and rushed me off, I shammed a faint, and they bundled me onto the pack horse unbound whilst they collected their belongings. I saw my chance to escape, and by great good fortune eluded them and made my way back. I found myself on a stout mount, and by the time the Saxons missed me and gave chase I was deep in the woods, and they never picked up my trail."

"They used an exceeding noble steed for a packhorse, " commented Cadell wryly, and she knew he wondered what she was not revealing. But he let it pass unchallenged, and she breathed more easily. She snatched a surreptitious glance at Clydog, knowing he'd heard her words, as she'd intended, and saw the relief on his face that she'd not given him away. But she saw something else there—a virulent hatred in his eyes so strong it was almost as if he struck her. She felt a deep misgiving, knowing his expression boded naught but ill for her future.

The documents from the Saxon leader's saddlebag galvanized the Court. Aroused by these indications of imminent invasion, all attention was directed at mounting a strong defense. Her father plunged into the deliberations, and she could see his former vigor returning. Tara was excited to find herself included in their counsels, reading it that they thought her mature enough to be worthy of heeding. And even better, it seemed to be creating temporary surcease from the company of her chastened betrothed.

For Clydog made no effort to press his attentions on her, but avoided her as far as possible. Contact at mealtime was unavoidable, but he said little and avoided any discussion of the affair in the Black Mountains. Thinking it best to ease his embarrassment, Tara sought to fill the awkward silences with talk of other matters. There was talk at table about the Danes massed at Lichefelda, perhaps planning to march south against Alfred, and she asked if he thought Danes might be natural allies.

"None but a fool would trust a Northman," he said sourly. "Saxon, Dane, Pict—they're all one. I'd kill the lot and be done if I had the say what to do."

"But surely we have need of the Dane today against the Saxon. If we try to stand alone, he can overrun us in a single campaign." She was not sure this was so, but it made a good subject to engage the surly Clydog, and she wanted to keep it going. "Belike Alfred's only fear is what the Danes may do if he exposes his flank to them. King Cadell says…"

"Oh, yes…'King Cadell says', and all must jump to list when he speaks." She could sense in his tone the frustration he must endure at being all but ignored in the councils. His voice was so strident that she darted a glance to see if the High King heard. "Let me tell you, my gel, all is not so just because my father calls it so. When I am ruler…" He stopped abruptly, and looked nervously toward his father, but Cadell was too absorbed in discussion with Llywarch to hear. "These affairs are too deep to speak on lightly, or with women. We've said enow."

For the first time, Tara began to comprehend something of the pressures nagging at the Prince that made him act as he did. If only he could take pride in himself, then who knows…

Stop, she told herself. Clydog's faults lay deeper than competition with his father. He must harbor a madness within him that could burst out with terrible fury one day. Pray Lug his path and mine may separate after this visit, and never lie together henceforth.

But in that prayer, she was destined to be disappointed.

From the day the Saxon plans were uncovered, patrol activity increased. Small patrols went out secretively, with no panoply or word to the Court to mark their movements. They were in the field longer, sometimes a week or even two, before they stole back into the compound to report their findings and lick their wounds.

For wounds there were, though infrequently. More than once, a party would creep in with bandaged men clutching their saddles tightly, or groaning figures lashed across the horses' backs. Clydog was prohibited from joining the patrols, at which he made no protest. Maddeningly, Tara also was kept back. She stood it for a time, but finally exploded to her father.

"Sire," she said furiously, "am I not your chosen heir?" And when he had to agree that in sooth she was, she continued. "And unless you have changed your mind, and now desire that I marry Clydog, we have agreed that a wedding will not take place. Therefore," and her glance as she spoke was fully as steely as his, "I will be monarch of Dyfed one day, and commander of her troops. But if I be not allowed where danger threatens, I must decline the crown when it is offered."

She stopped, breathless at her temerity, awaiting the explosion. But there was none. He expelled a heavy breath, and spoke gravely. "Very well, Princess. I have seen you stewing to the boiling point, and knew this time would come. I place no further obstacles in your path. You must follow your gods as you think best, and if that means going on patrol, so be it." He took her hand, and she felt his depth of feeling. "But guard yourself as well as you can, lass."

Tara's first patrol was led by Sir Pumphrey, and instead of a token one-day foray into the Black Mountains, they left in pre-dawn darkness to head southeast to Caerwent on the Hafren Channel, moving by night and hiding in the glyns and cors by day. Twice they spied Saxons to the east, and once they ventured out on the tongue of land protruding into the channel to spy out the Wessex shore. The patrol lasted ten day, and she returned exhausted, but with a clearer picture of the strategic situation.

On her third patrol, at her strong insistence—and with the quiet support of Llywarch—Tara assumed command. It was a small force, her lieutenant a sober veteran as backup to her inexperience. She was becoming familiar with the Cymri tribesmen who formed the bulk of Cadell's army. Magnificent fighters, their primary occupation was training for war. Under Cymri law, they were on call at any time, and spent the bulk of the warmer weather on army duty. They were not husbandmen or farmers, prisoners of their harvests and restless to return to their flocks, but warriors by choice, accustomed to traveling light and subsisting on the land, with but a bowl of whey and a handful of mountain goat cheese in their packs. They wielded the scramas axe, and their fierce javelin charge was an awesome display, but their weapon of choice was the Gwent longbow, made of wild elm, rude and rough but able to pierce a mailed shirt or the thick leather armor of a mounted knight. Their wild look evoked fear, with their swarthy faces and squat bodies, but Tara came to realize that they were ideal soldiers for the rough clandestine duty. She frankly admired these wiry, uncouth marauders, and in return she was accorded the worship they would have given a goddess, had they encountered one.

Her patrol took them southeast to Caerleon, thence southwest to Llandawa, at a cove in the Hafren Channel, whence word had come of possible Saxon incursions similar to those early forays at Tenby, suggesting that Alfred could be seeking staging areas for troop landings. Tara knew she would not be in the area if Cadell or her father thought a Saxon encounter likely, but at least this was an authentic patrol, and she intended to make the most of it.

They made camp in a thick grove of saplings, offering a view of the Channel in both directions, and after a quick reconnaissance posted a sentry, and her lieutenant suggested that she bed the party down for sleep campaign style. Tara found it a strange sensation, but had to admire its utility. They formed a circle, heads at the outer edge and feet touching in the center, weapons ready to hand. A single trooper, wakened by a foreign sound, could bring the entire force silently alert and ready by a few surreptitious nudges of his feet, with no word spoken.

Their vantage point was on a promontory of the Channel. Across the Hafren to the south lay historic Wedmore where Alfred's first victory had changed the face of Britain, and the bogs of Aethelingay where he had licked his wounds and regenerated his strength to defeat the Danes at Ethandun. He had infiltrated the Danish camp, assuming the guise of an itinerant harper, even performing in their chieftain's tent, all the while garnering intelligence and noting weaknesses to use against them on the battlefield. Why could not I do the same, she mused.

Consulting with her lieutenant next morn, Tara decided to move the troops down to the banks of the inlet at dusk, leaving a party of four men to stand guard to the north. The tribesmen moved silent as wraiths, and she strove to emulate them. As they approached the inlet, only a handful of fishing lights could be seen. On reaching the shore they fanned out in two directions, Tara's men south toward the sea, her lieutenant's north toward the tref. They would rendezvous at the starting point before dawn.

For two full hours they crept along, until Tara judged they were near the mouth of the inlet where they stopped, and there still was no sound. Suddenly a tribesman touched her sleeve, and pointed across the water. Following his finger, she made out a faint silhouette against the hazy moon. Belike naught but a herring fisher, she thought, but the boat carried no light, and herring do not school so close in. The whole group, alerted now, froze in place and watched the craft ghost toward them on the fickle night breeze. Its keel grated softly on the pebbles just south of where they stood, and by listening keenly they could detect muted whispers.

If they stayed out of earshot they could learn naught, but any movement to close in would alert the intruder to attack or flee, and neither action would provide the military intelligence she must gather. She gave the signal, and her small force silently melted back into the trees.

The next morn Tara led a small force away from the landing site, toward Caerleon. They concealed themselves in the brush while three tribesmen put aside their weapons and entered the village outskirts. Soon they were back, and set before her a large bundle, their usually impassive faces relaxed in grins, showing their blackened teeth. They undid the wrappings to disclose a village fisher girl, a filthy rag stuffed in her mouth, her face rigid with terror.

"Do not fear, lass," said Tara in what she hoped was a reassuring tone. "You'll not be hurt, and when eventide comes we will free you. You can help your King and Cymru, by loaning us your clothes, and the fish in your pannier. No, don't fret," she said hastily, noting the girl's trembling. "We'll just exchange clothes for the nonce, you and I." Slowly the girl's terror subsided, until she was calmed enough to risk removing her gag.

Adjusting the filthy garments, Tara took up the pannier filled with new-caught herring, and wondered if the intruders would find her convincing. Her own dagger was sheathed inside her thigh, and a borrowed one tied lightly along her left arm where a quick tug would break it free. She felt naked without her sword, as she strode back along the shore path. Knowledge that her noiseless troops were paralleling her path inside the tree line reassured her somewhat, but she knew her plan was mightily perilous, and she stood in deadly danger if aught went awry.

"Awell, wench, has t' fotched feesh for sup?" The sudden voice startled her, and she jumped back with an alarm that was not feigned.

"Foosh, lass, t'has nae need t'fright so. Us'll just take yer feesh 'n' thankee." The speaker stepped from the rushes along the shore, and his garb spoke plain that he was a Saxon, even if his strange speech had not. She feared that her own accent would betray her, so without speaking she turned as if to flee, knowing he would grab her. A moment later she was within the mashed-down reeds, surrounded by five men. Their crude effort at disguise scarce hid the fact that they were soldiers.

She stood trembling, only part feigned since her fear was real, and her captor spoke up again. "Ye'll be free 'n' on yer way quick, gel. Us'll jis have yer feesh forst." But she would not be on her way, she knew, for they could not let her tell her tales. Were she a real fisher girl, the night tide would carry her lifeless body out to sea for the crabs to eat.

She decided to risk speaking, since belike they knew not how village girls spoke, and she saw no other way to gain information. "Who be ye, sorr, and what're ye aboot, ahidin' in t'rooshes?"

They looked at one another, seeming not to question her identity as a village girl, and then one spoke up to the others. "Nae harm tellin'; t'puir lass'll be carryin' nae tales." Rude laughter followed, and then to her surprise they told her why they were there, and what it might portend. She tried to look thunderstuck, which was not difficult, as in sooth she was.

As the laughter died away, the one who seemed their leader muttered, "Us'll gie ye yer geld now, gel, 'n' thankee fer t'feesh." He reached meaningfully to his belt, but instead of a purse he drew out a wicked dagger which he tested with his thumb. Tara thrust her hands inside her kirtle, and made as if to shrink back. Cautiously her hand crept down her thigh to close on the hilt of her dagger, and she eased it free.

The soldier suddenly lunged at her, plunging his blade into the bulky folds of her kirtle with a force that would have near disemboweled her had it struck home. But it found no flesh or bone beneath the garment, for she twisted her body out of the weapon's path so it met only the folds of cloth. He stumbled forward, thrown off balance by the lack of resistance—and ran full tilt onto Tara's dagger point. Simultaneously she thrust upward with all her strength, and the keen blade slid beneath his rib cage into his lung cavity before he knew he'd been attacked.

His fellows could not see Tara's weapon, and his body shielded her thrust from view. He gave a muffled cry, which could have come from her, and when she let go the dagger to fling herself prostrate on the sand, it must have seemed that she had received a death blow. But their confusion would last only until their leader fell, and she waited with pounding heart for her men to take action. The next instant she heard the welcome thrum of bowstrings and the sibilant hiss of arrows finding their targets.

One of their quarry still lived when they returned to the castle. Even better, their ambush at nightfall had proved a grievous surprise to the Saxon craft, when it returned to shore again. And the maps and plans it contained, together with its two crew members, who had neither time nor heart for resistance, provided a rich lode of information bearing on Alfred's strategy.

The information Tara's force garnered guided Cadell's decision a fortnight later, when a foreign troop appeared at the Mark, trumpeting for entrance. Tara was seated at the high table when Cadell's steward ushered the visitors into the Great Hall. Never had she seen so huge a man as the bearded blond giant who came forward and flung his bona fides on the board. She looked for King Cadell to bridle at the apparent affront, but instead he let out a roar of pleasure, and they pounded each other on their backs as if long-lost brothers. The panter at once fetched a cask of mead, and menials scurried in with trenchers, whereupon the guests laid aside their pointed war helmets and great battle-axes, and fell hungrily on their food.

When the board had been cleared, she learned that the boisterous guests were Danes. Though they parleyed crudely in Cadell's language, they lapsed into their own tongue to speak among themselves. She thanked the fates that Father Eliswen back at Aber Castle had thought it best to drill the language of Denemearc interminably into the reluctant heads of the pages, for she found much of their speech understandable, and to their surprise and open delight made herself understood to them. Cadell seized eagerly on her ability as interpreter during their parleys, which to her quiet satisfaction made her privy to the elements of their joint strategy.

With enormous excitement, she learned that matters between Cymru and Wessex were coming rapidly to the boiling point, and great affairs were afoot. A Norse freebooter called Hasteinn, who had fled across the Narrow Sea to Normandy when Alfred subjugated the Danes at Wedmore, had since then devoted his energies to harassing the coast of Britain and rebuilding his force. He had come to land off Cantia at the eastern tip of Wessex, with three hundred and thirty sail, a part of his force seizing the fort of Apuldore in the Rother whilst the reminder with Hasteinn himself invested Bamflete near the Isle of Canvey, and threw up quick fortifications. But there Alfred overpowered Hasteinn's forces and captured his family, forcing him to flee once again and dispersing his forces. Splinter marauding packs from the once powerful Viking force seized and fortified a base at Shobury, in the mouth of the Thames, from where they marched inland along the river to Boddington in Gloucester. This had happened just recently, and now they were throwing up heavy entrenchments there, under the command of a freebooting Northumbrian Dane named Sigefert.

Sigefert hoped to use this strongpoint in the heart of Britain as a base for pushing Alfred into the sea. He expected that quick slashing attacks by his Vikings would throw the Saxons off balance, preventing Alfred from bringing his experienced siege troops to probe the inadequate defenses of the hastily constructed Danish citadel. But speed was essential to the success of this strategy, and Alfred's greatly superior forces must not be given time to gain the initiative.

As this stirring tale unfolded, Tara relayed its gist as best she could understand, and was breathless with excitement as she concluded the translation. She thought Cadell would be astonished at the great news of this powerful ally, but he merely nodded soberly as though all this was known to him beforehand. So acts a true king, she decided, keeping his own counsel, not becoming rattled, not shouting all he knows from the rooftops. So will I conduct my affairs when I am ruler, she vowed.

But, she wondered, when she had a chance to think it all over, what recked this stunning news? How could Cymru use the Danish threat against Alfred to its own advantage?

She learned that Sigefert's forces were battle-ready, hardened by years of raiding from Ponthieu to Brittany, but vastly outnumbered by Alfred's levies. Too, they fought on foreign soil, in unknown terrain, and far from their sources of supply—indeed, they had no sources of supply, save what they could seize by rapine and pillage. They stood in great need of allies, with larger numbers of fighting men, and local knowledge of conditions, and were here to enlist Cymri support for their campaign, inviting Cadell to join them in war against Wessex.

To her, the strategy was stunning in its scope and simplicity. Concerned with details of single patrols, she had given no thought to the long-term future of Cymru, the broad policy needed to insure its permanent freedom from the Saxon yoke. She had sought to be involved in action, with scant thought to what such action could achieve. As she thought through the plan, she realized it might be Cymru's only opportunity for independence, and agonized lest Cadell turn it down.

But he did not turn it down. As the discussions proceeded, it was apparent that the alliance had been cemented, and all that remained was settling the details of how the High King would marshal the realm's resources to reinforce the embattled encampment at Gloucester, scarce a day's march across its borders.

I must accompany them, she thought in high excitement. And I will lead Dyfed's contingent! Visions of the heroic Elen Luyddog ran through her head, and of the legendary Queen Boedicia of the Iceni, who sacked Londinium and slaughtered 70,000 Roman invaders. I will go, she vowed, intoxicated beyond measure with the glory of it all. This is what Atheurin meant, when he said the gods had a great quest in mind for me.

I am ready!

Her euphoria lasted until she placed the proposition before her father, and then, of a sudden, all her hopes were dashed.

CHAPTER 11

"It's too star-crossed an idea even to consider, Tara," Llywarch stated, as he and Tara lazed in the bower for the call to supper. "Aside from the matter that you are a woman, you seem not to ken that you are not yet e'en a woman grown. How old are you?"

Tara brushed his question impatiently aside. "I am your heir, your Crown Prince," she said defiantly. "You wat not how we scorned Clydog hanging back from any true patrols—shall I be scorned so by your Court? My responsibility and my right are to follow you into battle, Sire, as your heir, and I demand my right!"

"Demand and be damned!" Llywarch thundered. "Tell me not where my duty lies! Were you of age, Tara, I'd say yea, though with no pleasure. But child, you are not yet sixteen years grown! Were you not a princess of the blood, ye'd still be back in squiring camp."

"But I am a princess! And have I not the size and strength of a woman grown?"

He looked at her, affection and admiration mingling in his face. "Yea, you have that. And I wat you have a fearsome skill with the sword, for one so young. But e'en sixteen does not bring the maturity and judgment of a commander on the field of battle."

"The Queen of the Britons was but sixteen, Atheurin says. Boedicia was my age when she took Londinium from the Roman centurions. Think you I have not the skill of an untutored Briton?"

"Mayhap she was sixteen, and mayhap not. For that, such a queen as the bards hail may have existed, but many think her unreal. All we have for the truth of that tale is the song of the bards, and they sing many a tale that ne'er happened, were the truth to out."

She scowled indignantly. "Certain there was such a queen as Boedicia, Sire, and well you know as much!" She tossed back her head, the red-gold tresses grown to all their former glory glinting in the sun's waning light—emphasizing the very femininity she sought to deny. "Let bards sing wondrous tales in years to come of how your Crown Princess rode out to save the realm when danger threatened!"

"Belike they'd sing of a half-grown lass riding off to a bloody battle and being hacked down by some nameless Saxon thrice her size, for no cause save that she was there." He fell silent, contemplating the gloomy scenario.

She rose impatiently, helpless to shake his resolve. "You hold me in lowly esteem, Sire. We'd best drop the matter."

She got little sleep that night. She could think of naught to sway her father. Direct disobedience to his commands? He would but bundle her off to home in ignominious disgrace. Joining the force of another king? None would take her, once her identity was known.

How I wish Crosbey were here, she thought. She wondered if he had found a fair maiden to assuage his hopeless yearning. A sudden fierce resentment flared up inside her, as she pictured him bestowing his favors on another. She summoned up his image, and dreamily pictured the two of them together. This must be love, she thought, savoring the wonderful sweetness of her feeling, lost in the delicious euphoria of her yearning to be embraced in his strong arms, all of her problems vanishing in the security of his love.

The delicious feeling was rudely broken, and she sat up erect in alarm. Crosbey would go into the battle! Her father must needs levy on Eorl Skomer, as on all his lairds, and Skomer would draw his levies from all uchelwyr holding land in fee and fief within his domain. Crosbey would be called!

And be slaughtered, belike, she thought, despair weighing like a heavy stone on her heart.

She considered the long odds they faced at Gloucester. Recalling her father's accounts of the Saxon campaigns against the Dane, and the peace that finally evolved, she realized that the Danelaw had every reason to stand with Alfred, and precious little inducement to side with this feckless freebooter, Sigefert. She remembered studying a long-forgot pastoral, its preface writ by this same Alfred, portraying him as a ruler who treasured books for how they could help his people—while the Viking Danes were harrying the land, and burning all such treasures.

With a sudden clarity unusual in one so young, Tara realized that Cadell was throwing in his lot with an adventurer and buccaneer who had but slight chance of defeating the Saxons, or even of saving his own neck.

On their return to Dyfed, Menevia Castle and the surrounding cantrefs plunged into instant preparations for the expedition to reinforce the Gloucester garrison. Tara saw and felt the eager fascination war holds for those who lived in penury and hardship. They never could be sure of the next meal, they stood forever at the mercy of powerful overlords able to seize their holdings, clap them in jail, or see them hanged. To such as these, a campaign was a grand escape; all was well ordered, with food enow, a chance at loot, and release from the cares of husbandry. The maiming and dying happened seldom, and were in the unseen future. The carefree levies would have no thought of battle until it hit them. Llywarch, expounding on the matter, laughed grimly. "I must confess that I feel it too, and I have endured many campaigns." He took her face in his hands. "You, too, hear the siren singing of this evil mistress. When you long for the battlefield, do you picture the wounds and pain and heedless slaughter, or the blaring trumpets and the battle pennons whipping in the wind?"

His painful question stung her, and she had to admit that the dark side of battle was never in her mind. But I still must go, she insisted to herself, not for pleasure or even glory, but rather because I am the future ruler of Dyfed, and my sacred duty lies there.

Several years had passed since her last talk with Atheurin, though she had felt him at her side when she languished sick abed at Roch Dinas Abbey. He would expect her, a woman grown, to meet her own problems. But had he not made her a solemn promise that if ever she needed him he would be there? She'd be committing a folly not to seek his help, since it appeared naught else could change her Sire's stubborn mind.

But finding him was another matter. She called for the rangy stallion unwittingly presented her by the Saxon back in the Black Mountains, and rode through the wood to the old clearing, but to no avail. She searched in vain, but there was no sign of her old mentor, nor could she sense the bard's presence. She became utterly frustrated at her failure to reach him. What was she to do, she wondered forlornly.

Then a sudden thought found its way somehow into her mind—the old cromlech inside the thorn hedge beyond the Presceli Hills.

The black stallion, always hard for her to control, seemed unduly restive and unresponsive to her strongest tugging on his reins, but her pulse quickened as she recognized the trail on which he took her, the same along which she had raced on her little Cymri pony. Atheurin awaits me, she told herself eagerly. All I need do is crawl through the tunnel of thorns and find him! She rode on, scanning the side of the trail intently for the telltale hole she'd scrambled through. But it was not to be seen, nor even the thorn hedge she remembered so clearly. With difficulty she turned her mount, and backtracked her path, but it was not there. Discouraged and wearied, she was close to abandoning the hopeless search. How can I find you, Atheurin, she cried out aloud in her frustration.

She was distracted by her troubled thoughts, when suddenly a huge wild boar, tushes dripping red from some forest encounter, evil eyes glaring, darted from the brush directly into her path. The big horse reared in alarm at the sudden apparition and the beast's hot scent, and his sudden lunge hurled her to the ground. Her hip hit hard, twisting her body, her head struck the edge of a moss-covered stone, and she slumped into limp unconsciousness on the grass.

The boar turned in fury, readying for a charge on the prostrate figure, cloven hooves furrowing the ground. But the big stallion, thoroughly aroused by the confusion and the disturbing scent of blood, reared up and slashed out viciously with its forefeet. The boar had feared little in its turbulent life, and feared nothing now, but had learned which battles were best not engaged. Glaring at the murderous hooves of the aroused stallion, it turned and trotted into the concealing brush.

The horse finally calmed, uncertain what to do. It nuzzled Tara's head, flaring its nostrils at the odor of blood congealing darkly in her fair hair. It drew back, on the brink of galloping off, when something in the hush of the wood stayed its flight, and it stood motionless over the still figure.

Tara opened her eyes, drawing strength from the grass carpet underneath her, and looked about bewildered. Her head ached painfully, and when she reached up to touch it she felt the sticky blood that had oozed from her scalp. When she could think clearly, she concluded that perhaps it was no serious injury, or she'd never have regained her senses.

The stallion lifted its regal head, ears erect at an alien sound. Seeing this, Tara listened intently for the noise that had alerted the animal, but at first she heard nothing. Then she detected a soft footstep on the sward behind her, and focussed quickly on the horse. It looked at something behind her, showing no signs of alarm. Her hand crept stealthily to her dagger, but the sheath was empty.

"Your weapon came free when you fell, my Princess. It lies beside you on the sward. But you have no need for it."

That voice!

Recognition flooded back. How oft it had calmed her fears. How long it had been since those soft tones had comforted her.

Atheurin!

She felt a strange reluctance to look upon him, but without her willing it, her eyes were drawn upward. He stood before her, his gaze fixed on her, and reached over her to stroke the stallion's neck. Every detail of his appearance came back to her: the tan jerkin dappled by sunlight trickling through the leafy cover, the phrygian cap of soft deerskin, the sandals turned up at the toes, the gold flecks amid his curls.

"We must see to your wound, Princess," he said, his quiet voice borne on the forest breeze sighing in the trees. She was about to greet him, but he held up his hand. "Time for that when the healing has started," he said, and from his garment he produced a vial, the contents of which he trickled onto the ugly gash, without touching her, until the pain began to subside. Then to her lips he placed a horn of liquid, from whence she knew not, and the fluid was warm and soothing to her throat. Her eyes grew heavy, and once more she slept.

When she awoke, and they were sitting together on the sward, she asked the question to which she expected no answer. "How is it you know to come when I am in distress? What spirits summon you?"

He smiled, with his old enigmatic look. "Events are as the gods ordained e'en before your birth, and they would not have the prophecy o'erturned by happenstance."

She thought about her fall, and about the fierce wild boar that had caused it, and saw in his eyes that he read what puzzled her.

"No, Tara—they do not plan each littlest happening. They set a river flowing to the sea, without seeking to avoid each tiny pebble, which may ripple its path but cannot turn it from its destination. Whom the gods would use, they guard from harm. The mists I peer into oft are hazy, and no bard always reads clear what he may see, but thus far the foretelling holds true."

She perked up, thinking how he could help her reach Gloucester. "If the gods will me to fight alongside the Danes..." she began eagerly.

"If the gods wish it, you will go," he interrupted. "Return to the castle now, and fret no more about your wound, for it heals apace. Make your plans for Gloucester, and if it be in your stars, you will find a way." He handed her up into the saddle, her stallion strangely calmed, and she rode off, knowing she'd see naught if she looked behind.

If Llywarch guessed what occupied her or no, he did not deign to ask, and for her part Tara wondered how she'd ever contrive to manage the large force Dyfed would send—if the gods wished it so, she was quick to add. On the Caerleon patrol, every soldier had been within the sound of her voice. I need an equerry, she realized, to report back to me all that is said or done in my force, and to transmit my commands without any alterations to suit his private aims. In sum, I need one I can trust.

In a flash the obvious name came to her: Crosbey!

No other had been so steadfast a friend as her confidante at Aber Castle. She could trust him to the death, and mayhap beyond. He had stood ready to lay down his life for her, even when she offered little enow in return—naught but her undying friendship, and a warmth of feeling disturbingly close to love. But was that really so little? She conjured up his sturdy stance, his handsome face so free from guile. Had she not been of royal birth, and he a lowborn grwda, their paths well might have merged.

When she asked her father to assign her a mission that would take her to Aber Castle, Llywarch looked narrowly at her, seeking to discern some ulterior scheme to circumvent his wishes. Her request seemed innocent, however, and indeed there were messages dealing with the levy of troops that must be delivered. Skomer was devilish quick to take offense if he read a slight to his position, and sending the heir to the throne as emissary could mollify any injured vanity he nursed from Llywarch's demands. "Yes, lass. There are dispatches to be sent, and it truly can be a timely visit. I grant my permission, but charge you to return straightway and no detours."

She was restless to be off, but her father insisted on dispatching a messenger to Aber Castle to make sure the visit suited the prickly Eorl. Not until that was asked and answered did Tara's party ride out from Menevia Castle, along the old road that skirted Saint Bride's Bay and Newgate Glan. When they passed Saint David's, Tara rejected the impulse to visit the Convent, and by early afternoon was closeted in Aber Castle, receiving the Eorl's florid welcome, so patently insincere she was happy to beg his leave for a private tete-a-tete with his Countess.

"I would scarce have known you," said that shrewd lady, in frank admiration of Tara's metamorphosis into so sturdy a young adult. "I cannot picture you as the timid lass who trod so soft as a page."

"Was I so timid, Milady?" asked Tara. "Indeed, and I did not feel so."

"Well, in sooth, now I think on't, most probably you were not timid at all. But you knew how to give that impression." She gave Tara a shrewd look. "And the artifice served you well."

Is she meaning my plea to them to be my advisers on my accession to the throne? I never believed the artifice would serve, but she made as if it did. "I've thought oft on my happy days here, Countess," she said, shifting the talk to safer ground. "Belike I'll not find such happiness again. And I have much to thank you for. And of course, the Eorl," she added hastily.

"Of course," agreed the Countess dryly. "I'm certain you found little cheer in the nunnery. I did not think the stay there would help you, or change you into a puling sister." The dry tone was replaced on the instant by one of seeming warmth and sincerity. "I told the Eorl as much. My heart went out to you, when the Bishop turned his wrath upon you, for I saw a frightened lass, with nowhere to turn, unable even to weep because you were playing the part of a stalwart squire. You cannot know how I suffered for you then." Her look bespoke such depth of feeling that Tara found herself touched by the Countess's sympathy. She had a sudden impulse to unburden herself to the Countess and relate her plan, until she recalled Atheurin's warning words: 'No matter how warm you feel in the glow of her affections, never trust her.' Inwardly furious with herself for such naivete, she resolved never again to fall victim to such soft words.

The Countess, watching her keenly, saw in her face a hint of that thought process, but let it pass without comment. "Well, how will you entertain yourself during your stay?" she asked briskly. "I fear womanly pursuits appeal to you not at all. Can my Eorl take you ahawking? Or would you like to hunt? Stags have been seen to the north; would you like a chase up there?"

To the north! Toward Saint Nicholas Castle, where Crosbey had been appointed squire to the elderly knight who tilled its meager acres! She had puzzled how to reach him, and here the Countess was dropping it in her lap. "A stag chase would be mightily pleasurable, Countess," she said, careful to hide her eagerness. "But you must know, I need no escort. I know well the lands that way, and require but a brace of beaters if they be available."

"Very well, Princess," said the Countess, and Tara thought chagrin was hid beneath her ready smile. "I'll bid Sir Elwain make arrangements."

The north area was the Eorl's private preserve, a hunting area reserved for distinguished guests, and others seldom ventured there, except for occasional intrepid poachers. By devious questioning of the old gamekeeper, Tara found where Saint Nicholas Castle lay. Finding a pretext to dismiss Sir Elwain's beaters as they approached the preserve, she was left with only two of her own escorts from Menevia Castle, and thus free from any who could spy out her actions and report back to Skomer or the Countess. When the beaters were well gone, she spurred eagerly toward Saint Nicholas, excitement building up within her.

The old pile, built long ago to guard Deheubarth's border against Seisyllyg in the early tumultuous days, was crumbling into disrepair, but the guard at its gate presented smartly at their entrance. Her standard had been recognized, incredible though a royal visit must have seemed, for the guard captain stood await in the cramped keep, snatching off his helmet and sweeping it low. "We are honored you see fit to visit our poor castle. I regret Sir Egelwain finds himself indisposed, but he bids me present his respects, and ask how we may serve you."

Tara was exceedingly dubious that the ailing old knight had sent such greetings, or indeed that he was sensate at all, but it was a right courtly speech, and she was much impressed by the loyalty of the faithful captain, and conveyed her thanks and good wishes. Deftly shifting the subject, she managed to inquire after Squire Crosbey.

The captain's face reddened with embarrassment. The estate had no reeve for the nonce, he explained, and until they found another reeve Squire Crosbey had consented to perform those duties. He would be in the fields or the byrne.

So it fell to poor Crosbey to farm the lands in his stead. Good patient Crosbey, who had so rejoiced to find this post and be breveted Esquire, reduced to tramping dusty furrows and tending ailing livestock. He would be mortified to be found in such lowly estate, but she had come too far, and the matter was too urgent, to turn back now. She thanked the captain, wheeled her horse, and rode out into the fields to find the man she had journeyed so far to see.

Four or five taeogion could be spied out at the far perimeter of Egelwain's slender holdings but she saw no sign of Crosbey. It looked unpromising, but for want of any alternative she rode toward them.

Their large transport cart seemed to have lost a wheel, for it canted crazily on the remaining three, its load tumbled out in the dirt. The group, intent on their task, failed to notice her approach until she was upon them. Then one spied her, and sprang to his feet. She saw that the axle had broken, and the artisan appeared to be splicing on a temporary section without renewing the entire crosspiece. It was a makeshift affair, but an ingenious artifice to get back in operation without delay, and she admired the man who had contrived it. As she watched, he looked up, and their eyes met.

It was Crosbey! Crosbey, on his knees in the dusty field of a shabby farmstead, toiling like an humble wheelwright to patch a dilapidated cart ready for the dunnage heap. Crosbey, who had come to her with stars shining in his eyes, when he brought word of this appointment, now reduced to such low estate. They both stood frozen in the shock of recognition. Tears stung behind her eyes, and she blinked furiously to hold them back.

He jumped to his feet as she slipped from the saddle to meet him. "Tara!" He spoke the name softly, as if her name were too precious to speak aloud. "Tara! Is it truly you?"

She looked at him, in his rough taeog garb, soil clinging to him, his face grimed with sweat and dirt, and thought never had she seen so splendid a person. With all her being, she longed to reach out to him, to be enfolded in his strong embrace, ignoring the onlookers in total submission to him. But she could not. She decided she'd best get to her purpose before she broke down in tears.

"Crosbey!" She spoke as soft as he, that none around might hear. "Yes, Tara in the flesh, come all the way from Menevia to fetch you away—if you'll come."

"Fetch me? If I'll come?" Bewilderment and wonder struggled for mastery in his face. "What can you mean?" An impossible hope shone in his eyes, and instantly she regretted her words, so easily misunderstood.

"Naught of so great moment," she replied hurriedly, seeking to dampen his unreasoning hope. She spied a thin cluster of trees just beyond the furlong line. "Can we go yonder, so we might speak where none may hear?"

She sat on a rotting stump, and he crouched on the ground before her, both suddenly shy at being together with none about. Looking at him, she lost her train of thought. His shabby garb could not disguise that sturdy build, and the field grime could not hide the warmth and honesty of that face, on which she had looked once with such pleasure—yes, and with such love.

"You see me as I truly am, Tara," he said ruefully. The old knight had been a fine man, he told her, but all his fire was gone, and lately some of his mind was wandering as well. The noble Eorl ground hard in extracting his rents, and once his bailiffs came and went, precious little remained to keep Saint Nicholas alive. "You see me garbed as a farmhand, Tara. I like it as little as you, but there's no other way to keep afloat. Without me there is no one. No one."

He gave a big sigh. "But enow of our troubles. I wat you did not come to hear of them. I've wished so many times to hear of your fortunes. When they snatched you off to the convent, I thought the sun had sunk forever, so dark and gloomy was it without your happy smile. I've made shift to follow your fortunes, but we get little news here and it is impossible that I leave."

"But that's why I came to find you, Cross. I came to ask you to leave."

"Leave? But how? I've just told you…"

"If a reeve were sent here, could you not be spared? A real reeve, with experience, and with geld enow for seed and food and stores? And another from Aber Castle as esquire?"

He stared, dumbfounded, not daring to hope. She berated herself again for permitting her inner feelings to creep into her tone. "Cross, best I explain. The High King has allied Cymru with the Danes at Gloucester, and will take the field against Alfred of Wessex. Skomer has been levied; you must have heard tidings of it." He shook his head, and she continued. "Dyfed is to send a force, and though my father has not yet given his consent, I expect to accompany him as his Lieutenant. I want you with me—as my Equerry if you want it in formal terms, but truly as my trusted friend." There, she'd said it, and now to see how he'd react.

Crosbey's face fell imperceptibly, and she could see the wild unreasonable hope fade from his eyes. Then, replacing it, she saw the excitement begin to build, and when his eyes started to shine she knew he was hers.

The dusty messenger come from the Eorl found her back in the keep, making breathless plans with a rejuvenated Crosbey for the campaign they had no least doubt would materialize. At the sober news he bore, she left at once for Menevia, pausing only long enough to assure Crosbey she would make all the promised arrangements, and to adjure him to hold himself in readiness for the summons that would be coming very soon.

The tidings were frightening, and as she sped along the old Roman road toward Aber Castle she could put her mind to naught else. King Llywarch had suffered a seizure, and she was commanded to return at once, against the possibility that...

No! That eventuality was one too shattering to entertain!

CHAPTER 12

Tara was desperately anxious to be off, but one matter needed to be placed in the capable hands of the Countess first. "I urge secrecy on you, Milady, for the King has not yet agreed. I intend to accompany the Dyfed force to Gloucester, and I need Crosbey for my Equerry, but he will not quit Saint Nicholas unless satisfied he can be spared. I beg you to urge upon the Eorl to find a competent squire to replace Crosbey. I will contrive to find an experienced reeve to manage Sir Elwain's holdings, if you make no objection to my intruding thus on your affairs. Your Lord may know that Sir Elwain has not all his senses at times, and the estate stands in desperate need of good management. And, if I may speak on a sensitive matter, he needs your Christian charity, to remit his taxes for a time, until the fortunes of Saint Nicholas are somewhat restored." She hesitated for a moment, wondering how to bring the solicitation to an end. "Do I have your assurance, Milady, that this may be taken in hand?"

"Certainly, Tara," said the Countess with little grace. Her eyes were cold and calculating, and Tara saw her as the undoubted enemy she was.

Twilight was darkening the interior of Menevia Castle when Tara raced up the stairs, to learn that the gravity of the King's attack had been exaggerated in the telling. "I was not happy at Gruwent summoning you back, child," he said when she clasped his hand in hers, "but he thought it folly to have you in a far corner of the realm whilst I was bedded and near helpless." Llywarch sat up with difficulty. "But I am not as helpless as they picture me. Another week will see me back in harness again."

Tara, far from reassured, wanted to know more. "What happened, Sire? How did you first ken you were unwell? And how can you know you're on the mend?"

Settling back, he thought how best to put it. "'It was in the midst of dinner," he said finally. "I'd bit off a cut of mutton, and washed it down in ale. But it lodged square in my windpipe so catching my breath was precious hard."

"You strangled, Sire?"

"So I thought then. At the first cough it came up, and I recked all had been put right, until my chest gave me a stab like a mace blow, and I still could not draw breath. They tell me I dropped like a poled ox, and nigh on an hour passed ere my skull cleared and the hurt eased. The friar would have me bide abed for a time, and belike he's got the right of it."

"Does you chest still have hurt, Sire?"

He hesitated again, thinking back. "Betimes it does, the same quick stab of pain. But it passes fast, and then I feel healthy as a babe."

"How oft come these pains to you? Every day? Every hour?"

He squeezed her hand, grateful for her interest, but as well relieved to unburden himself of the worry that gnawed at him. "Only the two days are done since I was laid low, and in that time I've felt a clutch of pain mayhap five times, no more. When it hits, it seems as if a giant fist lays a stout blow on my chest, and I can think of naught else; then when it leaves I've little memory how it felt. The friar is firm that he must bleed me again…"

"No! You cannot let that happen, Sire!" One look at his pale countenance told her he had no blood to spare. "Sucking the life fluids from your body will not help the cramping in your chest! I'll enjoin him from laying hands on you with my last breath. If he even speaks of it again, Sire, I will stand at your door and forbid him entrance, with my sword if need be!"

"Very well, Tara, he'll slice me no more." He looked at her admiringly. "By the gods, you've turned devilish firm of a sudden, ordering your king about like a scullery maid." But he did not look displeased.

"Someone must, Sire," she said firmly. "And I've another order: it's time you rested again." She thought to hear his demur, but he made none, and when she rose to draw hangings over the windows she saw his eyelids fall. He needs rest more than he knows, she realized, and sat beside the bed until his breathing grew measured and regular, then cautiously stole out.

Tara had come in to her father's sickbed as still a child, but when she returned to her bower and thought over the encounter, it was as an adult that she pondered what must be done.

Though the King's malady was not easily understood, his general appearance and clear mind showed he was in little danger of dying, but belike he could sense how close the grave had beckoned. She felt sure he accepted within himself that he could not take the field for the coming campaign, and if she handled it right, the command might devolve upon her for lack of any alternative.

Her father had acquiesced with surprising lack of argument to her order that he not be bled, and this suggested to her that he might stand ready to accord her a voice in weighty decisions touching affairs of the realm. The revelation buoyed her spirits enormously and she needed solitude to think it out. She sent for supper in her room, not to emerge until the following morn.

The first overt sign that Llywarch might be submitting to the mailed fist couched in her silken glove was the surprising waiting upon her by the Guard Captain. He was there, he told her, with no sign on his face of what this might portend, to discuss the marching disposition for the force. Thereafter, with no signal that it was in any way unusual, they met every morning to go over the details of staging the troops, until she whipped up the courage to ask him outright if he was to be her

Lieutenant. He responded obliquely, by declaring that he'd be honored to assume the post, if such were the wish of his Lord.

She remembered to requisition from Sir Gruwent the experienced reeve she'd promised Crosbey, to be sent to Aber Castle, with a private note to the Countess asking not only that he be dispatched to Saint Nicholas, but that Crosbey be freed to return with the escorting troop.

The day Crosbey's party arrived was a poignant one for Tara. Their arrival was heralded by courier and Tara was at the parapet when they reached the Mark. She made out the familiar figure riding the Reeve's former mount, and her heart was light as she hurried to greet him.

"I declare you look monstrous elegant, Sir Crosbey," she said with simulated formality as he dismounted. "I'd not take you for a tiller of the soil today." And indeed, his attire was uncommon fine, for one just completing an arduous and dusty trip. She kept pace with his long strides, looking covertly at him, thinking no knight had ever cut so splendid a figure.

"I confess, Princess," he said with a smile, "I bade the escort commander bide in the wood short of the Mark, whilst I changed to garments suited to the Court. Now you know my deceit, mayhap you'll send me straightway back to Saint Nicholas in disgrace."

"Send you back?" said Tara happily. "Oh Cross, you cannot know how glad I am to have you here. I have such need for a trusted friend, one who thinks as I do. We have so much yet to do, and the day of our departure draws nigh so swift I scarce can credit it! But come along with me and see for yourself." She grasped his hand to tug him along, then dropped it in mock dismay. "What am I thinking of? You arrive from a wearisome trip, and I give you no chance to rest or fresh up. What manner of hostess am I?"

"I'm in need of no rest," he said at once. "The trip was as naught, and I was buoyed up betimes, dreaming of the great honor of serving as your Equerry. Let us be about it, Princess; I've much to learn."

She thought to tell him to have done with 'Princess' and call her Tara as he always had, but realized he was right. The Court's formal setting demanded chivalric courtesies, and opinion would fault her new Equerry if he slighted them. But no formality must hinder our close working together, she vowed.

She had Crosbey join the next meeting with Tellicho, and breathed a relieved sigh at how smoothly they worked together from the very first. Crosbey deferred to the experienced Guard Captain, and for his part Tellicho admired the staunch young squire's selfless devotion to the Princess, whom Tellicho himself held in the same high regard. He said as much to Tara later. "Command is a lonely position; you are well served with such a loyal Equerry."

Command! He had said 'command'. Was it a tongue slip, or something boding well for her aspirations? Did it mean…? She had to know at once. "May you not tell me straight, Captain—is it the King's plan that I command the Dyfed force?" She waited, surprised at her temerity, scarce daring to breathe.

"Aye, Princess," he admitted. "I'd no thought to say direct, as it's the King's place to tell you himself, but I saw you'd divined as much, and we've not the time for playacting. He knows, as do you, that he's in no shape for such a parlous campaign. I break no faith with the King to tell that his wish is for you to command the force, and to post me as Lieutenant."

Command the force! The thought was too overwhelming for speech, but Tellicho waited for her acknowledgement, so she forced herself to respond. "Naught could please me more than to have you at my side. With you there to guide me and show me the right, our standard cannot falter. I pledge all my efforts to our cause! If ever I act the part of a heedless maid, I entreat you to rein me in at once."

The old campaigner, too embarrassed to speak, glowed with pleasure and deep satisfaction at her words. The news delighted Crosbey as well, but he strove to treat it lightly. "Sure, you knew all the time, Princess. Or if not, belike you were the only one not to know. Your daily briefs with the Guard Captain were clues enow to everyone. And I can say true, there be few in the force but rejoice that you lead us."

"You jest, Cross," she said indignantly. "Don't make sport of me. I hoped to be Sire's lieutenant, but scarce the Commander. How could they know, when I did not? And how can they accept to be led by an untried girl?" How could they indeed, she wondered.

"You are too close to see it. The King could do naught else. As to being untried, they ken your combat prowess, for word of that has swept the gwlad. Believe me, they want not some swaggering prince, blustering and roaring, like to rush blindly into a fray like a mad bull. I tell you, common soldiers far prefer a leader with wit and coolness to fight when odds favor us, and to await a better day when they do not. They think you such a commander, and will follow you, as will I."

She was deeply touched at his words of encouragement. Crosbey had turned her painful feeling of inadequacy into a surge of optimism, and of hope that she might be equal to the task after all. Buoyed up beyond measure by the expectation of support from her men, which would be needed in full measure to counter the heavy odds against Cymru, she vowed to give her very best in return.

Command required one heavy sacrifice that she decided must be put off no longer—the cropping of her glorious red-gold mane of hair. The ordeal of growing it back on leaving the convent had been unbearably slow, and she'd vowed never to shed a strand of it again. But the commander of Dyfed's forces must not bring ridicule to her troops. She could not ride forth with a ribbon gathering in long tresses that flowed enticingly from beneath her helmet, or she'd be a laughingstock, hardly to be taken seriously in her new office. There would be struggle enow to get acceptance, without flaunting her femininity to distract them from the stern business of a hard campaign. Sequestered in her bower, she brushed her long hair nostalgically, luxuriating in the feeling, postponing the fateful deed as long as possible. Finally she pulled on her helmet, called Crosbey into the forbidden precinct, and handed him the shears.

"Here, Cross," she said firmly. "Before I lose my resolve, crop off all my hair below my helm." Horrified, he objected strenuously, but she was adamant, and in private he heartily approved her decision. She shut her eyes tightly as he cut, refusing to watch her hard-won locks fall to the floor. When he was finished, and no trace of her womanly glory could be seen beneath the rude iron helmet, she thanked and dismissed him, and wept in solitude over the loss of her femininity.

The overall march would be 140 miles, 90 to reach Brecon and join up with Cadell's force, and 50 more to the Danish encampment at Gloucester. While still safe in Cymru territory, Tellicho drilled the disparate groups from the various Dyfed cantrefs, trying to weld them into some semblance of a single functional force. This necessitated frequent stops to adjust the order of march, and on one of these he explained the historical precedent to Tara.

When the Romans invaded Celtic Britain they were vastly outnumbered, he told her, but the Britons fought as an undisciplined horde, while the invaders had specialist teams that could adjust to the shifting tides of battle. Their army comprised Legions and Auxiliaries, the former highly trained Roman citizen volunteers, the elite of the Roman army, and the latter conscripts from nations conquered on Rome's march through Europe. A legion had 5000 heavy infantry and 120 mounted scouts, with five or six Tribunes commanding its major units of 1000 men each, and with a centurion leading each century of 100 legionaries. An auxiliary unit, usually a garrison for smaller forts, had lightly armed infantry cohorts of 500 to 1000 men who bore the brunt of battle, and cavalry detachments protecting the wings. With such an army, vastly inferior in numbers but made up of full-time professional soldiers, Rome conquered all of Britain. When Rome pulled out to meet the Hun invasion of their homeland, some Cymri commanders adopted the same battle organization. Though not every

Cymri commander did, King Llywarch was a staunch advocate of the system that had extended Roman sway over so much of the world, and the Dyfed force would organize so.

"We cannot expect the performance of a Roman Legion, Milady," Tellicho said flatly. "Dyfed's is a hobbledehoy army, patched together of levies drawn from all across our realm, each with its own fighting style. They've not had time to learn how to pull in harness and not work at cross-purposes, and most have no liking of the change. Worse, at Brecon we join still other gwlads, whose ways in battle will not be as ours. Cymru's army is a huge blind beast, each gwlad's force a different leg, and all its legs running where they will. We do the best we can, and the Cymri tribesman is a tough soldier, but a fighting force is not built o'ernight."

Tara was flattered to have tactical matters explained in detail, and to be treated with the respect accorded an equal in combat experience, but Tellicho's harsh criticism of their fighting qualities perplexed and frighted her. "But I was told from the cradle," she protested, "that our forefathers were second to none on the battlefield, stouter fighters than e'en the Romans. Did not the Briton Queen Boedicea rise up against Paulinus in the first century of Jesu, to sack Londinium and slaughter 70,000 Romans? Was that not Briton against Roman?"

Tellicho hesitated, reluctant to gainsay her but it had to be said. "Mayhap she killed 70,000; some say as much. More like it was a tithe that many. But those were not Roman legionaries, Princess. Paulinus was off campaigning in the north, leaving but a garrison behind. Most of the dead were plain people—tradesmen and tinkers, women and babes. When Paulinus returned with his 40,000 troops, he swept her from the field, and put 80,000 Britons to the sword. Her cause would have been better served had she studied the enemy."

"What do you mean?"

"As did the chieftain Caratacus, who led the Silures nation bordering the Saefern, nigh to Gloucester where we be bound. When Caratacus was defeated by the Roman general Scapula, he made peace to save his people.

They got more than their lives, for Rome brought them law and letters, built fine roads and great works, and helped their barren ways of living. Caratacus once had visited the Eternal City, where he learned the Roman yoke rested lightly on those she subdued, bringing more good than ill. Boadicea, untutored queen of the wild Iceni tribe, knew naught of such things when she fell on Londinium, reducing it unneeded to ashes, and stirring Suetonius Paulinus to fury. She signed the death warrant of her people. Glory she had in plenty, but only the glory of the grave."

"But what of the great Elen Luyddog, descended of a Briton chief, Queen to the mighty Macsen Wledeg? Her great victories cannot be gainsaid. They were in Roman times, but never did a Roman general defeat her."

"True, Princess, but Queen Elen Luyddog was a Roman's wife. The general of whom you speak was a true Roman, and his real name was Magnus Maximus. He brought his forces to Caernarvon and put down Caratacus, sire of Elen Luyddog, and married Elen as just one of his spoils of war, and took her back to Rome. Our bards dub him Macsen Wledeg, and would have you think him Cymri, but though it's true he founded a great Cymri line of rulers he was Roman himself. He died in Gaul, and only then did Elen return with her son Constantine and some of her Lord's loyal legionaries, to defend her Cymri dominions—but from other Cymri chieftains, not Romans. The famous road from Neath to Brecon, that they call Sarn Elen, was Roman built. It's well to take pride in our countrymen, but the field commander who would win in battle must see his troops for what they are, and not be cozened with Mabinog tales."

Tara could think of naught to rebut his dry analysis. In that instant, she was humbled by her vast inexperience, realizing the degree to which she was dependent on men whose years of fighting, planning strategy and gauging the enemy reduced to almost nothing her scant training. Yet they call me their leader, she marvelled, vowing to learn all she could from her veterans. As for the brave tales of her childhood, she wondered how many other tales sung by the bards were fabricated to please the simple. How was she to sift out the kernel of truth inside these stirring accounts? Tellicho knows how, she decided. He knows what to expect of ill-trained levies fresh-drawn from the plough, and will reck the odds before throwing down the gage of battle. Please Lug she might learn from him, that she would know to do the same.

On the march for Carmarthen, Tara saw buglers with brazen horns gleaming in the sun, bowmen with wild elm longbows, wiry foot-soldiers with swords in their belts and javelins thrust aloft, and mounted scouts flitting through the flanking trees. The armored knights made a compact force in the van, attended by their squires. Admiring their stirring appearance, she was shocked to hear Tellicho scorn them as a component whose presence must be endured, but whose cumbersome armor was vulnerable to the deadly shafts of the mountain men. "True, they can make a difference when we need a quick galloping thrust to gain some key hilltop, or strike chill in the stomachs of ill-trained levies unused to the thunder of their charge, but knights cannot stand up to the longbow."

Tellicho bade the force halt for the midday meal, and when men and animals were fed, he gathered his commanders to confer on the campaign. Each of Dyfed's cantrefs was represented and Tara worried lest the levies from Aber Castle be led by Eorl Skomer, who'd take unkindly to orders from her, but the leader of the Mathry contingent was a lean and rough-cut soldier she'd not seen before. As Tellicho introduced the commanders, she scanned their faces for any distaste for her youth or sex, but if any was disaffected he hid it well.

"The Roman strategy would be to separate bowmen, foot soldiers and cavalry, Princess," Tellicho told her when they were again on the march. "Then if the shift of battle calls for one or other at some beleaguered rampart, we've but to dispatch the proper century. However, your father's uchelwyr are mightily jealous, and we are unable to pull their contingents apart so."

"Do they not understand the gain from such a plan?" asked Tara incredulously.

"They understand naught. Not one commander in the force has fought in a combined army, or ever had need to divide troops in the frontier skirmishes that have been his training. It may surprise you, Princess, but none here is more experienced than you, for the campaign we face at Gloucester. You saw them, and listed as they spoke. Heard you one who understood how to withstand attack against the scanty earthworks the Danes have tossed up at Gloucester?" His demeanor was solemn, and pondering all he had said on the march she wondered at their folly in facing an experienced field commander like Alfred.

"How of Cadell?" she asked hopefully. "Sure he must be a skilled campaigner."

"If he be, I know naught of how he became so," said Tellicho gloomily. "Sure not on the Mercian frontier where he served, for their largest skirmish was two-score men to a side. No, Princess, we plunge into unfamiliar waters, and we may find them deeper than we wat."

"Cross, I had no least idea how ill-prepared we be for this adventure," she announced, her morale low after talking with Tellicho. "There is none in Cymru understands what we face."

"Aye, Princess," he agreed. "The Cymri training is only in border tussles, not army against army. But I see the Dane far more skilled at battle maneuvers than Cadell. Sigefert led a great force against the Saxons, and we'd best ally with him if we're to prevail against Alfred."

"I hope you are right, Cross, if only Cadell sees it so." But she felt a grim foreboding, and saw the campaign no longer as a great undertaking, but as a perilous and ill-conceived venture.

It was while Tara and Crosbey were on an impromptu tour of the line that she experienced something to sink her spirits to their lowest ebb. She had been about to rein in and suggest they drop back to talk without being overheard, when a snatch of conversation from troopers riding ahead floated back to her.

"Hast seen t'wench who struts about at t'front?" The speaker made a gesture she did not understand, and his mates broke into ribald laughter.

"Aye, 'n' calling herself a soljer," said another. "I ken t'kind uv soljer her be."

"'N' wot kind, then, Catogg? said the first speaker, poking his mate heavily in the ribs. "Wot kind, then?"

"A doxie soljer is wot. One toss in t'bed wif me 'n' her wouldna strut sae proud. Ye'd see."

There was general loud laughter. "Garn, ye be'nt man enuf t'bed her, Catogg," said the one who had spoken first. "Happen ye need me t'help?"

Crosbey's face turned deep red, and he snatched his sword angrily from its scabbard. "No, Cross!" she whispered urgently. "No! Come back to the rear with me." She wheeled her horse without waiting to see if he heeded her command. Reluctantly he sheathed his weapon and followed her.

"They are naught but loudmouth soldiers, Princess," he said, when they reached a secluded place, and his hot temper had cooled enough for speech. "I was aching to run the varlots through. We would have had a parlous affair, had you not restrained me. But in sooth, Princess, they were but empty-headed words, not truly meant, spoke mainly to keep their spirits up, and help them forget they may be riding to their death." He looked at her with deep concern. "I do hope you take it so, Princess. If a commander were to call up all soldiers for what they say in the guard room when they think to be alone, half his force would be hanged in a fortnight."

"I know, Cross," said Tara wearily. "I wat all you say is true, and of course it is naught after all. Let us say no more on't. Belike we should be getting back, before Tellicho sends out a guard to collect us." She spurred her horse, storming past the cavalrymen so fast their heads jerked up in surprise.

They will see, she vowed to herself bitterly. I will show them what manner of frightened little wench it is who rides at their head and leads them into battle. Before Lug, they'll learn full well what I can do!

CHAPTER 13

The Dyfed force was met at the old border fortress of Saint Clears on the River Taf by emissaries of King Brechnor of Ystrad Towy, and escorted the last few miles to his castle. The prospect of seeing Brechnor's historic old castle excited Tara. It dated from over five hundred years earlier, in the later stages of the Roman occupation, and from its position on a broad plateau commanded a view of the Towy River valley. Perhaps less impressive than the castles of other Cymri monarchs, it was highly functional, and its network of underground hypocausts, carrying heated air from the furnaces to all parts of the structure, made it in winter the envy of all Cymri princes.

The troops bivouacked outside the wall, and Brechnor's emissary ushered Tara and her staff through the colonnaded gate to the keep, where the King waited in welcome. She was touched by the warm greeting of the rubicund old monarch, looking like a great elderly bear in his befurred robe.

"Lug's blood, Princess Tara, what a splendid commander you do be," he roared as she knelt, snatching her erect and smothering her in a hug so enthusiastic she could scarce breathe. "Let us look at you." He thrust her out at arm's length. "When last I saw you, you were but a tiny lass, though a spunky one. And now, you be a brave young warrior, and did I not know the truth I'd vow you a bonny prince instead of a princess. In sooth, Llywarch must be aburst with pride at what you've grown into!"

He turned to Tellicho, booming his hearty greeting. "It's too long since we last met, Sir Tellicho. You be very welcome at Carmarthen, and it eases my old bones to see a fighter who's forgot more than most ever knew. Now, honor me with introducing your 'centurions', as your King would term them."

Tellicho, warmed by Brechnor's greeting, made introductions while Tara gathered her wits. Though she feared the old king's praise would have her commanders smirking behind their hands, his wondrous warm welcome put a most pleasant cap on their arduous trip, and she could not but like their jolly host.

He turned to her after the cantref leaders packed were off, and inquired of her father. When Tara told him an attack prevented Sire from coming, Brechnor's cherubic face turned serious. "What manner of attack, lass?" He took her hand. "Mayhap I'm discourteous to address you so, but I find it devilish hard to term a young and beauteous maid aught else, when the last time we met you were scarce quit of swaddling cloths. But about Llywarch: what ails the man?"

Briefly, Tara described the onset and continuation of her father's malady, then turned to the King's unspoken question. "...and I thought it best...that is, he decided that it would be best, if I rode at the head of our levies, with Sir Tellicho commanding in all but name."

King Brechnor picked up her momentary slip of the tongue. "So, it was you thought it best, eh lass? I warrant you mow a heavy swath there at Menevia, with your dear mother passed away, and now your father ailing. You were right to keep him home. My beloved queen was stricken so two years past, but naught I'd say could keep her from fretting about—digging at her flowers, riding her palfrey in the orchard, seeing to the menials, calling on the sick. I was speaking only to the wind. Like you, she was, strong-headed. She refused to slow her pace, until her grand old heart gave out." He blinked furiously to hold back tears. "And mark me, Llywarch will be the same, unless you contrive to slow him down. Slow him down, gel!"

Left in privacy in the women's bower, Tara rearranged her hair, and was amazed at how attractive her butchered tresses looked when she brushed them into an aureole of light red-gold locks. She kept on her field tunic, open at the top and showing the delicate golden torc about her neck, and buckled her mother's girdle of jeweled gold around her slender waist. Sadly, her field kit boasted no perfume or emollient she could enlist in her subtle campaign to distract her leaders. She bethought of Brechnor's queen, whose chambers these were, and wondered if she'd used such witchery. Searching about, she found in a small alcove between the windows a delicate inlaid chest that opened to disclose a treasure trove of womanly artifices—perfumes, powders, ochres for shading the eyes, and other dainty ingredients she did not recognize. Perching astride the little stool, she felt a moment's regret that her martial regimen had left her no opportunity for experimenting with the arts of allure.

She found a tiny porcelain vial of scent that rekindled an elusive memory of her beloved Mama. She moistened the tip of her finger, and as her mother had done, she applied perfume behind her ears, in the little hollow at her throat, and on the inside of each wrist, then brushed her moistened hand through her hair. She selected a dark ochre powder to shade her eyes, their darkened lids accenting the golden highlights in her hair.

Viewing her faint image in the tarnished reflecting glass, she was astonished at the remarkable effect these few subtle changes created, and knew the overall transformation would captivate the men below. A pang of guilt touched her for outwardly proclaiming her soldierly masculinity, while secretly using these womenly artifices, but she was doing it in a serious cause, and as she left the bower she laughed aloud.

She was in the Great Hall but a moment before she discovered how wondrous well this cosmetic artistry worked. First to come up was the brash young Prince Pwyll of Narberth, who made to kiss her hand, only to be shouldered aside by a red-bearded giant identifying himself as

Eorl Blefwyn, and expressing perplexity as to how to address an army commander who also was a comely young lass.

"A lass, Eorl?" responded Tara, determined to stamp out such patronizing at the outset, but smiling to soften the reproof. "Best not to think of me so. I am trained for the field, not the bower, and I hope to convince you my skills are adequate."

"I be convinced already, Princess." It was the uchelwr heading Eorl Skomer's contingent. "I am Skyll Emrys of Mathry. I watched you defeat the overstuffed squire with the quarterstaff. in the tourney for your King, and heard how you bested two renegade soldiers in swordplay at Dewi Sant—though it was anything but play for the one you sent to the Otherworld, I warrant." He smiled slightly. "And murthered an outlaw with your blade in Priory Wood."

She saw eyes widen at this testimonial to her prowess, as she turned to face another who was greeting her. "So bonny a Princess, to soil her weapon on outlaws," he said, with a great bow. "I am Edwal of Castle Flemish, but already I fear I misspoke greviously when I termed so gallant a duelist 'bonny'. My apologies for speaking what my heart advised."

"You've every right to your opinion, Eorl," responded Tara with a smile of greeting. "You must give your heart every chance to be heard." Lug knows how hard I worked to appear bonny, she thought.

A broad smile broke over Edwal's face. "Well, that's my opinion in sooth, Milady, if I be hanged for it. I'm proud to follow you, but bemused betimes, for it's the first time I've been bewitched by the beauty of my captain. I trow you've used sorcery to capture our hearts so swift." And little does he wat, she thought, how close his 'sorcery' lies to the truth.

The others clustered around like bees at honeysuckle, and she was at a loss which to address. She spied an older man in the back, and made her way through the press to greet him. "Pray tell me your name, Sire," she said. "I know all too few of you."

"I am Aelfgar of the Fishguard troop, Milady. Your exploits reached me direct, through the eyes of my son Cadfan who was a page with you. I never thought to meet you, but now that I have I'm proud to offer you my sword." He drew his blade, and tendered the hilt to her.

She thought to speak with him about his son she'd known so well, but all her thought was on the question of how to respond to his chivalric gesture. "You do me honor, Sir Aelfgar," she said, and at a venture touched the hilt to her lips and presented it back to him. It must have been sufficient, for they cheered lustily. Her face burned with excitement and triumph, and she wished with all her heart that Sire could hear.

"Come, lass," said King Brechnor at last. "Join me at table and let us toast our bold venture before you faint from hunger." Once seated, she swept her gaze raptly over the assembly of Dyfed's battle commanders. So stern and awesome had they seemed on the march, and now all were as friends. As she watched them lift their flagons in toast, and rise one by one to pledge fealty to Cymru, she thought of the great tales of heroic knights who had pledged their lives and sacred honor in the legendary Court of Gwyn-ap-Nudd. She was in a trance, her happiness more complete than she could have dreamed. Naught, she vowed, could mar this occasion.

But in that, she was mistaken.

Glum in the midst of the jollity was one who sat dour and silent, emptying his goblet as if seeking to drink himself senseless. Distracted by his sour countenance, she asked the King who he might be.

"Why lass, did you not meet him?" he asked with a chuckle. "That be my son, Prince Wulfdune. He marches with us on the morrow as my Lieutenant. Forgive me the oversight, my gel, but my sin is soon remedied." At a word from the King, a menial tapped Wulfdune on the shoulder and delivered his father's summons.

"Ho, Wulfdune," cried Brechnor jovially when the Prince stood scowling before him. "Hast met the commander of the Dyfed force, Princess Tara? Didst ever see so fair a Tribune, lad?"

There was a lull in the conversation, and the Hall fell quiet. Annoyed by his son's silence, Brechnor raised his voice. "Didst hear me, Wulfdune? I charge you to welcome our fair Princess, and honor her as becomes her rank. A woman, and in command of Dyfed's troops! Speak up, lad."

The silence grew heavy, as it appeared the Prince was determined to maintain his rude silence, but at last he found his voice. "I know well she's the Princess. I heard King Llywarch had a lass, and heard the stories that she fancied men's garb, but I never thought to see such with my own eyes." He swayed slightly as he spoke, but his words were free of slurring.

King Brechnor was about to call down Wulfdune for his lack of hospitality, but Tara stayed him. "If it please your Majesty," she said clearly, "I would respond." He sat back with disgust into his ornate chair, and she rose to her feet.

"Does my garb so much offend you then, Prince?" she asked softly, but with an edge in her voice.

"A lass should know to keep her place," he said distinctly, his manner abrupt. "She should not push her way into men's tasks, when she has not the skills nor wit for it. I say give up this charade. Return to your bower. Leave fighting to fighting men."

Tellicho rose slowly to his feet, his countenance black, and with murmurs of disapproval several other officers rose in protest. I'd best stop this lest it grow out of hand, Tara decided. She waved Tellicho down.

"Pray take your seats, men of Dyfed," she said. "I need no succor." She turned to face the Prince again. "You find me unfit for fighting, Milord?" she asked calmly.

Wulfdune laughed scornfully. "No maid is fit for fighting. All know as much. What would such as you do if be it you met a real soldier?"

"Are you a real soldier, Prince?" demanded Tara frigidly.

"Aye, my lass. Soldier enow to best you with my single arm, were you so heedless as to meet me in combat." He turned to face the other guests, his face flushed with drink but his speech still understandable.

"How can any lass claim to be a warrior, when the least raw recruit in her force can strike her down?"

Tara, feeling the blood rush hotly to her head, tried to remain detached and gauge her tormenter's condition and strength. Were they alone, she could ignore his hostility, knowing it stemmed but from jealousy that she commanded her force whilst he was but lieutenant in his. She was torn, not wishing to cause a spectacle before the genial King Brechnor, but knowing that the whole assemblage watched and gauged, and that her new-won credibility could not survive a retreat from this rude challenge. She weighed the choices, and made her decision.

"Are you man enow to wrestle me down, Sire?' she asked.

"You must be addled, gel! I'd not wrestle a maid. It would be unseemly to pick on one so weak and ill-suited to a tussle."

She recalled how she had baited Grosseteste so he would lose his temper and throw caution to the winds. She must manage as much here, to have any hope of besting the sturdy Wulfdune. E'en with her best efforts, she'd find a tussle with this young Prince a most chancy enterprise.

"Do you fear me so, Prince Wulfdune? Look about you. See how all are watching. Will you have them think you too afeard to fight me?"

He flushed hotly, and she knew the thrust had gone home. "I fear no one," he shouted. "Least of all a puling maid who has not the strength of a babe. Do not tempt me, gel!"

"Very well. If you will but apologize, my Lord, and say you meant not what you said, I will excuse you from the bout. If you do not, honor demands that I hold you to it."

There was a roar of laughter coupled with a scattering of cheers, inflaming the Prince as would a crimson rag a bull. "Come out then, you foolish wench," he challenged. "Ye need a lesson taught." There was a rumbling of disapproval in the hall, but he seemed not to hear it.

Tara turned demurely to her host. "By your leave, King Brechnor. Your son has called me out, and it would be a stain on the honor of Dyfed and all her commanders were I to decline." He thought to demur, hesitating for a bit and shaking his head, then reluctantly acceded to the inevitable, the while whispers spread out from the high table, as her words were repeated throughout the hall.

The two contestants took their places in a cleared area just before the high table, where jongleurs and minstrels might perform, but tonight the audience would be watching a more serious entertainment. As Wulfdune took his position, she tried to gauge how he'd comport himself—cautious circling of his opponent, a deceptive retreat to make her commit, or as she devoutly wished, a headlong charge to end the bout quickly. The hot anger in his face gave her hope that it might be a rush, and she thought back hurriedly to the practice bouts with Crosbey, wherein he'd shown her how the very force of such a charge might bring its own defeat. The timing was precious close, however, and it could not work if Wulfdune had any inkling of her intentions.

"Goad your enemy," Cross had exhorted her. "Raise his blood to fury, so he thinks of naught save smashing you in the dust. He must hate you if he's to lose his head, however you bring it about. The way you make him so I leave to you, but do it!"

He waits for me to make the first sally, she realized. He's not so addled with drink as to abandon all strategy. I must bring him to charge headlong. Putting the thought to the deed, she stepped close to him, put her right hand on her left shoulder, then swung it out smartly to deal his face a stinging backhand blow that echoed throughout the hall.

He recoiled in surprise at the totally unexpected assault, lifting his hand unknowing to his reddening cheek, then ducked his head and charged furiously at her with both arms extended. Anticipating the move she'd all but invited, she fell backward onto the rushes, thrust her upraised feet hard into his unguarded stomach, and reached up inside his arms to grasp the loose folds of his tunic. Even as he was attempting to shuffle forward against the pressure of her feet to regain his balance, she rolled back, giving with the force of his rush. Simultaneously she pushed upward with her legs to lift him off his feet and tugged on his tunic with all the lithe young strength of her sinews.

The results were spectacular. He grasped at her, first furiously, then frantically, but could not manage to connect with her body tumbling so swiftly out of reach, and before he knew what was happening found himself somersaulted clear over her to land heavily on his back. Momentarily immobilized by the shock of landing, he scrambled up as best he could, and looked around to see where she had got to. She stood calmly by the head table, smiling demurely, not a golden strand of hair disarranged, savoring the deafening cheers. Goaded beyond endurance, he rushed madly at her again, but she evaded his charge with the slightest of movements, and he crashed awkwardly into the head table in front of the King's place.

"Enough!" Brechnor shouted, springing to his feet, his face reddening with anger. "Have done, Wulfdune! Our guest has answered your challenge clear enow. This is no wrestling pit, but the Great Hall!" He looked over the audience, paying no further heed to his maddened son. "Pray someone escort the Princess Tara back to her place, and let us put an end to this spectacle."

She felt her arm grasped, and looked up to see Crosbey at her side, pride glowing on his flushed face. "Did I follow your teachings aright, Cross?" she whispered.

He said naught, but the admiring look he bestowed on her spoke eloquently. When he handed her into her chair beside the King, she squeezed his arm impulsively, wishing she knew how to thank him for all the weary hours he'd spent training her for just such a moment.

The cheering of her officers was sweet music to her ears, but her shining moment came next morn. As she took her place at the head of the force, a scattering of cheers originated among the mounted troops—the same cavalrymen whose rude unthinking slights she had heard but one day before—then swelled to a crescendo that enveloped the whole force.

"Elen!" they shouted. "Queen Elen! Elen Luyddog!"
And it was of her they shouted.

CHAPTER 14

"A sad mischance thrust me into that wrestling bout, Cross," she said in vexation, as the two rode along together. She was regretting shaming the hapless Wulfdune in front of the diners. "I was wrong to react so. I've a new enemy, before ever knowing him as a friend."

"The matter is not so grievous, Princess," responded Crosbey reassuringly. "There's a good and a bad to all things. The good in your tussle lies in the respect you gain with our force. You mayhap garnered one enemy, but you earned many score of friends. You heard their cheers last night. You know how high they hold you. And you heard the ordinary troopers just now."

She turned to face him squarely. "In sooth, Cross, do they see me as their commander? Yes, I heard the officers last night, and the sound was sweet in my ears. Ne'er did I reck to hear such from so noble a company. But Cross, was it mostly their surprise and pleasure at seeing a drunken lout tossed by a maid—their maid? Do we not hear the same plaudits for a dancing bear, that he does something for which he's so ill-fitted? Does just the one toss make me a qualified commander?"

He hesitated in answering her. "Belike there was summat of that in their cheers. The moment you stepped forward so bold, you caught their fancy. They liked your rare spirit, and they thought ill of the churlish Prince. All there wished him laid low, and how much sweeter if the deed were done by their own beautiful Princess."

He looked suddenly flustered at having spoke too free. "I mean...there was no call for me to term you so. I mean, just that..."

"It's all right, Cross," she said happily, touching his arm. "Call me beautiful any time you will. The term ill-fits a squire who knows no feminine wiles, but if aught in my appearance won over our centurions, then I'm grateful for as much. But a battle commander has scant need of a fair face." She smiled ruefully. "Tell me true, Cross: how can they go willing into battle, with their general a maid of scarce ten and six years?"

"That's easy to answer. As one small thing, Tellicho is at your side, and in all Dyfed there is none so experienced as he. But they look not only to Tellicho—they look at you as well. A soldier on the way to battle needs augers, to show him the gods favor his cause, and if he finds none, his courage flags. In you they see a maiden with special powers from the gods, and they read it as a portent of success. Even the uchelwyr read it so." He paused a moment. "Even I."

She pondered his words. Her victory in the Great Hall had been a stroke of fortune, due more to Wulfdune's many flagons of ale than any skill of hers. His superior strength would have overborne her in the end, despite his muddled senses, had Brechner not called a halt when he did. But was it more than good fortune, mayhap one more piece in the complex plans of the gods in which she was little more than a helpless pawn? If so, it was writ that she would challenge Wulfdune, and that he'd come hampered to the affray. She'd best cease fretting on what she could not control, and focus her attention on affairs of the march.

But it was not quite so easy to free her mind of another nagging thought, and the closer they came to Glamorgan Castle the more it troubled her.

Clydog!

It had been common knowledge back at Menevia Castle for near a month that she'd ride in Llywarch's stead, ample time for Cadell's spies to get word to Glamorgan. She shuddered how ill Clydog would take it, and how he'd try to force his attentions and his plans on her. He hated and feared her: hatred because she had seen his cowardice close to, and fear lest she expose him. As her betrothed, he had every right in law and custom to control her, and that meant he'd make her dance to his piping—which included nullifying her command of Dyfed's levies.

She forced herself to address an idea gnawing at the edges of her mind, a reckless notion she'd refused to entertain. But the closer they got to Brecon, the more she thought on it. Her eyes turned to Crosbey, riding so proper and erect beside her, ever poised to do her bidding.

What if she were to marry Crosbey?

It was the first time she'd said it so plain, e'en to herself. Instinctively she turned away from him in confusion, terrified lest he notice and somehow divine the cause. She knew he would accept at once. And her tremulous excitement, the tightening in her chest, the heavy pounding of her heart, were signals all too clear of her own feelings. A lifetime with Cross—she experienced a sudden thrill at the thought of his warm glance...his strong young body...his loving caresses. A delicious shivering assailed her, and she felt short of breath. Tears sprang unbidden to her eyes; she was at once terribly happy and unaccountably sad.

I must cease this, she told herself, and whipped up her mount to ride on ahead, anxious to be by herself and think rationally. What if she were to marry Crosbey? What could Clydog do?

There was much he could do. He could have the marriage annulled, or King Cadell could do so. He could simply take her as his concubine, imprisoned in his chambers with no further mention of marriage, her position little better than slave. He could even...!

The realization agonized her. He could have Crosbey put to death! For Cadell—or for Clydog, in his name—a simple matter of giving orders. It would violate the law, but Cadell was the law. To whom could she appeal? While she and Cross were in Glamorgan Castle, there would be no safety for either one. Such a marriage would destroy all she held precious.

The tears flowed freely, tears of rage and helplessness at the crude
varlot waiting ahead, with all the power of majesty at his command, and
of sorrow for the stalwart young man who held her heart in his strong
hands. For Tara was forced to acknowledge to herself that Crosbey was
more than a true friend and ally.

Was she in love with him?

When she reined in to drop back alongside Crosbey, weary and
drained from the storm of her emotions, he looked questioningly at her,
but they kept to the rutted stone road in silence, each deep in thought.
Gradually Tara forced her mind clear, to focus on her surroundings.

"The Towy River keeps pace with us, Milady," Tellicho informed her.
She had joined him, determined to turn her mind to matters of the
moment. "It lies to our south as we march, and our bivouac for food
will be on its banks. Before the Romans built their road network to link
up their fortresses, the Cymri took to the river in their coracles for want
of a better way. This road is another of the debts we owe our Roman
conquerers; without it our trip would take twice the time." A sudden
thought hit him. "Had you a wish to ride on ahead, Princess?" he asked.

"Nay, Captain. I would remain with the main body. The more I am
with it, the better I learn how it moves. I have much to learn of fighting."

He rumbled with quiet laughter. "I would say, Princess, that you have
little to learn of wrestling. I was fair raging when that popinjay of a
Prince spoke so rudely in the Hall, but you took his measure like a veteran. Your Sire would have been proud how you tossed him onto the
rushes, like a wrestler born."

"I fear I've made an unneeded enemy, when I knew I heard only the
ale talking. But how could I back down in front of all?"

"Mayhap you could have found a way early on, but when you
stepped up so bold, none of your uchelwyr but hoped by a miracle
you'd throw him down, though none truly thought you'd prevail. I
might have told them different, but none asked my opinion. Now
you've spilled him, they're like to think you can draw on more sorcery

and lead them to victory. That's ever the way of soldiers across the land, to seek magic portents, and if belike they think they've found one in you, so much to the good. Today every least soldier will be clamoring to follow your standard and none other. No commander in history ever won over new troops so quick!"

His remarks were mightily comforting, confirming what Crosbey had said, but they did not truly address the point worrying her. "I am flattered to have their confidence so easily," she said with frank directness, "but you know I truly have no experience in leading fighting men."

"You know, and I know. But the rest do not. Or if they guess, they choose not to believe so. You need not fret the matter, Princess; I have some small experience in warfare, and I will be at your side. If you allow me to advise you betimes, we will do as well as the others."

The meal stop was brief, in light of the long trek ahead for the foot soldiers that day. Tara thought of riding over to Brechnor's encampment, to make her peace with his son and defuse the ill feeling she had stirred up, but scarce was the quick meal over than Tellicho had her call the order to take up the march.

The evening started quiet enough. The Dyfed force was quartered just off Llandovery, on the Llandingat ruins of an old Roman fortress, with ample room for the eleven centuries of troops to encamp. Tellicho threw up a command post tent and a smaller nearby for her, and after the troops were fed, the centurions gathered to plan their arrival at Glamorgan next day.

"Would you like to speak a word to your officers, Milady?" asked Tellicho as they stood outside the tent waiting for the group to assemble. "Mayhap they'd like to hear from you—it scarce matters what you say, but it reminds those who need reminding that you lead the force."

A quick tremor of apprehension shot through Tara at the thought of addressing the forbidding group, until she recalled their jollity the previous evening and knew her fears were groundless. These commanders are not faceless subordinates, she realized; they are friends, albeit of very short tenure. She started to ask Tellicho what to say, but knew he'd prefer her to make that decision. "If you think so, Captain," she agreed, with a calm she did not entirely feel, and proceeded ahead of him into the tent.

As soon as she stood before the gathering, her momentary apprehension left her. The uchelwyr greeted her with enthusiastic clapping, leaping to their feet when she appeared, and their pleasure at seeing her was plain to see. She'd not planned out what to say, but in the warm glow of their welcome the words came to her unbid.

"I pray, noble gentlemen, that I hear no challenge to another wrestling bout, for I am much fatigued by the ride and indeed have little enow strength to spare." She smiled engagingly as she spoke, and hoped they would not find her words unseemly, or unduly frivolous.

The group roared with laughter, under cover of which she asked Tellicho his intentions, and when her audience quieted she spoke again, "Enough talk of fighting among ourselves. Sir Tellicho and I have been discussing the higher priority of fighting the Saxon, and there are matters enow that we must take in hand before we reach the High Court." She turned to the waiting Guard Captain. "If you please, Sir Tellicho."

The ensuing discussion had been going on for near half an hour, and darkness had fallen, when they began to hear a disturbance outside the tent. Shortly thereafter, a sentry poked his head cautiously through the flap, eyes wide with apprehension at interrupting the gathering. He blinked and gaped, but no words came.

"Well, man?" rumbled Tellicho. "Speak! Speak! What say you, fellow?"

Thus admonished, and with all eyes on him, the man found his voice. "Saxons!" he croaked. "Saxons they be, Sorr!" At his words the uchelwyr poured pell-mell out of the tent.

As their eyes adjusted to the deepening twilight, they made out signs of a melee on the western perimeter, where the Fishguard force camped, and another disturbance on the southern boundary guarded by the Castle Emlyn levies. They scattered at once, each heading for his own bivouac area. Tara stood for a moment undecided, until she felt a hand on her arm.

"It's back in the tent for us, Princess," said Tellicho, pulling her gently along. "The commander does not belong in the thick of things. And best you bid the young Sir join us."

"I'm here, Captain." She looked back to see Crosbey behind her in the flickering light, and realized he'd been at hand throughout, standing unobtrusively aside but ever alert to her need.

"I feared something of this sort," said Tellicho in his deep voice. "We'll find it's Saxon patrols in some strength, trailing us to learn our plans. Now they jab at our flanks, blooding us a bit to unnerve our levies."

Tara noted his calm air, and thought about his words. If he was right, they had naught to fear from a token enemy force. Belike it's little stronger than the patrol I commanded out of Glamorgan, she thought. Recalling how her tribesmen stole noiseless through the wood, never showing themselves in the open, she realized it was not surprising the Saxons were undetected.

"But if they be so outnumbered, will we not slaughter all of them, now they've shown themselves?" She lifted the tent flap and peered out, but there was naught to be seen. "Sure they all be murthered by now."

"We'll not find it as easy as that. They struck at us in their own time and place, jumping a green sentry or two in the gloom, then loosing a quick shower of arrows into the camp, to hit whatever targets they would, and melting back into the trees. I misdoubt not what fighting we heard was Cymri against Cymri, in the confusion and dark. The Saxons be safely away by now, and we'll hear no more from them this night."

And so it proved. Eorl Blefwyd burst into the tent first, roaring a string of oaths that he cut short at once when he saw Tara. "Gone!" he growled. "The accursed varlots struck from beyond the palisade whilst our watch was changing, and the sentries were pounding through the bushes like so many war horses. One volley they unleashed and fled off like hares." He turned to Tellicho. "Belike you ken the rest of the fight was raw levies drawing bow at shadows—and at their fellows. The sentries gave no cry; they'll be lying out there with their throats slit."

Sir Aelfgar arrived a moment later with the same story: the sentries were killed whilst they chattered away like magpies.

"Best they learn the first night," said Tellicho dryly. "We'll see a tighter sentry-go now; this blooding will teach what no word from their uchelwyr could—walk in the shadows, step with care to remain silent, and open your eyes and ears."

It seemed to Tara that they were showing far too little worry about their assailants. "But are you not afeard the Saxon may strike again, as soon as the men settle in to sleep?" she asked.

"Nay, not this night. They've learned our strength and line of march, and rattled us a bit, which was what they came for. They be spurring for Sabrina now, to report what they found."

When the three of them were alone once more, Tara asked the question foremost in her mind. "Were we not remiss, that our sentries let themselves be surprised so?"

"Aye, we were that. We be grievously unready." He looked keenly at her, and went on in a wearied voice. "But think, Princess: with a score or two of picked Cymri tribesmen, I could surprise the outposts of any army encampment. A camp is full of noise and wanderings about, and how is any sentry to know the one snapping twig amongst many that bespeaks a foe?"

"Then what can we do?" she almost wailed. "How can we prevail at Gloucester?" Tara was in a nightmare of confusion, not daring to wonder what the future held.

"Do not put it quite so black. At Gloucester the Saxons must expose themselves against skilled warriors behind fortified earthworks, and Alfred has his green levies just as we. And the Danes are not ploughmen and shepherds called up to the colors, but full-time fighting men. I'll not be fretting about what this skirmish tells about our fighting strength, in any case."

Tara felt an instant alarm at the note in his voice, and looked quickly at Crosbey, to see him nodding agreement as if he understood Tellicho's unspoken fear. "What is it?" she demanded, anxiety lending an edge to her voice. "What deeper meaning lies in tonight's skirmish?"

"Alfred's knowledge of our movements means he has spies at the High Court. He knew where we would camp tonight. Belike he'll know our overall dispositions as well, when the combined army leaves Brecon. I ask myself, were I he, how would I use such information?" Never had she seen Tellicho's expression so grave.

She wanted to speak out urgently, pressing him, demanding an answer to his troubling question, but she kept silent, and after a time he continued, as if speaking to himself.

"Were I he, I'd use it to pinpoint where each of Cadell's generals pitches his tent, where he sleeps. I'd kill each one silently in the night, to destroy the brains of this ill-trained force 'ere it reaches Gloucester, winning the battle before it starts." He looked somberly at Tara. "And such could be his aim."

The march next day was a subdued affair. To the troops, the easy slaying of five sentries was a disturbing display of the Saxon's ability to breach their defenses at will. To Tara, the Guard Captain's analysis of the raid's deeper significance was profoundly disturbing, the more so as she wondered if Cadell had the skill to guard against such a possibility. Indeed, she had doubts if the thought would occur to him, or if he had enough experience of large-scale combat to give it credence. But that hazard lay in the future, after they left Brecon. A more immediate worry was the disaffection of her troops, under the impact of what was only a minor skirmish.

"I don't like it, Cross," she said, perplexed. "And I don't understand it. Tellicho's thoughts are gloomy enow, but heavy notions such as his are not what trouble the men, for they've not the wit to reck such things. It seems as if the Saxon attack, in sooth but a minor skirmish, has bewitched them enow to make them think Alfred invincible. Do you read it so?"

"Aye, Princess. Soldiers are strange creatures, naught but feathers for brains sometimes. Half their life they live in what I would call unrealistic hope of some great fortune, the other half in mindless fear of things they know not what. I've little doubt the morrow will hear their shouts and laughter again. It is not their fretting worrits me." He fell silent, and she knew in a flash of insight what he meant.

"You mean my worrying, Cross. Is that it?"

"I do, Princess. I know you've a downcast heart over the prospects for our cause. And unlike the mindless churls who march with us, your fears are no idle vapors. Tellicho's words, e'en though he'd be the first to own his theory is but guess, have you wondering as to our real chances, when and if we reach the Dane's encampment at Gloucester."

"In sooth, our chances against Alfred are not good, are they?"

He hesitated before answering. "I'd say no, not if it were left to the Cymri force alone. But we must pin our hopes on the Dane. Sigefert has held off Alfred's best strikes all the way up the Thames to Boddington, and no makeshift warrior could have done that. We must look to his army as our bulwark, with Cymri naught but an auxiliary force to build up his overall strength." Again came that disquieting hesitation, as if he were reluctant to say more. "I'm just thinking that..."

"What, Cross? Just thinking what?"

"I worry if King Cadell be too proud to serve a Danish commander. If he thinks to fight apart, with no experience at siege warfare, but unwilling to bend to a foreign freebooter, I'm afeard the encampment cannot stand."

It was with a troubled mind that Tara rode under the great forbidding portico guarding the entrance to Glamorgan Castle, and pulled up in the keep. Brechnor's party had arrived ahead of them, and the High King had escorted him into the castle, evidently delegating a subordinate to meet the Dyfed contingent. Tara hoped fervently this would not be Clydog, but in this she was disappointed. Scarce had she reined in, when she made out his overfed figure, and her heart sank.

"Our respectful greetings, Prince Clydog," boomed out Tellicho, sensing Tara's distress and seeking to draw away the Prince's attention. "The Princess Tara has the honor to present the Dyfed detachment, ready to join your standard."

Clydog did not acknowledge the courteous salutation, or give sign that he heard, but instead came brusquely up to Tara's mount and grasped her arm. "Come, wench!" he growled, tugging so hard she almost lost her balance. "You've been a devilish long time in coming. I've been cooling my heels for nigh onto an hour."

"Good morrow, Prince," said Tara, trying unobtrusively to free herself from his grip. "We had no thought to keep you and the High King waiting. I'm satisfied we maintained a smart pace." She was seething inwardly at his loutish behavior, and wondering how to terminate the encounter.

"Come! I'll be kept waiting no longer! Curse you for a saucy baggage, to keep my couch empty so long." He tugged angrily at her arm again. "I'll have a foretaste of your charms ere the night is done, so come along with me, my gel." He was pulling at her in earnest now, and she kept her seat only with an effort.

His fingers dug painfully into her arm, and suddenly he yanked so brutally that she lost balance and fell heavily from her mount, landing directly atop him. Clydog lost his footing and sprawled on the ground beneath her. Hastily she scrambled to her feet, embarrassed and shocked at the spectacle her thunderstruck retinue must be witnessing.

Shaken by his heavy fall, Clydog rose slowly and shook his head to regain his senses. The sight of the accursed girl so seeming calm, as if mocking him, drove him into a rage afresh. He lumbered toward her, hands thrust threateningly out, for all the world as if to throttle her.

Tara, dizzied herself by the fall, felt herself drawn aside, and saw Crosbey standing before her, shielding her with his body. She panicked, knowing what could happen if her equerry laid hands on a prince, and realized only her quick action could avert a terrible disaster.

"Stand aside please, Crosbey. I will attend the Prince as he requests. Pray see my equipage to my chambers, and I will be there anon." Not daring to meet his glance, she squeezed his arm, and stepped up to the fuming but now motionless Clydog. "I am ready, Sire," she said stiffly. "Pray lead the way." But not waiting for him, she brushed past and strode rapidly toward the castle entrance with all the dignity she could muster.

Inside, she stopped to allow the befuddled Clydog to collect his senses sufficiently to catch up with her. She had no plans beyond her hasty move to defuse the explosive situation back in the keep, and her nimble brain seemed to have deserted her. All she could do was wait, alert to any overt act on his part, ready to take her cue from his actions.

They were not long in coming. He stormed in after her and seized her wrist again. "High time you come to your senses, gel," he growled. "Come along with you, and no more of your foolishness!" He made as if to drag her, but suddenly she was unable to bear any more of his atrocious behavior.

She brought the heel of her free hand down sharply on the tender nerve at the base of his thumb, and yanked her wrist free. "My apologies, Prince Clydog," she said in silken tones. "I find myself too tired from the trip to do aught save rest. The supper hour is nigh; I will join you and the King there." Awaiting no response, she turned and hurried at almost a run, not daring to look back, toward the bower where Princess Meuriga had sheltered her many years ago.

CHAPTER 15

"Where be your mistress, goodwife?" Tara asked the befuddled hand-maiden, once she was over her shock at seeing what appeared to be a trooper entering the bower. "I will speak with her, if she be near."

But she was not near. In stumbling fashion, the maid managed to convey that the King had bundled his daughter off to Saint Catwg Convent, for sanctuary while rough soldiers would be about the castle, and Tara realized to her great relief that she had the bower to herself. Belike the chatelaine planned it thus, she decided, and dispatched the serving maid to find Crosbey, and to bring up her baggage.

"Come in, Cross," she urged, when he hesitated to enter the forbid-den zone. "As well I be hanged for a wanton as a reluctant bride. Besides, did we not work in the bower at Carmarthen Castle? Come in!" She smiled at him with more composure than she felt. "Who's to see you?"

"The Prince, Milady," he reminded her. "Were I he, I'd be lying await outside this very chamber, thinking to catch you when you leave—and belike scanning all who come and go."

"I never gave heed to that," she said, her smile fading. "But is it really likely? He has scant patience for such a waiting game. I escaped him the moment we entered the castle, saying only that we'd meet again in the Great Hall at supper. But Cross, I want not to go down to the Hall so soon. Can I not sup in the bower?"

She knew the answer before he spoke it. "Nay, Princess. It would be taken as a slap at the High Court, were you not there for King Cadell's welcoming. You must appear."

"I knew as much, Cross," she said wearily. "Then how if I have Tellicho report that I'm vastly fatigued, and beg leave to tarry in the bower until the drinking is done and it's time for eating. You can come for me in good time, and until then we'll keep Clydog at bay."

It was decided so, and after Crosbey left with the message she sat at Meuriga's boudoir, letting herself relax in complete privacy for the first time since leaving home. She'd no need to pretty herself tonight, lest it just tempt Clydog to press his suit the more. But she must fresh her appearance. The maid was sent for jugs of heated wash water, and helped Tara to bathe. Her hair was in disarray, and heavy with trail dust, and knowing the men would tarry long at their drinking, she bade the maid wash and dry it, and dress it in simple style befitting her military status—if indeed the maid had any such skills, which she thought unlikely.

When she was bathed and shampooed, she toweled her still moist hair vigorously until it was dry, and after the maid had done her awkward best to arrange it, she dismissed her. She combed idly through Meuriga's meager store of ointments, undecided if she should do any more. The commanders would be too deep in their cups to notice. Certainly she'd do naught for the foul Clydog—she grimaced at the notion. But something incomprehensible urged her to take pains with her appearance, and of a sudden she knew what it was.

It was for Crosbey! She yearned to appear attractive to him. And also for him I applied the fragrances and jewels at Brechnor's castle, she told herself in wonderment. But was it not to win over my uchelwyr, she argued with herself, only to have her inner voice respond that her mind was on Crosbey when she sought to beautify herself that night. Eyes closed, she leaned back, envisioning his strong body, as the disturbing but irrefutable new realization burned itself into her consciousness. Her lips parted into a soft smile as she surrendered to her sweet imaginings.

Then she sat up abruptly.

Marry Crosbey? Had she not thought it out before, only to be convinced that such a union was impossible? She was a princess, and e'en were she not promised to Clydog—which she was, seemingly inescapably—marriage with one so low in rank could not be countenanced. She had worried at it from every angle, and her mind was clear that no prospect existed for such a marriage.

But her heart, hitherto near silent, now was beating out an urgent message to the contrary.

Scarce aware of her actions under the spell of these troubling musings, she applied perfume and eye-shade as before, buckled on her jewelry, and half-unconsciously adjusted her garb to display her figure to best advantage. That done, she waited with heavy and confused thoughts, until a knock alerted her that it was time. Her heart was pounding as she opened the door, but it was only a messenger, with the word that Crosbey was detained in conversation with the King. Silently she followed down to the Hall, her strange new feeling holding her so in its grip that she had no recollection of the way they took.

She saw Clydog the instant she reached the Hall, and he moved at once to intercept her, but she maneuvered to put a tangle of carousers between them, and by the time he was wise to the stratagem she was enveloped within the comparative security of the royal presence.

"My apology, your Majesty," she said respectfully, kneeling before him and reaching for his hand to kiss. "I came as soon as my ailing stomach would permit. I bring you greetings from King Llywarch, and present his troops under my command to join your standard."

Cadell courteously took her hand in his before she might kiss it, and handed her to her feet. "Good eve, my dear," he greeted her. "I recall an ailing head took you from the Hall, when last you graced our board." But his expression was pleasant, and she decided such feminine subterfuge had not displeased him unduly. "Sir Tellicho tells me your King's ailment was too grievous to permit him the trip."

"Yes, your Majesty," she responded. "He bade me come in his stead, for the friars told him he would not survive the campaign." And how will King Cadell take the substitution, she asked herself nervously.

She could make naught of Cadell's faint smile. "There be many among us who mayn't survive this campaign," he said. He hesitated for a pregnant moment. "But we intend to make certain that you be one who does."

"Thank you for the kind wish, Sire," she said lightly. But the ominous portent behind his last words could scarce be misunderstood.

The supper was of brief duration, most of the toasts having been drunk already. Tara steeled herself for the ordeal of sitting beside Clydog, but to her surprise was seated at Cadell's right hand with Tellicho beside her. She attempted with great care to draw out the King on his final enigmatic remark, but he refused to take the bait, and when she returned to the bower she still was none the wiser. She slept fitfully, half expecting a clandestine visit from Clydog, but it did not come. Belike he was too far besotted for such an amorous excursion, she concluded, and managed finally to drop off to sleep.

Dyfed's force was assigned to the extreme rear of the formation, and Tara was moving to her station, when a messenger came with the unwelcome tidings that the High King wished to see her. She found him with his officers, foregathered on the Common.

"Good morrow, Princess," he said pleasantly. "I planned to speak with you earlier on this, but the evening did not allow opportunity."

"Yes, Sire," she said, wondering if he wished to issue a last-minute marching order, and regretting she'd not brought Tellicho.

"You may regret what I must say, lass, but I do it for your own good— as well as for that of the succession. Perhaps you can guess my words."

With a premonition of total disaster, she waited, hoping her fears were unfounded, but knowing with terrible clarity what he would say.

"This mummery of yours, parading as a soldier, is over. You may not accompany the force, as Dyfed's commander or in any other capacity."

He went on to talk about it being no life for a maid, about the necessity of keeping her alive as a bride for his Crown Prince, about the disruption her presence on the field must cause. But she took in none of what he said, conscious only of the bitter sting of tears behind her eyes.

She obeyed in dumb resignation as he beckoned to the Chatelaine who materialized nearby, and turned her over to the lady's charge. The unctuous lady escorted her briskly up to the bower, and when they were inside and the door closed, spoke for the first time. "The King has commanded me to see you clothed in suitable garments, Milady." She was visibly nervous, but pressed doggedly on. "Pray make no difficulty, Princess. You must allow me to do as he bids."

In grim silence, seeing no alternative, Tara stiffly let herself be attired in the hated feminine kirtle and bodice. The Chateleine's hands were shaking, but she persisted, encasing Tara's hair in a silk-threaded net with an absurd linen barbette under her chin, as if she was some plaything of a doll. All the time, Tara's brain was racing furiously to devise some steps she could take to end this nightmare, but to little avail.

"Come now, Princess," coaxed the Chateleine, taking courage from Tara's apparent lack of hostility or sign of resistance, her voice taking on a silken wheedling tone. "The King will be coming to the door soon now, to see and approve the vast change we've made. Come now, we must wipe off that black look. We must not distress the King!" She all but pushed her out, and Tara's heart sank to its lowest ebb to see a guard posted stiffly at the door. She was a prisoner!

After a long wait, the anxious Chateleine bustling busily about the unmoving Tara the while, to touch up her garments, Cadell came up the steps and stopped in front of her. He looked her over briefly, and nodded his head in approval. "Women's attire becomes you enormously, my dear," he said, his cold voice nullifying the compliment. "Your place is here, awaiting the return of your Prince from the field of battle. Put those other addled plans from your mind. Princess, and all will go well with you." Leaving the implied threat hanging in the air, he turned on his heel and strode away.

As she passed the guard on her way back into the bower, Tara noted his vacuous look, and began to think how she might contrive to make his oxlike stupidity play into her hands.

Her idea was only half-formed, but its first steps were plain, and she could worry out the rest as the circumstances dictated. She would act the part of innocent before the Lady Elinor, no matter how distasteful that subterfuge would be, hoping to disarm any suspicions in that lady's mind as best she could. Then she'd turn her attention to the more difficult problem of outwitting the stolid guard.

"I vow it truly is peaceful in the bower," she said sweetly, the words near sticking in her throat. "Mayhap I really should not go soldiering on this parlous adventure, the only woman in the midst of all those rough troopers." She made as if to laze back in her chair. "I'll just bide here in quiet, trying not to think on it, and mayhap nap for a bit." She closed her eyes, and forced herself to lie back motionless, for what seemed an interminable period.

After an eternity, she opened her eyes the narrowest slit and peeked at the Chateleine, seeing her motionless, her head sunk onto her chest—but whether she was asleep or no Tara couldn't tell. In an agony of impatience, she forced herself to wait silently for another eon, the while watching the Chateleine intently. Presently the woman's breathing took on a regular rhythm, betokening a deep sleep from which it was hoped she'd not easily awaken.

With exquisite care Tara retrieved her dagger, held it by the blade, and tiptoed to the door to open it a crack. Instantly the guard thrust his lance across the door, barring exit, but she made as if she didn't see his weapon. "Lady Elinor has taken a fit!" she gasped. "You must come at once! She needs help, or I'll vow she is like to breathe her last!"

He stood stock-still for a long instant, his slow brain digesting her words, then finally lay aside his lance. Awkwardly he entered the unfamiliar bower, clearly uncomfortable in these forbidden surroundings, and approached the sleeping woman. Once his head was turned away, Tara raised her dagger cautiously, and brought the hilt down smartly on his head. He slumped heavily to the floor, unconscious. Hastily she slashed free the window cords, and trussed up his hands and feet behind him. Snatching the hated kerchief from her head, she jammed it tightly between his slack jaws and tied its ends behind his head. With a feeling of great release, she pulled her uniform from the cabinet, and threw herself into it.

She knew what she must do next, distasteful though it would be. The Lady Elinor was rudely awakened, to face an apparition so horrifying she thought it a nightmare—a fierce outlaw pressing a vicious dagger to the starched wimple about her wrinkled neck. Even as she realised it was no nightmare, the compliant young Princess of a few moments earlier was saying with appalling seriousness that her throat would be cut if she tried to scream. The Chatelaine, cowed past any thinking, mutely endured the indignity of a gag stuffed in her throat, made no demur when her hands were pinioned to the chair, and remained motionless as her eyes were bandaged with a strip of sheeting. In an agony of fear, not knowing what she heard, she listed to the sounds of a sword being buckled on, a dagger sheathed, the door opened and closed, and a key turned in the lock.

Tara gave a silent sigh of relief as she entered the byrne, to see none but stable lads. At her calm request, they made haste to ready her big stallion. Pausing only for a quick look to see that the way was clear, she threw herself into the saddle and spurred ahead, thrilling as she felt the great muscles respond.

She knew the knights forming the rear-guard could not be far ahead, and as the trail was empty she could maintain a strong pace. Once past the knights, who accepted her presence with no questioning, she caught up with the Dyfed contingent and took her place alongside Tellicho. He greeted her with no apparent surprise, which meant he had no inkling of Cadell's harsh orders.

"I thought you were riding up ahead with the High King, Princess," he said, perplexed.

"He did have a few words with me," she said, "though not bearing on the march." Except to tell me I would not be part of it, she added silently.

Crosbey returned her casual greeting, but with unanswered questions in his eyes that told her he knew all was not well. But how could he have learned of Cadell's decision?

No hint of her presence must reach Cadell, that was sure. If she remained sheltered in the bosom of the Dyfed force, it seemed unlikely anyone would spy her, or report her presence to a member of the High King's retinue. And belike Cadell would not have discussed with any of his subordinates the extraordinary action he'd taken. If she took care to stay out of sight, she would be safe.

Tara's tent that night was pitched adjacent to the command tent where Tellicho and Crosbey were billeted. She retired early, not up to explaining her predicament to Crosbey, and dropped off into a wearied sleep. She slept too soundly to hear the altercation outside her tent, waking with a start just in time to see the tent flap thrust aside, and a frightening figure outlined massively against the pale moonlight.

She groped for her dagger, but he was atop her instantly. The fetid reek of ale on his breath told her at once who it was. She struggled furiously to dislodge him, not wanting to call out and attract attention to herself. With a ripping sound, the cloth at her throat tore open. In another moment he'd have her naked from the waist. Her fury at white heat, she felt in the darkness for his face, found his nostrils, slid her fingers up to find an eye, and thrust her thumb savagely into the socket.

He reared back with a scream of agony, clawing at the tortured eye, and giving her the freedom to wriggle free and leap toward the tent opening. As she did, she collided heavily with a frantic Crosbey, his sword drawn, and behind him, in the dim moonlight, she recognized

Tellicho with weapon in hand. Both came to an abrupt stop as she emerged, disheveled and with her tunic ripped half away.

"What has befallen, Milady?" demanded Crosbey urgently. "Whoever did this, is he still in there?" He started in, and frantically she pulled him back.

"Cross! No!" The urgency in her voice stopped both men. "You must not go in there!"

"Who is inside, Princess?" The steady voice was Tellicho's. Even in the dark, she could see the fury in his face.

"Clydog!" She mouthed his name hoarsely. "He stole in when I slept, though how he knew." She broke off, perilously close to hysteria, but determined to maintain her composure.

"Let me fetch him out, Princess," pressed Crosbey. She was warmed to see him standing there so firm, so ready to do what could only lead to his arrest or worse, wanting but a word from her to thrust himself into irretrievable trouble.

"Oh, Cross, no!" she cried, and grasped his arm.

"Nay lad—not you," commanded Tellicho. "I'd best go in myself. Belike Cadell will not quite have me hanged for it, as he would be like to do to you, if you made so bold." But neither had to enter, for at that moment Clydog burst forth, his hand pressed to his eye, looking bereft of his senses. Tellicho cleared his throat and stepped forward.

"Come, Prince Clydog, time you returned to your tent," he said, speaking as if to a child. "I'll see you home." He took the now silent Clydog firmly by the arm, and led him unresisting toward the royal compound.

The next morn an officer from the High King arrived, with word that Cadell wished to see the Princess Tara in his tent at once.

When she presented herself before the High King, he paid her no notice, keeping at his documents as though she didn't exist, until her mood gradually changed from despair to hot anger. At last he looked up, his expression hard.

"So you would ignore my explicit orders, Princess?" he said with an icy calm more disturbing than any furious shouting. Raising his hand to still any reply, he went on. "Heed what I say, and woe be to you if you cross me again! You will be sent back from Gloucester by the first caravan, under close guard. When you arrive, you will be stripped of these mannish clothes, which will be burned while you watch. Then you will be locked in your chamber, and there you will remain until my return, when I will deal with this. Do you understand?"

She nodded dumbly.

"You will have word, when we are ready to send you back. Now, get out of my sight!" He terminated the audience with a peremptory wave of his hand.

She would be imprisoned like the lowliest criminal, decked out like a strumpet to wait in shameful captivity for the day she'd be compelled to minister to the depraved sexual demands of his detested prince. Dashed were all her high hopes of achieving Sire's vaulting dreams of a brighter future for his subjects, of writing another chapter to the glorious Cymru history in the tradition of Boedicia and Elen Luyddog. In one brief, vindictive command, Cadell had ended any possibility of her realizing her ordained future.

Through the mists loomed the great Dyke running from the Irish Sea to the Hafren Channel. Built by King Offa of Mercia a century earlier to defend against marauding Cymri, it was the largest structure Britain had ever seen, and through the years had proven a stubborn defensive barrier. When the Dyfed troop arrived at its base, however, they could see that no Saxon force had been deployed to contest the Cymri army's passage. This was a surprising stroke of fortune, for even unopposed as they were, Cadell's engineers were hard put to move the unwieldy mass of straggling soldiers through the inadequate gates in any sort of order.

"We see the Saxon's first major error," announced Tellicho with a show of relief. "And mine as well. I read his first skirmish as a signal that he'd harry us on the march, not only seeking to kill our leaders in their tents, but certainly contesting our transit of the Dyke."

"Then why was he not here?" demanded Tara. "Has he mayhap some deep plan that we cannot read?"

"I'd say not, Princess. He's made an error is all. Belike we do our cause less than justice when we term Alfred all knowing, as if he were a god. He's but a man who can't be everywhere at once. The faint-hearted amongst us can take heart from his omission."

The Guard Captain's words were encouraging to Tara. "I've been one of Tellicho's faint-hearted band," she confessed to Crosbey. "The events of the past days have left me so down-hearted I stood ready to grant the Saxons victory e'en before we reached Gloucester."

"Tellicho sees things clear," Crosbey commented. "But you have other things to fret you than defeat or victory. Cadell's order leaves you in hopeless case. What shall we do about it?"

"What's to be done, Crosbey, but submit? I try to make myself believe the press of affairs when he reaches Gloucester will push me from his mind, but that's a slender reed to build on. Had you seen and heard him, you'd know."

He reined his horse alongside hers, and her pulse quickened as he took her hand. "We've all too little time left, Tara," he said huskily. On the morrow, or mayhap even this eve, you may be taken from us—from me—never to be together again. I would speak free, with your permission or without, on a matter that long has torn at me."

She nodded mutely, not trusting herself to reply, a deep longing for him welling up in her heart.

"Just this, Princess—Tara. You are a great lady, destined to be a Queen, and I born to a humble grwda. You lead the Dyfed army, and I serve as your faithful Equerry." He stopped, too full of his emotions to continue, and she feared the precious moment would be lost without her encouragement.

"Yes, Cross?" She fair breathed the words.

He took fresh heart. "I must tell you…Tara…you are more precious than e'en life itself to me. I know not how this battle will end—if we win the day, or more like, crawl home in defeat—but I will survive. Mayhap there will be some glory in the field for me, more like not. But I will return to Cymru when all is done, and I pray you find a small place in your heart to hold private for me. I care not that you are a Princess, or will be Queen. I care naught for such things. I think back on how close we were at Aber Castle, and in my dreams…" He fell silent, and she knew he was repenting his boldness, and might not find the courage to say more.

"Oh, Cross," she whispered, unable to check the tremor in her voice. "I feel as you. You are the only one I care for. In my dreams, you are ever there. I know not what the future holds for either of us, but I want you to know that you are dearer to me than any other ever will be." She took both his hands in hers, and they looked at one another, their emotions overpowering both. Without speaking, Crosbey took the reins from her unresisting hands, and led her horse off the trail into the woods. They rode thus between the trees, until the sounds of the march behind them were muted, when he pulled up his horse in a grassy clearing. Dismounting, he went to the side of her horse, and lifted her wordlessly to the sward. In the next moment she found herself pinioned in his strong arms, her body pressed tightly to his.

The strong male scent of him, and the warmth of his rough cheek against her face, made her heart pound with an unfamiliar excitement, and every nerve tingled with anticipation—of what she knew not. Breathess, she felt Crosbey's heart thudding against hers, and sensed the strength of his desire as she clung motionless in his grasp, making no effort to pull away, awaiting his pleasure. All rational thought deserted her. Subconsciously she knew she had ached for this moment, and she was suffused with so deep and strong a longing that her feeling transmitted itself without words being spoken. He draw apart enough to gaze down tenderly into her upturned face, and the expression of love and desire passing between them emboldened him to take her chin in his hand and tilt it up, drinking in the sweet wonder of her eyes, and kissing the soft, unresisting mouth.

Paralyzed by the wondrous magic of his mouth pressing so hungrily on hers, and his strong young arms holding her as if they would never let her free, Tara knew not how long they stayed thus. She sensed only that she had never tasted such sweetness, nor dreamt her heart could be so full, willing the moment to last forever. She longed to be fully and completely his, in a way that would bring them totally together, never to be separated, in a glorious unforgettable memory they could savor forever...making them one...enduring all their lives. He was asking, in her imagination, if she wanted him to seal their union so, and joyously she responded.

Yes! Oh, my dearest love, yes...yes!

An explosion erupted in her head, dazing her, and frantically she attempted to struggle to her feet, but there seemed to be a furious struggle going on above and around her, and she could not find her footing. Her vision was blurred, and she blinked furiously to clear it so she could see what was taking place. Instinctively she groped for her dagger, but ere she could get a firm grip a flailing foot knocked it from her grasp. She had a sense that there were several assailants, but her head was dizzy from the blow, and she could not seem to focus clearly. She wanted to faint, but she must not!

"To me! To me!"

Crosbey's shout! He was calling for support, urgently summoning any within hearing to rally to him.

So they must be under attack!

Saxons!

In a flash Tellicho's words came back to her. He had expected an attack here, then decided Alfred had made a blunder when none barred their way at the Dyke. But Alfred had not made a mistake!

The awful realization seemed to clear her vision, and suddenly she could see them plainly. Crosbey was engaged in a violent struggle, beset by two assailants, and the three were tumbling and thrashing about around her and atop her. She made a supreme effort and rolled clear— and as she did, she could make out a fourth man. He held a crossbow, and with a horrified gasp she realized his purpose. He waited for a clear line of fire, that he might release his bolt at Crosbey…pierce deeply into that beloved body…to kill…kill!

At Crosbey! Acting on instinct, she spun about and dug her fingers painfully into the ground, scrabbling frantically to scoop up a handful of dirt. Alerted by her sudden movement, he shifted his aim to her chest, and at the same moment she flung the soil into his eyes.

She heard the 'twang!' of the bowstring, and stiffened to meet the shock of the arrow, but it flew wide. She got a momentary glimpse of the bowman trying to clear his eyes, and knew that only her stratagem had made him miss.

She must help Crosbey—and trust to the gods that the bowman was blinded enow for the moment that she could safely turn her back on him.

Crosbey was fighting desperately, but the odds against him were lengthening. One of the attackers, looking twice Crosbey's weight, had his arms wrapped about Crosbey from behind; the second had managed to break partly free from Crosbey's grip and was grasping urgently at the handle of his sword to clear it. Tara could see how close he was to succeeding, and once he did, she knew naught could save Crosbey.

She searched wildly about her for a weapon, knowing if none came to hand in the next few seconds it would be too late. She spied a moss-covered stone in the grass directly at her feet, snatched it up, leaped over to the man with arm upraised, and with a primitive drive to save her mate smashed it savagely down on his bared head. With a feeling of wild exultation she saw the skull cave in under her blow.

With one opponent eliminated, and the other momentarily unnerved at his partner's shattered skull, Crosbey broke free and his sword flashed from its scabbard. Tara looked for him to engage his remaining adversary, but instead he stared past her in horror and rushed frantically toward her, shouting.

"Drop!" he cried in agonized tones. "Tara—down!"

He was upon her before she could comprehend his meaning, raising his arms, crashing directly into her, bearing her painfully to the ground underneath him.

Suddenly the glade was filled with soldiers—her soldiers. Rescue was at hand! With a huge feeling of relief, Tara rolled Crosbey to one side and got to her feet. She put her hand down to help him up, thinking to lighten the tense situation by teasing that he'd be too tired for the effort himself. But he didn't take her hand.

"Not just yet, Princess," he said softly.

A terrible, horrifying fear assailed her, a fear so awful she could not bear to face it. She wanted to ask him what he meant, but was afraid to find the words.

"I think we forgot the crossbowman."

As he spoke, she saw it—the feathered shaft protruding from his back. His body, rolled to one side when she pushed him off her, had deflected it sideways, but she could see clearly enow to know he'd sustained a terrible wound. She cried out urgently for assistance from the soldiers searching the encircling woods, but his raised hand halted her.

"Help would come too late, my love," he said. "My eyes are dimming already, and I can feel the bleeding inside."

"No! I'll get help—let me get help!" she started to turn, but again he stopped her.

"We've too little time, love; don't waste it on calling for help that will arrive too late." He found her hand, and pulled her to him. "Come closer—I can see you but dimly."

Her body shaking with great retching sobs, she dropped beside him, and cradled his head in her lap, wiping small wisps of grass from his face, not knowing what she did.

"I must tell you this, my dearest love, whilst I still have my senses. I've been greatly honored that I was picked to save your life for Cymru and her people who need you. The gods were good, letting me play a part. I've always said I loved you more than life itself, but that was just talk— until now." He was convulsed in a fit of trembling, and his eyes closed. After a time it subsided, and he spoke again, so soft she had to put her ear to his mouth to hear.

"If there is an Otherworld," he whispered, "I'll be watching for you, praying for you...loving you." He closed his eyes again, and Tara thought he was gone, but he opened them once more. "If not...if not..."

His head, cradled in her lap, fell sideways, and she knew his bright and glorious spirit had passed forever from her.

She looked up at the soldiers gathered around, and as if hearing her unspoken wish they melted away and she was alone. She bent her head down until her cheek was against his, and her tears fell on his face.

CHAPTER 16

Cadell deployed his force on the plain before the Gloucester encampment, and a mounted Danish troop thundered out toward their position from a slit in the earthworks. The lead horseman carried a standard bearing the figure of a raven interwoven with strange devices—the enchanted Reafen, which legend said the fighting men of Denemearc held dearer than their own lives. From her vantage point on the left flank, Tara could see little through the obstinate veil of tears. Preoccupied with her own agonizing grief, she could not bring herself to find any interest in the dramatic joining of the two forces, and the days ahead promised only a dreary continuation of the paralyzing sadness that overwhelmed her.

Both her martial training and her instinctive awareness, however, precluded a complete shutting out of her surroundings. Distracted as she was by the haunting torment of reliving the previous day's agonizing events, nevertheless she continued to observe the newcomers, and—with no conscious effort or realization that it was occurring—to evaluate what she saw. The Danish troop pulled up at the High King's command post, easily identifiable by its position in the van and its flying pennants, and the huge leader flung himself lightly from his mount. What took place was too distant to be made out, but after a lengthy palaver the group broke up, the royal party accompanying the Danes into the compound while equerries scattered through the force with instructions for the entry.

The encampment, ten times vaster than the compound at Aber Castle, was bounded by a high wall appearing to be of great antiquity, for great gaps appeared in it where it either had been breached or collapsed of its own weight. These many openings had been filled with raw earthworks scarce shoulder high, atop which were planted new-cut wooden palisades matching the height of the existing wall. That such flimsy fortifications would be impossible to defend told Tara that the Cymri cause was well nigh doomed. Realization of their fatal vulnerability, together with her overwhelming sense of personal loss, plunged her into profound despair. As they entered and she looked about, she felt a helpless rage at Cadell for leading them into this trap. Oh, my beloved Cross, how you would have railed at such stupidity!

Mightily disturbed, she assailed the Guard Captain. "Sir Tellicho, however can this place be held against a Saxon army?"

"That is uncommon easy to answer, Princess: it cannot. This old Roman wall was built nigh onto a millennium ago, and serves today for little more than decoration. If Alfred lays siege to Gloucester, he will breach it in a score of places. If he elects to starve us out, I wat the Dane has not had the time or facilities to garner supplies for a long campaign, so we starve."

"Then what will we do…?"

"Our only hope—and it must be our allies' hope as well, for it is how the Viking fights—is to use Gloucester as a base for raids on Saxony, striking swiftly at many points and vanishing before Saxon forces can be deployed so many places. The hope is that it will keep Alfred too busy protecting his broad frontiers to launch his own attack. This Sigefert will be skilled at such. The strategy cannot bring victory—only delay the final conflict a year or so."

Tara realized that Alfred, a seasoned campaigner with experience against Sigefert already under his belt, would not be long turned aside by pinprick raids. It was more wish than reality.

An equerry interrupted them, summoning leaders of the gwlads to meet the Norse Jarl. She decided Tellicho must go to represent Dyfed, since Cadell had stripped her of command, and the sight of her might produce a public confrontation. Aching with dejection, she turned away from the group, when it was as if she heard Crosbey's voice, come from across the divide. Eloquent, with the impetuosity of youth, his words rang strong inside her.

Your King Llywarch appointed you to command Dyfed's forces, and no one, not even the High King, has the right to override his appointments!

So distinct were the well-remembered tones, so clearly his, that she looked quickly about her, nourishing a sudden irrational hope. But no…she was alone. Yet it was his voice. E'en from the Otherworld, he watched over her still!

Crosbey had laid down his life for her—his supreme sacrifice, that she might realize the destiny the gods had laid out for her. What right had she, whatever her own wishes, to turn cravenly aside and abandon her birthright and Sire's dreams for Dyfed, to satisfy a selfish whim of the High King?

I will go, Cross!" she declared aloud.

"Cadell will expect you," she told Tellicho, "but if he sees us both, he'll find it too easy to dismiss me. I should go up alone."

To her surprise, he agreed. "The High King exceeds even his authority, removing you from command. We be his levies, not his pawns, to move on the board or discard as he wishes. Be sure your father would read it the same."

The monarchs proceeded into the Hall in order of march from Glamorgan, placing Tara at the rear. Sigefert and Cadell shared the platform, and as each ruler stepped up he was presented to the Danish chieftain by Cadell, with a recital of his escutcheon. As she neared the front of the line, it was the Jarl, Sigefert, who caught and held her gaze. He was a towering giant of a man, near a head taller than Cadell. His short, straw-colored hair was cut with a fringe down his forehead that he thrust impatiently back from time to time. His reddish moustache imparted a powerful fierceness to his strong face. Naked to the waist, he displayed huge biceps, and heavily corded stomach muscles that rippled as he moved. His full pantalons of bright blue fabric were cinched by a broad leathern belt, and gathered in below his knees to disclose muscular legs bare to his sandals. A huge two-handed sword hung at his side, and a great broad-axe with flared blade was socketed in his saddle pouch. Silver bracelets and bangles gleamed at his wrists, incongruous on so heroic a figure.

He exuded such magnetism that Tara found herself strangely disturbed by him, the spell broken only by the equerry's arrival for her. Oddly flustered, she stepped up and bent her knee in salutation.

Clearly disconcerted by her almost mutinous presence, Cadell hesitated so long in his introduction that it took Sigefert's questioning glance before he deigned, with evident ill-grace, to recognize her.

"Princess Tara of Dyfed, Jarl Sigefert," he said at last, his anger clearly showing through. "Dyfed is one of our leading gwlads, ruled by the gallant King Llywarch, whose health prevents his coming." He spoke in the Cymri tongue, and Tara wondered if the fair-haired giant could follow.

But evidently he did. His deep bow was faintly mocking, as if to ridicule a woman with the temerity to march to war. "I greet you, Tara," he said, his heavily accented voice oddly melodious. "Tara of Dyfed, you say? Is correct?" He seemed to be searching his memory, then suddenly roared with delight as he recalled what he sought. "Tara! You be the maid! I lack your speech to say it well…" He paused, groping impatiently for the proper words.

Tara had a sudden impulse to speak in his tongue, though her knowledge of it was imperfect. King Cadell would be slighted to be cut out thus, but why else had Father Eliswen—or mayhap the gods themselves— pressed study of that language back at Aber Castle? And what did she owe Cadell, who gave such short shrift to her wishes? "Shall we speak in your tongue, Jarl?" she asked, in the language of Denemearc.

Sigefert stared at her in astonishment. "By Odin's beard," he exclaimed. "You speak our tongue, wee Princess! And just now I recall…I know of you! On a raid, we took a Saxon our prisoner, and he sang all he knew before joining his ancestors. He told of a beauteous Cymri maid in soldier garb—a Valkyr!—caught by Edward, son of Alfred, while spying on your land. Thinking her a wanton, brought along for pleasuring, he tried to make free of her…" He paused, and Tara reddened, reading in his glance that for an instant he pictured himself that Prince. "But she pricked him with her fotbitr and stole his mount." He studied her with intense interest, as if assessing her physical capability for such a deed, and unconsciously, she stood more erect. "I wonder…I ask myself…Princess, could it be you were that Valkyr?" He turned to Cadell and spoke rapidly to him, but in her astonishment at the Dane's remarks she gave no heed to what was being said.

Excitedly, she went over the incident in her mind. Son of the Saxon king himself? Impossible! And yet…thinking back, picturing the man's sturdy posture, the patrician look of him, she knew he could have been noble born. But to stab the Saxon Prince! But had she not acted as she did, he'd have violated her. But she only pinked him! Inexplicably, she felt relief to learn she'd not brought death to that healthy young figure, whose only sin was being a man.

Her countenance must have betrayed her thoughts, for the big Dane boomed out, "So, Lady, did you not know who you blooded? Well, now you know—the enemy Prince himself!" She saw frank admiration in his eyes, and she blushed, partly with embarrassment but also with a glow of pride.

Sigefert perceived that glow, for her turned to Cadell and asked impatiently, "Are all not met now?" He clapped his great hands, and a boisterous contingent of Vikings poured into the hall, shepherding a monstrous foaming cask that turned out to contain honeyed beer. When all the horns were filled, Sigefert lifted the thunderstruck Tara effortlessly to the tabletop, and sprang lightly up beside her.

"Drain your horns for the Princess Tara, who met the Saxon Prince and bested him in fair fight!" he cried. "Be all our troops such robust fighters, and we'll feed the Saxons to the ravens!" He went on, with embellishments of language that Tara had not the skill to follow, but that drew great roars of delight.

"The gods smile on you, Princess," commented Tellicho when they were alone again. "I was told what the Dane said to Cadell about your encounter with Edward, and saw his jaw drop as he worked out what really took place that day on Black Mountain—his son playing the craven and you the battler. Cadell will lack the courage to tell his new ally he's banishing so stout a fighter. And you're safe for another reason: our High King has too much on his trencher to waste thought on't. He and Sigefert meet in the morn to hammer out their battle plan, and I warrant they'll soon be at sword's point on how best to fight the Saxon."

Tara took heart from Tellicho's hopeful view of her own situation, but baffled by his other comment. All their differences should have been ironed out long since. "Are not the two as one on how to defend the encampment?" she asked.

"That we'll know better after the sun sets once more. But I trow the twain will not see it the same, for their fighting styles be far apart. We'd best pray our cause will not suffer in the squabbling." Cadell, he explained, raised on siege warfare, would hold the first priority to be for-tifying the encampment as securely as time allowed, in hopes the Saxon would spend his strength fruitlessly against its barricades. Sigefert, weaned on lightning raids and swift retreats in the Viking style—and with vast experience in real battle—naturally would push a strategy of harrying the Saxon countryside everywhere, to distract Alfred from mounting an attack. The two would be hard put to find agreement.

And so it proved, over the days that followed. After increasingly acri-monious sessions that divided the two forces into increasingly bitter factions, Tara asked Tellicho his opinion. "Are you for awaiting Alfred's attack, or taking the fight to him?"

"Neither, Princess. Waiting here for him would be suicide, for he can overrun our meager defenses in a day. Nor can we seek him out as Sigefert wishes, for we know little of his defenses on the lands that lie across the Saefern, and cannot tell where best to sting him."

His answer confused her mightily. Did not Cadell or his advisors have full knowledge of Ethandum, Ashdown, Ellendun, Reading, and all the boroughs nigh to Chippenham—which e'en Father Eliswen had listed in his Priory geography lessons? If as a child she knew of them, the High Court must know them well. But, she bethought then, Cymri patrols had no cause to venture beyond the Saefern, taking risk of discovery for no gain—and realized how pitifully scant was their knowledge of Saxony.

But had not Cadell planned for this war? "Does not the High King know all of Alfred's main boroughs, and how best to raid them?" she demanded of Tellicho, hoping against hope for a positive response.

"We know pitifully little, Princess. And think what portends. We must know where Alfred defends, in what strength, and for how long, to avoid running into Saxon hornet nests. Cadell will argue that, since we know not where danger lies, we can strike nowhere, but Sigefert, drawing confidence from his past successes, believes he can prevail even where he's heavily outnumbered. He speaks with authority, for he's done such many times past."

"So how may it be resolved? Precious time leaks away whilst they squabble." Glumly, Tara wondered how Crosbey would have chosen, but found no answer.

"Aye, Princess. But make certain Cadell will commit no Cymri unit until we spy out Alfred's forces."

Cadell and Sigefert were closeted in the council chamber when the equerry escorted Tara in. She knelt before the King, as was his due, but he waved her impatiently forward.

"Jarl Sigefert has a task for you," he told her sourly. "I misdoubt it will come to aught, and know not why you be chosen, when we have experienced spies, but he will have none other." Without knowing the mission, she read in the High King's eyes the hope and expectation that she would fail. "He conjures up this venture, and he'll tell you of it himself. I charge you to obey him as you would your own King!" He rose abruptly and stalked out, leaving her alone with the huge Northman.

"Come sit beside me, wee Princess," Sigefert began. Then, sensing her hesitation, he went on. "Nay, goddess of the dragon's horde, fear me not; this is serious business. Come, look at Alfred's domain." He spread a tattered map, and she seated herself beside him. He was changed into field gear: a short drab corselet of padded leather with what she took as plaques of bone inserted in its set of narrow front pockets. Without further preamble, he indicated a section of the map, and her uneasiness was dispelled as she came to see he'd no thought of her.

"This is our only picture of Wessex. The Ashdown monks were persuaded to donate it to us." He laughed briefly. "Whether it is true to the land I know not, but my Skald finds its smell good. We must use it. What say you?"

Clearly he expected comment on the map. Caught thus, she was nonplussed, but he was waiting for her opinion, so she made shift to satisfy him if she could. "I have studied some of those boroughs, Sire," she said hesitantly, "but I have never visited Wessex."

He nodded briefly, then indicated the Wessex shore of the Hafren Channel, south of Caerleon. "You know this country, no?"

"I've led a patrol out here, Sire," she said, indicating the promontory where they surprised the Saxon landing party. Encouraged to tell him about it, she related how, disguised as a fisher maid, she had penetrated their hideout. When she told of stabbing the Saxon who would have murthered her, he applauded admiringly, and she began to like this forbidding Dane.

"Splendid, wee Princess! Our gallant Freyja would find you a worthy daughter. Did I not tell your old woman of a King we must have someone like you?"

"I don't understand, Sire—in what role?" she asked, but with a nagging fear that she did understand. A part of the Viking force holding the encampment had sailed up the Hafren Channel to Gloucester, and the remainder had come up the Thames—that she knew from her interpreting back at Glamorgan Castle. But now she was learning that Sigefert would take their longboats on a hazardous foray down the Saefern, to scout Saxon concentrations along the Wessex shore. And she would accompany them, the only Cymri so honored. But why her?

Foregathered in the chamber, the scouting party awaited orders. Tara's pride turned to bitter humiliation when Sigefert tossed her a bundle of filthy rags. "Put this garb on, Princess," he commanded. "Make haste—we take to the boats within the hour."

"What are these shabby garments, Sire?" she demanded hotly. "I am well clothed!" Could it be his purpose to ridicule her before his men? No, she'd seen no meanness in him.

"Why do you think we take you?" he asked, seeming surprised at her question. "These are from a Saxon milkmaid, which is what you'll be, when we put you ashore to learn the lay of the land. Put them on— time to talk after we embark." As she hesitated, his expression hardened. "Did you not hear your king? Obey me as you would him. Dress now, argue later!"

He turned abruptly to other matters, and she knew objections would be fruitless. Outraged and shamed, she pulled the tattered kirtle over her clothes, and wrapped the grimy kerchief about her hair. She resolved the problem of her sword by securing it under her shapeless garment, despite its revealing bulge. She would not go on hostile ground weaponless!

The two hundred or so Vikings appeared to have no baggage save their accoutrements. She wondered briefly what they would eat, but recalled childhood tales of Norse depredations, and remembered that farm animals always were part of their prizes. So we live off the land, she concluded, with an unavoidable feeling of sadness for those who would endure the raids.

The rhythmic thrust of the long oars pulsed in her ears, the motion of the boat almost soothing. She had found a place in the bow, curled up awkwardly against the great prow as shelter against the night wind, and only when the sound of the keel scraping over sand awakened her did she realize she must have nodded off. Overhead, a leafy canopy of branches obscured the moon. The dim shapes of nearby boats told her they were safely at their first objective. Fearing to be left behind, she searched out Sigefert. "What is our plan now?" she asked, reluctant to bother him but impatient to understand.

"Sleep," he replied laconically. "Find a place." Without another glance at her, he stretched out in the grasses and pulled his cloak about him. Tara found a spot where the rushes provided some shelter from the penetrating breeze. Troubled by conflicting impressions, still tormented by her inability to put aside thinking of Crosbey's violent death, she curled up and tried to rest.

"We're close on Wedmore. What can you tell me of it?"

Sigefert had summoned her at earliest light, firing the question the moment he caught sight of her. Ignoring the hunger assailing her stomach, she racked her memory for scraps of Father Eliswen's teachings. Wedmore was the nerve center of Somersetshire, where Alfred conquered the Danes, and consigned them to the Fifburghers in Mercia, to live under his suzerainty.

"I know its history, Sire," she offered.

"Let off Siring and Jarling me, Princess. I am Sigefert to my Vikings, and Sigefert to you. Call me so."

"Aye…Sigefert. And I am Tara."

Her retort, with its insolent sarcasm, caught him up sharply, and a spark of respect glinted in his eyes. He laughed briefly, then at once turned serious again. "Aye, Tara it is. Now, Tara, are we to learn Alfred's plans if we go to Wedmore, or no? Will troops be quartered there?"

"I think no, for they expect no danger from the Hafren Channel."

"And why not? Am I not here? Am I not danger?"

It was true, when he put it so. "We would be danger, were we here in some strength," she answered after a moment of thought. "But sure the Saxon's spies would catch wind of any invasion force."

"Well said, Tara. Then, if not troops, would we meet up with those who know where his troops be? A good place to smell out, no—this famed place?"

She wondered if the good burghers of Wedmore, so far to the west, could know aught of Alfred's dispositions, but Sigefert seemed to attach importance to the historic site, so at dusk two boats shoved off upriver to reconnoitre along the nearby shore. Tara still wore the detested dairy maid garb, again secretly tucking sword and dagger beneath her kirtle as they set out. Those few villeins they met on the road were too besotted to make sense, and one mounted thegn, splendid in bright cloak and belted tunic, proved too stubborn or afeard to speak, so they dispatched him and tossed the limp body into the bog.

The sum of what Tara learned, upon being deposited in a rude tavern on the outskirts, was that cowherds and shepherds were attracted to her. Acting the part of a harlot seeking a soldier, she mingled with the tavern crowd, enduring gibes and pinches, but hearing naught of troops thereabout. In trade for submitting in silent fury to one sodden wretch's clumsy pawings and bawdy comments, she did learn that Alfred's health was uncertain and son Edward now commanded the Saxon army.

"To learn aught of his movements, we'd best get closer to Chippenham," she advised the stubborn Sigefert on her return, but he paid her no heed.

After picking their way fruitlessly through treacherous Somerset bogs, achieving little save killing a farmhand they'd stumbled on, the Vikings decided to carve out a secure hideaway on the riverbank near the capital as their base, and Sigefert sent Tara forth again. This time, posing as a street wench and itinerant barmaid, she was hired at an inn where soldiers were reputed to mingle with villagers. Suppressing with difficulty her distaste at the rude surroundings, and seeking she knew not what information, she was keenly on the alert for any person in that motley gathering who would possess some small morsel of Saxon movements.

Only after two fruitless and wearing days did it appear her mission might achieve some success. She was serving a raucous crowd at a table near the door, when suddenly her attention was caught by the entrance of what appeared to be little more than a stripling, but garbed as a trooper—the first such she'd seen since she'd been sent spying out the region. Her pulse quickened at the sight of what he was clutching so nervously in his arms. By its look, it could be naught but a military dispatch case, bound and sealed with fresh wax. Why would such a low-level soldier be so burdened, unless he carried urgent messages? Could such a message be from a Saxon leader in the field, bound for the ailing King Alfred? Could she be so fortunate?

Abandoning serving her revelers, she focused all her attention on him, wondering how to get a look at what he carried without alerting any of the enemies round about her. He was wandering from table to table, trying to question whoever would list to him, but was having little success speaking over the loud shouting and laughing of the ale-soaked patrons. She moved closer, and tried to decipher his agitated speech. He seemed to be complaining about a lost horse…a horse he'd secured to a hitching post just up the way…a horse that had slipped its halter and bolted down the trail. He'd searched all along the roadway, but his mount was nowhere to be seen. He was much distressed, as he querulously demanded to know if the horse had come this way and been caught. He was on King's Business, he said, and must make godspeed. He was looking exceeding close to tears, that none paid attention to his problem.

None save a make-believe barmaid—who was thinking furiously.

He wanted to find his runaway horse. Very well, with the help of her gods she'd show him his horse—or if not his, at least an actual horse. There must be such in the byrne behind the tavern. She calmed him down as best she could, fabricating a tale about a riderless horse, caught and stabled in this very byrne, and before she had a chance to say more he grasped her arm in high excitement, and brusquely demanded to be taken to it.

"See if it be yer horse," she said, throwing open the byrne door, and as he rushed inside she groped beneath the folds of her kirtle to release her dagger. Scarce had she gripped it when the youth turned on her, suspicion heavy on his face.

"There be nae horse here, wench! What fool's trick is this?" he shouted, grabbing her weapon arm, not seeing the dagger she held.

"Not in t'front, sorr. Look in t'other part, jist aboot t'wall," she insisted, extricating her arm. Suspicion momentarily dispelled, he turned to where she pointed, and she seized her chance to reverse the dagger, that she might strike its hilt against his head. But he looked back, confused where she meant, and his eye lighted on the weapon.

"Devil spawn!" he screamed, backing away and drawing his sword awkwardly from its scabbard. "Now, wench," he cried, "what's t'game, I say? Speak afore I skewer ye!" With no time to clear her sword from its folds, she hurled her dagger at his face. He threw up his hand to ward off the weapon, which sliced into his palm and skittered off into the hayrick.

With the brief respite, she managed to draw her sword, barely in time to parry the trooper's furious thrust. His clumsy handling of his weapon told her he was no swordsman, belike just some new recruit off the farm, selected as messenger because he could do naught else. She was clearly his superior at swordsmanship—unless the kirtle hampered her unduly. Unexpectedly he charged, sword extended awkwardly in front of him, in crude parody of a duelist's style but disconcerting in its unexpectedness, and in the quick retreat forced on her a heel caught in her torn hem, and she tumbled sideways onto the dirt. Realizing that e'en in the hands of a novice, his sword could be a lethal weapon to an adversary sprawled on the ground, she frantically scooped up a handful of shredded straw and flung it in his face. As she was rolling desperately away, she felt the thudding impact of his heavy blade, penetrating the spongy byrne floor where she had lain just an instant past.

Overbalanced by finding no target, and blinded by the straw, the hapless youth sprawled to the ground. In the brief interlude, as he clambered clumsily back to his feet, Tara was springing up, ripping off the remains of her hated disguise, and snatching the kerchief from her head. The soldier, belatedly reaching his feet and rubbing his eyes, perceived dimly through his tears that the barmaid had vanished. In her place stood a beauteous golden haired apparition garbed absurdly in soldierly attire, a contradiction that to his confused brain lent the whole scene a supernatural aura. A wicked weapon had sprung from nowhere into the creature's hand, and her threatening stance was unlike that of any earthly female.

"Who ye be?" he quavered. "Ye're nae barkeep, fer sure! Be ye a Valkyr?" His hollow cheeks were ashen, his bloodshot eyes bulging.

A Valkyr? Does he take me for some fearsome creature from the Otherworld? Best I let him think so, she decided quickly.

"Yea, my lad, I be a Valkyr. Ye've no chance in fight against such as I. Best have done and throw down your weapon." But despite his evident terror, he was made of stronger stuff than that, and with a trembling hand raised his sword once more. Now unencumbered, and with her adversary offering scarce more hazard than a beardless page, Tara easily parried his half-hearted attacks, and when he gave her an opening thrust her blade under his hilt and sent his sword spinning. Before he could retrieve it, he felt the quick pain and warm sensation of his own blood trickling wetly where her sword point pierced his side.

"I've no wish to kill you, lad," she told him quietly, "but if you move I'll run you through."

He shifted weight fractionally, and felt a repeat prick of her sword. "Who be ye?" he whimpered, frozen into immobility. "Oh, Jesu! Ye be a Valkyr sure! I'll be murthered!"

"Nay, lad. Not if you tell me all. Where do you come from, where are you bound, and what message do you carry?"

In terrified, halting gasps, he told her. Edward had overrun Gloucester, and its defenders were fleeing under hot pursuit. The Cymri King had been slain in battle, and his standard taken, leaving the Cymri army in disarray. Many longboats had been torched, and all resistance had ended. He and other messengers had been dispatched across the land. The reports in his case were confidential tidings of the event, transmitted for King Alfred's eyes alone.

Her senses reeled at the magnitude of the disaster. The tragic memory of Crosbey dying in her arms, uselessly, for a cause that failed, pierced her heart like a dagger. She stood mute and stunned, wishing to die herself. Momentarily her attention turned inward, until the prisoner's slight movement, and the now calculating look in his shifting eyes, recalled her to the here and now.

"I will spare you, soldier," she told him firmly, "but bound, lest you spread alarm." He submitted to lying face down for binding, and she stunned him with a smart blow to the head. She tore strips from the hated kirtle she'd wear no more, to truss him up like a pig for the sticking, finishing with a rude gag to stifle his cries. Then she dragged and lifted him into the small feed bin, out of sight.

Forcing herself to accept the calamitous tidings calmly, she composed herself for the long vigil that lay ahead, until she could return under cover of the dark to the rendezvous in the bog.

In each moment of solitude she'd been granted since Crosbey's tragic death, she had relived bittersweet moments of their years together—moments, though she had not read them so at the time, that built inexorably to that final tempestuous encounter. She'd known then, with unalterable certainty, that she loved him with all the passion and strength of her being. She strove to evoke the sweet image that could have been her future as Crosbey's wife, sharing her successes with him, turning to him for guidance when beset by problems, drawing solace from distress in his comforting arms. She sought to call up the beautiful picture of what might have been, but the present kept intruding, blurring the vision. Despite her desperate efforts, the dream dimmed further, until no longer could she conjure up the soothing fantasies that had helped her accept the terrible finality of her loss.

Oh, Lug, she entreated, don't steal the memories of my dearest love! Don't make me forget! I want not to forget! So long as I can picture the two of us, he still lives. Allow me to remember, for ever and always. Oh, Cross, Cross, she wept, our cause failed, the cause for which you died! You offered up your life as forfeit, that I should sit on the throne one day.

I will see that day, my dearest Cross…will make it come…because you willed it!

Then, at long last, she was able to visualize the bitterly poignant beauty of those final moments in his arms—his fine looks…his sweet words…his achingly tender love. Bereft, she surrendered herself to uncontrollable sobbing.

CHAPTER 17

So High King Cadell no longer lived to upset all her plans. As Tara pondered that news, a sudden thought struck her that it must have been the gods' doing—striking down any who dared tamper with their plans. But that could not be so, for Atheurin had told her that whoever the gods favor must play a large part themselves, and sure she'd played no part in Cadell's timely death. Moreover, the unsettling thought reminded her, Clydog now would succeed to the throne—if throne there was, after this disastrous defeat. Naught had changed, she realized.

She made her way cautiously into the ravine Sigefert designated as rendezvous, only to find it empty. She could not suppress the clutch of panic at finding herself alone in this alien land, and her unease grew as time went by with no sign of the Danes. Was it the wrong place? There stood the twisted oak, the crumbling stone hedgerow fronting the stream bank, and the stream bed itself. Had she been told to find them farther down the dry stream? Was there perchance another ravine very like this, the Vikings e'en now grumbling at her absence…or e'en deciding to leave without her? Terrified by the thought that she might be abandoned in this foreign land, she hastily retraced her steps, to see if she'd overlooked a fork in the path.

The going was difficult in the dark. Once a huge, ghostly shape burst from the gorse to brush her face as it hurtled past, and her sudden terror was stemmed but slightly to realize it likely was but a hunting owl startled from its perch. A fierce barking erupted dangerously near at hand, and she fingered her sword nervously, but the beast's noise quieted to low growling and finally to silence. Distraught, she sank to the ground, trying to collect her rattled thoughts. The day's travails had levied mightily on her courage, leaving her reserves perilously low, but there must be no giving up. It was the right place, she knew, and drew resolve from some untapped reservoir of strength to stand and plod back to the twisted oak.

She had regained some mastery over her fears, and was telling herself she had no reason for panic, when she was borne brutally to the ground, and a huge arm was wrapped suffocatingly about her throat.

Even through her terror at the sudden assault, her military training did not desert her, and she clawed with her free hand for the dagger sheathed at her thigh, preparing to stab blindly at her assailant, when there was a muted chuckle and the powerful arms fell away.

"So, back at last, wee Princess? We gave you up nigh two moons past, woman! Where in Odin's name have you tarried so long?"

Relief washed over her. She lay silent for a time, trying to still her trembling. She was lifted up, and in the faint light made out the reassuring shape of Sigefert's face looming close to hers.

"Can you not speak?" He shook her vigorously, the rough handling oddly stemming her tremors. "I fear'd you'd been taken. What befell you? Where were you?" Even as he spoke, she saw shapes materializing, and realized the Vikings must have been closing in silently about her ever since she arrived.

Sigefert's arm bumped into hers, and he caught sight of the dagger clutched in her hand. He laughed ruefully. "I'd forgot your little battlestormfish, and your way of blooding your men. We took you for some drunken thrall with a bellyful of ale, not a fierce little Valkyar with fire in her belly. I'll take more care next time. But tell me—what kept you? What have you learned?"

She told them everything. At the outset they were refusing to credit so overwhelming and swift a rout, but when Tara recited to them the cold words of the dispatch as best she recalled, they could disbelieve no longer. "You did well," Sigefert told her, but stiffly, as though praise was unfamiliar. He turned to the others, and announced gravely, "Our ponts are burnt then. There will be no going back."

There was a muttering at that, and a large Viking strode out from the group to stand before Sigefert. "Such would be a craven thing!" he growled. "We must go back! Do we let countrymen die without avenging their remains? I say we return at once—tonight!"

"You are crazed, Oddune!" said Sigefert quietly. "What boots it to dash ourselves against the Saxon rock, and spend our lives to no end? We do not play at Hnefatafl—we are at war! Did not Tara's message say many Danes broke through to the east, and escaped down the river to Shobury? Do they hurl themselves senselessly back into the conflict to die? Nay, we will save our force, and live to fight another day when the odds are more even. That is my order."

Oddune would not be stilled. "Our friends and brothers lie dead there—Odin's oaks! You may hang back like a craven, if you've not stomach enough for a brawl, but my bloody branch goes back to avenge my comrades!" His eyes swept swiftly over the group. "There are many things more to be feared than death. Who among you would seek the Court of Odin with me, and do battle with Geri and Freki, and find your places in the Web of Destiny?"

A groundswell of growling and muttering among the Vikings turned the atmosphere suddenly tense. Tara sensed a mortal challenge brewing to Sigefert's authority, and watched anxiously to see how he would stem it.

He measured his pace to Oddune, his manner deceptively calm, until they stood eye to eye, scarce a mote's difference in their heights. "So you term me a craven, do you, Oddune?" he asked softly. "Few men have called me so, and none who did lives today. This matter is simple, no mind how hot your blood boils—we will not go back to throw our lives away, as long as I am Jarl. But you make it a different matter when you question my courage. So we will fight a holmganga at dawn. Tonight we lie here quiet, not to rouse the countryside. Return to the longboats." He strode off, not looking back, toward the setting moon glowing redly just above the horizon, and to Tara his silhouette seemed that of a god who walked the earth.

The holmganga, she learned, was a formal ritual, fought with sword and shield inside a square scratched on the sand. It ended by custom when first blood was drawn, but as they matched off in the murky light of early dawn, Tara heard quiet predictions that it would be a battle to the death. Sigefert had inspired little affection in her, but she prayed to her gods that the duel's end would not see his strong and vital body lying lifeless on the beach.

As they stepped into the square, each man wore a girdled tunic falling just below his waist, tight pantalons, and pointed leathern helmet framed in iron. Each bore a huge single-handed broadsword and heavy wooden shield. Their faces were ominously grim.

There was no thrust and parry, as in a Cymri sword fight, but tremendous slashes by one, caught on the heavy shield of the other. In the hands of these two giants, the force of their heavy swords seemed nigh irresistable, but repeatedly the massive shields strapped on brawny arms turned them aside. There was a ritual quality to their struggle, as though they were two performers in a macabre dance, but they fought in grim earnest, and she saw clearly that a misstep by either could mean his death. She wondered anxiously which would die this day.

The breathing of the contestants grew labored, and the pace slowed, as if each husbanded his energies for some supreme effort. Oddune was the first to change the routine of slash-and-parry, charging suddenly, shield clashing against shield, thrusting Sigefert backwards and off balance as he strove to stay inside the line, then sweeping his sword savagely upward. Sigefert twisted violently, but could not completely escape the extreme tip of Oddune's sword, which slashed open his pantalons, and through the rip Tara spied a thin red line etched on his thigh.

There were shouts of "First Blood!" and Oddone stood panting, his sword tip lowered. "Yield!" he shouted hoarsely. "Do ye yield?"

"Not if it means we go back," growled Sigefert through compressed lips. "If that be your thought, fight on!" With evident disappointment, his fatigue plain to see in the hunch of his shoulders, Oddune lifted his sword and the duel continued.

The attacks were slowing and their force lessening, both men showing the strain of their enormous effort. There were shouts of "Enough!" but neither paid attention. Tara felt tension building, and had an inescapable impression that events were building to a critical climax. Even as she sought for a reason to explain her strange premonition, Sigefert dropped to a sudden crouch, his huge sword slashing like lightning beneath Oddune's shield, and in a climactic blow that drew gasps from the onlookers struck Oddune a paralyzing blow on the outside of his unprotected calf. Oddune stumbled back, dragging his wounded leg, and fought desperately to recover his balance. As Sigefert stood immobile, his expression inscrutable, the leg suddenly collapsed under Oddune, and he fell heavily out of the square.

A muted groundswell of approval erupted from the Vikings, their pent-up emotions released, and a dozen willing arms were extended to carry their fallen shipmate across the beach and set him carefully down on the grass.

Sigefert turned his back on the scene, and walked toward the longboats. "Embark!" he said tersely. "We set our sails for Northumbria—unless there be another who would question my order." He did not look at Tara, as she hastened to board his craft. From her station in the bow, she turned to see how Oddune fared, and saw him dropped unceremoniously in his longboat like a sack of meal. So much for the vanquished in the harsh Viking regimen, she concluded.

Thinking Sigefert's slash might require tending, she threaded her way back to where he stood in the stern sheets. "Shall I bind your wound,

Sigefert?" she asked, kneeling and moving the torn fabric aside, but he brushed her hand away.

"No time," he said curtly, and grasped the steering oar. "Launch boats!" he ordered, and she hastened forward between the rowers' elevated oars, taking her place in the bow. The keel grated across the sand, and the boat glided onto the glassy surface of the Saefern.

Broad water lay ahead when the word was passed to step the mast. Tara was watching the evolutions with interest, when she heard Sigefert call out, "pass the Princess back." Before she knew what portended, she was snatched up by the foremost oarsman, and tossed casually aloft from hand to hand, until she found herself deposited at Sigefert's feet. She started to object, but decided there was no harm done, and held her tongue. Why did he want her back here with him? She darted a look at him, catching his eyes on her, but he glanced quickly away, and she could read little in his expression. The quick exchange of looks unsettled her, and she turned her back on him as if to watch the rigging of the sail. There was no physical resemblance between Crosbey and him, yet the furtive flicker of interest in his eyes reminded her again of the longing she had felt for Crosbey—her cherished Cross…her friend…her squire…the first sweet love of her innocence…the forever champion of her life's dream.

Feeling the bitter sting of tears as the memory gripped her, she forced herself to look away, and for distraction she studied the stubby mast, socketed in a massive hollowed-out stone. As she watched, strong hands pivoted it up to the vertical, bringing taut a line running from its peak to the bow. A great furled sail was set across the deck, and spread open to the wind by hoisting its upper spar with a line run over the peak and down aft to serve as a backstay. The moment the striped square of cloth was spread, it billowed out, and she could feel the surge of power as the longboat accelerated through the water. It recalled vaguely to her that long-ago trip with Sire, but try as she might to recapture it, the image was lost in the shadows of time.

All day the wind held fair, and the flotilla stayed its course down the broad Hafren Channel, hugging the Cymri coast to slip past Wessex coast watchers or Alfred's lion-headed ships. She expected they'd set her ashore near Caerleon, and shuddered at the realization that with Cadell dead, Clydog would be High King. But when they cleared the mouth of the Channel, they made no move to put in. Shortly thereafter, the lookout sang out the sighting of Caldey Isle, and she knew Tenby lay close to hand. But by then it was growing dark, the wind was freshening, the long rollers were coming in from the open sea—and the last chance for being put ashore in Cymru was lost while Tara was too seasick to care.

When night came on, bringing a lessened chance of discovery, the flotilla sought shelter along the Damnonia coast, but they were bucking a head sea, and gray dawn was breaking as they reached close enough under its lee to moderate their heavy rolling and pitching. The skies threatened, and thick fog hugged the coast to screen their passage. For the first time, they had a respite from the constant strain of alertness—and finally, a chance to give thought to their destination.

"Could we not have sought shelter at Milford Haven in Cymru?" asked Tara, still nauseated from the turbulent passage. She hesitated to approach the grim chieftain, but the thought of being so far from her homeland filled her with a nameless dread.

"And put ourselves in the lion's mouth?" Sigefert replied, scarce concealing his scorn. Alfred, he explained tersely, would learn at once where they'd sought sanctuary, and would bottle up their boats in the small harbor for destruction. Even if they survived that danger, word of their escape route would filter back to him, and his fleet would pursue them. "We'll have a conference of captains to decide where we go, but there be few choices, and Alfred can work out our likely route near as well as we," he concluded, less gruffly.

After much arguing and disagreeing, the conference broke up and the flotilla was underway again. They would 'provision' at the Scilly Isles. From overheard fragments of conversation, Tara began to comprehend why the Northmen were forced to raid peaceful farmlands, though with no excuse for their oft needless atrocities against the hapless peasants. It depressed her enormously that she was part of the Norse maraudings, and the more she thought on it the less she could bear to look at Sigefert.

The onset of their second night, close under the nearby land, found the seas smooth. Sigefert informed her that they skirted a place called Cornubia, whose barren soil and sparse population enticed few to call there. He gave a grunt of a laugh at his words. "Strange I describe it so," he said, "for it is as if I speak of Denemearc. That is just such a cold and hostile land, yet Vikings foraying all over the seas long ever to return there." He paused, pondering his words. "I will land on the Cornubia shore one day, and see if it has the smell of Denemearc."

Whatever small comfort Tara enjoyed earlier abandoned her late in the night, when they cleared the last tip of land, to face the full brunt of the wind howling across the open ocean. Sail was shortened until only a small scrap of cloth was aloft, but it sufficed to drive their craft boiling through the long combers. Sleep was impossible in such heavy going, and she wedged herself tightly under the rear thwart lest some rogue wave snatch her overboard. They'd be on short rations until the Scilly Isles, and though she'd scarce eaten a bite she felt bitter bile rising in her throat, and retched uncontrollably, dry heaves seeking to dredge up food from her empty stomach.

Morning found her too exhausted, when the cry of landfall went up, to sit up at the rail and scan the horizon. But the errant sun came out at long last, and under its welcome warmth, combined with moderation of the seas, her distress lessened and she felt able to look about her.

The seven boats, now formed in line abreast, approached the forbidding shore at what seemed to her breathtaking speed, to grind to a sudden stop on weed-strewn stretches of sand. The instant each craft beached, its crew sprang ashore to seize the gunwales and haul their boat clear of the breakers. Tara fervently hoped she would not be joining the raiders, and thankfully her wish was granted. "You stay, Tara," Sigefert said, tossing the words over his shoulder as he joined the party climbing the steep bank. "You'll not have the stomach for this."

They returned in a surprisingly short time, laden with transport baskets that they upended into the boats. Within minutes, the flotilla was well offshore, sails hoisted again and the boats heeling under the lively breeze. "And did you kill any peasants today?" Tara asked Sigefert scornfully.

"There was no need. They fled at sight of us, and we took what we needed and left." He looked narrowly at her. "We slaughter none for sport, but only to protect ourselves."

He puts a broad meaning on 'protect', she thought acidly. However, eating the welcome bit of curd and chewing hungrily on the dried meat, she was forced to admit that the unwilling hospitality of the Scilly Islanders was most timely, as she'd been near starvation.

When the flotilla changed course, shifting the mid-morning sun around to the starboard bow, Tara asked where they were bound, fearing as she did to hear the reply. "Up the Oceanus Britannicus, if you ken the name. We stop at a tiny isle off Normandy for more provisioning."

Normandy? Vaguely she recalled the name from Father Eliswan's geographer, but had no notion where it might be. "And after that, we cross the Ocean?" she asked.

"We cross it now."

The thought of traversing the vast waterway the Cymri oddly termed the 'Narrow Sea' would have terrified her a month earlier, but much water had flowed beneath their keels since Gloucester, and she drew reassurance from the nearby shore on their left hand. If weather threatened, sure they could seek shelter there.

When she said as much to Sigefert, he roared with laughter. "The shelter of the grave," he said mockingly. "Yon is Saxon land, woman. The only shelter they have to offer is the gibbet. Vikings must earn their shelter with their weapons. No matter how stormy your Narrow Sea, it is friendlier than that shore."

It was the following night before the smoothing swells, and the sight of sea birds about the rigging, told that land was nearby. They furled their sails to creep in under oars, beached the boats, and spread out to catch what sleep they could until dawn.

Evidently these farmers were made of sterner stuff than at Caldey, for some Vikings bore wounds when they returned. They embarked in haste, without speaking, and were barely off the beach when pursuers could be seen at the crest of the hill. "Now you ken why we avoid the mainland," Sigefert said laconically. "Were this the Normandy coast, boats would be on our tail before we reached the channel. These islanders lack sufficient boats to follow."

Once at sea and under sail again, Sigefert deigned to disclose their plans to Tara. "We head nor'east for the Flanders Strait, but in the open sea now, since both shores are unfriendly. The trip will be over 70 leagues, and it can make up stormy." He watched keenly to see if mention of rough weather frighted her, but she took care to hide the apprehension she felt.

"I forgot one small thing," he added. "Alfred's fleet is like to lie in wait for us there."

The promised rough weather never materialized. Instead, gentle swells rolled in from the south, and the sun ruled a cloudless sky. She wondered if Sigefert had exaggerated the risk of bad weather to alarm her, and confronted him with her suspicion.

"You've a woeful lot to learn, Tara," he said, with an unexpected bit of a grin that lighted up his face. "The Oceanus Britannicus won't disappoint for long those who yearn for rough weather. Be patient, and it will show you."

But the weather held fair. Scanning the star-studded bowl of the heavens, Tara's heart ached with the sheer wonder and beauty of it all. Never could she have imagined the majesty of the night skies from a ship at sea. Tears welled up as she thought of Crosbey, longing for him to be here beside her, glorying with her at the spectacle. Despite her anxiety about losing the memory, she recalled clearly her last poignant moments with him. She could feel the tenderness of his arms, his fingers stroking her cheek. Oh, why did the gods take him so; why did he spend his entire young life in her defense, only to be snatched so cruelly away? Cross, Cross, my beloved! Do you hear my thoughts of you? Can you feel these tears? Do you know, even where you are, how much I will always think of you, and love you? Pray Lug he be safe and happy in the Otherworld, she breathed, and cried herself to sleep.

Sigefert sent a single boat stealing into their selected landing place, and the dawn was just breaking over the shore when he cautiously led the remainder of the flotilla to the beach. Sentries were posted at once atop the low dunes at either end, the boats were swung about and deployed in line abreast at the water's edge, oars in the rowlocks and sails ready for instant hoisting. The Vikings were spread thinly along the sand, to avoid vulnerability to surprise. Only then did Sigefert relax his guard somewhat, and let a little of the tension drain off.

"Come over here, Tara," he said. "I would speak with you for a bit. Come, sit beside me."

Full of wonder that he should pay her such notice, and a little unnerved by the attention, she did as he bid. The warm sand was pleasant, and relaxation with no thought of danger was a huge relief. At last, she rejoiced, no foe was nearby and no harm threatened.

CHAPTER 18

There was a great shout from the lookout, followed at once by an urgent horn blast, signalling an imminent attack. The Danes were up in an instant, shields unlimbered, swords gleaming in their left hands, great battle-axes brandished at the ready—an ugly surprise to the bone-weary Sigefert. He had just relaxed from the turmoil of their headlong flight, and started to recharge his energies in the sheltered inlet, but he sprang up at once, assessing the threat even as he readied his weapons. He is tireless, thought Tara; if only I were the same. However, she drew her own broadsword, slim and light as a toy beside the massive Viking weapons, but lethal enough in her competent hands. Belike the situation was one of deadly peril to their little band, and she noted the rapid throbbing of her heart, but her senses were too keenly focused to feel any fear.

Strangely, instead of charging headlong into the fray, the aggressors seemed to be standing their ground on the crest of the bluff, and their fair-haired chieftain doffed his helmet in the Norse signal for a parley. On guard against treachery from this new threat, Sigefert bade his troop maintain their vigilance, but to ignore a truce call meant dishonoring his standard, so he raised his axe arm to hold his men where they stood.

The opposing bands stood motionless for a brief time. Then, slowly, the enemy chieftain raised his sword to touch its hilt to his lips, and returned it to its scabbard. Tara wondered if it was trickery, but Sigefert must have decided it was not, for he set his axe aside and sheathed his sword in the same ceremonial manner. The two approached each other across the sand, met, halted and spoke together, their words inaudible.

In the atmosphere of confrontation, so charged Tara could feel it crackling, the two came down the rise toward the silent Northumbrians, and the stranger scanned the hard, merciless faces of men who would strike him down at a single false move. His head was proudly erect, his manner as confident as if presiding over some military ceremony. Seen at close range, he was very young. He's scarce more than a boy, thought Tara, but his accoutrements marked him as a person of rank. His wooden shield was worked in silver, its boss cut in an intricate pattern. His sword hilt was carved in intertwined serpents, gleaming of gold. The helmets of his men were of leather, but his was of heavily embossed iron. Unlike the others, he wore no beard, and in the waning sunlight his hair was bright and fair as a maid's, but he was large framed and sturdy of build. Incongruously, Tara thought she'd never seen eyes so crystal blue.

"Men of Northumbria," announced Sigefert, when the two had come to a stop, "this be the Prince Gormsson, grandson of King Gorm the Old of Denemearc. He has come Viking along the Ponthieu coast, but an ill tempest drove his boats on the rocks. He stands ready to do battle if it be our wish, but they are Danes, and would join us. What say you?"

The fierce expressions relaxed slightly, and Tara noted here and there a lowering of weapons, an almost palpable easing of tensions. The battle lust was draining off, their postures slowly returning to normal. Atop the bluff, Gormsson's men maintained their readiness, but with the same relaxation in their stance. We are with friends, realized Tara with vast relief. They are countrymen, and my courage in battle will not be tested this day. Breathing her silent thanks to the generous gods—mayhap to Atheurin as well—she lowered her weapon to wait.

No word was said, but Sigefert read in the faces of his men that they accepted the pact. "So we are allies, Prince Gormsson," he declared, loud enough for those atop the cliffs to hear. "Join with us in our camp, and we will drink on it."

Tensions fell away, and the beach erupted with boisterous laughter as mead was broken out from their meager store and the two groups told their tales. The newcomers, it turned out, hailed from Denemearc itself, while Sigefert's Vikings were Northumbrians from the north of Britain, second generation Danes who had never seen the motherland, but they shared jokes and bawdy tales one on another as old friends. All of them castaways, they provided much-needed reassurance on an unfriendly beach along a foreign shore. The air that night rang with their singing and carousing, and the monks in the monastery of Sainte-Mere-Eglise, ten miles inland, triple-barred their huge iron-studded door, and told their beads in vast unease.

Gormsson's five longboats had been sorely battered, two beyond repair, the others little better. His expedition had brought no shipbuilding tools, leading Sigefert to mutter that the young had no concept of misadventure and hence made no plans against it. Without the Northumbrians' supply of adzes, augers, chisels and hafted wedges, plus stores of luting, tar and linen thread, Gormsson's situation would have been hopeless.

Fascinated, realizing again all the skills of which she knew naught, and determined to improve at every opportunity the knowledge she should have as Queen, Tara watched the battered vessels slowly take shape. All three keels were judged sound, and there were enough stem timbers, but much of the side planking had splintered on the sharp rocks. The Danes salvaged what iron nails and roves they could, while Sigefert's master shipwright set his men to felling and splitting logs for fashioning new planks. Tara was put to work stripping hair from hides of whatever animals they could hunt down, and mixing it with pine resin to caulk the larger seams. As the replacement planking rose up the sides, internal support timbers were set in place, and Tara's maritime vocabulary was enhanced by learning that bite crossbeams and snelles were secured to them with whittled trunnels. Although a few oars had splintered in the tempest beyond repair, the inventory from five long-boats sufficed to outfit the surviving three.

Sigefert rushed the repairs all he could, working day and night with little thought of rest, while the combined squadron was immobilized and virtually defenseless, and long before Tara had thought it possible, Gormsson's boats were ready to deploy. His problem of too few boats for too many Vikings was solved handily, as Sigefert's seven longboats had set sail originally from Gloucester only for a reconnaissance mission and were not fully manned for ocean travel. The combined force of ten well-manned longboats constituted a formidable squadron, but Sigefert well knew that the hasty repairs could not withstand sustained heavy weather.

The one overriding worry weighing on all was the prospect of Alfred's vastly superior fleet laying await off the Kentish promontory, blockading the Narrow Sea at its narrowest point, ready to deny them passage by sinking and capturing them all. The flotilla's only hope was contriving to slip through chinks in Alfred's lion-headed warship patrol. To a man, Sigefert's force clamored for a simple frontal attack to redden their weapons as fighting men, and feed the ravens on Saxon corpses, but he knew how outnumbered they were, and that most of the corpses would be their own. Impatiently overriding the popular view, he decided on the prudent strategy of hugging the far shore, hoping to creep past in the dead of night.

As they approached the narrow neck where Alfred would mount his blockade, they proceeded at single file under cover of the dark, close under the Frankish coast at Flanders on the east, as near as Sigefert dared approach. At early morn they dragged the boats into the marshes and covered them with brush for concealment, and Gormsson was sent north with a scouting party, to steal horses and reconnoitre.

In mid-afternoon he was back, with dried blood on his hastily-band-aged arm, impatient to report his findings. "The lion-heads lie off the second headland north, and stretch across the channel like a pont, as far as we can see. They be a score or more to our one."

Sigefert digested the gloomy tidings, which came as no surprise to him. "Think you we can find concealment in the shallows, to walk the boats past without alerting the lookouts?" he asked.

"I would swear by Odin's beard it cannot be done. They lie moored in a line that comes up to the shore, with a lookout perched atop each mast. It's clear they look for us to try such an inshore route, and are bound the inmost ships will sound an alarm."

"Aye, that must be the right of it. Were I the Saxon commander, I would plan it so. The cursed part is, if we sneak under the shore we go not in battle array but single file, and if they attack, then our force is ill-disposed for a fight. No, we cannot chance it."

"Then we must attack head-on, at the weakest point in the screen, and fight through. It is the only way." But Gormsson's worried face showed his pessimism at that strategy.

"It is no way. Thor himself could not prevail against so great a mismatch. We must find a better plan."

Both men fell silent. Both were brave fighters, used to facing unequal odds and battling through by the fury of their attack, but the lion-heads bore seamen as stout as they, and it was folly to ignore their overwhelming superiority in numbers.

Suddenly Sigefert struck his open palm with his clenched fist. "By Thor," he exclaimed, "I know how we must do it! Call your men together; we plan the night's pleasure for the Saxons."

The Saxon sentry in the crow's nest was vastly bored with staring into nothingness along the dark shore. He fought to keep awake by recalling tittilating memories of the saucy barmaid whose pallet he had shared back on the Isle of Sheppey. For three hours he had seen naught, and yet a dreary hour dragged out ahead, until his useless vigil would be done and he back in his warm hammock. He savored the warmth and comfort awaiting him there, and he drowsed.

A garotte tight about his neck snatched him cruelly from his dream, to plunge him into one from which there would be no awakening. Simultaneously, the forecastle lookout felt the searing heat of steel in his vitals, the pain enduring but an instant. Shadowy figures with bare feet and blackened faces crept catlike throughout the ship on their silent business, and soon it was all over.

Sigefert saw his attack team over the rail, then slid down the anchor line himself, leaving the ghost ship to continue its vigil with sightless eyes. They waded onto the shore, and ran catlike on their toes back to where their longboats waited.

"How went the venture?" demanded Gormsson tensely.

"All is done. Quick—scant time remains before the dark will lighten; time to speak when we are well clear. Take you the lead boat, and not a sound. Go!"

The longboats ghosted silently inshore of the lifeless Saxon ship, wading men panting from the sustained exertion as they breasted the dark combers. Now and then a muted curse signalled collision with submerged obstacles. After a long hour, the last boat of the flotilla was by the blockade line, but Sigefert made them continue their slow trek until the enemy ships had disappeared in the gloom astern and it was safe to make sail. Early morning light found the longboats meeting the seas under a lively quartering blow, and Sigefert knew Alfred's larger and more awkward vessels would find them hard to overtake. But that they would be giving chase he never doubted; the moment they boarded the death ship they would know what had happened, and would devote all their energies to the pursuit.

The wind blowing up the Channel from the open sea stirred up long swells, and Tara's stomach turned queasy as the boat settled into a rhythmic motion, accelerating down the slope of an overtaking comber, then slowing as the bow mounted the crest. I will not be sick, she vowed, and forced her mind to other things, but the taste of bile in her throat was ever-present. Unconsciously, she snatched a guilty look at Sigefert.

He was watching her, and laughed in scorn when he sensed her condition. "If these little ripples discomfit you, Frigga help you when we hit the full brunt of the Northern Sea."

"I have not been a sailor," she said firmly. "My life has been in the wood and the hills. Were we chasing a stag in the King's Forest, you'd not find me wanting."

"Then it is an unhappy thing that we be not in the King's Forest, but this is the sea. Here all pull their oars. A longboat has no room for one ignorant of the sea."

"Then I will learn," she said indignantly. "Why do you not teach me of the sea, so I will learn? Do you growl so at all your men, when first they take to the sea—or do you teach them?"

He cast his eyes upward, as if calling to his deity. "Odin's wounds, loose me of this fey creature! I have no need to teach them! They are seamen born, and they know the sea in their blood. Were they goatherds, they would know the barnyard, without need for teaching. Were they merchants, they would know their tally sticks." He paused. "And were they women, they would know the hearth."

There it is, she thought. His real problem is that I am a woman, and he recks this a man's demesne. "Then since I am but a woman, you think me fit for naught but the hearth?"

"The ocean is no place for a woman," he said tersely. "The sooner we drop you ashore, the better for all."

She started in shock at his dismissive words. Drop her ashore? She had welcomed flight with him, partly to escape a Saxon rope but mayhap more to flee from the dread prospect of a life with Clydog. In her haste to flee, she'd given little heed to what lay ahead, and his chilling rejection devastated her, the more so because unconsciously she must have imagined a future in his company. But how could she have done that, with the memory of Crosbey so fresh within her? No—she simply had not thought it through. Or had she, in some dim unplumbed corner of her mind? The matter of her feeling for Sigefert confused and upset her even more than what he had said.

This was no time for such musings, she told herself. Certainly she would not seek to be with any man who held her in contempt. She would be glad to see the last of him. But why, then, did her heart feel so heavy at his words? Furiously, she turned to look stonily back at the wake bubbling out astern.

By nightfall, they were well into the Northern Sea, and Tara was cold, wet, seasick and miserable. She curled up in the cramped space forward, under the high carved stem, and slept fitfully. In her dreams she saw Sigefert's scornful face, and read the contempt in his cold eyes. When she awoke, her face was unaccountably wet with tears.

The morning brought wind howling in earnest, stirring the sea into a confused chop that wracked the longboats cruelly. Sigefert eased his boat astern, anxious to see how Gormsson's boats were taking the pounding, and what he saw was far from reassuring. Two of the three were making heavy weather of it, and Gormsson's own boat was wallowing heavily and losing way. Sigefert pulled abreast it, and shouted across.

"Are your seams holding?" The wind swept his words away, and Gormsson could not understand. Sigefert found it impossible to make himself heard, but even as he called he saw the port garboard strake pulling open at the seam. The boat's nose dipped into the sea under its growing load of seawater, and despite the steersman's desperate efforts to head it into the wind it was too sluggish to answer the helm. Sigefert saw it was doomed, and pulled alongside at once, his grappling irons securing the two craft together.

"Aboard me, all hands!" he cried, and instantly Gormsson's crew were abandoning the stricken craft to spread themselves through his now overladen boat, looking stonily ahead, not turning to see their longboat breaking apart. Gormsson stared silently off with unfocused eyes, and Sigefert did not intrude on his grief. The steersman put over his long steering oar, and the Northumbrian boat picked up way as the slatting sail hardened to the wind.

Sigefert spread the refugees among the nine surviving craft, and gloomily took stock. The wind was freshening still, and it was essential to put in somewhere in order to assess damage. Postponing plans to head for the Humber, they veered toward the East Anglian coast, painfully aware that any delay was dangerous with the enemy fleet in pursuit, but recognizing that there was no help for it. Besides, Alfred's fleet would be having weather problems of its own.

By nightfall they had found a quiet inlet along the East Anglian coast, to beach the boats in calmer water and lick their wounds. Sigefert bade the wearied shipwrights inspect Gormsson's surviving boats at once, ignoring their grumblings. He ignored Tara as well, and her injured pride made her act impulsively. Scarce able to bear the sight of him after his scornful remarks, she decided that if he wished to drop her ashore she'd save him the trouble. Father Eliswen had told of Colchester's great abbey in the north, where he took holy orders. They would extend sanctuary to a pilgrim, and she could make further plans from there. Recalling that it was on the water, she decided she'd come upon it if she walked south along the coast. The prospect of going alone, afoot, and by night was daunting, but she was driven by anger, and the idea of remaining unwanted with the aloof Sigefert was worse. Hastily gathering her few possessions, she stuffed her pouch with dried fish and stole away into the dark.

She reasoned that if she kept the beach close at her left, she could not lose her way, so she headed seaward, but the moonlight scarce penetrated the overcast and it took an eternity even to reach the shore. She started trudging southward down the beach, but hearing sounds in the woods she broke into a run, her angry resolution replaced with a mixture of irritation at her foolhardy action and fright at the unknown. Suddenly a dark shadow loomed before her, and as she tried to avoid it she stumbled and fell, her knee striking a jagged stone edge. Pain shot up her leg, and she was close to fainting.

Total desolation swept over her. Irresolute, she lay motionless for the moment, seeking to call on reserves of strength. She tried to stand, but the pain was too intense, and gradually the seriousness of her situation became brutally apparent. Gingerly cradling the injured knee, she pulled her tunic about her and tried to rest, hoping the swelling she could feel would subside enough by morning for her to walk.

The night mists blew away, and the full moon rising behind her swelled enormously until it seemed to fill the sky. In its depths, hazily, she could make out a forest glade, and as she stared the figure of a little child materialized, sitting on the grass. Disbelieving the evidence of her eyes, she watched as the scene cleared, and saw that the child was herself—and there on the log was Atheurin! In the silence she could hear the child, asking "but what if I am far away from you, and caught out in the dark—and afeard?" The answer came distinctly. "Then you must close your eyes, and call for me, and I will be there with you. Remember, little one, you are never alone. Near, or in a distant land, whenever you have need for me, I am there." She tried to call out to Atheurin, but the picture faded away and the dark enveloped her again.

A murmur of voices awakened her. So she had slept! Then through the grasses she saw a torch, and another. Struggling to her knees, ignoring the shooting pain, she hastily drew her sword, realizing as she did the futility of attempting a defense from such a position.

The grasses were thrust apart; she was blinded by a torch thrust in her face, and her sword was kicked aside. Her instant terror turned into a great surge of relief, as she recognized the furious visage of her nemesis, Sigefert.

"By the rood, lady, what in the name of Freyja are you playing at?" he demanded angrily. "Know you how long we have searched for you?"

A small spark of anger intruded on her feeling of great relief, and she made herself remember that she was running away. "You had no need to search for me. I am leaving!"

"Leaving? And just where were you headed, in this Niord-cursed land?"

"I will seek sanctuary at the abbey in Colchester. You will not be burdened by a useless woman any longer!"

"You would have walked all that way, through these bandit-infested woods?" He shook his head in irritated disbelief. "Are you then a Volva or a Valkyr, that no harm will come to you?"

"I have my sword, and know how to use it. Already it has killed three bandits who thought me easy prey."

He snorted, but his eyes told her he was seeing her speculatively, in a new and unfamiliar light. "Then why are you not on your journey now, since you are so deadly with your little fotbitr? Why lie lazily here?"

"I do not lie lazily here!" she snapped, wondering why his words had such power to infuriate her. "I have cut my knee. It needs healing before I go on. It will be better by morn, and I will go about my journey."

"By Odin's blind eye, I ask myself why we wasted time hunting you! We should have left you here to die on the grass."

But he was bending over her as he spoke. He was not leaving her here to die on the grass. He was lifting her in his arms, and carrying her!

The trip back did not seem long, and miraculously the throbbing in her knee was lessening. But she wondered why, if he meant to put her ashore, he had come searching for her. She decided to ask him, when they reached camp, but he dumped her unceremoniously into a boat and disappeared. She shifted to ease the pain of her bruise, and heard the keel scraping over the sand, and immediately they were underway— as though, miraculously enough, their departure had waited only for her safe return. Before she could puzzle out what had taken place, the wind began its high-pitched keening in the rigging, and the boat started pitching—and she could think of naught but keeping her stomach from climbing up into her throat.

All night they ran north before the same quartering sea as before. Whenever she essayed to open her eyes, she saw the pole star swinging drunkenly as the swells tossed the boat. She was wet, sick and miserable, and the pain in her swelling knee bade fair to deny her any sleep. Sigefert was nowhere to be seen, and the figure looming over her at the steering oar looked like Gormsson. How badly Sigefert must have wanted to get rid of her. Very well, she would stay as far from him as possible. He'd have no more worries on her account!

The rhythmic creaking of the beitiass spar, and the thrumming of the backstay, coupled with the boat's regular motion, proved oddly soporific, and she woke to a leaden morning sky.

Gormsson had left the steering oar, if it had been he, and now squatted athwart a rowing bench. "So you awoke at last," he said, smiling down at her. "I thought our chieftain had put a spell on you, and you would sleep forever."

She tried to orient herself to what was happening. "Why did we leave so fast, and at night?"

"Alfred's fleet was coming up from the south—we saw their running lights. The inlet would have been a trap. We had to put to sea again, though we were unready."

"Your boats—were they repaired?"

"One was. We are riding it now."

"And the other?"

His smile faded. "We had not the time to repair it. Unfit as it was, the Storm God would have swallowed it before the day was out."

She was silent, sharing his grief. Of his five longboats, only one survived. She wanted to say how sorry she was, but knew he would be shamed by her words.

"Sigefert was a man possessed, when we could not find you," he said. "He stormed out on your trail, with no heed for the Saxons coming up from the south. It was Frey's blessing that he found you quickly, or we would have been bottled up by the lion-heads, and ripe for plucking."

"But he wanted only to be rid of me," she said, mystified. "He told me as much."

"Odin says a man should be wise, but not too wise. Sigefert spoke of putting you ashore to remind you that you are but a woman, and that may be wise of him. But if he puts you ashore, and loses you forever, then he is too wise. Your Northumbrian is not too wise."

"But you did not see his face when he said it. He wants to be quit of me," she said, then added, "and I of him."

"I give you one more of Odin's sayings, from the Havamal. 'Better not seek to know your future, if you want a more carefree present.'" With which remark he rose and went forward.

The blow abated, but the wind stayed fresh, and Gormsson assured her the lion-heads could never equal their speed. At dusk the lead boat hailed land to port, and they lay offshore to enter the Humber River after dark. Morale at reaching the Humber was high, for here they were in the Danelaw and free of the Saxon threat, but prudence demanded that they await darkness.

When the boats were beached, Sigefert went to each boat to summon the captains for a council. When he reached Gormsson's boat, she was prepared to be ignored, and turned away, but he twisted her about. "You come, too," he ordered her shortly.

Out of place among the longboat captains, Tara sensed a remoteness, almost a hostility, in their eyes, but none commented on her presence. Gormsson, seeming her only friend, had eyes and ears only for Sigefert and his message.

"You Northumbrians know well where we are: we have reached a land controlled by Danes. Upriver is the place of the Danish Althing for this region, and they'll make us welcome. There we can make repairs, replenish our supplies, and ready ourselves for the balance of our trip to Northumbria. We camp here tonight, and go upriver at early morn."

"What of Alfred's fleet?" asked one.

"The Saxon is little liked here. Alfred will not venture this far north, lest his beard be singed. We need fear no attacks from here north."

Shortly, the meeting was adjourned to make camp, and Gormsson steered Tara back to his longboat. "I have a strange feel, Princess," he told her.

"What does that mean? Feeling about what?"

"If we were in such mortal danger just down the coast, how can we be in mother's arms here? If Alfred controls the nearby seas, what is so different here?"

"Because Sigefert says this is a Danish homeland," she argued, surprised and alarmed at his doubts.

"And was not East Anglia a Danish homeland as well?"

She realized with sudden enlightenment that he was right. The Yare River was Danish territory, yet Alfred pursued them there. Why would this be different? Confused, she knew not how to answer his argument. However, they would know on the morrow, so she put it from her mind, and rolled up in her tunic to prepare for sleep.

The Danish capital of York was six hours upriver. They started at first light, gliding smoothly through blessedly calm waters, flanked on each side by verdant forests so reminiscent of Dyfed that a lump formed in Tara's throat. She found herself admiring the precise rhythm of the oarsmen's muscular bodies as their blades bit in unison into the still waters, leaving precise little patterns of eddies in their wake. She had never imagined a watercraft could be so swift.

Coming round a bend, they saw the palisades of the capital. Armed men were massed at the landing stage, and in the fields men were seen dropping their implements to buckle on weapons and run toward the river. The atmosphere was disturbing to Tara, as though she was witnessing troops readying to repel invasion. They show us a chilly welcome, she thought, glancing at Gormsson, but his expression was unreadable. Seven of the boats closed ranks and roped stern posts together, while Sigefert's boat slowly approached the landing stage.

They spoke at the landing for a long space. Sigefert did not disembark, and Tara knew all was not well. A feeling of unease came over, and she could see the same emotion in the eyes of the Northumbrians.

The conference broke up, and Sigefert returned. He stood at the bow and grimly addressed the crews. They could not stay, he said. Guthram had made a pact with Alfred, and was pledged to treat them as pirates. The local commander had orders to seize them on sight, but told Sigefert he would not see them if they were gone by sundown.

The grim conclusion they were forced to draw from this news was that they'd find no sanctuary anywhere in Britain. They must leave, stopping along the river only for game and water, then had no alternative but to set sail for Denemearc. To the Northumbrians, none of whom had seen that bleak land, it would be exile. And to her as well.

Glumly they made camp near the river's mouth, and Sigefert immediately sent out hunting parties. Tara was sure they'd laugh at the idea of a woman on the hunt, so when all eyes were on the departing hunters she grabbed her bow, and stole unseen into the woods. She headed west, keeping the sun at her back, drinking in the sounds and sights of the forest. She unlimbered her bow, set the bowstring to the notch of a hunting arrow, and crept across the sward as she'd done countless times before. She was in her element. She'd show Sigefert what she could do!

The soft ground bore ample signs of deer, so she knew she had only to be quiet and patient. At the edge of a small clearing she spied a doe with two young fawns, and one trustingly came up to her. The wee thing would have been an easy kill, but the mother's agonized anxiety touched her heart, and she shooed the trio away. Mayhap she was stupid, but she was glad she'd spared them. I seek bigger quarry, she told herself, and searched again for signs marking a game trail that she could watch.

A slight noise through the trees made her freeze, while she peered carefully about. On a slight rise to the east stood a large buck, its back to her, its ears turning about as it tried to locate the approaching hunting party. She raised her bow with exquisite care, waiting for the buck to take fright.

It turned, and bounded in her direction. I will let fly when it reaches the gap in the trees, she told herself, her heart beating faster but her nerves icy calm. The antlered head came into her view, and she let the arrow fly.

For an instant she thought she had missed, for the buck bounded on. Then it stumbled, and she saw the arrow piercing its chest below the shoulder. A perfect hit, she exulted, and ran in pursuit. The deer disappeared into a thicket, and she drew her dagger, knowing a wounded buck was deadly dangerous. Hearing naught, she cautiously reached forward, and parted the bushes so she could see, and found the deer lying dead. She dragged it forth, and started dressing it out.

When the first hunters arrived, she had it eviscerated and skinned, and was starting on the hindquarters.

"Sigefert now knows you can hunt," said Gormsson happily, as they exited the Humber estuary and hit the open sea. "Yours was the first game taken, and seemed to me the most noble beast. Where did you learn to do that, Princess?"

"I grew up in the forests of Cymru. I hunted almost before I could walk."

"How did you know where the deer was? You must have headed straight for him."

"I didn't know where he was. You never know. I lay await beside a game trail, and the excessive noise of the Northumbrian hunters flushed him out, and drove him down to me."

"And did you tell them that?"

"They did not ask me, so I did not tell them."

"Good woman! And Sigefert, did he give you compliments?"

Tara frowned. "He said nothing to me. Nor I to him." She tossed her head defiantly and turned away.

Again the boats turned north, into the trackless Northern Sea, and again the long pitching motion began. The skies were clear, and the day was fair, but Tara had never felt such keen loneliness. This trip was different, for when they had put to sea before, it was always for a port in a land she might call home. But this time, they were embarked on a long and difficult voyage, across a vast unknown sea, bound for a cold and remote land she had never seen. Every roll was taking her irretrievably, and for all she knew permanently, farther from her beloved homeland. Away from her Sire, from the Bard—and from the unforgettable place where she had held her dying lover in her arms.

She choked back a sob. Oh, Atheurin, Atheurin, where are you now, she cried silently. But the gods that once favored her seemed to have abandoned her as well.

CHAPTER 19

Even under shortened sail, the vessel drove powerfully through the oily rollers, stinging spray inflicting a chilling bite that gave the Northern Sea its forbidding reputation. Tara tried to shelter herself against the spume, but gave it up as futile, and curled into an uncomfortable ball to retain what heat her thoroughly soaked body could generate. But surprisingly, the longboat's monotonous heaving did not sicken her as much as before, and when gray streaks in the black sky signalled the onset of dawn she asked Gormsson why.

He manned the heavy broadoar, holding the yawing craft as close to its course as the seas permitted. "You're getting your sea legs, girl," he answered cheerily. "Some find them fast, some slower, some not at all. Thank your gods that you're one of the fortunate.

"Does that mean I'm through being seasick?"

He laughed. "Not so, the more pity. Come the next blow, you'll rue the day you were born."

"Why do you Vikings never get sick?"

He laughed again, merrily. "You've been
heeding to Loki, the Prince of Lies, I trow. Who said the sea never strikes us down?"

"I thought...belike I just took it the sea was life and breath to them. Do you mean your men get seasick, too?"

"Half my crew will sicken in a heavy storm. They try to pass it off, hoping their mates don't notice. And oft they do not, being sick themselves. Even the older ones, born to the sea, feel Thrym's iron fist clutch their vitals when it blows up. They look sourly on me when the seas kick up, for I be one of the blessed—despite my tender years, sea-illness passes me by."

"Then when next it blows up a storm...?"

"You'll be sick as a herring, and with company aplenty."

Tara fell silent, contemplating that unhappy prospect. At least I'm well enow now, she thought—were I not wet to the bones. The thought reminded her anew of her clammy garments, and a fresh chill went through her shivering body.

Gxormsson read her mind. "Tonight, if the wind does not blow up fresh, we'll sleep dry. We used no tilt over us on leaving, lest it slow us if Saxons were afoot, but they're not like to catch our scent so far out."

"How far out are we? Or...what I really mean is..."

"You mean how long have we yet to sail to fetch Denemearc?" She nodded. "I answer with great care, Princess. I must acquaint you with Norse tradition, so you ken why I make no hasty reply. So attend my words."

Gormsson swept his arm around the horizon. "We are at the pleasure of many gods and giants," he began. "Hrim-Thurs, the ice giant, can send his monstrous ice floes into our path when he will, but this is not quite his season. If our sails feel the frigid breath of Bergelmir, the frost giant, they turn to sheets of ice and refuse to propel us. Though the fiery shafts of Thor, the mighty thunder-god, may not slow us, they can fright us so we forget our way, or, if fortune be so foul, can set our very ship afire. Mother Frigga, goddess of the raging seas, and Gialp, giantess of the storm, are the two with most power to drive us from our course, or even fling us back to where we started. We must cross the great sea stream known as Ifing, which can be playful or deadly to mariners at Ifing's whim.

"But if all goes well," he said more reassuringly, after a glance at Tara to see if she was suitably cowed, "the shining mane of Skin-Faxi can reflect bright sunlight upon us, and the giantess Gna, on her mighty steed Hofvarpnir, can summon up pleasant breezes to blow our way. If we meet but the last two, and evade the rest, the trip will take four days. If not…" he shrugged philosophically, and Tara marvelled anew, as she had many times before, at the complex characteristics making up these strange Viking creatures. Fearlessly aggressive in battle, brilliant at times in skill and strategy, they were oddly humble before the confusing multitude of ruling gods of their danger-fraught world. With their giant bronzed bodies, weather-hardened faces, and piercingly blue eyes, they were as gods themselves, she reflected.

"Then since we have been gone near a day, the trip will take but three days more," she mused aloud.

Gormsson smiled at that. "Have it your way, Princess. But prudent sailormen never predict the sea's behavior."

Not until evening, after the tilt—a rude cloth shelter spread from rail to rail near the full length of the boat—had been rigged, did Tara ask the question that nagged at her most: their destination. She chose a time when the boat was making good headway under sail, the crew mostly settled in to sleep, and she and Gormsson sat in the extreme bow looking at the heavens. He had just pointed through an opening in the clouds at a crescent of stars he termed 'Frigga's spinning wheel', and told her they used it as a guide to hold mariners to their course.

"What is our course?" she demanded. "Where are we bound?"

"Bound for Denemearc, Princess. Where else?"

"For Denemearc, I know," she responded impatiently. "But where in Denemearc? What do we seek there? What will we do?"

She could sense his hesitation. "First, we hope to make a landfall on the Frisian Isles in the north, the Isle of Sylt if our reckoning holds true."

Tara had an unpleasant memory of pillaging on the other isles in their path, and prayed they'd not do as much here, so close to their own homeland. She waited, hoping he'd say more.

"We pass well to the north of Sylt," he continued finally. We are bound for the port city of Ribe, a trading center upriver from the coast.

The name meant naught to her. "I've not heard of Ribe," she said. "Why do we go there?"

"Because it's as good a place for us as any. Neither your Sigefert nor his Northumbrians come from Denemearc, so one place is as good as any other to them. They are homeless now, with only their sword-arms to barter. I picked our destination."

"His Vikings may have their sword-arms to sell, but what have I to offer?" The moment her words were spoke, she flushed crimson at the obvious answer. "I mean…" she broke off in confusion.

"I know your meaning, Princess. Don't fret. And the plain answer is: I cannot say." He hesitated. "You will forgive my plain talk, but have you hopes of going on with your Sigefert—staying with him?"

The blunt question shocked her, said so abruptly. But it only brought into the open what she realized had been her unconscious thought.

Gormsson sensed her confusion. "Come on, Princess," he said kindly. "Tuck yourself under the thwart and sleep well. You may not sleep wet tonight, unless Gialp has it in for us, and from the look of the heavens she sleeps herself. We'll talk again, and try to solve the questions gnawing at you."

Gialp must have awakened, for she turned the weather brutal in the morn, and Gormsson was fully occupied. The tilt came down, to keep it from blowing out in the fresh wind, and the mounting seas crashed frighteningly against the fragile hull. They crested against the nearly submerged lee rail, intermittently spilling their tops into the boat. The crew kept bailing, but despite their best efforts the bilges sloshed ominously with their heavy cargo of seawater.

All through the day the weather remained foul, and Tara concentrated miserably on staying warm while she was soaking wet. Sometime that night she heard shouted commands and hurried movements among the crew, and the subsequent lessening of the wind's howling and the sea's fury told her they had turned about to run before the storm. The flooding of the seas over the rail ceased, and the falling water level around her told that they were gaining on their bailing. She wondered vaguely if the other boats were running downwind with them, or if they were running alone, mayhap to be abandoned and lost. They must be sailing away from their destination, which would make the interminable voyage even longer, but she was beyond caring.

The end to her constant drenching finally enabled her body to generate some soggy warmth despite her sopping garments, and the easier motion brought an end to her painful retching. Exhausted from her continual stomach cramping, her resistance at lowest ebb, she sank into a comotose state and finally into half-sleep.

A ray of sun peeping through a hole in the gray overcast fell on her upturned face, and she woke. Gnawing hunger assailed her stomach, but no longer did she actually hope for death as she had during the interminable night. She summoned her energies, and rose slowly to her knees.

"We are back on course, Lady." The voice came from behind her, and she twisted about to see an older man, his face deeply creased and browned as if he'd passed a lifetime at sea. His yellow hair was flecked with gray, his beard scraped shorter than the usual Norse style. He was stretched full-length on the rowing bench, and sat up to make space for her. She rose stiffly and sat beside him.

"Are we lost?" she asked, for she could see no other longboats about.

"Nay, Lady." Following his pointing finger, she managed to make out indistinct shapes against the rising sun. "Three boats make way there, and two others are coming up in our wake." She craned her head, but could not find the two.

Six boats. But there had been eight when they left! "Does that mean two are lost?"

"Not lost. Just not in sight now. When the sun burns off the mists, we should see them as well."

"What will we do if we don't?"

"Then we'll join up in Ribe."

"How can they find their way across the ocean?" She recalled now that he was the man Gormsson consulted often on their course. "How can we find the way? You're the one who sets our path, are you not?"

"Aye, I am navigator. And there are many signs to show the way. The swells come mostly from the same direction, and Denemearc lies at this angle to their path." He angled his arms to demonstrate. "I carry what navigators term a Star-Oddi scroll. It tells how close the sun lies to the east-west line when she rises and sets, and how high she rises in the sky at midday." He drew from his tunic a tightly rolled sheaf. "And when the night skies are clear, if we hold the pole star at constant height, we sail due east."

Despite her discomfort, she felt a stir of interest in this new concept. "Then we sail east?"

"Not quite. We make a little northing," he pointed, "so the pole star climbs a little higher each night. The sky is clearing, so she will show tonight, and I can check my course."

A quick fear assailed her. "Is Sigefert's one of the missing boats?" she asked, a quaver in her voice betraying her incipient panic. "Is he lost?"

"No boat is lost, Tara," said Gormsson, appearing beside them. "We were separated when the weather worsened, as always happens. Now we are turned back to our course, and they the same."

"Could they be sunk, from the storm?"

"They could, as could we. The sea is not kind to fools. But Sigefert is not a fool, and the storm was not so fierce. Why should you think so experienced a seaman sunk?"

It was not that she'd actually thought him sunk, for she knew how capable he was. It was only that the idea of an existence without him inexplicably left an aching void...

What am I thinking, she demanded of herself angrily. How can I lose something I never possessed? I am naught to him, and he owes me no favor. She sat in gloomy silence, longing for a familiar land, familiar faces, and the security of being in control of her destiny. She was desolate at the bleak realization of how completely alone she was, and utterly ashamed of her faithlessness to Cross's memory. Gormsson, understanding a little of her jumbled feelings, wisely kept silent.

When the boat had been cleansed, and lines respliced, food was set out and portions passed up the line of rowing benches. "Usually our fare is fish in all its varieties," said Gormsson dryly. "Smoked, salted, pickled, dried—whatever you wish. But we departed the Humber in haste, if you remember, and must settle for the deer meat and birds we took in the woods. However, we have plenty of what we have. Allow me to offer a bit of half-dried meat, fit for a king, or of course a Princess."

She accepted it gratefully, finding it far from dry and emitting a rancid odor, but surprisingly satisfying. The crew had rigged a sail to collect rainwater during the night, and as she drank she wondered aloud to Gormsson that anyone had nerves or energy for the task in such a furious storm.

"The night blow was no worse than we encounter on most crossings," he told her. "The ship's work goes on, and if all allowed ourselves to give in to the storm there'd be none to tend our jobs. Then we'd founder in truth."

His words brought her back to the possible plight of Sigefert, but she kept silent on that matter. "You say we head for Ribe. Will Sigefert...the Northumbrians...will they stay there?"

"Not so. Ribe is a city of merchants and traders. Your Northumbrians are fighters. I will guide them overland to Jelling, where my august grandfather holds Court, and seek for them work more to their liking than bartering furs and fish."

"You mean they will be part of the King's army?"

"Just so, if it be he has a place for them."

And me? Gormsson saw the question in her eyes, but she left it unspoken and he did not try to answer it. Bitterly, she regretted her failure to be set ashore when they'd passed Tenby.

The storm giantess must have taken pity on the wayfarers, for the weather was bright and fair the balance of the trip. Shortly after dawn the fourth day, the lookout on the prow sighted land, and all hands crowded forward to peer eagerly at the hazy speck showing intermittently above the wave tops. Finally it was distinct enough for clear viewing, and the concensus was they had raised the Isle of Sylt, dead on target. The mood in the longboat turned loud and raucous, and crewmembers who had not smiled the whole voyage now smote one another boisterously as they contemplated the pleasant thought of land. But only some of the men in this boat be Danes, thought Tara, and this is their homeland. They'll be returning home, but the Northumbrians will be casting their lot in a foreign and belike inhospitable land.

The course was adjusted northward, and soon the rugged Frisian shore was abeam to starboard, and then dropping astern as they boiled on under full sail for the mainland.

"There be but a scant six or seven leagues more to Denemearc itself," announced the grizzled navigator, allowing himself a brief flicker of a smile. "The shore on the coast is bare from the winter winds, but you'll see greener lands upriver."

"But not much green land, and not so green at that." Gormsson had taken the broadoar, and stood with feet widespread directly behind them. "Denemearc is my birthright, and I'm bound to call it fair, but it wins few beauty prizes with visitors."

Tara heartily concurred, when they came in close enough to see clearly. The landscape was depressingly flat, and seemed to be mostly wasteland, rugged heath, and sand dunes. But, she thought in an effort to lighten her melancholy mood, so might some wild reaches of Dyfed appear to castaways.

As they approached the estuary, two longboats rowed smartly out to greet them, and with a feeling of joy Tara recognized the reassuring figure of Sigefert athwart a forward rowing bench. "And there's your man, Princess," said Gormsson jovially. "You see—a far better sailor than any of us." She hoped Sigefert's boat would come alongside, and perhaps even take her aboard, but he passed with only a cursory wave.

Tara's first view of the touted trading settlement was disappointing. The crowded waterfront consisted of a jumbled cluster of log buildings, none but the watchtowers over a single story in height, jammed so tight behind log palisades she wondered the populace found room to move. The longboats threaded their way through a harbor crammed with vessels of all shapes and sizes. The cluttered beach curved around in a jagged crescent, terminating in a treeless spit dotted with rude animal-hide tents. Gormsson's boat ground to a halt before a conical-roofed watchtower, and just in front of a squat turreted gateway.

Despite her previous ache to have the voyage end, Tara felt an inexplicable letdown from the sudden release of tension, and was oddly reluctant to leave the boat. Gormsson extended his hand across the rail to her. "Come, Princess—best face it straight on," he said with surprising understanding, and she stepped awkwardly out of the beached craft. The sand felt unsteady, as if it moved under her feet, and she stood stock-still to clear her senses.

The Northumbrians were gathered uncertainly about Gormsson, awaiting his guidance. Tara scanned the restless throng, searching for Sigefert, and was unable to suppress the rush of emotion that filled her at the sight of him. His eyes fell on her at the same moment, and he came up quickly and grasped her hand.

"It is good to greet you, Tara," he said with unexpected warmth. "I am glad the seas were kind to you. Your looks are good."

His compliment was far from the truth, she knew. Her hair was caked with ocean salt, and matted past combing out, her clothes streaked and rumpled from the ravages of passage, and her face thin and drawn from her bouts of ocean sickness. But despite knowing he spoke false, she gloried in his flattery.

"I worried for your safety."

Her words were out before she thought, and she found herself speechless to say more. Pray Lug he did not think her a foolish wench, opening her heart so to the first man looking her way.

But her remark seemed to have no untoward effect, for he squeezed her hand and lifted her downcast face. "And I for yours as well, Princess," he said softly. He patted her gently on the head. "May all in this strange land be just as you wish it."

His words seemed full of feeling. He cares for me, she exulted. He'd not have spoken so did he not hold me special. Breathlessly she waited for what he would say next.

But he said no more to her, turning to converse with Gormsson. His pat on the head evoked faint memories, long forgot, dashing her soaring hopes of a moment before. Thus Sire had patted her when she was a small child, to signify fatherly affection. Sigefert did not see her as a woman grown, with ripening affection to offer the one who could capture her heart, but only as a child with adolescent fears, who needed comforting.

Tara expected they'd be put up in Ribe, and could scarce wait to fling her exhausted body onto a pallet. But their apparent host, the Captain of the Port, upon learning his guest was King Gorm's grandson, hastened to put immediate transport at their disposal. "I'll bed down your crew here for the present, young Master, and your personal party can take horse to Jelling at once," he announced. "The trail is good this time of year, and if you leave now you'll reach the necropolis by nightfall." So, bone-weary from the voyage, Tara found herself being tendered only a bite of bread and cheese before the three of them were riding out, on half-tamed little Birka horses, along the main road to the Court city.

In addition to Gormsson and Sigefert, their party included a ten-man escort pressed on them by the Port Captain, to guard the precious person of the royal grandson. "I trow we could defend ourselves if pushed," said Gormsson, but he seemed pleased, and Tara was relieved as well not to face the way's unknown hazards unaccompanied.

They rode three abreast, giving Sigefert his first chance since York to speak at length with Gormsson. "And how may we be welcomed by your King—if he chooses to see us?" he began.

"He'll see us, no fear," said Gormsson confidently. "I am his favorite grandson, for all that I be his only grandson. He'll scarce turn me by without a word."

"But I am not his grandson," said Sigefert reasonably. "Nor my men, nor the Princess. What of us?"

"You forget you saved me from an unmarked grave on a lonely foreign shore. Gorm will not be blind to his debt. He will see the three of us, never fear."

Tara knew she had saved no one, and doubted King Gorm would feel any obligation to her, an outlander and a woman, but thought it best to hold her silence.

"Tell him we are fighting men, and stand ready to join his standard, when and where he wishes." The words were stalwart enow, but betrayed by a tentative note in his voice.

"You will tell him yourself. Rulers in Denemearc stand on little ceremony, and you may be surprised how plain and simple he conducts his affairs. You can tell him everything."

Sigefert's doubts remained unresolved. "And how might he make use of us?"

"As you just said. Any ruler needs experienced fighting men, particularly those who fall in his lap with no work on his part. I cannot say when or where you'll be billeted, but you've my word he'll take you on somehow."

Tara sensed Sigefert's unease at the vagueness of Gormsson's response, but her own uncertainty far exceeded his, for any offer of enlistment to the Northumbrians that the King made scarce would extend to her. He'll have scant need of a woman whose only training is for the queenship, she thought wryly.

The royal necropolis at Jelling was far handsomer than Ribe, and Tara's spirits rose despite her doubts about the future. They had reached Gorm's Hall just before dark, and she was much impressed by the vivid green of the grass, and the thatched roofing of what must be the palace. Its primitive simplicity surprised her, but Gormsson had explained the scarcity of building materials, and she had to admit it looked less forbidding than the somber grey stone of Menevia Castle back home. The approach took them between two great grassy mounds of earth marking the entrance to the palace. Gormsson noticed her curiousity, and pointed out two rune stones planted beside the entryway.

"No need trying to read what's writ there, Princess," he advised. "I have some scraps of learning, and was born in the shadow of the palace, but even I struggle to decipher it. They taught me as a boy that it says 'King Gorm erected this memorial to his wife Thyri, who was the adornment of Denemearc.' She lies buried in a chamber deep down inside that mound to the south."

The simple inscription, solemnizing the massive mounds built by a lonely monarch to memorialize his lost love, struck a responsive chord in Tara's heart, and she swalled hard at the thought. "He must have loved his Queen dearly," she said, when she could trust herself to speak.

"I trow he did. Queen Thyri was claimed by the gods before her time, and he has taken no other wife to him since."

"What a lovely thing to write! He must be a good man."

Gormsson laughed. "Do not count on that. He is King, and kings must take care not to be too good, lest they lose the throne. He is fair, much of the time, and that's enow to ask for."

The unprepossessing structure serving as King Gorm's palace was larger than it had appeared at first sight. The arched central pile rose two stories high, and from it extended four large single-story wings. Gormsson passed by the main entrance, and took them with great assurance around to the side, where he bade them dismount at a small postern entry and secure their mounts, then led them into the building.

"We have come to the best part of the palace," he told them. "The cooking wing. It is where I stayed as a child when we came here. My happiest memories are of the wondrous smells from the kitchen hearth. We'll find safe haven here, and after we settle in they'll take up word of our arrival. When the King gets over his shock at our arrival, I trow he'll make space for us in his audience schedule."

Tara's bones ached cruelly from the ride, and she was near total exhaustion from lack of rest, but the aromatic odors were too enticing to ignore. Six or eight women worked in the low-ceilinged room, one of them kneading dough in a wooden trencher, while another baked flat loaves over the embers of an open fire. A third stirred the bubbling contents of a huge iron cauldron suspended over the hearth pit, another baked platters of fish or meat in the oven, and yet another roasted what looked to be a whole pig, turning the rosy carcass on a great spit. A half-grown girl ladled liquid from a vat like those in Menevia's dairy, filling large horns set into a rack at her feet. The panorama evoked such nostalgic memories of Tara's childhood in the kitchens at home that she could not have left had her life been in the balance.

Gormsson escorted them expansively to a low bench against the wall, and bade them sit. "Food will be brought us very soon," he assured them. "Freya smiles on us—we arrived at mealtime."

Sigefert looked dubious. "Is it meet to steal the King's hospitality without invitation from him, or even his knowing?"

Gormsson beckoned the women to serve them, as he answered. "The old runestones praise liberality in the kitchen above all other virtues," he told them. "The Skalds write 'when a guest does arrive, chilled to the very knees from his journey, he must be given fire, food, and dry clothes.' Guests we be, and whether chilled to the knees I cannot say, but sure we arrive from a journey. No household in Denemearc would turn us out, or deny us the best from its cooking pot. Eat! When we are done, we shall sleep."

Seldom in Tara's life had she savored a meal more pleasurably. She had forgotten how hungry she was, until the steaming meat stew was placed before them, to be followed by trenchers of savory baked fish, bowls of fresh hot bread, and horns of foaming milk. The hearth flame roared its cosy welcome, the warmth and fragrant odors created a delicious drowsiness, and a warm feeling of security she'd not known since leaving home, and she fought to stay awake sufficiently to finish her meal. The last she remembered was being scooped up in the strong arms of Sigefert, and deposited on a soft pallet, where she sank into bottomless slumber.

She was awakened, in the dead of night, not knowing why. She opened her eyes with difficulty, seeing naught in the darkness of the chamber. She rubbed her eyes drowsily, and looked about her once more.

Atheurin was by her side, and e'en in the dark she could see him plainly. His presence gave her no surprise, and she followed unquestioningly as he led her into a great hall. The view was blurred, as if she dreamed, but she knew she was not asleep. She realized gradually that the hall was not empty—there was a throne at the end, and a figure sat the throne. His face grew more distinct, and she saw that it was Clydog, King of Cymru. He was speaking to a stranger.

She approached, and as her eyes shifted to the stranger she realized he was no stranger at all, but a Dane she'd seen at the Gloucester encampment. He made no sound, but somehow she knew he was reporting that she'd fled to Denemearc—and with Sigefert. Then Clydog spoke, and though she heard no sound she knew he was swearing a mighty oath to send to Denemearc and find her, and bring her back to throw her into the bower like a prisoner, as his wife. She turned in extreme dismay to Atheurin, but he was gone, as she knew he would be.

She sat bolt upright. Was it but a disturbing dream, brought on by the stress of the voyage just ended, or a vision from the gods of a real happening? If Clydog plotted so in fact, why did not Atheurin speak with her...bring her solace...advise her what she must do? Never had he come to her in the past just as a silent apparition. It was beyond thought that he'd done so now!

No—she'd seen no true vision, but only a fool's dream, and one best forgot.

Chapter 20

The mists surrounding her were annoying, and she shook her head to clear her vision. Then came another annoyance—a rude buffeting that flung her unpleasantly about. Irritated at being snatched from sleep in this manner, she tried to lash out at her assailant, but her arms seemed to lay flaccid at her side, as though mired in quicksand. Frustration at her comotose state drove her at last to open her eyes.

Her perplexity cleared, as she realized where she was. Her pallet was in an alcove off the kitchen, and the mists arose from a steaming cauldron over the hearth. She saw immediately the root of her annoyance; it was Sigefert, bending over her, and reaching out as if to shake her again. In the intimate environment of her bedchamber, it seemed to her as if his strong bronzed body had attained a sort of masculine magnificence, and she found herself strangely unable to speak.

"Arouse yourself, Tara," he commanded, his words ill-formed as though he, too, had just awakened. "They let us laze abed, with half the morn gone. This is no day for me to play the dullard, or you either." His firm hand shook her again. "Up with you! We've a king to see."

Collecting her wits yet again, Tara sat up and threw off the prickly woolen coverlet—only to snatch it instantly back, at the discovery that she was stark naked underneath. The shock brought her fully awake. How to explain her state? Who had disrobed her while she lay half-unconscious with exhaustion? Who?

Sigefert saw the shock in her eyes, and laughed. "Yes, girl, I stripped you for the couch. Your garments were caked with sea salt and trail grime. You could never have greeted Gorm so. I had the women wash them as well as you. Your maidenhood was at no risk, if that be your worry; I ached for sleep as much as you. By Freyda, your trim body was sorely tempting, but I could think of naught but rest." His blue eyes held hers, and his look of frank admiration, telling her he had thought of more than sleep, was unexpectedly arousing. Her cheeks flamed, and she looked down hastily lest she reveal her confused emotions.

What had taken place, while she lay naked and helpless under his bold appraisal? Had Sigefert indeed contented himself with feasting his eyes on her, or had he gone further...? And if he had, would she have known? She looked up, flustered by the intensity of his gaze, knowing her thoughts were all too obvious. He smiled roguishly at the tangle of emotions in her expression.

"Do not fret, lass, that our weariness robbed you this time. Another time it will be different, that I promise you."

Tara felt embarrassed and humiliated, more at the clear meaning of his words than at knowing he had stripped her bare while she slept. Confused, and feeling guiltily disloyal to Crosbey that she could allow Sigefert's words to arouse her so, she felt unable to handle such bandinage. "Where are my clothes, then?" she demanded uncertainly, tugging the covers more tightly about her.

"There." Following his eyes, she saw her clothes neatly folded on a bench against the wall, cleaner than she had imagined they'd ever be again. "I'm off to find Gormsson, so make yourself ready. We may be called before the King on scant notice." Before she could respond, he was gone.

The kitchen women seemed to ignore the episode, but their probing eyes told her they wondered what sort of creature graced their presence, and how the young Prince meant to use this trophy he'd brought back from the sea. Little do they know Gormsson's complete lack of interest in her as a woman, she thought, unaware how wrong her conclusion was on that matter.

She and Sigefert were finished with their hasty breakfast, and he was striding restlessly about the cooking area, when Gormsson arrived and flopped down on the bench beside her.

"Where have you been?" Sigefert demanded irritably. "The women knew not where you'd gone! We thought you dead."

"The gods refused to allow me near you," said Gormsson lightly. "You could not be spied above your covers, and I concluded you'd clapped the Tarnkappe on your thick head to become invisible. Princess Tara lay in deeper sleep than Brunhild, and I was no Sigurd to wake her."

"Where were you?"

"To see my grandfather, as you asked."

Tara's quick glance noted the mix of excitement and concern on Sigefert's face. "What did he say?" he asked, striving for calm. "Has he a mind to put us on his rolls? What did he say?"

"What did he say? Well, let me think. First, he said he was glad to see me. Not that he put it quite so—actually he said it was high time he got his men and longboats back."

"Did you not tell him all your boats were lost save one?"

Gormsson laughed ruefully. "He'll learn that in our next conversation."

"Well? And what else?"

"What else? Well, he said it was about time I started earning my keep in his army."

"Gormsson! Cease this running around the runestone! I want to know if he'll have us in his forces. What did he say to that?"

The mocking expression disappeared from Gormsson's face. "To tell truth, he said he has but slight regard for defeated warriors."

"Defeated warriors! Because we refused to spend ourself in certain death against a force thrice our size, he'll not see us? Well, I have a message for your king!" Sigefert's expression was black as a thunder-cloud, and Tara knew he'd explode if he heard more. At all odds, she must prevent him from burning his last pont to a satisfactory future for himself and his men.

"He has not refused to see you," she reminded him quietly. She turned to Gormsson, her eyes imploring him to support her in her question. "He will see Sigefert, will he not? Was it not just his way of not granting favors too easy? He will give an audience when he's ready, is that not so?"

Gormsson's eyes softened at the overt supplication in hers. "Of course he will see us," he reassured her. "He may not even know it yet himself, but when I tell what doughty fighting men I've brought, he cannot turn them down, for Gorm never has enough soldiers. But it cannot be today. I need a little more time, good friends."

And with that they had to be content. Sigefert took the delay badly, striding about like a caged bull, then bursting out upon the grounds and pacing furiously, as though to force the audience by the sheer power of his nervous energy. Tara felt deep sympathy for his travails, and sought to put his mind on other things.

"May we not use the time to bring your forces from Ribe?" she suggested. "If you'd have the King offer a commission, he must see your Northumbrians, to know for himself what fine fighting men they will be in his force. You'll have time enow to get them and return."

"Nonsense!" he growled. "The moment I take horse to Ribe, that's when he'll send for us." But she caught the thoughtful look on his face, and was wise enough to let the rest come from him.

"No," he said shortly. "I must hold myself in readiness here at Jelling. Kings like not to be kept spinning their thumbs." A speculative expression came over his face. "You could fetch them in my stead."

Her surprise was total. Would he actually entrust her—after all his taunting her as naught but a woman, fit only for the hearth—with such a mission? She wondered if he jested, but his was not a jesting mood, and there was no hint of ridicule in his face.

"Do you mean it? You would trust me so far? Or do you but make light of me?"

"Why not? Are you not a Crown Princess, trained to lead fighting men? Do my Vikings not know as much? Did they not see you as a hunter? They'd be but a small command for you beside the army of Dyfed." He chucked her casually under the chin, and she felt a thrill of excitement at his touch, but was careful to hide such womanly feelings. "As Odin is my witness," he declared, "I've never been so serious. Have you not the stomach for the venture?"

"I have stomach enow for it," she retorted, womenly feelings banished. "My resolve is full as stout as yours. See you to their quartering when they get here, then, and I'll go."

She left that very morn, in company with the Port Captain's returning escort. "I'll give you a note to the Captain," Gormsson had said, "and Sigefert can write an order to his men." He had added hopefully that he might accompany her, but Sigefert had vetoed that curtly, and only later had thought to add that, with Gormsson not here to press Gorm, there'd be no audience.

The sun was still climbing when they set out, with provisions coaxed from the scullery maids and a horse from the royal stables for Tara. The land, seeming so barren and forbidding only yesterday, now smiled on them as they rode. So much for controlling her destiny, she thought. She knew not what the future might hold, for her as well as Sigefert, but would savor the day without thought of her uncertain tomorrows.

The afternoon was still young when they rode into the Port Captain's tidy compound. On reading Gormsson's note, he sprang to her bidding, arranging for the Northumbrians to leave at first light the next day. "And now for your quarters, Lady," he said genially. "My sleeping room is yours. We've no palace here, such as you've come from, but you'll be snug and safe." She was reluctant to oust him from his quarters, but knowing he'd prefer it so she accepted the offer graciously.

His cabin, overlooking the harbor, was surprisingly liveable. The room below, where he conducted his affairs, doubled as eating chamber, and she was expected for the evening meal. He had donned a fur-trimmed tunic in her honor, and had a well-scrubbed look. The table was spartan, but each place had its socketed horn of milk, the baked fish had an inviting aroma, and the bread was hot and tasty. Her host had extended himself, and she said so.

"I was surprised to see a Briton Princess," he said. "Have you visited my country before?"

"Nay, Sire," she replied. "This is my first visit. We'd not be here now, had not the Wessex king given us such a hot sendoff. I am Cymri, from the west of Britain, and the King of Wessex seeks to invade my homeland. He is our enemy, as he is enemy of the Danes."

"How come you to speak our tongue, Lady? Few Britons make the effort to do so."

She told him something of herself, why she had studied his language, how she came to be here. Then, because he reminded her strongly of her father, she unburdened herself to him.

"I know not what my future holds in your land," she confessed for-lornly, as her tale came to an end. "Even Sigefert's Northumbrians, and they be Danes by blood, find little welcome in King Gorm's court. If brave and capable fighting men, tried in many a battle, and prevailing in all save this last against overwhelming force, find no door open, how can there be any need for an untried lass—no matter that I am trained almost since birth to the sword?"

His seamed face warmed in sympathetic concern. "You say King Gorm makes no place for your Sigefert? Then why do you take your Northumbrians to the necropolis?"

"We're not yet sure he'll turn them away. Prince Gormsson tries to talk his grandfather into a change of mind. He and Sigefert thought if the King just could see them—how stout they are, what seasoned fight-ers, the look of them—he might change his mind."

The Port Captain smiled his relief. "If the young Prince says he'll talk the King into enlisting them, depend on it. That young Sir has few years on him, but he can move mountains, and is the pride of his grandfather's eye. Gormsson's father, Crown Prince Harald, rubs sparks with the King; men say they are too alike. So all favor fastens on his grandson. The lad knows it well, but takes care never to overplay it." A thought struck him. "You said you rescued him from a stranding, and more? Then take heart: King Gorm will find a way to make repayment, in his own time. He likes not to be in any man's debt."

There was more conversation, but it bore on other things, and Tara was too happy at his reassurance to pay it close attention. She excused herself as soon as good manners and gratitude for the Port Captain's hospitality permitted, and repaired gratefully to her pallet.

On her arrival at the Northumbrian compound next morn, one of them stepped forward from the others, and she recognized the big Viking who had fought Sigefert.

"Oddune!" She was pleased to recall his name. "I am happy to see you again. Is your leg well healed, then?"

"Healing. Not yet healed." His response was civil, but lacking in warmth. Behind him a hostler held the reins of two horses saddled for the trail. So he'd be riding with her.

Oddune followed her eyes. "You and I will go mounted; you as leader, I because I cannot yet walk well. The rest go afoot."

"Are you not in charge of the force, Oddune?" she asked.

"I have been so, Princess. Now you are put in command."

His resentment was palpable. How could he be otherwise, she asked herself. Belike he saw her as weak, no warrior but only a lass, and a foreigner as well, usurping his place by her wiles with Sigefert. If only he knew how little mind Sigefert had for her.

She must bolster his pride, if she could; she had few friends as it was in this forbidding land. "I am not leader, Oddune," she told him. "I am a messenger, who brings tidings from Jelling and knows the trail. Let us ride together, and I'll relate the matter bedeviling Sigefert."

They kept their horses to a walk, pacing themselves to the marching speed of their men, and Tara explained at length how they were at the mercy of King Gorm's whim, with any hope coming only from his feeling for his grandson. Oddune was unresponsive.

"Would your men like to hear from you how the land lays?" she asked when they pulled up at midday. "I wat you can explain to them better than I."

To her surprise, Oddune declined. "I've not been at Jelling," he said abruptly, "and can know only what you tell me now. They will want to hear it direct from you." Not wishing to go against him, she agreed, though uneasy at her imperfect command of the language. When he called them together she scanned their faces, both surprised at how many there were and unsettled by their impassive faces. It must offend these veterans to learn their fate from a woman, she knew, and scarce could blame them for that. Girding herself for the ordeal, she spoke out, groping for words at first, but picking up confidence as she got into it.

They listened silently. When she was finished, she awaited questions, but there were none. They simply turned away and formed up again for the march.

Disconcerted, she looked to Oddune for explanation. "It was as if they understood naught."

"They understood well enough. They knew before you spoke it would be a chancy thing."

"But how could they know that? Sigefert looked to Gorm to seize the chance of recruiting an experienced force. He must need fighting men."

"They are Danes. Gorm is a Dane. Were any of them king, they would see it as does Gorm. Why should he jump with joy at turntail refugees crawling to him, begging for another chance? If Gorm puts us on his rolls, it will be for his grandson, not because he wants us."

Thinking about it as she rode glumly along, Tara saw the logic of his view. Why indeed would any monarch welcome recruits with a history of defeat? Kings needed troops who could win. Mayhap a canker takes seed in fighting men who flee the battlefield, destroying both their self-respect and their will to conquer, even infecting others barracked with them. Gorm was an experienced ruler, and belike he read this blight on Sigefert's Northumbrians as an auger of their future utility in his service.

Beset by this pernicious thought, though she realized it was absurd, it was a discouraged Tara who led the taciturn troop into the barracks area. It stood nigh to the palace, behind a circular rampart higher than a mounted horseman. They entered through a tunneled opening, and proceeded along a dirt street between two quadrangles, each formed by four buildings around an open court. The hour was late, but there was activity in the near buildings.

"The fates are kind," said Gormsson with a welcoming grin, as he indicated where Oddune's force would go, then escorted Tara through a low gabled entrance. "Gorm's house guards are south at Ravning Enge just now, clearing a bridge site at the Vejle River, and their barracks lie empty. A month earlier we'd all have slept under the stars. Even so, I had Loki's own time getting permission to use them. Come, Princess, be introduced to your quarters."

As he spoke, she felt his hand grasp her arm. Startled, she looked up at him, and was disconcerted by the intensity of his expression. His clear blue eyes bore into hers with a directness she found oddly upsetting, and she looked down in embarrassment.

"I missed you, girl," he said huskily. "The light went out of my day while you were gone. The moon refused to show her face, and I was miserable. I fear'd you'd not return. I'll...we'll not let you out of sight again." He sighed deeply, and his serious demeanor gave way to his usual jocular attitude. "Come see, child," he said, in an entirely different tone. "Quarters fit for a Queen."

Where was Sigefert? She was far more concerned about his where-abouts than her sleeping area, but she felt that in his present strange mood Gormsson would not welcome questions about the Northumbrian. Besides, he still held her tightly, and she had no choice but to follow.

"Here we are," he announced, throwing the door wide and drawing her inside. "The better part is, you've this lovely chamber for your use." He hesitated. "The worse part is, we share it. However," he went on hurriedly, "you'll find it better than the sleeping area we shared in the longboat. My only question to you is: will you be able to bear my company?" His tone was bantering, but she caught a plea in his eyes she'd not seen before, and he looked so young and shy she could not bear to hurt him. Later, she decided. Later, I'll tell him—but not right away.

His manner turned brisk, his distasteful task done, and she knew he was embarrrassed at his own temerity. He's scarce older than I, she thought, and unskilled at the language of dalliance. She liked him the better for his inexperience, and thought oddly of Clydog, comparing his boorishness and misshapen build with Gormsson's kindness and clean-limbed young body. How sad Prince Gormsson was not Cadell's heir, rather than Clydog, she thought, and at once banished the unworthy notion. Gormsson was but a good friend. She closed her eyes, seeing in memory another good friend who had come so close to being her lover. Oh, Cross, her heart cried in longing, why did the gods snatch you so cruelly from my arms?

The scene faded, and she still wished to know Sigefert's whereabouts. "Where is he, Gormsson?" she managed. "Sigefert—why is he not here?"

A look that could have been guilt flashed across Gormsson's mobile face, to disappear at once. "A great opportunity for him!" he said. "I arranged for him to meet Jarl Bjornsson, who commands the Revning Enge unit, and they rode out there at morn. If the Guard Commander takes to Sigefert, he could persuade my grandfather to make a place for the refugees." He looked at her woebegone face, and some of the lightness left his. "Did I take too much on myself, girl?"

"Not so; it was a happy thought, and can but help." But she was unable to hide her disappointment. "When will he return? How can we best use our time until he gets back? Can you try Gorm once more? Mayhap he's had time to reflect on the great prize he rejects."

"I'll go ask him, and come back to tell what he says." Gormsson turned abruptly and left, before she could say more. And I did not even thank him for the barracks, she thought ruefully. He cannot be blamed if he tires of doing so much, and with no proper thanks from me.

Then, belatedly, she realized how he'd thought to be thanked, and her heart sank.

Gormsson's return was delayed, and Tara expected he'd thought better of his boldness in thinking to share her quarters, but when he did get back he burst in on her excitedly, scarce able to contain his news. "You'll think me an ignorant changeling," he said, unable to suppress his jubilation. "I had to bring you the tidings just yesterday that Gorm wants no part of the Northumbrians, growling that he'll have me flogged if I continue urging him. And today, what?" He took her hands. "I have been proven the King of Liars!"

Tara could not trust the hope that wanted to fill her heart, lest she be disappointed again. "Proven how? What is it? Tell me, Gormsson—let off torturing me! What did your grandfather say?"

Gormsson beamed with pride. "He'll see Sigefert at midday tomorrow, and may have a place for him. He'd not say what it is, but it's something big—I could see that plain, from the way he spoke."

"But Sigefert's down south with your Jarl! How will we get him word to come back?"

"By Asgard—I forgot!" Gormsson's rueful expression was ludicrous. "I suppose it falls to me to fetch him back." He smiled sheepishly. "So, Princess, you sleep alone after all. You must know, I could not have mustered the courage to sleep here. Not that I'd not jump at the chance, if you gave me an ertog of encouragement." He looked at her hopefully.

She gave his arm a friendly squeeze. Why, he has the look of Crosbey when he talks so, she thought, and they're of an age. Her mind flashed back to the way Crosbey looked, his warmth of manner, his faithful devotion…his undying love. Enough—she must thrust such bittersweet remembrances aside. "If I believed half what you say, I'd be addle-pated. Now be on your way, and take all my grateful thanks with you, to speed your passage."

He deserved more than that from her. She'd have to express her appreciation better than those few words. "It was very kind of you to go speak again to your grandfather, and don't think I'm not grateful. You're the only one who could have done it, and we'd be lost without your help—for that and so many other kind deeds to us…to me. You are more than a friend!"

His face crimsoned, and he stood motionless, unable to respond. On impulse, Tara pulled him close, stretched up, and put her lips lightly to his. "You do me honor to wish me to stay with you, Prince," she whispered. "And I cannot deny, the invitation is tempting. But you must know how impossible it is."

He found his voice at last. "Sigefert?" he asked huskily.

Taken aback, she knew not how to respond. Could he be right? Had she such a feeling for Sigefert, not admitting it to herself? She stared at him dumbly.

"Then I'll ride out and fetch him back to you," he said, reading the answer in her face. At the door, he turned. "If he fails to see how bright Valfreya smiles on him, I'll slice his thick head from his body." The tone was joking, but his expression, as the door closed, had never been more serious.

Tara was stunned by what awaited the three when they were admitted to Gorm's audience chamber. She thought for a moment that the King hadn't yet arrived, until Gormsson nudged them toward a rudely garbed figure, slouched in a fur-covered chair. He wore wrinkled boots of unscraped hide, into which were tucked loose trousers of undyed wool, and a plain reddish tunic bearing no marks of rank. His unkempt hair perhaps once had been blond, but grey streaks had turned it dull, and it was cropped as carelessly as that of any taeog back in Cymru. But to Tara's surprise, he was not an old man; she realized he likely was younger and fitter than her father.

He regarded them silently, chin sunk disinterestedly in one hand. Tara wondered fleetingly if she should kneel, but Gormsson and Sigefert remained erect, so she stood with them.

"You," he said finally, tilting his head toward Sigefert. "You're the fierce freebooter who terrorized the Saxon coast?"

Sigefert hesitated. He wonders if an answer be called for, thought Tara. Belike Gorm has this way of belittling those who come before him. But the King waited, apparently for a reply.

"We harried the coast of Britain," Sigefert said at last. "With Hasteinn. And we raided along Normandy these three years past. Tales of our raids there may have reached you."

Why doesn't Sigefert say more, she thought impatiently. Why not relate how we ran Alfred's blockade? Or how he rescued the King's own grandson from shipwreck and inevitable capture by the Franks? Why is he so tongue-tied? Fretting to tell of Sigefert's exploits, she came near speaking herself, but held back, belatedly realizing how unseemly it would be for a woman to speak unbid in the King's presence—or to usurp Sigefert's authority.

"Your men—what manner of fighters do you rank them? True Vikings, such as we breed in Denemearc, or soft like women in the warm clime of Britain?"

Sigefert stared back at Gorm angrily. The King stared back, a mocking smile on his face, making no effort to end the awkward silence that followed on his dismissive words.

"If you'd like a test," Sigefert began at last, his voice soft in a way Tara knew masked his fierce anger, "you may set any in your force against me, with broadsword or battle-axe—or with bare hands if you will." He hesitated a moment. "Any man—common soldier, or the King himself!"

Tara gasped. He'd thrown a raw challenge in the King's teeth! But he was not done. "You speak of being soft like a woman. We've a woman in our force, who stands before you," tossing his head to indicate Tara, "who'd be glad to show your Danes how soft a woman is." He gestured toward the entry, where stood an accoutred guard, massive but markedly overweight, with fierce drooping moustaches, and thick braids that fell down the sides of his chest. "Perhaps yon sentry would hazard crossing his sword with the Princess Tara here, your Majesty, that both of you may gauge the softness of her blade. I will avouch that she may make shift to change your view."

Tara froze in astonishment, and not a little horror, at the provocative and all but insulting words. Automatically her eyes darted toward the guard, checking the heft of his sword, appraising his size and probable strength, assessing his likely endurance for a protracted bout, probing for any point of weakness to exploit if, against all odds, a fight should materialize. She felt her hand tighten and prepare, and stepped shoulder to shoulder with Sigefert, easing her sword in its scabbard. Her posture stiffened, and her weight shifted to the balls of her feet. Had Sigefert taken leave of his senses? At best, the King would accept Sigefert's bold challenge; at worst he'd clap Sigefert in irons, and toss him into whatever passed for a dungeon in this accursed land. She stared at Gorm, waiting for the inevitable explosion.

It did not come. Instead, the bleak smile on his hard face broadened, and he emitted a snort of humorless laughter. "We'll do better than that," he said. "If you and your band, and this mettlesome young Valkyr whose valor you hold so high, aspire to become Einheriar and feast with Oden in Asgard, we'll give you Northmen to fight. The sooner all of you may reach Valhalla," he added with a grin. "Will that assuage your bat-tle-lust, Northumbrian—and that of your shapely young maid?"

His eyes brushed over Tara, appraising her, then shifted back to Sigefert. He waited for some reply, but none was forthcoming, and he continued. "I've a fortress to build, north on the banks of the Limfjord, to serve as a rampart against King Harald Haarfager of West Norway. It's not a post for faint hearts. Are your Codbiters and Stiffbeards men enow for the task?"

Sigefert returned his cold gaze, stare for stare. "And the name of this cold fortress?"

"Aggersborg."

If Sigefert was taken aback at this news, he failed to show it. "I'll call my men together and put it up to them. For me, I accept, but I cannot speak for freemen."

Gorm turned aside, and began examining a wood carving at his elbow. Apparently the audience was at an end, for Gormsson beckoned them to leave. Tara could not believe the lack of Court manners, that they would not bend knee and back away, but just walk out as if they quitted a horse-byrne. This was Denemearc, and she'd best learn their ways if it was to be her homeland.

But was it to be her homeland? She realised that her future was far from settled. Hurrying, she caught up with the men, whose long strides had left her behind while she mused.

Gormsson led the way outside. "We'll not be overheard out here," he said, his tone grave. "You need to reck the facts of this posting before you rede your Northumbrians, however restless they may be at their inaction. I'd best tell you of Aggersborg."

"What, then?" asked Sigefert, clearly impatient to be about it. "It sounds a lively duty, very like what we've been at these three years past. Is there something Gorm chose not to tell us?"

"Aye, there is. Aggersborg is on Gotland Norrejyske, on the upper tip of Denemearc, and will be a great fortress defending our northern border.

Will be—not 'is'. Jarl Bjornsson told me something of it in private last night, when I rode to fetch you. Gorm himself told me more before he summoned you. First off, though the ramparts are up, the barracks are scarce begun. Much of your soldiering will be carpentering."

"And we've done that before. We can do it again."

"Second, there's yet no town outside. There's a name for it—Lindholm Hoje—nothing more. There'll be scant diversion for your men this first year, or longer."

"There were few diversions in the longboats, but we survived then, and we can survive now. What else?"

"The third thing you'll not much like, though I misdoubt you'll be surprised. You've not yet Gorm's complete trust, so he sets me to watch you."

"What does that mean?"

"I'm to be posted as your Lieutenant, with my men. Gorm reasons that if you have schemes of your own, I'll learn of them in time to argue you back to loyalty, or report you to Jelling."

Sigefert pondered that. "Well," he said at last, "I cannot fault him for that. My speech with him was not that of a friend. Come along with us then, and enjoy yourself."

"I'll not enjoy it. I have little appetite for the cold northern Isle of Gotland. My grandfather could be rubbing my nose in it for losing his ships, rather than sending another. But at least I'm the devil you know instead of one you don't. And it seems we have no choice."

"Is that all your conditions, then?"

"No, there's yet a fourth, one I was saving for last." Gormsson hesitated, uncertain how to put it, deciding finally to come out with it direct.

"No women may go to Aggersborg."

Sigefert jerked back as if struck. "No women!" His eyes went to Tara, though what was behind them she could not tell. "Tara cannot accompany us? She's a warrior, not a woman. I told Gorm as much. She goes!"

"She does not go. I vow to you that Gorm will hold to that, and even Loki barring the gates of Valhalla would not shake him. Let me explain how it is in our fortresses. The men live in a common central hall, about 75 to a barrack, sleeping on a long bench around the sides. The rules are strict: only men, and they between 18 and 50, all must avenge a fellow as a brother, never speak a word of fear, all booty even divided, all news goes to the leader first, no absence over three nights running, no vengeance on a fellow. And a few more I've forgot. The fortress soldiers are a brotherhood, as in a monastary."

"Those are good rules for a fighting force. We hold to near the same in the longboats."

"Except for that one final rule: no women may enter, ever."

It took them both to restrain Sigefert from rushing back into the throne room to hurl King Gorm's offer in his teeth. If Tara could not step across its threshold, then no more would he! Curse him for a craven if he'd allow any man, fancy Danish king or no, to decide who would be in his force! Tara's heart was near bursting with pride at this token of his feeling for her, though whether it came from desire for her company or stubbornness she was not certain.

But she would not—could not—allow him to burn his bridges in this unfriendly land! He must not turn his back on such an opportunity. If he rejected this offer, he'd get no other. He must consider not just himself (and her, if she read him aright), but the men who trusted in him as well. She would shut out any thought of what would become of her. He had to accept!

The tension was becoming unbearable, when Gormsson spoke up. "I knew of this problem yesterday," he announced, "and I sent a messenger to my great-uncle in Fredericia. He is a trader—a merchant. Indeed, he is a rich merchant, as befits the brother of my mother's father, with many storehouses bulging with goods and many ships that trade along the rivers of the Rus. He is rich, but he grows old." He turned to Tara. "And he has great need for just such assistance as you can provide."

"What are you suggesting?" demanded Tara, bewildered and not a little suspicious over this new direction their talks were taking. "What sort of help could I render him? I have no training as a trader; what could I do for him?"

By this time both Sigefert and Tara were staring questioningly at him, and he found it hard to explain. "Well…many things. He needs…that is…" He collected his thoughts for a better start. "He is an aging man, and his wife of many years who was his right hand in record-keeping died last year. I'm sure he's found none who can be trusted to replace her. He will jump at the chance."

Tara forebore to ask how Gormsson could know so much of Fredericia, when he was fresh from a long sea-quest. Above all, she wished to put no obstacles in Sigefert's path, and it seemed he'd not accept the Aggersborg post until he was sure she had a safe haven. I must pretend excitement at this, she thought, and try to believe Gormsson's unlikely story of how much his uncle—who belike had not been sent any message at all—needs me and wants me.

"It sounds a fine place for me," she assured the doubtful Sigefert, pretending a satisfaction she was far from feeling. "This is the best way to find a home where I'm truly needed, as Aggersborg will be for you and your Northumbrians. Let it be settled. Make your plans."

"It's no spot for you, girl." Sigefert's voice was firm, but she sensed irresolution, and with a sinking in her heart knew her deception had half convinced him.

"A year is not long," she went on bravely. "By year's end the town will be built, you heard Gormsson say as much, and then I'll come—if you still want me," she forced herself to add.

"Still want you? By Odin, naught do I want more! And if you don't show up, I'll come to get you, no matter if the King himself says me nay." He grasped Gormsson by the arm. "This uncle of yours—he's a good man…to be trusted?"

"He is. And too infirm to do more than hold your Princess safe, while you ready Lindholm Hoje to be a fit place for her."

Tara stepped away as the two arranged her future. She knew she had no real claim on Sigefert, no cause to make him sacrifice his future on her behalf. Even the concern he showed now about her well being in Fredericia was more than she had any right to expect. Why, then was she so unaccountably sad?

When they fell silent, Sigefert turned to Tara. "It seems I am caught up betwixt my men and my Lady," he said, his mind apparently made up. "But I say it again. If you fail to come at year's end, I'll be back to take you, by force if need be." He took her hand, and his eyes burned into hers. "I made you a promise that morn by the scullery, when you lay bare beneath your bedding. It's a promise I mean to keep!"

He grasped her shoulders in his strong hands, and Gormsson, sensing his depth of emotion, moved apart from them. Then his arms enfolded her, and she felt for the first time the raw power of his pent-up feelings at the thought of losing her. "Mark you, my love," he declared, his voice husky. "You are mine! We separate now, for a time, because the Fates will it, but you are mine always—and never forget it!" He tilted her back until her spine was near to breaking, and his lips found and pressed against hers with an urgency that left her breathless. Things were happening too fast for her. She held rigid for an instant, willing her body to resist, but the force of his assault was overpowering. Gradually, despite her resolve, she felt herself responding, returning his kisses, pressing her body against his. For an instant, she was lost in the exquisite fulfillment of the moment, thrilling at the fullness of her new found feeling.

The next instant he released her, and turned brusquely away. She watched unsteadily, excited and disconsolate by turns, until he turned the corner out of her sight. He's back to the business of the moment, she knew, his thoughts turned entirely inward to what he must tell his Northumbrians. So quickly do the passions of men rise and fall, she realized, weeping within, while women, weak creatures that they are, must find strength to endure the agony of parting.

So she would go, suppressing the pain inside her. Go, to an unknown and unwanted place called Fredericia, to take up the dreary existence of a trader in the service of one who neither knew her nor wanted her. Go, far away from her only protector, belike never to see him again despite his passionate vows. Go, and try to live on the futile hope that time would dull the ache of her broken heart.

CHAPTER 21

It was a warm day, as weather in Denemearc went, when Tara arrived in Fredericia. The clothing Gormsson had hastily cobbled up for her was caked with dust from the trail. The men-at-arms waited at a distance, impatient to start their return trip, as Tara walked up the log path to the largest house in the trading compound, and knocked at the door, not thinking how her appearance would startle her host. The brown tunic belted at her waist, the blue cape fastened at the shoulder with large silver pin, and the bronze helmet encasing her red-gold hair, had been parting gifts from Gormsson. "You may as well appear for what you are, girl," he had said as he personally pinned the tunic in place, "a warrior who just happens to be a lass as well." Supplementing her own slim broadsword buckled at her side, he had accoutred her with a smaller version of the Viking's broad-axe, and a bossed wooden buckler. A leathern bag, dangling now from her shoulder, held her scanty personal baggage.

Bentorm's face showed a comical look of dismay as he read Gormsson's proferred letter of introduction, and was given to understand that the militaristic creature before him was to be his housekeeper. In a land of near giants, Bentorm was painfully slight, towered over half a head by Tara, and with her sturdy build dwarfing his thin frame. He wore a loose-fitting tunic with high neck and full sleeves, and a bright red fur-trimmed cap perched atop his snowy-white hair. Sharply waxed moustachios upturned at the tips, bright ferret's eyes, and a severely pointed beard, gave him a look of mock ferocity, but he had the hollow cheeks of an old man. His ill-concealed distress at Tara's arrival made him appear almost ludicrous, and she decided he most closely resembled the tree-elf pictured in the old book Mama once read to her at bedtime. She stifled a smile, miserable as she was, at his confusion.

He read the letter once, carefully, then again. That done, he stood courteously aside and admitted her to his home.

Tara's position in Bentorm's house was not set forth at all by him, and its slow clarification over the passage of several days required much trial-and-error, coupled with forceful initiative on her part. The first night, her host invited her to share his table, but for the most part the meal passed in silence, and she had ample opportunity to note the slatternly behavior of the serving maid. There were clods of mud on the unswept floor, and through the open kitchen door she saw the scrawny cook's torn kerchief and badly stained apron, and absorbed the penetrating odor of her unwashed body. Tara's pervasive impression was of an unsupervised household staff, gotten far out of the old man's control. This, she decided, was where she'd concentrate her efforts until Bentorm could determine how best to employ her, and the work would take her mind off the desolation of her separation from Sigefert.

At the outset, she tried to encourage more neatness and cleanliness among the household staff, but her tentative suggestions elicited only resentful mutterings, and the slovenly service continued. Clearly, stronger measures were called for, to secure for Bentorm the comfort and good service he deserved.

After a particularly unsavory meal of underdone pork and watery porridge, Tara summoned the grumbling servants in a body to check off a litany of their shortcomings that she'd observed. When she was finished, all of them filed back into the kitchen except the gaunt cook. Fierce resentment flaring in her tone, she objected furiously to Tara's comments.

"Who be ye, missy, to think ye can burst in here unbid, and tell them as has worked here afore ye was spawned how to tend our hearth? Us got no call to take orders from such as ye! It's takin' this straight to the Master, I am! I be listenin' to no more of yer scoldings!"

The outraged woman turned to stalk back into her kitchen, but a strong young hand grasped the folds of her apron, twisted her about, and yanked her up until only the tips of her toes touched the floor. More outraged than alarmed, she emitted a shriek, and struggled vainly to free herself.

"List to me, goodwife," said Tara evenly. "Clean yourself up, and mend your manners, or you'll be whipped and sent packing, long before your master returns! First, throw away this filthy apron." She snatched the foul garment over the thoroughly subdued woman's neck, and flung it to the floor. "Next, you'll go at once to the bath house for a scrub, and don't come back until you smell as sweet as new-baked bread! Then I'll tell you what else needs changing." She gave the wretched creature a push that sent her stumbling toward the kitchen entry.

This confrontation produced an immediate effect on the awed menials who witnessed the startling encounter with the stiff-backed harridan they secretly disliked and feared, and the improvement in service was salutary. But Tara knew that any such change would be fleeting unless she followed up with precise directions. As the old man had given her no instructions on her duties, she took free rein to institute sorely needed improvements. Rooms were swept and scrubbed daily, the floors oiled and polished to a satiny gleam. The dining table was scrubbed down and rubbed with rotten-stone until its surface gleamed white. Cobwebs were chased away, and Tara supervised weekly stripping and washing of bedding, with thorough beatings of the straw mattresses. Regular bathing was instituted for all staff, whether thrall or free, and orders given for soiled clothing to be laundered daily. Meals began to arrive on time, and served both attractively and with ceremony befitting the table of Fredericia's leading merchant.

Gratifyingly for Tara, the serving maids seemed to hold no grudge for her strictness, but indeed held their heads higher. Even the old cook, initially surly after her scolding, warmed slightly, and eventually took to calling Tara 'Mum'.

It was Tara's second month of residence, and she had despaired of receiving any direction from Bentorm, when he addressed her at table, asking her diffidently to dine with him and his guests the next evening. His invitation was the longest speech she'd heard him give, and it gave her a pleasing glow for the balance of the day. She was flattered to be wanted, even if only as dinner hostess to two old merchants, and she made sure to acknowledge as much, "It is an honor to be invited to join your guests, Sire," she replied appreciatively.

She repaired at once to the kitchen, and worked out with the now compliant cook detailed plans for the most savory and elaborate menu she thought their limited culinary skills could manage. That in hand, she realized that her appearance would have to be as a real hostess, rather than a warrior, if she were not to embarrass and shame her host. On impulse, she decided to consult with the cook, as most senior servant, for advice, and sent a serving maid to fetch her. When the cook arrived, red faced from the fire, drying her hands on her spotless apron, Tara explained her need for feminine attire.

The old woman screwed up her face in thought. "The old Master's Lady," she offered. "He kept all her finery in t'chamber cabinet after her died. Happen ye'll find a kirtle and camisole to suit ye."

"But will they not be too small?"

"Nay, Mum. Her wuz nigh as tall as ye. Bigger about t'middle, but I'll take it in so's it'll fit ye. Come along if ye please, Mum, 'n' see wot's to do."

The wardrobe of Bentorm's late wife was not extensive, but the quality of her clothes was surprisingly good—as befitted the Lady of a trader to Eastern climes, Tara decided. After she tried on her final selection, she could scarce credit the remarkable transformation. She studied herself before the ornate looking glass, admiring the long skirt of delicate blue silk, the cream silken blouse, and the snug vest of red and gold cloth. The pinned-up garments accentuated delightfully the shapely young figure her military garb had hidden. The cook, now enthusiastic about her task, found a magnificant full-length cloak of scarlet, edged in blue and white embroidery, and gathered it at her shoulder with a silver broach that left it open down the front.

The senior serving maid, a stout red-faced elderly woman, offered shyly to dress the mistress's red-gold locks. She arranged it as attractively as its shoulder length would permit, brushing it until it shone, combing it in a center part to fall in soft waves on each side, then tying it at the back of her neck with a deep blue velvet ribbon. "Ye look a fair lovely one, Miss," she announced proudly when she was finished, holding up a Rhenish reflecting glass so her handiwork could be admired all around.

Tara caught her breath at the sorcery the new clothes and hair arrangement had wrought. Gone was the soldierly Valkyrie in drab battle-garb, replaced by a beautiful maiden who could stir any masculine heart. Unaccustomed to heeding her appearance, she could not credit her new beauty. They've turned me into a lady of the court, she told herself, hiding the real Tara behind cunning feminine artifices. She smiled at the deception, but as she savored the miracle her attendants had achieved she turned thoughtful. Could it be this soft and feminine creature looking back from the glass was the real Tara?

The repast, though falling far short of the gala feasts Tara recalled at Menevia Castle, would be sumptuous indeed by Bentorm's standards. She had planned wild hare, trenchers of fish baked with leeks, a tasty slab of spareribs, and a succulent leg of mutton smothered in its juices. The vegetables consisted of mushrooms, wild apples and cloudberries, and the savories included curds, nuts, fresh herring and hot flatbread. Tara doubted the cook could bring all the food to completion at the same time, but looking in the kitchen during its preparation, she was gratified to see no less than six helpers assisting to ready the feast.

With an intense desire to leave naught undone in perfecting her appearance, Tara combed through the former mistress's cabinets, discovering ochre, rose petal, kohl and other cosmetics. She applied these dexterously to bring a delicate glow to her cheeks, seductive color to her lips and eyelids, and an unfamiliar but doubtless feminine fragrance overall. All that done, she composed herself, feeling somewhat ridiculous at playing the part of a beauteous maid, but withal proud of the breathtaking loveliness she and her helpers seemed to have created. And if Crosbey once had loved and desired her, as—she was certain— Sigefert did, belike he'd seen past her male attire, to a hidden radiant beauty she'd never taken for granted.

And from the stunned look on Bentorm's wizened face when he beheld her, and the proud flush on his cheeks as he introduced her to his two unabashedly smitten guests, Tara knew she had made a thoroughly gratifying impact. She was delighted she had taken the trouble to bring pleasure and pride to the old man, realizing it added to her own enjoyment and pride as well.

She had never heard of Hebedy, but from the conversation of the well-fed merchants she gathered it was a trading city more important than Fredericia. From their flowery descriptions, she painted for herself a picture of a bustling metropolis, bulging with splendid goods from all the empires of Europe and the East, from such storied names as Holmgard, Gnezdova, Kiev, Berezany Island, and the fabled Miklagard.

"A pity you cannot join the trading expedition down the Varangian Way, Lady," said the elder of the two. "Just one sight of the dread Turcic Petchenegs would haunt your memory for a lifetime. And men say that to view the Golden Horn of Miklagard is to pass on to Asgard content."

When Tara showed her keen interest, one of the portly merchants was happy to explain. "Our caravan heads east and north in deep sea knarrs, up the great Varangian Sea to Lake Nevo where there is a fortified trading settlement, Aldeigjuborg. There the knarrs must be left, since they be too deep-drafted for the long fetch down the Volkhov to the Lovat. At Velikiye, they empty the boats and portage them overland—thralls carry them on their very backs, Lady, and upside down to provide a bit of protection from the Tater arrows—to the upwaters of the great Dnieper River for the balance of the trip."

The other merchant spoke up in a sonorous voice. "You omit the exciting part, Knut. The Dnieper, Mother of Rivers, leads to the trading center of Kiev, and traverses the most fearsome rapids in the world. Only during the months of high water can we get through them at all, just after the spring freshets subside, and then only with some loss of boats and thralls."

"But when at last you reach the Isle of Berezany, that guards the entry to the great Black Sea, all is clear sailing to Byzantium," said the first.

"Except for the Thracian pirates lurking there," Bentorm put in. "And the Byzantine Navy, supposedly our friends, but sometimes the worst pirates of all."

Tara was entranced by their exciting tales. She had not imagined the life of a merchant trader could be so adventurous, and looked at Bentorm with new respect. "You must have great courage, all of you," she said admiringly.

Her comment drew prolonged laughter from the guests, and even Bentorm chuckled. "Oh, Lady," said the older merchant. "We do not go ourselves. No merchant would make such a trip. It is far too dangerous! We have our trading agent. It is he who braves the dangers for us. He is, of course, well paid."

"Unfortunately," added the other, "his life tends to be a short one. It is said that he is not paid more, only faster."

The talk went on then to other matters, but Tara heard with but one ear. A bold thought was taking shape in her head, one she dared not voice, but could not put aside.

The two Hebedy merchant traders were Bentorm's long time partners in an annual trading voyage down the Varangian Way, their combined forces harnessed to fight off bandits that plagued the voyage. Only the wealthier merchants were able to finance such a venture, and Tara concluded that to this Bentorm owed much of his prosperity. She also deduced, from the jokes his guests made about the state of Bentorm's records, that he sorely needed an energetic and literate aide to return his accounts to the order his wife had imposed. She, Tara, would become that energetic and literate person—while awaiting the task of which she dreamed.

It proved surprisingly difficult to persuade Bentorm to her thinking, even after pointing out her training in such matters by Eorl Skomer's Countess. It took a week of importuning him, to the point of veiled threats that without more challenging tasks she might grow stale at her housekeeping. Tara concluded it was only this unpleasant prospect of returning to his previous slovenly existence that won him over in the end.

"Well and good, Princess," he said, appearing to capitulate. "On the morrow you'll join me on my morning inspection, and see the extent of my holdings." She realized he thought to overwhelm her with the size of her proposed task, and frighten her away from it, and bravely vowed to be on her mettle, showing him she was equal to any burden he could inflict.

Despite her brave front, the tour dumbfounded her with the sheer volume and complexity of his establishment. There were huge stacks of reindeer hides, fur pelts of every description, clay jars of honey and wax, weapons of all types, spindles and looms, pottery weights, coulter and mould-board ploughs, carts, wagons, sledges, oak planks, wattle, footwear, dried herring laid out on flats, all sorts of iron implements—anvils, tongs, hammers, mallets, files, chisels, shears, shovels, plough-shares, rakes and hoes—as well as bronze castings, carved figures in bone and antler, beautifully worked objects of leather and wood, huge bags of bird feathers and down, walrus ivory and heavy ropes woven from walrus hide, high stacks of soapstone vessels and artifacts, beads and sticks of multicolored glass, jewelry worked in amber and jet, combs and playing pieces from the antlers of red deer, schist whetstones and querns, broaches and other jewelry articles—more objects than she could imagine, filling the big warehouses to the rafters. Out in the paddocks and cages were animals and fowl of every breed.

There was another valuable commodity she did not find stacked with other goods, but learned was a major element in Viking trade with Byzantium. That commodity was thralls.

Tara asked constant questions, determined to learn as much as Bentorm would tell about warehousing and stock-keeping, and as well to convince him of her competence. Privately, she was near overwhelmed by the scope of the task, and dubious about her ability to handle such complex matters, but was determined not to let him know her doubts.

"I can keep your records, Sire," she declared confidently. "I was trained so because I am a Princess. In my land, the ruler must be manager as well as warrior, so I am trained in both."

Greatly to her relief, he acceded to her proposal, specifying only that she would give up the project if a four-month trial proved her unable to improve matters. Long before these months passed, there seemed to be an implicit agreement that the record-keeping job was hers.

Bentorm made one strange request, which she realized she must not refuse, though carrying through with it would be both inconvenient and annoying. Ever since the night she'd appeared in woman's garb for his two guests, he had wanted her to dress so. Her hair was growing, and she had taken to wearing it parted in the middle with two short braids down her back. She found that one side of her welcomed his wish that she dress as a woman, for she recognized the feminine allure and budding beauty awakening beneath her rugged military posture. Her fighting clothes were put away with some reluctance beneath her pallet, and she consoled herself with the realization that the day inevitably would come for donning them again. As one private concession, kept from Bentorm, she was never without a dagger concealed in the folds of her voluminous kirtle.

It was a cold and blustery morn in the waning days of winter, and Tara was accompanying the old merchant on his daily rounds as was her wont. All was in order, until they reached the fur warehouse, to see the lock on the door hasp missing. Bentorm was quick to conclude it was only the carelessness of his stores chief, until he stepped unsuspectingly inside—and saw spread on the floorboards a pile of bear pelts that had not been there the day before. His wrinkled face clouded with alarm, and Tara felt her hand tighten on the hilt of her dagger.

"Thieves have been at our furs!" cried Bentorm excitedly. "Had we not come along, he would be off with my bearskins now! He fled when he heard us!"

Tara did not believe the robber had fled, for they blocked the only exit—and the dark corridors between the stacks offered ample places for concealment. She urged leaving to get reinforcements, but the merchant showed a reckless courage by plunging at once into the shadowy interior, and she had little choice but to follow. She was hurrying to keep him in sight, when she was alerted by a slight sound coming from a dark passage on her right. She spun about, to collide heavily with a figure that burst out from between the stacks. Knocked off balance, she doubled into a ball as she'd trained at Aber Castle, and rolled back on her feet.

The thief, seemingly taking a kirtle-garbed woman as no threat, sprang on Bentorm and bore the old man to the ground. Tara caught the flash of a knife upraised, and hurled herself upon Bentorm's attacker, her dagger poised for the thrust. To her horror, the thief's knife already was plunged into his victim's frail body. Rage at the attack on the old man giving strength to her arm, she plunged her weapon deep into the attacker's side, feeling it slide as through butter. She could hear the wheeze of his rank breath becoming labored and quickening, and see the gush of his blood pooling on the decking around them.

His screams subsided to a gurgle as his life-blood spilled, but Tara had no eyes for him. Urgently she hacked away the old man's cloak to lay bare the slash, feeling an agonized pang of pity to see his painfully thin body so ill-used. With hands she could not prevent from shaking, she tore her underslip into strips to make a pad, and pressed it firmly against the wound to stem the welling blood. Through the dizziness overcoming her, she heard assistance arriving...

Helping hands pried away her stiffened fingers from the reddening pad, and carefully lifted up the silent old man. She felt curious eyes on her, and wondering looks at the dead intruder, but there were no questions. Drained and dizzied by the encounter, she followed slowly behind the procession that took him back to the house.

"I'd no notion you were such a she-bear with the dagger," said Bentorm in awe, once his wound had been dressed and he had recovered a measure of composure. The clumsy knife thrust had scraped his rib and been deflected, producing an ugly slash that bled copiously but did not penetrate his vitals, and he seemed to have surprising reserves of strength. Tara sat silent on a low stool beside his cot, not knowing how to respond.

"Had it not been for your bravery and quick action, Princess Tara, Bragi would be welcoming me to Asgard. One more thrust, or one deeper, and I'd not be speaking with you now! I marvel you could dispatch such a man so quick. Few of my guards could do as well."

"I was trained to the sword, Sire," she murmured in embarrassment, uncomfortable to be so praised for doing her duty.

"I was very wrong about you, Princess. I tried to make you a woman of the house, taking the place of my blessed wife. I had you in kirtle and apron, to make myself think I did right in seeing you so." He paused, his labored breathing seeming loud in the quiet of the chamber. "I was wrong to ask it."

"Nay, Sire," said Tara hastily, distressed that he should blame himself for aught. "I am a woman. You took me in when I had no other place to go, my man sent off by the King to a fortress on the far off northern border. My duty was to serve however you wished."

"I was wrong—I say it again. Your body may be that of a woman, but in courage and spirit you were born a warrior. I will treat you as such henceforth. Your destiny is elsewhere—I see it now. I have no power to make you a battle commander, but there is a post within my reach that may please you and your gods. It is yours if you will have it."

Could this be it, at long last? She held her breath in an agony of anticipation, fearful lest it not be what she hoped.

"Chuef Trader of our Byzantium expedition," he announced grandly, emphasizing each word. So she was right! "There will be a battle escort, with its commander, for the actual fighting that will take place, but you will have command of the cargo and all who handle it. Much as I will sorrow to lose you," the open regret on his face testifying to the sincerity of his feeling, "the post is yours, Princess. If you wish it."

The fleet consisted of six Roskilde cargo knarrs, massive deep-sea traders for traversing the broad and often rough Varangian Sea. To their good fortune, the weather giantess, Gna, lavished such bountiful winds on their sails that on the fourth day they rounded the north tip of Gotland Island, and scudded past the Isle of Osel, to enter the broad sheltered delta of the west Dvina River. Bentorm had routed them via the Low Road, chiefly because the Swedes who ran Aldeigjuborg had turned quarrelsome, and the merchants dared not risk the loss of their ships and cargo there. At the point where the delta narrowed, they stopped at a small fortified settlement, to transship from the knarrs to smaller river boats suited for traversing the shallows.

Tara was interested to see the rowing schedule, oarsmen rowing for two days and resting the third. They passed with scant attention rude fishing villages of the timid Livonian Rus; danger of attack from shore, said the Guard Captain, would come later. They even camped ashore at night on this leg, with no fear of attack, but drawn close to their campfires by eerie forest sounds of unknown beasts and birds.

When they reached the first portage, which Tara had been dreading, the boats were emptied and dragged along the shore to open water ahead, where the hand-carried cargo was restowed. But as laborious as that undertaking was, the Guard Captain warned that a far greater challenge lay ahead, when they left the Dvina at the Great Portage and dragged or carried the trading cargo overland to Gnezdovo, to the great Dneiper River that flowed into the Black Sea.

The crew fished every night, and the catch was bountiful. They ranged inland to hunt, not only the familiar elk but also great bearded oxen reputed to be sacred to the Polotjans, who, said the Captain, would avenge the beasts ferociously if word of the slaughter reached them.

At the Olla River, Chief Halvden told Tara they'd arrive at the dreaded Great Portage next day. "We're safe until then," he announced. "This be Dregovite land. Viking slavers have hit them so oft they give all Northmen a wide berth. We've naught to fear from them." At that moment, an errant arrow from the woods took him in the neck.

Tara thought back many times, during the ordeal of the Great Portage, to the event that thrust her into command, pondering the fateful happenstance that made some unseen archer's ramdomly launched bolt kill the Guard Chief. Was it naught but blind fortune, or another in her life's ordained turning points, each playing its role assigned by the gods, guiding her toward some predestined future? Like fateful entries on the Norn Mother's scroll, they were burned in her memory: the omniscient Bard Atheurin...the storm that routed the pirates...Bruh killing the mastiff...escape from poachers on Presceli Top...outlaws prompting her escape from the convent...her sudden miraculous recovery at the Abbey...Sire's inability to command Dyfed's force...the wrestling bout with the hapless Wulfdune...her fortuitous absence from Gloucester when it was overrun...finding a post with Bentorm...the attack in his storehouse.

All those...and now this!

Was Halvden's death an accident, nothing more? Could all these have been just blind fortune? Or were they all planned, to build her destiny?

CHAPTER 22

One part of her fearful, but with a keen exhilaration she'd never known, Tara reveled in the challenge. Instinctively taking advantage of the momentary command vacuum arising from Halvden's sudden demise, she contrived to appear as a leader of positive action amid the universal confusion. She did so not by making any announcement or declaration, but simply by acting in command. Immediately after Halvden's bizarre death, with his troops shocked into inaction by the loss of their commander, she provided an outlet for their tangled emotions by directing the flotilla ashore, to consign the body ceremoniously to Valhalla. That done, she gave the order to get underway, and none arose to question her right. She selected the stopping point for that first night, and when she posted sentries against the belatedly recognized Dregovite hazard, the reasonable step was accepted almost as a matter of course. With each new initiative on her part, it became more automatic for her orders to be followed. Without really planning it, or thinking it through, she played to the universal need of a suddenly leaderless group for someone—anyone—who could step forward immediately in the midst of confusion, and reestablish a comfortable routine.

In taking this course successfully, Tara was the beneficiary of certain elemental forces not really understood even by her. The rugged Vikings of the Guard would have scorned to fight under a woman in any other situation, but they'd all heard about Tara's slaughter of Bentorm's assailant, and seen the lethal accuracy of her bow against the mighty eastern elk. Many of them had been regaled at second hand by Gormsson's cleverly planted accounts of her Cymri battle exploits. But impressive as these were, no tales would have sufficed without the unconscious aura of invincibility that emanated from Tara's being, suggesting to the credulous among them that she was blessed by the gods, or possibly a goddess herself. Nourished on superstition as was this warlike race—ranking high the heroic virtues of valor and skill in battle, immersed in a mythology grand and tragic, taking as gospel Scaldic runes of gods and giants, werewolves and elves—their minds provided fertile soil for believing that the Norns had sent another Brunhild to make them invincible. Tara sensed this atmosphere, without understanding the cause, and it provided the impetus for her decision that she should take overall control of the expedition—its fighting forces as well as its trading activities.

She selected a huge oldster named Olof as her deputy, and hungrily absorbed all he told her of the voyage's hazards. There was the Slavic city of Kiev, whose Prince conscripted soldiers from passing craft. There were the fierce rapids below Kiev to batter them. And there were the far more deadly Turcic Petchenegs, who saw all passing on the Dnieper as their lawful prey.

Tara depended also on a fortunate addition to their flotilla—a half-breed Byzantine Dane named Ahpuliet, who had fled his Byzantine jailors and found a fulfilling career in Bentorm's employ. A skilled navigator and chartist, he earned his stipend by negotiating the labyrinthine trading customs of the Golden City as well. He showed her his map of the Great Portage, overland bridge between the Dvina and Dnieper river systems, and gave her assurance of an easy resupply after the portage, at the Viking settlement of Gnezdovo. He half-convinced her of his vast knowledge of all things related both to navigating and trading.

Tara felt an unbelievable thrill of pride at the way she was settling in to command, even if the gods had ordained it, for she well remembered

Atheurin's warning that the gods helped only those who made every effort to help themselves. Oh, Sigefert, she whispered exultantly, how it would nourish your pride and ease your mind to see this Cymri lass in her new life! I was not born to the sea as were you, she told him in her imaginings, but now I, too, am a captain afloat, e'en if not quite of any ocean sea!

How sturdy a captain she was, she was soon to find put to the test, when her small flotilla unexpectedly encountered a Gotlander heading upstream. She'd thought to be alone on the river, when with a creaking of oars against the thole pins a mighty vessel materialized around the bend ahead. She was a formidable craft indeed, boasting twenty-odd pairs of oars, and with the bulwarks bristling with fighting men. Tara's heart was pounding, but taking care not to disclose her misgivings, she confidently called out orders to prepare to repulse boarders.

"What men be ye?" The hoarse cry came across the water.

"From Denemearc, bound for Miklagard," shouted Olof back. "Who be ye?"

"We be Gutes, bound for home and long overdue. We've home on our minds, and we're not bound on battle, but you hamper us at your peril!"

"Give a thought, Lady," whispered Ahpuliet. "They'll be carrying cargo from the Golden Horn that we could seize, and we'd need voyage no farther."

"Nay," replied Tara, momentarily tempted but quickly dissuaded. "From the look of them, their cargo is mostly armed men. And from what you tell, I misdoubt so deep a craft transited the rapids downstream, or ever saw the place you call Byzantium. We'd be risking too heavy a loss of life, against the slim chance of what we might win."

Whether her decision was right or no, neither side took any overt action, and in short order the strange vessel was well astern and soon to be out of their sight. My first test is behind me as well, she thought with a great feeling of relief.

The next possible port of call was Kiev, commanding the heights of the Dnieper's west bank. She learned it was first raided by Norsemen before she was born, and conquered soon after by Oleg of Holmgard. A province of Sweden, it purported to be a friendly stronghold for the Rus, but mindful of Olof's warning of sometime conscription of those who passed, Tara had her flotilla hide in wooded shallows on the east shore until nightfall. Paying no heed to the Vikings' grumbling about such unnecessary effort, or their disappointment at being denied the delicious pleasures of this bawdy capital city of Kievan Rus, she steadfastly held firm. At dark she emulated Sigefert's clandestine passage by Alfred's blockade, towing the boats silently past in the dark shallows. Morning found the force wearied from the unpleasant ordeal and lack of sleep, but safely downstream from the danger, if danger there had been.

"And what hazards do we face next?" she asked of her two deputies when they had picked up the pace once more.

"Until we reach the weirs, Lady, naught," volunteered Ahpuliet. "But when we hit the rapids," he lowered his voice dramatically, "we will be in the abode of the fiercest savages in all this accursed land!"

Tara recalled the lurid accounts in the same vein that Bentorm's partners had related, and was prepared to believe at least part of these grim prophesies, but realized she needed hard first-hand information if she were to plan a workable defense. Olof and Ahpuliet, pressed for factual details as veterans of past voyages, needed little encouragement. They both swore that the truly deadly obstacle would be the mounted Petchenegs, who habitually launched showers of arrows from horseback well out of range, forcing the impotent Vikings to take what shelter they could, with no way of closing to make a real battle of it.

This gloomy scenario, which could scarce be the whole story or there'd never be successful voyages, started Tara to thinking. She was confident that the Vikings, man for man, were far superior in battle to any such barbarians, but only if they could turn the encounter into hand-to-hand combat on foot. The Petchenegs' overwhelming advantage lay in their mobility, and how to neutralize that was the question. Olog, a veteran of past caravansaries, told her that when they neared the Weirs, they hid by day and proceeded only by night, seeking to give no advance warning of their coming. But this did little more than postpone the inevitable, since the barbarians inevitably would spot them at the first rapid.

It was clear that to counter the Petchenegs' crucial advantage, a completely new strategy was needed—and Tara, whose principal training was in the arena of mounted combat, thought she might have puzzled out one that might work. It was chancy at best, demanding the fullest cooperation from her skeptical Vikings, and their willingness to entertain a form of combat in which they had little experience. Despite repeated gloomy predictions of failure from the unconvinced Olof, and the silent disapproval of Ahpuliet at such madness, she held firm. Over and over again, she rehearsed the glum Vikings in their role, until she thought to detect in some faces the ghost of a budding enthusiasm for the project.

The flotilla, with no effort at concealment, pitched camp on the left bank of the river, just above the raging shallows. At nightfall Tara gave the signal, and shadowy figures with blackened faces stole quietly into the bordering woods, and silently headed southeast behind their forward pickets, not knowing what awaited them in the dank reaches of this alien territory. It was slow going, the blackness of the night and the overriding need for absolute quiet making it all but impossible for the men to stay in close formation, and the failure to make any contact with an enemy made the discouraged Tara almost ready to cancel the enterprise. Suddenly there came a sibilant hiss from the patrol up ahead, and the creeping Vikings froze in their tracks.

Tara touched the arms of the two nearest Vikings, alerting them to follow, and crept silently ahead, her heart beating so hard she was irrationally afraid its pounding would give her away. The trees were thinning out ahead, and the extra effort of moving told her the land was rising toward a hillock. When they broke free of the treeline, they could see a faint lightening of the horizon from the nascent moon. Behind them they heard faint rustlings, telling them the rest of the party was coming up.

At first, as their eyes swept the hilltop, they could see nothing. Suddenly, as if materializing out of nothingness, a lone figure on horseback stood silhouetted against the sky. Even as the motionless Viking party silently watched, two other mounted men appeared over the far brow of the hill to join the first. They were perilously close, their sibilant whispers borne faintly on the night breeze. For a long period they stood together in consultation, and Tara prayed to the gods that they would not ride into the Viking patrol and spoil her plan.

But her gods must have been with her, for even as she silently mouthed her prayers the three turned eastward, and shortly disappeared down the far side of the hill.

Tara set her column in motion, following the riders. Walking silently in the uncertain light was painfully difficult, and she was not certain that, with the imperative need to be completely quiet against discovery, they could keep up with mounted men, but by another dispensation from her gods the horsemen were in no hurry. As they proceeded, walking their horses, apparently feeling secure that none followed, their voices grew louder. They had been proceeding downriver for near an hour, when other voices and the flicker of campfires warned that a camp lay ahead. At that point, the horsemen whipped up their mounts and galloped into the camp. The loud cheers of welcome made it obvious that they had no fears of discovery.

They report that our flotilla has arrived, thought Tara, and count on their distance from it to release them from any need for silence. Pray all goes as planned this night, so they'll never reap any benefit from that knowledge. With exquisite care to avoid alerting the Petchenegs to their presence, she beckoned the two Vikings to come close, and instructed them to reconnoitre the camp's perimeter, in particular to learn where and how the fierce nomads tethered and guarded their horses. Recalling the unexpected success of the patrol she led to Caerleon from King Cadell's court, she prayed Lug would smile on her again. After they left, she retreated to the woods to round up the main body of Vikings, and assemble them up to her vantage point.

The first of her spies returned very soon, reporting that he'd circled the camp as far as the river without coming upon horses, but as the camp extended too close in that direction to pass he'd taken the prudent course of terminating his search at that point. The second spy was gone so long the Vikings feared he'd been taken, and there were whispered suggestions that the party move in to free him or recover his body, but the lack of any shouting or clash of weapons seemed conclusive enow evidence that such fears were groundless. Nonetheless, she was feeling the heavy burden of holding back fighting men eager to take action, and was afraid they'd soon brush her aside in their lust for battle. The situation was becoming tense, when to her great relief the other spy suddenly materialized in their midst. He'd found the horse pasturage, he reported, with but two Petchenegs with the horses—and they huddled together over a low fire, making no effort to keep silence. They were not sentries, it seemed, but only herdsmen detailed to keep the herd from wandering off.

Instantly the strain was relaxed, and the Vikings' fiery urge to rush the camp was replaced at once by their eager readiness to steal the horses—precisely Tara's plan. Simultaneous axe blows dispatched the two unwitting guards with no outcry, and the Vikings melted in among the herd to carry through with their ambitious plan.

Back at the flotilla's camp, at the entry to the rapids, plans were made for the transit. They could envision the plight of the hapless Petchenegs, awaking to find themselves bereft of their horses which constituted their principal weapon, and thus with their teeth pulled by removing their ability to attack on horseback. While it appeared they'd have no recourse but to return to their pasture grounds on foot and disgraced, Tara had no intention of relying on the fierce nomads to act rationally. The tall and large-chested Petcheneg horses were far superior to the little Birka mounts of Denemearc, and when Olof called for volunteers to form a mounted troop he was almost trampled to death in the crush of volunteers. This troop took the landward route alongside the boats, prepared for any assault, but none materialized during the whole passage.

"You'll find it different on the return, Lady," warned Ahpuliet portentously, somewhat miffed at the success of a plan in which he had no part. "They'll be on guard for any repetition of our raids."

"No, they won't," said Tara impatiently. "We even carried off the sentries' bodies to deceive them. Did you not tell me they are ignorant barbarians, ready to blame misfortune on cruel spirits? And besides, we'll find a way to pasture our horses, and pick them up on our return, so we'll be mounted as well as they."

"The Inland Sea weather will be quieter than at home," predicted Olof, and so it was. After finding suitable pasturage for leaving the horses at Berezeny Island, they entered the broad waters of the sea. They stayed well off the coast, the Thracian mountains but faint smudges on the sky-line, to avoid coastal pirates, and after a swift transit they reached the Golden Horn. When the chain was dropped for their entry, they sailed triumphantly into the packed harbor, and hove to before the massive sea walls of the fabled city that Danes called Miklagard, some in the East called Byzantium, and the Romans called the City of Constantine.

"New Rome is a metropolis such as you've never seen," said Ahpuliet grandly, giving the city yet a fourth name. "Five thousand fine mansions, a score of Christian churches including Saint Sophia, Church of The Divine Wisdom and the greatest church in all Christendom—and ten or twenty palaces of emperors and empresses, including of course the Great Palace of the Emperor Leo."

"But where do we land, Ahpuliet?" demanded Tara.

"The Capital Fleet patrols the Horn, governing travel of all foreign vessels. They, and they only, say when we may land, and where, and…" he broke off, looking at something behind her. "Ah, here is the Dromon now."

A massive naval craft loomed threateningly over the small Viking boats, its broad lateen sail emblazoned with a monster imperial eagle, menacing war engines on turrets at bow and stern, and no less than three banks of oars penetrating its lofty sides. A helmeted marine clambered up to the stemhead, and there followed a brief exchange in Romaic Greek.

"We're directed to beach by the Venetian Quarter, and wait upon the City Prefect," translated Ahpuliet importantly. "He tells us what merchants we may trade with, and sets our prices." His face took on a sly look. "But I still have a few friends here, and they have their ways. If fate is kind, I can dispose of a small part of our cargo at better prices through them."

From the tiny quarters assigned them in the city, Tara looked down in fascination on the dusty streets, where foreigners congregated in every imaginable dress. She was entranced by the constant rumble of wagons, the ring of hooves on the stone pavement, even by the mingled odors of olive oil, animal droppings, cooking fires, and human sweat. But above all, she was eager to bathe and shampoo her hair, which she did as soon as water could be found. On impulse, she left it unbraided and brushed out in all its red-gold glory. The Prefect had impounded their weapons, but her dagger was strapped carefully inside her thigh.

In addition to silk, silver was the Danes' main interest. Bazaars of the goldsmith and silversmith guilds were located prominently along the main arteries, within easy walking distance of their quarters, and the Saccellarius required traders to surrender their wares to these at rigidly controlled prices. But through the secret offices of the dark, large-nosed Anatolians, with whom Ahpuliet seemed on good terms, the majority of their goods were sold at prices in Arabic silver coins double the official rates. Tara understood why Bentorm closed his eyes to some lining of Ahpuliet's pockets, for without his shadowy associates the expedition's profits would have amounted to less than half what it did.

Obtaining exit clearance from the Prefect was a drearily slow process. His office was in the Augusteion, hard against the wall of the Great Palace, and Tara came there daily to wait for the Prefect's summons. Foreigners of all races were drawn magnetically to the shining city of Constantine, which the New Romans termed the center of the universe. Tara's eyes took in the towering parapets of the Imperial Palace, spying immobile figures of the Emporer's Hikanati Guard, resplendent in their gleaming armor. Though they appeared foppish to the plainly-garbed Vikings, their regiment was one of the privileged four in the Tagmata, a mighty fighting force whose armored heavy cavalry, the infamous Cataphracts, was the scourge of the civilized world. These heavy cavalry troops, when joined with the Trapezitic light cavalry forces, formed the nucleus of the finest and most capably commanded army ever fielded. Within the impregnable structure of the Imperial Palace, Emperor Leo VI, at thirty the ruler of the world's mightiest empire, may have been cloistered with his frail Queen Theophano, rumored on her deathbed even as her husband ogled all women he saw in search of a well-favored replacement. Tara, bored with waiting for the Prefect's summons, wandered off and found herself beneath the parapet overlooking the main palace gate.

A figure stood on the balcony, impressive in gold and silver vestments, obviously a person of consequence. He regarded the crowd with a gaze so intense that Tara imagined for a moment that it was fixed on her. He turned to an attendant and pointed, and this time she was sure it was at her he pointed. She felt a momentary unease as the attendant saluted, turned smartly, and disappeared from view. The dignitary stepped back, and she put the incident out of her mind.

She did not see the tall, fair-haired soldier until he stood directly before her, so much like Sigefert that for a breathless instant she thought she recognized her own precious Viking. Then she looked more closely, and saw with disappointment that they were not alike at all.

He spoke first in a tongue vaguely familiar but not comprehensible to her. At her look of bewilderment, he spoke in Danish, his words oddly slurred together and lacking the harshness of speakers in Denemearc.

"Can you understand what I say, my Lady?" he asked.

"Yes," she said with relief. "You speak the tongue of Denemearc. I was surprised to hear it in this land, so far from home."

"I am from Birka, in Sweden," he explained. "Just now I am a Kentarch in the Varangian Guard, serving the Emperor."

The Varangian Guard! The famed elite military unit, composed exclusively of Northmen, who served as the Roman Emperor's personal shock troops. This man could be an ally! "What would you have of me, Sir?" she asked him.

"The Emperor would have you wait upon him, my Lady. He appreciated your beauty from the balcony, and prays to have a word with you." She stiffened quickly with caution. "It is an honor many would seek, my Lady. Do not hesitate."

His words were reassuring on the surface, but the hint of steel in his voice disquieted her. For the first time, she noticed four Guardsmen standing stiffly in back of and beside her, and realized that she was a prisoner. On this busy thoroughfare, she was a prisoner!

"I seem to have little choice, Kentarch."

"No, my Lady. But do not fear." He took her arm courteously, but with a clear hint of overwhelming strength, and she knew resistance would be futile. She drew herself erect with dignity, and walked with him at his bidding.

Leo VI, Vicar of God, Protector of the Christian Church, bastard son of Michael III and his mistress, Eudocia Ingerina, a learned man of delicate manners, Emperor of New Rome, and ruler of the great Byzantine Empire, reclined languidly on his couch and inspected at length the interesting woman kneeling before him. Her appearance piqued his fancy, beginning with her hair, a beautiful reddish-gold, rare in his land, and the way it flowed down her shoulders as she bowed her head tittilated his jaded senses almost beyond tolerating. Her outlandish garb was that of a soldier, albeit an effeminate and shapely one, rather than of a maiden. He would not have been surprised to see the ultimate absurdity of a deadly scimitar tucked in at her trim waist. And finally, she was neither flustered nor excited at being summoned before his Presence, as a maidenly supplicant should be, and showed little or no apprehension. Indeed, outlandish though the notion was, he thought to detect a thinly veiled irritation.

"Who is this complex creature, Kentarch?" he demanded of the Varangian who brought her. "Why have we not seen her before?"

"She is a Viking, Majesty. From my country." This was not quite true, but the Kentarch thought it best to simplify.

"Oho! We now understand the costume she affects. And do all the women in your land masquerade as soldiers, Kentarch?"

"No, Majesty. Only some of them."

The Emperor's eyes feasted on Tara's charms, camouflaged though they were, and he felt the familiar stirring in his loins that always beset him at the prospect of adding a delectable new damsel to his entourage. "Ask her to what we owe the favor of her presence in the Imperial City."

"I have asked her, Majesty. She led a Norse fleet down the Varangian Way, to trade here."

"Down the Dnieper? And she the leader? Indeed!" Leo was momentarily taken aback, but only until he considered the exquisite pleasure of taming such a vixen. His eyes gleamed with excitement at the prospect. "Pray ask her, Kentarch, how she managed to best the Patzinaks?"

The kentarch spoke briefly with Tara, then reported to Leo, his eyes a trifle wider. "She says, Majesty, that if you mean the Petchenegs, her men captured all their horses, and drove them off afoot."

Delicious! But surely there were limits to the absurdity of her claims. "And where are these captured horses now?" he asked triumphantly.

The big guardsman spoke again with Tara. "She says they are pasturing on Berezany Isle, Majesty, as they will be needed at the weirs for the
return trip. She says your Majesty may see them there, if you wish."

The Emperor looked displeased, suspecting the audacious woman of
mockery. "Tell her I'll not see these horses, if indeed they be there. And
tell her, Kentarch, that she'll not see them either, for when her caravan
departs she'll not be with it. Let her know she pleases me, despite her
less than respectful manner before the Throne, and she is invited to join
my Court."

This time the guardsman's discussion with Tara was contentious and
protracted. The Emperor waited in mounting frustration, finally unable
to contain his impatience. "Come, come, Kentarch!" he exclaimed
angrily. "Does the baggage not appreciate the honor we extend her?"

The Kentarch seemed to have trouble finding words. "She says,
Majesty…to thank you with supreme respect, but…but, she must decline
the honor."

Tara thought desperately how she might extricate herself from this
preposterous situation. Emperor Leo might actually believe she should
take the invitation as a great honor; doubtless any Roman maiden
would acquiesce eagerly. But she was no Roman, and she viewed the
prospect with horror. He had a queen, and proposed to take her only as
a concubine—one of many in his harem. This was far worse than
Clydog offered, for at least Clydog had proposed to make her his bride
and ultimately his queen, and she had resisted that with all her power.
She had not fled Cymru to fall into a situation infinitely worse!

But what could she do?

She asked the Kentarch to relay an urgent request to the Emperor.
"She begs to seek counsel from the Patriarch, Majesty," he said, somewhat bewildered.

"The Patriarch! What knows she of patriarchs? Does she not know
that my own brother, the Syncellus Stephen, is now Patriarch? Even if

he'd grant audience to one seeking to reject his brother's invitation, why would she speak with the Patriarch?"

Back came Tara's reply. "She says she is a virgin, sworn to chastity and to service of Mother Church, Majesty. She vows it will be her sacred obligation to take her life if she is forced to live sinfully." The Kentarch looked painfully embarrassed.

The Emperor turned livid with rage, forgetting the tittilating appeal of deflowering such a she-cat, in his anger at having his desires frustrated so. "She lies!" he screamed petulantly. "If she is sworn to the service of the Church, what does she on a Norse trading voyage?" He sprang to his feet and paced angrily about. "She claims a special call from the Savior— does she indeed? Very well, let us see if He will protect her! We will devise a test for her, Kentarch! A test she'll find ungodly hard to surmount!"

Tara was distraught at the translation of Leo's dictate, but strove mightily to maintain her dignity. She was sure the furious monarch would set her a test none could pass, belike one that would leave her dead, or worse. She regretted her hasty, and doubtless insulting, remark, but she could not retract it now. Frantically she cast her mind about, for any sources of help. Olof...Ahpuliet...indeed, anyone in her party? No, she could not get word to them, and in any case they'd be powerless— and weaponless—against the Emperor's crack Varangian Guard. As so often in the past, she would have to rely on herself.

"How much of what you told the Emperor was truth, and how much fabrication?" asked the Varangian as he led her to her prison cell. "I disbelieve the tale of being sworn to virginity, as does he. For the horses, I believe that much, looking at you."

"That much is true," confirmed Tara. "The part about the Church is false, as you guessed. But the rest, about killing myself if he takes me for his concubine—that part is true."

"I believe you mean it," he said. "We are countrymen, near enough, and I'd assist you if it lay in my power. I cannot help you to defeat his test, but I can tell you what it will be."

When he told her, she grew pale with despair. She was as good as dead right now. There was no way to extricate herself from this truly murderous test!

Alone with her fears, Tara felt abandoned by all who had cherished and sheltered her in the past. Sire?—old and sick, looking more to her for help than capable of offering support. Atheurin?—with his sage counsel, and his powers that had strengthened and protected her, but remote and silent in this hour of her greatest need. Crosbey?—whose stalwart arm was ever lifted on her behalf, but now rotting in a distant grave. And Sigefert?—off in his distant outpost. Did Sigefert even care for her? Would she live to see him again?

But if by some miracle Atheurin looked on from across the seas, he'd tell her it did no good to surrender herself to apathy, and simply give up. The gods would expect her to fight to the last, to bend her mind and all her energies to the crisis, and think only of how to surmount it. Energized by this thought, she resolved to put aside her fears, her frightening picture of the coming ordeal, and analyze how best to deal with this greatest challenge of her life.

Summoning up the shreds of her resolution, she tried to concentrate on the problem. She did have one advantage, which could be decisive if the gods were with her—a keen dagger out of sight, strapped to her thigh. Unless through an evil quirk of fate she was searched, she'd carry it into the Arena, and face the Ordeal with a weapon, puny though it was, that none knew she possessed.

The first visitor to her cell in the lower recesses of the Hippodrome, where she repined awaiting the age-old Ceremony of the Heretics, was the Propositus of Petitions himself, bearing a message from the Emperor. A gloomy, black-bearded oldster, with the gaunt frame and hollow cheeks of an ascetic, he wore the gaudily embroidered robes of a court dignitary, over which a pendant silver crucifix looked as incongruous as if a harridan of the streets were to affect wimple and veil. He

came on an errand that plainly discomfited him. Through an interpreter, another guardsman this time, he urged Tara to change her mind.

"The Emperor, in his mercy, is willing to forgive your blasphemy if
you will but join his household. He authorizes me to assure you that,
after the passage of a year, if you then desire to leave, you will be free."
And at that time, thought Tara, I know how he'll set me free—with a
knife across my throat. The dignitary was unable to believe her refusal,
requiring her to repeat again and again that she actually would choose
death over dishonoring her sacred vows.

The second visitor was the Kentarch who had apprehended her.
From his clandestine manner, she guessed the Emperor had no knowledge of his visit. "I've more to tell you of the Ordeal, my Lady. A pagan
heretic, doomed to die for blasphemies against Mother Church,
stands guard for the moment at the Obelisk of Theodosius in the
Hippodrome. He is chained by the neck, restricting his range of
movement to but twelve cubits from the Obelisk, on which lies a
parchment bearing a passage of Holy Writ. If he prevents you from
taking the parchment, his death will be mercifully quick. If he certifies
your blasphemy before God by killing you, proving you not under
Divine protection, he will go free."

"And if I evade him, and secure the parchment?"

"Then your sanctity will be demonstrated before all, and you will of
course go free. But he is very strong, and once his arms grasp you no
temporal power can save you. And he is so quick that if you venture
within his reach he will have you." He hesitated. "And, you must
remember, he is fighting for his life just as are you."

"What if I stay beyond his reach?"

Then you will die at the stake, a self-confessed heretic, convicted by
your own refusal to endure the trial."

"Then to have a chance of escape from death—though I be but a
brief visitor to your land, and guilty of naught—I must fight him."

"Yes, my Lady. I know not how you can prevail, unless there be truth in your claim to sanctity. I did supply the pagan secretly with hasheesh, which will make him wilder and harder to predict, but happily will slow his reflexes. It is little enow to do for a countryman, but I am powerless to do more."

"If I kill him, death will save him from the stake as well, yes?"

Her ally laughed humorlessly. "If you do kill him, yes. But of more import to your fortunes, it will save you from the stake."

"Then I will kill him," she declared firmly, with a confidence she was far from feeling.

The final visitor was the gaoler, who took her to the arena and there released her from her chains. She secreted the dagger, apparently still unnoted by the onlookers, in her left sleeve, where she could snatch it free swiftly. Only two spectators were with the Emperor. So this was the 'all' before which the Kentarch had said her sanctity would be demonstrated. Apparently Emperor Leo courted no public notice of his thwarted passions. She forced her eyes toward the Obelisk, and her heart fell like a leaden ball in her chest.

Her opponent was chained at the neck, true, but his huge arms were free, and the wild look on his face told her all too plain what she could expect if she ventured inside his twelve cubit radius. The gaoler escorted her to a point perhaps twenty cubits away from the pagan, almost within his reach. The pennoned lance was lifted high, and she knew that when it swung down her time would start. If she did not retrieve the parchment within the set period—and none had seen fit to tell her what that period was—the test would end, and she would have sentenced herself to be burned at the stake.

All too soon, the fateful lance fell. Her time of testing had begun!

She had rehearsed a crude and sketchy plan, but stood irresolute, sure it could not succeed. A sudden dizziness assailed her, and she rubbed her eyes to clear the film covering them, but the haze perversely grew thicker until she could scarce see the pagan or the Obelisk. Then from within there sounded a voice, so faint it could be naught but her desperate imaginings. For want of aught better, she listed to it, and, sensing rather than hearing, managed to decipher the single word whispered again and again.

Wulfdune...

Wulfdune!

From some forgotten depths of memory, she managed to dredge up a confusing vision...of Carmarthen Castle, eons ago...in a Hall, before an audience of uchelwyr...her Dyfed uchelwyr, under her command. There was a wrestling bout, and she strained to see who fought. The mist cleared somewhat, and she realized with a shock that she was a contestant! She looked to the other contestant, and again the scene cleared and she saw who it was.

It was Brechner's son. It was Wulfdune!

It all came back to her clearly then, in a miraculous rush of memory. It came to her how she had met the challenge of Wulfdune's attack. And suddenly, as if a gift from the gods, she knew what she must do, to put her desperate plan in effect.

Confidently, permitting herself no doubts, she strode purposefully forward to the point just out of her adversary's reach. The red glow of madness in his implacable eyes gave her pause, but a familiar voice bade her show no fear. He'd expect her to feint, to lunge in at one side and withdraw at once, leaving him off balance for the instant she needed to dart in on the other and seize the parchment. So e'en his hasheesh-dulled brain would warn him not to commit to either side too soon. He'll make no sudden lunge at me, she knew, lest he grasp empty air. Such a tactic on my part would play right into his hands—his huge, strong, clutching, murderous hands!

As if they played parts on a macabre stage, he held back, great arms widespread, waiting for her to make the first move. She stared deeply into his eyes, gauging the focus of his pupils. He watched her face, and down to her shoulders, nothing lower. She moved her feet just a trifle, testing him, but his eyes did not react to the motion. He doesn't see my feet, she decided—or he is a better mummer than she knew he could be—only my upper body. It's time to act!

She turned her head suddenly to his left side, and instantly his body turned slightly in response, his arms still widespread to intercept her. Savagely, then, she kicked at his groin, the toe of her boot striking home solidly, and instantly leaped back. Involuntarily, his hands dropped to his crotch. In the same instant, she swung her left arm powerfully, and dealt him a stinging open-handed blow to his eyes. Bellowing with rage and pain, forgetting his cautious tactics, he charged at her, his great hands reaching out for her neck to throttle her.

Now! The precise moment was here, and if she failed to seize it instantly the contest would be lost. Instead of recoiling, she charged him head first, knocking his arms awry, slamming with all her force into his protruding stomach. Through the fetid animal stench of him, she sensed the instant of confusion on which she'd planned, before he could bring his arms together to grasp her. And in that briefest of moments, she thrust her dagger forward and upward, driving with the full force of her strong young muscles into the swelling belly just above his groin, and penetrating deep into his stomach cavity.

For a terrifying moment, as the momentum of her charge pinned her against him, his wet pulsing flesh lay suffocatingly against her, and now she could feel his huge hands groping at her unprotected neck. As he moved forward, his great bulk was bearing her down even as his hands were finding her throat, bending her irresistibly back until it seemed her spine must crack. As she was borne helplessly to the ground under him, his leash hit its end, snapping his head back sharply, mercifully breaking the hold of his hands. Wildly he thrashed about, trying to regain his feet and relieve the agonizing pressure choking off his windpipe, seeming oblivious of his wound. He managed to draw back to his knees, freeing Tara sufficiently for her to tug the dagger from his stomach and roll free. His hands groped back, found and seized the halter, but could not sustain his weight, and again he fell forward, suspended by the collar about his neck. He hung there insensate, reddened eyes frozen open—a grotesque figure, denied the dignity of death.

Tara lay silent for a moment, waiting for her uncontrollable shaking to pass, then with great care reinserted the dagger into its hidden sheath, breathing a silent prayer that none would decipher her movements. A vital part of her plan—her hope—was to make the pagan's death seem supernatural, so the onlookers could have no doubt that it was divine intercession. She rose unsteadily to her feet, stared at the body hanging pathetically from its cruel harness, then slowly went to the Obelisk and took up the parchment. Forgetting why she took it, she looked at it a moment with unseeing eyes, let it slide from her fingers, and walked slowly toward the entrance.

"Where are you bound, my Lady?" The Kentarch appeared beside her. "The Emperor will wish to see you…to congratulate you on meeting the test…to confirm your piety."

"I am leaving now," she told him, continuing under the great arch as she spoke.

"I cannot allow you to go, my Lady, until the Emperor gives the word."

She halted then, turned to face him directly, and her cold eyes stared implacably into his. "Stop me at your peril!" she said, in tones of ice. "Touch me, and you will die, as surely as he!"

His hand, which had been lifted to detain her, pulled back hastily, as though he touched hot coals. He crossed himself, and stared at her in stunned disbelief, making no move to stop her.

She strode confidently through the main entrance, and turned the corner out of his sight.

CHAPTER 23

"Tell me again, lass, how you thwarted the Petchenegs," insisted Bentorm, as much entranced by the account of turning the nomads' horses against them as by the pleasurable profits of the expedition. For the third time, Tara recounted their night foray, explaining how seizing the Mongol horses for the Vikings to use had changed the situation from deadly peril to little more than harassment. For Bentorm and his partners, this meant that all future expeditions would be buttressed against attack by the dreaded Turcic plainsmen, and the profits increased most attractively. "I did not imagine you'd be so practiced a caravaneer, Princess Tara," he said, with something approaching awe in his voice. "Your gods must hold you high, to bestow on you so rare a skill in surmounting the perils that beset you!"

She wondered to what flights of fancy the old merchant would soar, if he knew how she had surmounted the far greater peril of the Emperor's foiled abduction. She had told no one about it, lest her femininity be seen as a special vulnerability, a risk liable to rule out future expeditions for her. Ahpuliet's sharp ears had caught rumors, and he had confronted her, but she'd responded so sharply he'd dropped the matter at once. Belike some distorted version would reach Bentorm's ears in time, but she'd say naught to confirm it.

In fact, a fairly accurate account of events in the Hippodrome already had reached Bentorm, and it was Tara's extraordinary ability to extricate herself, while hiding from the Roman court any hint that a dagger, and not divine intercession, had achieved her triumph, that led the cautious trader to an astonishing decision. Earlier he had impulsively considered, and then reluctantly abandoned any thought of making such a revolutionary appointment, as being too demanding for one so young and lacking in experience, and more importantly, as too dangerous an assignment for a young woman he had come to admire and even cherish. But her fast thinking and aggressive action to free herself from the Roman Emperor's clutches made it clear that she was in fact better equipped than most men to deal with unexpected emergencies. He would have to give the matter more careful consideration, before rejecting it out of hand.

Meanwhile, Tara was luxuriating in the environment of clean bedding, precious privacy, the delightfully sensuous feeling of feminine silken garments, and the other pleasures of her well-ordered existence at Fredericia. She had settled happily back into the comfortable routine of morning inspection rounds with Bentorm, with the hope that, for a time at least, naught would arise to disrupt her existence.

But that was not to be. She was accompanying Bentorm on such an inspection, when he halted before the fur warehouse and cleared his throat. She recognized this as a prelude to some portentous matter, and composed herself patiently to wait, reassuring herself that naught he could say was remotely likely to interfere with her secure and well-ordered life in Fredericia.

"We cannot trust even the daub on our walls, when we think to speak in private," he said, in the whispery voice he saved for important disclosures. "I would not have us overheard." Tara gave him her fullest attention as he continued. "The King has graciously awarded me a contract of some import, and I'm concerned how best to carry it out. Your comments will be useful to me, and I can promise they will be heard by none other."

Tara's interest was piqued, but she could not see how she would be directly affected. "What is the contract, Sire?" she asked. "What is he calling on you to do?"

"It is a task we've not done before," he told her. "A contract to out-fit one of his new fortresses—collect the supplies and provisions to put it in full readiness. And something more: to assemble a flotilla and ourselves deliver the cargoes to the site."

One of his fortresses! Was it...could it possibly be Aggersborg? Excitement built to fever pitch within her, and she chafed at his annoyingly deliberate exposition.

The King was dispatching a large contingent of people, Bentorm explained at length, and a provisioning fleet would accompany the passenger ships. He discussed in detail the supplies and provisions that would be included, the interactions between the contingents car-rying the people and the supplies, and what his responsibilities and duties would be under the contract.

He had told her naught so far! Was it Aggersborg, or another fortress? And the other 'contingent'—was that perchance wives and families going to Lindholm Hoje at last, as promised? More to the point, was she permitted there? And most importantly, just what did Bentorm have in mind? Was it advice only he solicited, or was he trying to say that she was involved?

"Sir!" she blurted out impatiently. "You must tell me at once! Could it be Aggersborg?" The precious memory of Sigefert, pushed resolutely from her mind these past months as best she could, came flooding back in a torrent of feeling, and she could not bear the old man's maddening slowness. "Pray, Sir, tell me at once!"

Bentorm looked puzzled. "How strange you should say Aggersborg. I wonder why that place came so quick to your mind." From his quizzi-cal look, she knew not whether he really wondered, or if he was indulging in gentle sarcasm.

"But is it?" she pressed. How much more irritating could he be?

"I cannot deny, Princess, that Aggersborg it is. The King has asked me to keep its identity close, but you guessed it without my help."

Then, in his deliberate way, he explained. Aggersborg and its fledgling town were completed sufficiently to house the families, and Gorm had authorized a provisioning force to transport supplies for the first difficult year, until crops and herds were well established.

"And who will head your caravan, Sir?" She thought that his cautious hinting had all but revealed that, but she'd misread such in the past, and had to hear it clearly.

"I thought of assigning Krohgarn, my Chief of Sentries, as he is a one-time longboat captain, and the most experienced of my force. Some say he was a wolfskin in his younger days, and he's still a sturdy fighter, though no doubt past his prime. But on his down side, his rage simmers close to the surface, and oft he acts rashly. I dare not put a vital Crown commission in the hands of a hothead who cannot control himself, yet I cannot choose one under him, as his loss of face would be extreme. No, it must be Krohgarn—or an outsider."

"And the outsider? Have you someone in mind?"

Bentorm's hesitation to say it outright was patently apparent. "Yes…there may be," he mused. Then, more forcefully, "There is."

"Who is it to be, Sir?" Tara asked breathlessly. "Do I know the one?"

"You should, Princess Tara," he said, chuckling a bit now that he was about to commit himself. "It is, of course, you."

Although she had entertained the thought, almost known the answer but not dared hope for it, she was somehow disconcerted now that he'd put it on the table. "But Sir…think you I have the experience for…" She broke off. Of course she did not have the experience, and both knew it. His great gift lay in handing her the honor despite her inexperience, looking instead at what he saw in her potential. Then another problem hit her. "And Krohgarn…how will he respond to being under a maid— one a third his age?"

"Badly, I fear. But I'll try to throw him a sop. If you raise no objection, he can accompany you as Deputy Commander."

Her enthusiasm was suddenly dampened, as she glumly considered the disadvantages cf such an arrangement. No matter what she did to smooth over the situation, belike he'd remain an implacable enemy, seeking to discrediting her whenever opportunity offered—or making an opportunity, if none presented itself. But she must remain silent with any objections, out of consideration for the great favor Bentorm was showing her.

He took her silence as acquiescence, but Tara was left with deep misgivings, and knew with virtual certainty that ill would come of accepting Krohgarn.

Still—Aggersborg! Being reunited with Sigefert! Her heart leapt at the prospect. How, she wondered, could she ever endure the days until they departed? Impulsively, she squeezed the old man's hand, thanking him again and again for his trust in her—and knowing she must not diminish in any way his wondrous decision by raising an objection to Krohgarn. Painfully embarrassed at the intimacy, but filled with pleasure at Tara's evident joy, the shrewd old merchant wondered if it came from pride at the honor alone, or more likely, some romantic attachment at Aggersborg. She was but a young lass, despite her warlike behavior. And to the young, love was all.

The voyage must complete before winter's storms closed in, so preparations proceeded at a feverish rate. The fighting men, navigational contingents, and her force providing security for the supplies, would travel by longboat, with commodious cargo knarrs for stores and livestock—and because of their better facilities for families, as well as smoother riding characteristics, for the wives and children. The longboats would be left at the fortress to supplement their fighting fleet, and the empty cargo knarrs would bring the transport party home. "So you and your men will have to sail home in the knarrs," Bentorm told her. "They are slow, but will give more comfort than the fighting craft."

One unwelcome bit of news clouded Tara's pleasure. Gorm was allowing only Gormsson's Danes to bring their wives. The Northumbrians, with no families in Denemearc but with the primal ache of all fighting men for the opposite sex, were allowed no women at all. So how could Sigefert find a way for her to stay? Would his conscience as leader prevent him from taking what was denied his Vikings? Best she leave that question in the hands of the gods, she decided. In any case, she'd see Sigefert soon, and that was joy enow for now.

The provisioning force, with Tara in command, joined up at the coastal town of Arhus with the dependents' fleet, which had put in there to take on water and fresh food, and provide the families a brief respite from the arduous ocean voyage. Tara worried how the wives and children would fare when they rounded the headland and breasted the stormy Kattegat. The 'nursery fleet', as Krohgarn scornfully dubbed it, was commanded by a dour mariner, and Tara's force would be under his overall command. His weatherbeaten face showed no surprise when she reported to him as provisioning commander; doubtless such an experienced sea dog would have seen near everything in his time. In any case, he simply handed her the sailing directions, as though it was commonplace for a party of seagoing Danes to be commanded by a young female foreigner. His embroidered orange tunic, and the massive jeweled belt around his ample middle, seemed incongruous in his rough environment, but the way his crew jumped to his commands gave testimony to the respect in which he was held.

Eager to quit Arhus and be on their way, the families grew less enthusiastic when they left the land's shelter and hit the open sea. Tara's experience afloat had inured her somewhat to the sea's turbulence, but she sympathized with these indomitable wives braving the fearful waves for the first time. She mentioned as much to Krohgarn, as they watched the helmsman tug at the heavy athwartships tiller against the yawing force of the quartering seas.

"They'd best not have come, then," he said sourly. "I hold not with women aboard ship—it's against the will of the gods!" She knew Krohgarn included her in his scathing assessment, and had hardened herself for a thorny relationship, but was grateful that thus far he'd expressed his resentment only by his surly attitude, rather than any harassment or open insubordination.

"How would they join their men, then?" she asked reasonably. "The King granted them permission, and decided they'd best go by sea rather than overland."

He did not deign to lower himself into argument with a woman, and particularly not with this woman. In addition to being deputy commander, he captained the largest longboat, a huge craft built in Sjaelland. She had wished mightily to take a different boat, but thought it best to have him under her eye, and perhaps more importantly they'd be in speaking range if any problem arose demanding that they confer. She knew she'd be subjecting herself to an unpleasant trip in consequence, but there was no helping it.

With the steady north wind now directly in their face, the need to tack back and forth gave them a crabwise advance which lengthened their trip, and it was a wet and weary band that finally raised the Gotland coast. With his human cargo so weak from seasickness, the fleet commander decided to enter the Mariagerfjord, and lay over at the Fyrkat stronghold. Tara was fascinated by this first Danish fortress she'd ever seen. Its immense timber-laced rampart and deep encircling moat made the place look impregnable, in stark contrast to the makeshift Gloucester palisades that Edward had breached so easily, and Tara thought with a pang of regret how different the outcome might have been if Gloucester had boasted breastworks such as these. But had they not been forced to flee so precipitously, she might never have come to know Sigefert so intimately. Worse, she would have become a helpless chattel of Clydog! She wondered fleetingly when, if ever, she'd be reunited with Sire and her homeland. So much had transpired in one year, it seemed at least five had passed since she left Cymru. Would she ever sit Dyfed's throne? Could she avoid marriage to the despicable Clydog? Would her problems never resolve themselves?

At beach call the next morn, after a night spent by the families recovering, enjoying the Fyrkat wives' hospitality, and regaled by tales of life in the field, the rejuvenated Aggersborg women glowed with anticipation. Tara, somewhat depressed by her reflections, envied the women for knowing what their future held, for knowing they belonged to men who presumably held them dear—for knowing they were wanted.

And she—was she wanted? She'd had no way to tell Sigefert she was coming. When she arrived unannounced, how would he respond? Would he welcome her, make her feel as secure as the fortunate wives now reembarking so happily? Or would he be cold, indifferent, seeing her as only a half-forgot creature of his past, an unwanted burden? She had told him, that day of sad farewell, that when the town was built she'd come if he wanted her. And he'd answered—how well she remembered—that naught did he want more. And that if she did not come in a year, he'd come to Fredericia and take her, if necessary by force.

But that was a year ago, and words were easy spoke. Time had a way of cooling hot spirits. As she turned away from the gaily chattering groups, stinging tears welled up, and stubbornly refused to be blinked away.

Tara had learned that Aggersborg was several hours' run west of the town, realized that the Northumbrians would have no wives to greet, and understood that the fortress never could be left undefended. Long ago, therefore, she'd steeled herself to the likelihood that Sigefert would not be at the town to greet them. But despite such cold rationalizing, when the fleet entered the Limfjord she scanned the beach eagerly, searching for his face. Neither he nor any Northumbrians she remembered came into view. She leaned listlessly against the rail, waiting for the debarkation to end, trying to bring her errant mind back to the work at hand. The main force would remain at Lindholm Hoje, to see all the passengers well housed before they left, but the provisioning group would be ready to proceed upriver to the fortress as soon as stocks for the town were offloaded, so command of the flotilla would devolve upon her. She'd continue on at dawn to Aggersborg; tonight she must try against all odds to fall asleep.

"Girl!"

She sprang up in confusion, to see who shouted at her so.

"By Odin's blind eye, can it be true? Is it actually the Princess Tara, in the body?"

Gormsson! It was Gormsson…her dear friend! Of a sudden, she felt light-hearted and happy. Eagerly she sprang to the beach, and broke into a run in her excitement to greet him.

"Tara, herself!" He wrapped his arms about her, snatching her off her feet, and spun her giddily about in a circle. Still holding her, he drew back enough to look at her, in unstinting admiration. "Yes—still the most beautiful soldier in Denemearc! We wondered if you'd talk your way aboard the provision fleet, did Sigefert and I. It's plain we needn't have worried."

"Oh, Gormsson! How wonderful to see you again! We've been apart such a long time. You might have died, for all I knew!" His warm and affectionate greeting so lifted her spirits that she began to cry. Scarce caring that she was commander, and oblivious to the obvious disapproval of the sourly watching Krohgarn, she made no effort to stem her tears.

"Here, here, Princess—this will never do." Clumsily he blotted her face with his sleeve. "Warriors are forbid tears. Does the sight of me sadden you so? Say the word, and I'll leave."

"You'll never know how much you were missed!" Impulsively, she threw her arms about his neck, and pulled him close to her, glorying in the warmth and hardness of his strong young body, and in how much he reminded her of dear wonderful Crosbey. "Not that I didn't love your uncle—he was more kind and forbearing than I had any right to expect—but it was not at all the same."

"And how did you talk him into letting you ship on with the provisioning force? Did you smile sweetly on the commander?"

She smiled inwardly in anticipation, savoring the impact of what she was about to tell him. "That would have been impossible."

"Why so?"

"Because…I am the commander."

That startling statement necessitated relating the complete account of her life since leaving Jelling. He laughed sheepishly to learn how surprised Bentorm had been at her arrival ("I knew he'd fall under your spell, as the rest of us did," he explained lamely), smiled proudly upon hearing how she'd stabbed the robber, clasped her wrist delightedly at the account of outwitting the Petchenegs, and stood aghast at her ordeal in the Hippodrome.

"By Valfreya, girl, Utgard-Loki's foul breath could have burned you to a crisp on that adventure! How is't you manage to seek out these perilous escapades? Why can't you stay home as other women do, instead of always tempting the Norns with your careless ways?" But his face showed his admiration, and she glowed with pleasure at his implicit praise.

Gormsson insisted she board his longboat, for the trip to Aggersborg next morning. It vaguely disquieted her to leave Krohgarn to his own devices for a single day, but that worry was thrust aside in the presence of a handsome young prince. The wind still held fresh from the east, and they sailed smartly up the Limfjord. For Tara, aching to learn about the new fortress, and flattered by the attentions of Gormsson, the time sped by.

"You don't ask about Sigefert, girl," ventured Gormsson finally. "Have you no interest left in the man?"

The bashful smile illuminating her face made him ache with longing for her. "I have, Sir Gormsson," she replied softly. "I might ask if he still remembers the refugee he brought from Britain."

"So you might. And the answer is—though he says nothing, for that is his way—I wat no day passes but you are foremost in his thoughts."

"Did he mention I might be with the provisioning party, or wonder in your hearing if I would…?"

"Of course he did, girl! Well…not in so many words, but I could read it in his face when he spoke of the expedition. Now, don't look for him to jump all over you for joy, as I would—as I did, come to think on't— for Sigefert's not the man to wear his feelings on his tunic. You must look deeper to read him." Suddenly he strode to the rail, looking silently out at the passing shore. When she touched his arm tentatively, he turned to her, hoarse with sudden anger. "Curse the man! I'd give my right arm if you felt for me half what you feel for him! And he does not e'en come to meet you!"

"But he could not know I'd come," she said reasonably, shaken by the depth of his emotion, and moved by the words he spoke. "I can understood why he did not meet us at Lindholm Hoje." But that's not true, she said to herself. It is not easy for me to understand.

"How could he not have known you'd come? I knew."

She squeezed his hand, not trusting herself to speak.

When they first sighted the fortress, they could make out no signs of life. Then over the water came the lookout's stentorian cry, and men spilled out the gate, with a familiar figure in the lead. Tara's heart sang with joy at the recognition, instantly forgiving all.

Sigefert! It was Sigefert in person, leading a welcoming formation such as she'd never seen! Her boats started beaching, and she saw his gaze sweep over each in turn. Not thinking to look in Gormsson's boat, his shoulders sagged and he turned away, disappointment so evident she ached to let him know she was there.

"Sigefert! Sigefert!" Crying his name, she leaped into the shallows and ran pell-mell up the beach, yearning to throw herself in his arms— but suddenly stopping, knowing how it might embarrass him before his men. Her pent-up emotions choked her, and she could find no words.

Sigefert spoke first. "You came!" The words were simple, even laconic, but looking past his speech and into his eyes, she saw with an overpowering rush of emotion, so strong she could scarce contain herself, that he loved her.

"Yes," she said simply, the excitement seething so powerfully within her breast she feared she would swoon. "I came."

He took her hand tenderly, and led her ahead of the others into the compound. Allowing herself to be led unquestioningly, she thought briefly of her responsibilities for the cargo, but they had become as naught to her. Krohgarn could see to them—or they could go unaddressed; she did not care. She was with Sigefert again; nothing else mattered.

Tara was more than a little apprehensive at being alone with the strong and hot-blooded Sigefert after so long a separation, but was almost disconcerted to find how ungrounded her fears seemed to be. He drew her into a small chamber resembling a counting room, offered her a seat at the center table, and seated himself opposite. Looking about her, Tara saw a second door, which belike led to his sleeping chamber. This was his apartment, then, where he handled the fortress business. The bleak chamber, and the awkward formality that seemed to build up between them, were somehow disturbing, as though she were not truly welcome. But what else could he have done? Were they not together, and in privacy? Had he not led her off at once, ignoring all the others? Had he not seemed genuinely happy to see her?

What more could she expect?

"Tell me now, lass, all you've been up to since last we were together." She could not stifle an errant wondering whether his request, breaking the awkward silence, bespoke real caring or just polite interest. "I've imagined wild and desperate deeds, knowing your venturesome nature," he went on. "Better I learn the reality, rather than the dreaming I've been doing."

Somewhat encouraged by that, she recounted what she had told Gormsson, trying to make her voice lively and excited. Sigefert did not show his feeling openly as did Gormsson, she knew, but his jaw stiffened when she described her narrow escape in the Hippodrome.

"You could have been killed," he said, frowning. "Bentorm must be addled to send you on such voyages. It must never happen again!"

She laughed, almost happily, at his expression of concern. "Sometimes I have the feeling that my life, my future…that it is charmed," she confided.

"Your life charmed?" There was no laughter in his voice. "Your adventures have sickened you in the head! How can you believe so, Tara?"

Trying to justify her remark, angered that justification was needed, she told him something about Atheurin, how he'd read in the omens that she was chosen by the old gods for a special destiny. "How can they let me die before that destiny is fulfilled?" she asked reasonably.

He was frowning again, as though she displeased him. Had Tara fully understood the love of a man for a woman, perhaps she'd have known that his worry came from the very intensity of his caring, but lacking experience in the ways of men, she found his criticism a chilly contrast to Gormsson's open adulation, and felt keenly tongue-tied.

"You talk nonsense," he went on, scowling. "Some addle-pated skald tells you the gods hold you special, and you think you cannot be harmed! Don't you ken they tell such tales to all who ask? They say what you wish to hear, with no grain of truth in their gabble."

Feeling unfairly assailed, she considered enumerating the many miracles Atheurin had wrought, but suddenly was too wearied for the effort. "Well, let it pass," she said finally, smiling as bravely as she could manage. "Tell me about your work here at Aggersborg, and of your wondrous progress. It seems the gods be on your side, e'en if not on mine."

Sigefert, taken aback, looked closely at her and said more gently, "I did not mean the gods are not with you, Tara. Just that the gods do not rescue fools who rush headlong into any danger. Many a brave man lies dead, who trusted the gods to protect him from all perils. You trust too much, I meant." His expression changed, and he went on. "Yes, lass, we've done well enow." His men had moved mountains, he said, disclaiming the major part his leadership must have played to complete the half-built fortress and rough out the town. "There've been no wars fought here," he said wryly. "We've been carpenters and smiths. Had enemies attacked, we'd have been obliged to defend with tools, for our weapons moldered on the shelves from disuse.

He went on, enthusiasm building as he talked. She could see that his mind was full of the small miracles he'd wrought, with no one to tell, no one to praise how he'd blown life into raw stones and sod, making Aggersborg a working fortress. She tried to give him what he craved, to exult with him, taking pleasure in his eager account and the glowing pride in his face. But though she knew not just what she'd hoped for at their reunion, certain it was not a recital of this barrack erected, this road laid, this hillside leveled. Finally she could hear no more.

"Sigefert, leave off!" she begged firmly.

She spoke hurriedly, lest she lose her resolve. "I've a question for you. I came all the way from Fredericia, facing heavy seas and harsh winds, holding my tongue against sneers and insults from the sourest deputy ever a commander suffered. And I am the commander, in case you may be interested. And I'll be put off no longer!"

He sat up straight at her outburst, astonished. "Let's have your question, then, lass."

"It's only this: have you missed me?"

Sigefert sat still, studying her, seeking for words. Finally, he replied, so soft she could scarce hear. "I have that, Tara. I've missed you sure."

Suddenly the dam broke on the emotions seething inside her, and the words spilled out. "The way you say it, it's not enough! I must know if you've missed me as I've missed you—waking in the night and unable to sleep for wanting to hear your voice—staring at strangers who pass, in hopes one will be you—eating food with the taste of ashes because it's not eaten with you—knowing life is scarce worth the living, without you to live it with! Have you missed me like that, Sigefert? Because if you haven't, well I'll just…I'll just…" She never said what she would do, because suddenly she looked pathetic and began to sob, hating herself for it.

Then surprisingly, miraculously, she was in his arms, and with gentle movements and great care he wiped her tears away. Then with a tenderness she'd not known he possessed, he lifted her. "Best we have done with talk, lass," he whispered. "Best I show you just how much I've thought of you, and dreamed of naught but your lovely face on my pillow this long year. Yes, and how I have missed you, my little Princess."

Cradling her then, he kicked open the door to the chamber, and carried her to the pallet, where he deposited her and knelt at her side. His kisses covered her face, at first feathery and gentle, but with increasing urgency. In the dim light, his body seemed to loom over her, huge and protective, and Tara sensed the intensity of his desire, and the fury of his impatience as he fumbled with the fasteners of her garments and knelt once more beside her, his breathing accelerating and his blue eyes half-closed with mounting passion. His lips found hers, and his hands on her silken body moved with gentle but urgent purpose.

A recollection of giggling yet fearsome tales, exchanged between Angie and Altie in the bower at Aber Castle, made her shiver with awareness of what was about to happen—accepting the penetration of her chaste body by something alien—e'en as she knew there could be naught alien about Sigefert!

Her warrior instincts made her stiffen and flinch, her body raising her defenses against the initial pain, and in that moment, sensing her alarm, Sigefert held her all the more protectively, his soft endearments soothing her anxiety, while Tara, in turn, sensed and shared his wondrous joy at finding her pure and untouched, exclusively his own.

"Tara!" He breathed it in so worshipful a tone that the mingling of pain and emotion made her tears run freely down her face—tears that Sigefert, in his love, kissed tenderly away.

So it must have been this strange magical ecstasy for Brunhild the Valkyr, thought Tara dreamily—saved from the lusts of ordinary men, rejoicing to discover the miracle of her womanhood with one special man—one special hero!

Oh, Sigefert…Sigefert!

CHAPTER 24

When at last she woke, Sigefert was already gone. She lay motionless for a time, reliving in her mind the wonder of the last evening, savoring the soft loving words, Sigefert's gentle touch. She hated to break the spell, but the day must be well along, and there was much to do, so reluctantly she rose and dressed. A thrall, waiting at the outer door of the apartment, reported that the commander had called assembly, so she hurried to be present. Her wondrous new life was starting, and she wanted to hold on to every glorious second of it—and every precious moment of Sigefert's company.

She knew many of the Danish-born soldiers would be at Lindholm Hoge, welcoming their families, but she looked forward to seeing the Northumbrians again. Oddly, when she entered the enclosure they were drawn up in rough formation at one end of the areaway. At the other end stood her Fredericia cohorts, with Krohgarn standing stiffly in front.

Sigefert turned as she stepped up to his side, and nodded slightly. His expression was oddly enigmatic, and she felt a shiver of unease. She searched the Northumbrian ranks for familiar faces, quickly spotting Oddune standing at their front, and he returned her salute with a solemn expression. She wanted to greet him, but Sigefert put a hand on her arm.

"Not just now, Tara," he said softly. "Time for that after the work is organized. But there's another matter—your deputy has a bee in his helmet that we must address."

"Krohgarn? He came to you direct?" Her eyes blazed in anger. "He has no business dealing with you; arrangements with the fortress are mine to handle."

"I must heed what he says." She could see now that his face was taut with worry, in a way she'd never seen before, but she had no hint of the cause.

"Nonsense! Send him packing! I'm in charge of the provisioning party. If he has something to say to you, require him to say it through me."

"In this matter I cannot." He spoke formally, in a manner unfamiliar to her. "He demands a holmganga."

"A holmganga? With me?" She was stupified. "What for? Why? What gives him the right?"

"He has the right, by the King's Law, to charge before the local commander that you have slandered him or treated him ill, and to demand an einvig or holmganga in defense of his honor and his reputation. Be thankful he does not insist on the einvig, for that is a duel to the death. The holmganga is done and honor satisfied when the first blood spills on the cloth."

"Honor? The man has no honor!" she scoffed, livid with fury. "And how does he claim he was treated ill?"

"He charges that at Lindholm Hoje you shamed him before his crew, by leaving his command without his leave, and taking passage with another to Aggersborg."

"Leaving his command? What is this? He's under my command!"

"He is under your command of the overall force, true, but when you take passage in his ship you are under his command as a passenger or crew member."

"But that's ridiculous!"

"Ridiculous perhaps, but the Law. A ship's captain must have unquestioned authority for his ship, and if you ignore his authority, others can as well. You must see that." His tone was almost one of pleading with her to understand.

Tara was thunderstruck. Was this stiff-backed stranger the same man who had held her with such tender and compassionate understanding just the night past? "And you entertain this charge, do you?" she demanded hotly.

"I must." Through her exasperation, she could read how the words pained him, and in any other situation she could have appreciated his scrupulous fairness, as would befit a commander. "But there is a way out," he went on. "All you need do is apologize to him for your behavior, and his right to the holmganga disappears."

"Apologize? You cannnot be asking me to do that!" Her exasperation returned doublefold.

"Is it not better than fighting, than risking death?"

Death! "But you said the duel ends when first blood flows."

"That is the Law, yes, but it does not always work out so. Many have died in the holmganga, first blood or no."

She remembered suddenly how Sigefert had scorned to stop when Oddune blooded him. "But Krohgarn well knows I meant no insult to him; if he has a brain, he must know I gave him no least thought, once I saw a familiar face. Oft I have ached to insult him, but not then. I shifted to Gormsson's boat only to visit with him."

"I wat he knows that well enow." Sigefert's tone was grim. "But he's thrown down the challenge, and by the Law it must be answered."

"You must know if I apologize on so montrous a charge, my authority over the men will be gone—e'en your Northumbrians will hold me in contempt. I may as well turn over my command to him and be done!" A flash of understanding hit her. "Belike that's his purpose. He seeks no duel with me, but just an apology—his way to hit back at me for being placed over him."

"Very like," agreed Sigefert. "But you must answer him one way or another. His witnesses say you left his ship without leave, shaming him before his crew, and we cannot gainsay that. His challenge demands you apologize or fight; there is no other way before the Law."

He reached to take her hand, but she drew it angrily away. "I beg of you, Tara—let us meet in my chamber privately, say your apology, and only we three will hear."

"And when the holmganga is called off, will not all the fortress know what took place there?" He was at a loss to reply, and she went on. "There can be no apology. I will fight him!"

Sigefert's face was ashen. In his worried countenance, Tara read admiration for her courage, compassion for her plight, and overshadowing all, a dreadful fear for her safety. "You must cool your anger," he urged. "This is no half-starved robber skulking in a storehouse, no clumsy outlaw preying on the poor. Krohgarn is a Viking, a skilled swordsman, and word reaches me that in his younger days he was a berserksgangr."

"His younger days are past! Think you I fear this...this bag of wind? No! We will fight!"

Standing at the edge of the cloth staked out on the ground, its stone border marking the duel arena, she knew a fleeting moment of regret for her hasty anger. Krohgarn presented a fearsome appearance in his unwieldy iron helmet and heavy iron corselet over knee-length mailed brynga, and armed with his double-edged sword and iron-bossed shield. Searching hard for a vulnerable spot, she suddenly realized how hard he'd be to blood. If it were a long engagement, of course, the weight of all he carried would wear away at his endurance. Powerful he was, but well past his prime, with a thick waist that meant more weight to slow him down. But his massive arms and legs betokened the strength to crush her with a single blow before he tired. And what did she have to oppose him? Naught but her quick agility, and the stamina of youth. And perhaps one additional crucial advantage—the strong likelihood that he'd underestimate her, belike disbelieving the tales of her Byzantium exploits.

She appraised him more carefully, searching for any sign of weakness, any telltale gesture betraying his intentions. She could imagine his lidded eyes gloating at maneuvering her into this encounter. She'd have to focus intently on those eyes, while seeming not to, in an effort to guess his target before he struck. His style would be a fearsome hacking attack, such as in the bout between Sigefert and Oddune, where first blood could be the cleavage of her skull, but his need to raise his sword first might give her just that crucial instant to evade the powerful downward sweep, or at least to try. Her tactics would have to be the lightning duelling thrusts of the Cymri, requiring no drawing back of the blade, giving no warning.

She knew her accoutrement astonished the audience, for she wore neither armor nor helm, and her left arm carried no shield but only the short dagger that had served her so well so many times. Her pantalons and tunic were light, and her feet bare. Her keen Rhenish sword seemed a child's plaything beside Kruhgarn's fearsome battle weapon. Their difference, she reflected, was that he was outfitted to absorb punishment, and she to evade it.

Pray Lug I can evade it, she breathed silently. If just one of his blows found her, it could end her life. This would be no ritual duel for honor's sake, but a naked attempt at murther. And belike the only end would be when one of them lay dead.

Briefly, she looked for Sigefert, to draw strength from his presence, but she could not pick him out from the milling throng of onlookers. Her pulse throbbed in her temples. How she longed to be free of this travesty and in Sigefert's arms, safe in the certainty of his protection! Why did I not apologize, she asked herself. I need not have done this. Oh, Sigefert…why did I not let you stop me…?

The lance dropped, drawing her abruptly back to the dreadful here and now, and the two adversaries moved cautiously into the square. The audience fell quiet, and in the sudden silence the ominous crunch of Krohgarn's heavy boots on the gravel beneath the cloth was the only sound. He held his shield well in front of him, tilted outward to deflect blows harmlessly aside. His shoulders were turned to one side, his sword arm raised high and bent, his wrist cocked back. He was poised to

launch a murderous downward sweep, but she devoutly hoped the preliminary tensing of his muscles to set shoulder, arm and wrist in motion
would suffice to give her the needed warning of his intentions.

She caught the shift of his pupils, tracing a path down and left across
her neck, then the sudden tightening of his jaw.

Now!

His powerful torso turned with unexpected quickness, and the sword
slashed down on the path she'd read. She spun clear, and as his heavy
blade cleaved the air she swept her blade backhanded, its point biting
into the mesh brynga protecting his shoulder. There was a quick intake
of breath among the watchers, but none spoke. Krohgarn pulled back
swiftly, and again they faced off.

He's blooded, she thought exultantly! The duel can end! Should not
the duel end now? But the hatred boiling in his eyes told her it was no
part of his plan to let her off so easily. Filled with foreboding, she steeled
herself to fight on.

He frowned, his manner more cautious now, and she knew his recognition of her skill would serve to make him doubly dangerous. He
stepped back, raising his sword, but launched no attack. He waits for me
to commit, she knew, hoping to catch me off balance as I did him. Not
willing to offer him such advantage, she waited. Neither moved for a
time, and she could hear impatient murmuring from the audience.

Krohgarn's eyes, which had been fixed on hers, shifted to focus
momentarily on her left shoulder. He thinks to dangle an opening
before me, hoping I'll repeat my riposte, she guessed, then shift his
stroke and catch me. But was she right? Could she read so much in that
darting glance?

She'd have to. There'd be no other warning.

Again his jaw muscles tightened, and she tensed. His sword slashed
down as before, and instantly she reacted, springing to the opposite side
this time, expecting his blade would arc to the side where she'd spun
away before. Too late she saw he'd fooled her; it was coming straight

down. Frantically she reversed, but the blade tip sliced down her tunic and she felt the quick pain of its tip tearing her flesh. As she sprang back, shaking involuntarily, she caught the gleam of triumph in his hooded eyes. We've blooded each other, she thought. Now she could drop her blade to earth, before the loss of blood whose warmth she felt on her chest weakened her, declare the holmganga satisfied, and it would be over.

But suddenly a burning anger churned inside her. No, she decided in cold fury—I will not take the craven's way and call it over. He will pay for this! Then they were back in attack position, and her chance to call a halt, to save herself, had passed.

I must not try to read his eyes. I must give up that advantage, she realized with sinking heart. He knows I try, and will deceive me with false signals. Sigefert warned she fought no doltish churl. If she waited again to react to Kruhgarn's attack, she would be lost. To save her life, she must carry the fight to him!

Her blade flicked out like a striking snake, catching his sword hand just inside the hilt, and blood spurted from a vessel in his wrist. Instantly it flashed out again, straight for his face, its tip sketching a thin red line down his cheek. Blood there was now, in plenty, but neither would call a halt while both were on their feet.

Maddened by the pinking, Krohgarn roared out, and furiously swung his sword in a mighty sidewise swipe that would have cloven her in twain had it landed. But it was high, and he had signalled his intent a bare instant before launching it, and Tara was dropping to all fours even as it started. She escaped the murderous slash by the merest whisper, and realized she could not be so fortunate again. He learns fast, she knew, and his next swing would be designed to catch her no matter how low she crouched. She must disable him now, before he could recover and launch that next blow, which an inner foreboding told her would be fatal!

Whether a voice came to her, or the thought was dredged up from her own frantically searching mind, she could not tell. But somehow the words echoed in her subconscious, as they had at the Hippodrome: Wulfdune! Wulfdune!

She faced off Krohgarn, stared directly into his flushed and furious face, leaned forward, and spat full in his eyes.

He recoiled, too surprised to seize the momentary opening she presented before she leaped back. Then he furiously swung his weapon above his head, strategy forgot in his raging need to avenge the insult to his pride and manhood, and slashed it down with blind ferocity, pressing forward so she could not evade him. But Tara did not seek to evade him. She, too, rushed directly forward, thudding hard into his stomach, even as his arm overreached her and his sword met empty air.

In that instant, his infinitesimal moment of vulnerability, she did as she had done at the Hippodrome. With her left hand, she plunged her dagger beneath his iron corselet with every ounce of her strength, forcing it in and upward, piercing his brynga like so much cheese, and driving the lethal little weapon to its very hilt, deep into his lung cavity.

He stumbled forward with the momentum of his charge, carrying her body to the ground beneath him. Even as she writhed to pull free, she saw his sword knocked from his hand to lie on the ground beside her. She could ignore the huge weapon, for he'd not have room to draw it back—but he still had his powerful hands, and she was pinned beneath him, helpless to defend herself. She could do naught but wait, in a strange mix of terror and lassitude, for those great hands to come together around her neck, and throttle the life out of her.

The hands clenched involuntarily—not about her defenseless neck, but at nothingness. His eyes, inches from hers, widened in astonishment, and she heard him call out incoherently, but his words were muffled by the blood spewing from his mouth and spattering her face. His huge body trembled as if he had a chill, then changed to muscle spasms, and his huge legs twitched. After an eternity, his movements ended, and he lay motionless, still holding her pinned down and unable to pull free.

Eager hands were pulling Krohgarn's inert body away then, were lifting her up, prying the dagger from her stiffly-clenched fingers, cheering as she could never imagine these stolid Northmen to cheer. Painfully, she struggled to a sitting position, wiped her face with her hands, and stared with mute incomprehension at the blood between her fingers.

Her eyes misted over, and she felt her stomach heaving. She grasped about her for support, but there was none to find.

Then, despite her desperate struggle to retain consciousness, she felt herself sinking into an abyss, and fainted dead away.

CHAPTER 25

A gossamer fragment of imagination drifted into her subconscious mind while she dozed fitfully—a phantasmagoria of the nether regions, in demonic response to the throbbing pain of her wound. But the image that came to her was pure and sharp and bright as a summer's day.

It was the dappled forest glade, Atheurin astride the chestnut log, unfolding before the little girl at his feet a stirring panorama of her Celtic origins, inspiring her with his vision of Cymru's future, dedicating her to the great role the old Druidic gods had fashioned for her. And e'en as she looked, from outside the vision, she was in it as well—as if at one with the child, looking direct into the Bard's eyes, drinking in his words.

"You must hew true to your path, Princess," he was saying, in his soft grave voice. "Oft it may be hard to discern, with its twists and strange turnings to test you and build your strength. But it is there, and will lead you back to Cymru and your destiny, as sure as the gods hold court in the Otherworld, for you are the chosen of the Ui Liathain. E'en when their way sends you far across the seas, always are you under the shelter of the great Manawyddan fab Llyr. The road you follow holds dangers and trials aplenty, but ever have you found the resource and courage to surmount the perils that beset you. I have called to Esus, Taranis and Teutates, the three great gods of the Celts, that they grant you stamina enow for those that surely lie ahead.

So the fortress itself must be part of her path, she concluded, awed by the warp and sweep of her conflicting fortunes, and the vastness of the great plan that guided her. But if it was, she needed answer to a sudden perplexing question.

How then, may I stay in the fortress, which bars all women? Am I not a woman?

You are a warrior. And you are a Princess. The code of the fortress cannot bar a warrior who will rule a kingdom one day.

But how, then, may I show that I am these things? How prove to the Fellowship, which thinks me but Sigefert's maiden, that I am more warrior than woman?

Did you not fight the berserksgangr? Have you not the wounds to show? Lies not his lifeless body on the funerary pyre in clear testimony of what you are? Who dares say you nay?

She shut out the scene briefly, thinking on his words. When she looked once more, the scene was sponged out, and she saw naught before her but the mute walls of Sigefert's empty chamber.

"I was near to thinking you bewitched, lass."

She had thought herself alone—no, she had been alone—but when she turned again, Sigefert stood over her. "You were moaning and calling in your strange Cymri tongue, your eyes wide but focused on naught, and I could not reach you. Where were you?"

She took his hand gratefully, a blessed security from the welcome pressure of his grasp infusing her. "Far away, my love. In a wooded glade back in my home. But the dream is ended, and I'm back here safe with you now." She smiled up at him.

"Thanks be to Freya!" His relieved sigh told her he'd been worried, and she felt warmed by his caring. She would learn later that, throughout the duel, he'd been poised at a point behind her, tensed and primed to charge to her defense had need arisen, honor or no honor. He would not let her die! "Your wound was not deep, only the flesh is badly torn. I dressed it as best I knew, and called to Odin that Krohgarn's accursed sword bore no pestilence." He touched her breast just above the wound gently. "How feels it now, sweet love?"

"There's little hurt," she assured him untruthfully. "I was blessed to escape so light. You were right, Sigefert—I did underestimate him, thinking him past his fighting prime. The gods of Denemearc and of Cymru watched over me together, to keep his sword from its mark."

"And I, as well, sought the gods. I called down the help of Tyr, god of martial honor, to be with you on the cloth. But my sense tells me Krohgarn's slaying was of your own skill, unaided by any gods, Cymri or Norse. It was as well you fought so nobly, for he sought no bloodletting for honor, but evil murther for one he envied and hated." He broke off, his voice hard with suppressed emotion, and Tara felt through the space that separated them the strength of his feeling. His free hand went to her brow, and gently he brushed back her golden hair, his fingers savoring its silken texture. "You were magnificent! Did I not know you are a beauteous woman, I'd wager Mimir himself that you be no woman at all, but a true Valkyr and Viking."

His flattering last words, choked as they were with emotion, minded her of a pressing matter to be settled. "Take thought on what you just said, for it bears on a thing of great import to me...to the twain of us. I ask you, as commander of Aggersborg, to rule that the law barring women from a fortress does not fall on me, for I am a warrior who has fought on your ground and by the laws of your Fellowship."

She had thought to see a reaction of grave concern, and was disconcerted by his sudden outburst of laughter. He released her hand, and walked around to the foot of her pallet. "I was wondering when that would out, lass," he said, smiling as though he'd won a gaming toss. "I've already taken a vote at our Althing. As commander, or chieftain, I need not have done this, but some might whisper that I favor one close to me. It was best decided by all the men in concert." He came back again and took both her hands, and Tara's heart nearly burst from happiness at his devoted look.

His cheerfulness, and his encouraging words, made it clear how they'd decided, but waiting for him to speak was needless agony. "And the decision? Leave off torturing me! Tell me!"

He wore an expression of commingled admiration and awe. "All who watched you fight are of one mind: you are more than woman, whatever the curves of your body tell. You are a warrior born, and you've earned your place as one of us."

It was not until mealtime that the other question struck her, and as she tried to ask she blushed deeply, not finding words. Sigefert was quick to read her thought. "Fret no more on that, Tara—you need not sleep in the men's barrack. You are warrior by day only. When night falls, you become a woman—my woman—and you share my chamber." He hesitated. "But only if it sits easy on you, girl."

She was too flustered to make answer. And though his invitation was her very heart's desire, the question must be pursued to its end. "But the men—your Vikings, and Gormsson's Danes—will they object?"

"And face me in the square, as Krohgarn faced you? No, lass, they'll not object. Envy my great fortune, more like."

The following weeks brought a time of such idyllic happiness that Tara agonized lest her excess of joy displease the stern gods, and induce them to end it. She could see that the Danes and Northumbrians alike bore no animosity toward her for joining their company. Rather, she was the object of their raucous toasts, the recipient of constant gifts brought from the lush countryside, and e'en the burden of their tuneless and bawdy songs around the evening board.

The fortress awed her by its immensity. With its internal diameter of near nine hundred Roman feet, and its ramparts better than sixty feet thick, it was quite the largest enclosure she could have imagined. Twenty-three longhouses were completed, with twenty-five more planned, for the ultimate fortress complement of over five hundred warriors plus supporting menials and thralls. The hastily erected buildings had timber-framed walls of wattle and daub, as there'd been no time for the sturdier construction of halved tree-staves. Though simple and rude, they would suffice to withstand the winter winds roaring in from the Varangian and Northern Seas. The gable ends of each main structure had small rooms apart from its main hall, and it was to one such that Sigefert had taken Tara for their living quarters.

The fortress lay on the Limfjord's northern bank, and the big Gokstad ships had to be threaded through a narrow channel. Bentorm's Roskilde knarrs were shorter, but too broad of beam and deep of draft for the canal, and were forced to berth at the landing stage. The seamen and soldiers from Fredericia, together with the Jelling fleet that had brought the families, went home in the knarrs, their numbers proof against the Norway pirates from Kaupang who swooped down like angry bees to harry shipping along the coast. Indeed, Gorm had established Aggersborg to hunt down just such as these freebooters of King Harald Haarfager.

Tara asked Sigefert and Gormsson to let her say a private farewell to Bentorm's force, and break her final ties to Fredericia. "The Master will be fair broke in heart you're not returning, Lady," said Dunstad, the respectful old soldier who fleeted up to command at her defection and Krohgarn's death. But had not the old merchant himself insisted she make this voyage, hard on her return from the punishing Byzantium trip? It seemed likely the wily old man had known from the start how desperately she ached to come, and had contrived to win the contract that she might reunite with Sigefert. And how tragic that the proud Krohgarn could not know the command would devolve on him one day later, and had to die a needless death. Despite his ferocious wish to kill her, the tragic denouement saddened her. He was well past his prime, and she could have apologized. The shame for her would have been small, soon forgot. Why had the gods pushed her to fight, and in the end to kill him? Then the sudden thought struck her: had she not fought, would she have been accepted by the Vikings to stay on in the fortress?

So belike his killing was one more chapter, planned by the gods. Oh, Atheurin, she pleaded, thoroughly confused, tell me if I see it aright. Tell me! But he gave her no sign. Belike he decided she needed none.

On her arrival at Aggersborg, Tara wore clothing from the store Bentorm had procured for the fortress complement, and thus was not easily distinguished from the men. When she was fully accoutred, with helmet in place, even with her long red-gold braids hanging down her chest, she resembled a soldier—especially since many Vikings wore braids also. Sigefert refrained from comment on her masculine attire, but she knew it displeased him. When one day he confronted her with it, she took it amiss, asking with disdain, "what would you have me wear, then—laces and silks and frippery?"

"And why not, lass? You call yourself a soldier..." He corrected himself hastily at her flash of anger. "You are a soldier, none disputes it. But you're a highborn lady as well, and I trow others have seen you as such. Just once I'd fain see you so myself. Can you understand?"

The reasonableness of his comment disarmed her. At night, snug in their chamber, there was no doubting his ardor—or hers. But she knew that her daily appearance could do little to stir his pulse. If she made shift to cobble up some bits of feminine finery, mayhap his eyes would keep shining on her the day long.

But no! She was no Jarl's baggage, to hang breathless on his words, to swoon at his glance.

And yet...

In the end, persuaded by his gentle coaxing, she allowed him to take her to Lindholm Hoge. Gormsson undertook to learn, from the wives of his Danes, where to find the best the frontier town boasted in feminine finery, and accompanied the couple on their shopping quest. "You must take care not to affright the women, girl," he chuckled. "They'll take you for a Valkyr in that attire, come to spirit their men off to Valhalla, and that without seeing you handle a blade. If they'd witnessed you skewering Krohgarn, they'd ne'er unbar a door to you."

"But we cannot beg them to share their meager store of clothes from Jelling," said Tara, not seeing how this trip could succeed. "And sure you'll not find clothes shops in such a new town so soon."

"Not true shops, as you had in Fredericia, but I think we'll make shift. The men's purses are full of silver from the back pay you brought, and where there's coin you can trust goods to appear as if by gifts of the Aesir. The problem, with supplies so sparse, will be to get fair value for our silver."

"If we find naught, there's no matter, for only Sigefert's fancy brought us here." She turned and bestowed a comfortable smile on Sigefert, to remove the sting of her words. "I've no real need for women's finery." And no wish for it, she added silently. But a small inner voice bade her recall her triumphant excitement in old Brechnor's Hall—the heady experience of seeing feminine artifices draw the uchelwyr swarming about her like bees to honeysuckle. Might it not be nice, just for a time, to luxuriate in soft-spun linens and delicate Eastern silks?

"I'll not insist, Tara, if your mind is dead set against it," said Sigefert, miffed nonetheless at her remarks. "I thought it might please you to bring some beauty to this dreary outpost, and to remember how you look as a woman."

"And not just you remembering," added Gormsson with feeling. "It will bring pleasure to all in the fortress."

Sigefert frowned, not entirely pleased with support couched so. "You'd wear trooper gear by day, of course," he declared firmly. "Kirtles and skirts would suit you ill on the ramparts. But at night…"

The women had outdone themselves, finding an out-of-the-way but surprisingly well- supplied shop. Its building was more substantial than the rough log homes, but the door frame was so low they were forced to stoop almost double to enter, and see what surprises it held.

Soapstone oil lamps hanging from the cross rafters shed dim light, but it sufficed to show several women, none so young as Tara, cutting and sewing jumbles of garments in various stages of completion. The fabrics that could be seen were of surprising quality, equaling those Tara had seen in Byzantium. On tall shelves behind the central table were piled bolts of silken cloth in shimmering blues and greens, rolls of Irish lace, folded piles of creamy linen and dyed woolens, hanks of woolen yarns, coils of embroidered tape worked in elaborate designs—an astonishing inventory for such an establishment in this rude frontier settlement.

The shopkeeper emerged as they entered, asking briskly how he could serve them. "A gown, perhaps? A fine embroidered apron? A laced bodice?" His own garb was drab brown: a long robe thrown over his shoulders and near scraping the floor. His black hair, long hooked nose and swarthy complexion, coupled with his dark and deepset eyes, betokened a Paulician or Anatolian, and Tara marvelled at the legerdemain enabling him to come from so distant a homeland to serve this lusty young town. His eyes lit on Gormsson and Sigefert, and he directed his attention to where the power lay.

"This lady must be garbed properly," said Sigefert shortly.

"But certainly, Lord. My greatest wish is to serve the Lady—and you, Lord." His obsequious tones disgusted Tara, but Sigefert seemed not to notice, and asked the shopkeeper to take her in hand and recommend what was needed.

The dark man's eyes lighted up with an avaricious gleam. "In such case, Lord, she'll need underslips, bodices of both silk and laces, woolen kirtles, aprons to wear in the morn, tunics for afternoon, capes for eventime…"

"Stop!" Tara impatiently cut off the unending recital. "I need but a woolen kirtle and linen apron." She looked about her. "Though I do admire your excellent stock, I need no inventory of it. If you please, show me kirtles and aprons."

The merchant humbly begged to explain: she must choose a cloth, a suitable style, and the seamstress would take her measure… But Tara, no longer attending his words, saw a kirtle of striped red and blue wool.

"This will do." She tossed it to him, and started looking for an apron, as the women stared openmouthed.

Unfortunately, the man stated in unctuous tones, the kirtle the Lady liked had been ordered for someone else, who would call for it on the morrow. "But may I suggest..."

"The Princess Tara wishes that one, shopkeeper!" Few merchants would have made bold to gainsay one with such an air of authority, who spoke in such a stern voice. He was starting to bow and acquiesce when Sigefert went on. "And pray you find her an apron—a fair one, with bright trim. We have no time for pettifogging; we leave within the hour."

The chastened merchant, recognizing the voice of command, prevailed upon Tara to at least try on the garments, that they might be fitted and adjusted. By the time they left the little shop, Sigefert had added a bright Shetland knit sweater with cap and mittens to match, and a velvet bodice to wear under the kirtle. The moment they were well underway on the return trip, he induced her to put on the cap and sweater for their viewing.

The Shetland sweater, though loose-fitting to provide winter warmth, sufficed to show off her healthy feminine body to splendid advantage, and both men were stirred unexpectedly by her gloriously altered appearance. When she adjusted the cap, so it showed to best advantage her lustrous red-gold braids set aglow by the northern sun, she looked, standing erect before them with unconscious pride, like the very embodiment of a Norse goddess.

"By Odin, girl—you're a beauty!" declared Gormsson, staring in unabashed admiration. "'Fore the gods, it is too much—so gallant a warrior, and so beauteous a creature withal!"

Tara's heart was warmed by the frankness and sincerity of his compliment. "What you see is happiness. I am happy...happy to have such good friends." She turned to Sigefert, and took both his hands in hers. "And so grateful to you, both for what you've bought me, and for urging me against my wishes to come with you and buy them."

She hoped he would echo Gormsson's easy words of praise, but though he looked at her with disconcerting intensity, he did not speak. I know he thinks me fair, she told herself, and would say so if he knew how. But if he would not speak, how could she know what really was in his heart? Did he take her as naught but a feckless maid, sexuality her sole tool, its revelation before men her main power? That will never be my way, she vowed in irritation. I am a Princess! I have no need of niggling female ways—not while my arm is strong and my blade keen! She turned quickly away, the warmth in her heart irrationally chilled, and stared unseeingly at the far shore.

That evening an unaccountable stiffness grew between them, that neither knew how to ease. She thought to put on her new clothes, and ached to go to him and openly confess her doubts, taking strength from the reassurance of his strong arms about her. But some unyielding inner reluctance held her back. And later, when they went to bed, each turned away from the other without speaking. She was miserably unhappy, but helpless to divine the cause. Their sleeping failed to wash away their mutual disaffection, and they went separately and in silence to their morning work.

When she first arrived, Tara had been accorded the place of honor at Sigefert's right hand, with Gormsson seated at his left, and it became her regular seat in the dining hall. Four others sat in the high seats: Oddune and a Dane named Hralf, sub-chieftains of the Northumbrian and Danish contingents, an older Northman named Kjell who was Chief Armourer and Weapon-Master, and the fortress Skald. The latter's traditional responsibility was to compose their poems, chronicle their doings, and prepare the Runakefli, with their cryptic Runic prophesies which were an essential prerequisite to any major undertaking.

Tara had taken to wearing her woman's clothing to the Second, or evening, meal. She did so at first as a peace offering to Sigefert, but he seemed scarce to notice, and never made reference to her finery. Her costume was such an instant and dramatic hit with the officers that they'd think it unseemly for her to abandon the practice once started. If Sigefert had intended the finery to be displayed only in front of him, he never said so outright, and she would not grant him a favor he thought too unimportant to request.

The first few times after she started dressing so for the evening meal, Tara repaired to their apartment as soon as she had eaten, but Sigefert remained at table in the Norse manner, and when he came to the room, it was usually to fall straightway into bed, his senses somewhat dulled from too many horns of local mead. She resorted to staying in the hall, as her only way to see him at night. The officers were much pleased to have her there, and she became the subject of joyful and oft ribald songs, the toast of boisterous drinking bouts—and more and more, the cynosure of all their eyes, and unwilling recipient of their half-drunken attentions.

Perhaps inevitably, the situation showed signs of getting out of hand. What started as harmless flirtation was becoming something serious, and potentially ugly. More than once, she had remarked a Viking, too deeply in his horns to ken what he did, clawing his way toward her with bloodshot eyes, restrained only by his laughing companions. It would be but a matter of time, she knew, until one made his way to her unhindered, and she shuddered to think of his inevitable confrontation with Sigefert.

And she would be the one to blame for the bloody scene that was likely to ensue!

She never should have come, to so woman-starved a camp, with the Northumbrians made even more restless by the enforced idleness of winter. They grew bolder and more discontented daily with their unnatural celibate existence, and she knew not how it would end.

When Sigefert would be occupied in discussion with others, she oft found herself conversing with Oddune on her right, and even with Ottar, the enigmatic Skald who sat next to him. One evening, when a drunken youngster had to be beaten back from clambering across the table to get at her, and sat nursing his bruises and glowering resentfully at her, Tara put the burning question to Oddune direct.

"What ails the men, Oddune? Can no way be found to salve their unease? Would it be best for me to leave the mess at the Second Meal, and eat henceforth in my apartment?"

"They are exactly as soldiers everywhere, Princess. They watch Gormsson's Danes off to Lindholm Hoge, one barrack each week, for their family leave, then must list to them return at week's end with loud tales of bedding their women. They need women of their own."

"But is there no curing it?" She was reluctant to speak out plain, but in Mathry Tref outside the walls of Aber Castle, in Menevia's tref, and belike in all such places, she had heard there were women who... "Cannot your Northumbrians have leave in the town as well?"

It took him a time to understand her meaning and reply. "Nay, Princess," he said after a bit. "The Northumbrians may not enter Lindholm Hoje. It is Gorm's order, and his grandson's real purpose here is to ride herd on us, and see all of Gorm's orders carried out, come what may."

"But why...?"

"Because he does not yet trust your Sigefert, nor any Briton. That is why, if it comes to a blowup, Gormsson's Danes outnumber us three to two."

"But Sigefert is fortress commander."

"Aye. Gorm knows his grandson has neither the years nor battle hardening to hold against attack by King Harald, so he must use a proven commander—Sigefert. But he likes him not."

"And meantime, forces all of you to live the lives of monks."

Oddune nodded in assent. The Skald, who had listed with great attention to their words, spoke up in his monotonous sing-song. "There will be no peace in Aggersborg while the men of Briton are imprisoned here! I see wounddew flowing, the Angel of Death at the gate, biers piled high with dead soldiers. I see, waiting at the landing stage, a royal vessel with high curving prow, and bodies lying thick about the mast sole, swords and armor stacked there, and the black raven perched at the masthead!"

The awful solemnity of the chant made a deep impression on Tara, and it was as if she actually saw before her the dread picture his words painted. "Is there no way out? Can naught be done? Does not Gorm know the effect of his orders?"

"Aye, he knows."

Sigefert had been listening unnoticed, and it was he who made further answer. "Gorm's mind runs deep, and his ways are hard to fathom, but I can tell you this—it is no part of his plan to leave a Northumbrian in command at Aggersborg."

"Then why does he not replace you now and be done?"

"He cannot…not yet. More remains to prepare Aggersborg. But the day will come when he is ready, and when it does…"

He left the sentence unfinished.

CHAPTER 26

"Why do we not return to Britain—to Northumbria?" If Gorm's intent was to discard Sigefert as soon as he completed the backbreaking task of building a new fortress, why should they not best Gorm at his game, and leave at their own pleasure? To Tara, the idea had seemed obvious, but when she set it before Sigefert, it earned her naught but an indulgent smile.

Ever since she'd been at Aggersborg, he'd shared no decisions with her. Bentorm had given her full rein, made her a person of consequence. At home she'd been the honored heir to the throne—and was the heir still, far off though Dyfed now seemed. She'd been trained to the arts of deciding and managing, and frankly enjoyed the exercise of power.

And perhaps that was the problem. She had not been raised to aspire to the subordinate role of wife. Yet, she realized, she'd come eagerly to Aggersborg, heedless of all else, apparently to fill that role. Would it suffice her to be naught but Sigefert's woman, living forever in his shadow, submerging her ambition and talent, doing and wanting only what would advance his career? And if so, would he truly hold her special, or was she but chattel—naught but his property? Property to be enjoyed, shown off...e'en on occasion admired. But cherished? Loved perhaps more than life itself? He did not ever tell her as much. And of late he'd been unduly preoccupied...inattentive to her...even indifferent at times. If it was to continue thus, mayhap she'd been ill-persuaded to come. The thought was deeply troubling to her.

Best to have done with such broodings!

"I cannot return to Cymru whilst Clydog sits the High Throne," she went on, in an effort to engage him in discussion, "but could we not repair to the land of your birth? That would be the Britain we both know, our native land, and you'd be among your own people."

Sigefert sighed patiently, a habit that was starting to annoy her. "Do you disremember York, and the reception they accorded us? Those were my people, near enough, but they had to bend the knee to King Alfred, and dared not let us remain. We cannot go there."

"But could we not make landfall higher on the coast?" persisted Tara. "Above the Humber, higher than Alfred's forces range? There's no fighting to stir up the Saxons now; why should his ships remain on patrol month after month, finding naught?" She looked keenly at him, to see how he was taking the close questioning. "I wat we'd contrive a safe haven farther north."

Sigefert took her face in his hands, tilting her head back until their eyes met. "With Alfred we've no chance but to be hanged as pirates. With Gorm—he can change. We've done his work, faithfully and well, not grumbling about delays, not scheming against him. No others could have done better. Gormsson will testify so. Gorm's bound to accept that, in time. I expect him to change, and accept us into his fighting forces as true Danes. Prime fighting men are not found easily, which is why he gave us this chance—as a trial. You list too much to what the men say, when they talk unthinking. Best you think your own thoughts, Tara."

She did not raise the question again.

Each week, a Danish barrack contingent boisterously took sledges, hauled by spiked-footed horses over the plains and frozen waterways, to visit their women in Lindholm Hoje. And each week, the Northumbrians watched glumly from the parapets. When they returned, it was even worse, their ribald accounts pouring salt on the wounds of those who could not share their boudoir pleasures. Each week, the resentment festered and smoldered. The tiniest spark in the tinder of their frustration could kindle a destructive conflagration.

Such a group had left just before the onset of a blizzard that now enveloped the fortress in deep snow. The snow had lessened on the morn they were due to return, but the weather had turned bitter cold, and Sigefert and Gormsson realized the expedition was ill-equipped for any extended exposure to the elements. They were expected before mealtime, but when the Second meal ended with no sign of them, Sigefert was seriously concerned for their safety.

"I like it not," he said, and called together a council of officers to consider whether a search party should be dispatched.

"The snow was not so heavy today," said Hralf. "Thorfinn is leader, and he's come through much heavier weather than this."

"I say the same," agreed Oddune, in whom resentment still rankled. "Northumbrians would take this weather for child's play. A pity some of my men were not in the party."

"So you think my Danes less hardy than your Britons?" demanded Hralf, glaring at Oddune.

"Leave off, Hralf," scolded Gormsson, urging the deputy back into his seat. But a red flush rose on Hralf's neck, and Tara could feel the atmosphere growing tense.

Sigefert knew the storm had blown itself out by then, but it could still be heavy to the east. "They may be having far more difficulty than we ken," he said. "It will not be easy for them to hew to their way in the dark."

Tara put words to a sudden chilling thought. "Could they have run afoul of a raiding party from Kaupang?" she asked.

All looked at her in astonishment. "In this foul weather?" demanded Hralf, forgetting how he'd belittled the weather moments before. More tactfully, Sigefert expressed his opinion that the Skagerrak would be too rough for raiders to venture out.

Finally Gormsson spoke up. "We must mount a search tonight. Morning could be too late. My Danes will go. This is not a task for Northumbrians."

Sigefert bridled at that. "This is not two fortresses, part Dane, part Northumbrian. What affects one affects all."

Gormsson accepted the judgment without demur, and it was agreed that two parties would go out, to cover the widest possible area eastward. One would go north of the Limfjord, one south, both staying close to the frozen waterway lest they lose direction in the blackness.

At once the two groups were dispatched, equipped for all eventualities: sledges breaking through a wind-driven opening in the ice, a spill that could break runners, a wrong turn in possibly still blinding snow— even an unlikely encounter with a hostile raiding party. The officers remaining behind coalesced in groups around the cooking house, speaking quietly, quaffing occasional horns of mead, reluctant to retire while searchers were out.

"One good thing may come of this," Gormsson said thoughtfully. "If Oddune's men find Thorfinn in need of succor, mayhap a rescue will restore some good feeling to mute the ill-will building up between us."

"A good hope," responded Sigefert. "Odin grant it does not work out just the opposite."

"The opposite? How could that come about?"

"I know not. A score of ways. The Norns twist things about cruelly when they've a mind to. All we can do is wait and see."

The discussion on that topic ended then, but Tara was left with an unsettling premonition, too vague to be set to words.

The two groups returned to the fortress late at night, dog-tired and half frozen from their fruitless searches. They had ranged far to the east, along both shores of the Limfjord, finding no trace of the refugees, and there was naught more to do until daylight. At dawn both parties resumed the search, and again those left behind maintained a restless vigil. Knowing they could hear nothing before noon, Tara sought to busy herself at sword drill, but found herself so snappish with the patient Weapon Master that she gave it up in disgust,

It was late afternoon when the lookout's cry drew all hands to the palisades—only to see the vacationers swaggering in, singing their raucous songs as if still on holiday. Far behind them trudged the bone-weary searchers, feet leaden with fatigue, faces black with anger.

The Lindholm Hoge party seemed genuinely astounded at the apparent concern of their welcomers, the entire fortress complement clustering about to ask what had delayed them. Sigefert pushed impatiently through the crush.

"Where in Asgard have you been, Thorfinn?" he demanded angrily. Where did you pass the night?"

"The night?" responded the surprised Thorfinn. "Why…at Lindholm Hoje, Jarl. We left only this morn."

Sigefert recoiled as if struck in the face. "You left this morn? Why not yesterday?

The leader sensed the bitter anger in Sigefert's words, and hesitated before answering. "The weather, Jarl. The snow was threatening, and I thought…"

"You thought! That's just what you did not do!" Sigefert's eyes were smouldering. "Come with me!" He turned and strode rapidly toward his apartment. After a moment of indecision, Thorfinn followed, half running to keep up.

The trouble was not long in starting. The Northumbrians from the search party sought only rest, but a group of their fellows—who had watched the roisterors arrive, been forced to hear their bawdy tales, and noted their callous indifference to the searchers' efforts—reached boiling point.

The returning Danes had scarce settled into their barrack, when an enraged Northumbrian band burst in, and set upon them without warning. The attackers were for the most part the young soldiers, lacking the steadying influence of their elders, who might have kept the affair from erupting into a bloody melee. At the start, the intruders kept their weapons sheathed, using only their fists and feet, but they were outnumbered by the leave party, that recovered quickly from the rude surprise and began to defend effectively. The flash point occurred when the Northumbrians drew their swords, and the blood of the unarmed Danes began to flow.

There became a gradual awareness, on both sides, of the gravity of the affair, and with it a lessening of the fighting fury, until soldiers on each side stood panting, glaring at each other, but striking no blow.

It was only then that the officers, belatedly alerted by the uproar, burst into the area and pushed between the two bands, effectively ending the melee. The room lay in ruins, with naught intact save what was too heavy to damage. But the real price was measured in human terms. Seven combatants lay dead, a score had suffered serious hurt, and scarce a man but had painful cuts and bruises.

Sigefert recognized with foreboding that, for all the heavy human and material cost, the real tragedy lay in the fact that the bloody encounter had settled nothing. The bitter emnity between Dane and Northumbrian—between those who visited the town and their women, and those who could not—was deeper than ever.

In the morn, Sigefert summoned his principal subordinates to a conference around the high table. Tara deemed the matter of too grave import to miss, and Sigefert made no demur when she took her seat. He asked for comments on the matter, calling first on Ottar, the Skald.

He is the same as a bard, Tara realized, the same as if Atheurin were in this chamber searching for a sign to divine the answers so desperately needed. But she could feel none of her Atheurin's power in this slight and shabby man—only a faint and ineffectual aura, promising naught. She looked hopefully at his staff, but found it cold and lifeless, and she sensed no strength emanating from it. It is but a carved trinket, carried to impress the ignorant, she decided. No true word from any gods would come through such as he.

"There are sacred groves in the countryside, but we seek them not," he intoned. "We have implanted no runic stones to honor the gods. Sveigdir chased a dwarf, and was seen no more. Fjolnir drowned in a vat of mead. There are kennings aplenty, but we read them not. We have slaughtered no horses, placed no bloody ox head on its pole. We have abandoned the gods in this place, and now they abandon us."

A bewildered silence followed his cryptic words. They were devoid of meaning, Tara knew, spoke but to hide his emptiness. Apparently Sigefert thought so as well, for he thanked the Skald curtly and continued round the table.

The Weapon Master rose next. He pointed out with some justification that the men needed more to occupy their energies, to tire their muscles and leave no strength left for such rampaging. He suggested more sword drill, and a schedule of wrestling games, to act as outlet for their anger. Sigefert nodded with scant enthusiasm, and turned to the next. "Hralf?"

"Dane and Northumbrian must be kept apart, not just in separate barracks as we do now, but in separate sections of the compound. We must make it two fortresses, with no contact between. Else there will be no ending these fights."

Sigefert's eyes flashed angrily. "Never! All here are Danes, and we will have but one fortress! What say you, Oddune?"

The big Northumbrian rose, to lend emphasis to his words. "The problem is plain. All here well know it. In plain words, our men need women. No more useless sword drills to tire their muscles, when it is not their muscles that trouble them. They need activity of a different sort. They are men, and they should have women—those who want them. So long as some of the men have women, while some cannot, that long our men will stand at odds." He spread his big arms apart in a gesture of discouragement. "The solution I cannot see."

"I can."

All eyes turned to Gormsson. He explained his thesis in bald terms. "The spring will be on us soon now. Norway lies just across the Skaggerak, in easy reach of our longboats. There are women in Norway."

There was total silence, as his meaning sank in. Temporarily ignoring her own mixed feelings, Tara studied the faces around the table, watching each man's reaction to the dramatic suggestion. She was interested in seeing how each accepted the implications of Gormsson's startling proposition—nothing less than a raid on people with whom they had no fight, to steal their women.

Sigefert found his voice first, to take sharp exception to the proposal. "And think you King Harald will not strike back at us with massive force, if we raid in the very shadow of the necropolis?"

"I have taken thought on that. We must raid him disguised as Swedes, to turn his anger elsewhere."

"And where would we fish, then?" Despite Sigefert's scorn, Tara sensed he was giving the radical proposal serious consideration. For her, tearing women from their homes and families, to submit to a harsh new life of slavery in strange surroundings, was a fearful proposition, but looking at it dispassionately, in the cold light of analysis, there was logic in Gormsson's suggestion. Tara was no stranger to the institution of slavery: her old nurse, Brigidea, had been a caethwas, as had many in Menevia Castle. They had enjoyed far more security and comfort than in the mean existence from which they were plucked. She had loved Brigidea, and that Brigidea had loved her she had no doubt. Most slaves, given opportunity to return to their former mean existences, would choose not to go. But still—kidnapping helpless women for the casual pleasure of rough and oft cruel Vikings raised a strong and silent protest in her heart. She was a warrior trained, but she was still a woman.

"At Agder, west of Kaupang," Gormsson continued, "is a likely settlement, where many a buxom milkmaid or fisher lass dreams of marriage to a brave warrior, and I wat would find it far better than passing her life amidst farm manure or herring entrails." He looked sidewise at Tara. "And there is a convent hard by, overlooking the sea…"

"No!"

Tara started with surprise, and only then realized the shouted protest was hers. But the thought of gentle sisters, such as those whose spartan life she'd shared at Dewi Sant, being ravished by Vikings was an unendurable horror.

"Don't fret, Tara; none of us has thought of profaning the convent," said Sigefert, his face softened with tenderness. "Gormsson does but tease."

The discussion resumed. Gormsson informed them that, although Agder lay close to King Harald's necropolis, it was by far a safer choice than Kaupang, the other settlement within easy reach. Suddenly, she realized, they had moved unconsciously from dismissing the project as a harebrained proposal to planning it out as a serious campaign. Sigefert took the first step in this new direction by ruling that, if the project materialized, only Northumbrians would take part, as they would be the chief beneficiaries. Tara surprised herself by joining the discussion, insisting that no captive be turned over to a man unless she agreed to accept him as a husband. As others broke in, looking at the tactical difficulties and how they might be surmounted, it appeared the initially foolish suggestion was close to being adopted.

The fortress law forbidding women could not be waived, so it was agreed that construction be started on a small settlement nestled against Aggersborg's south rampart. A hasty survey disclosed that, of Sigefert's more than two hundred followers, only the younger men desired wives, so it was agreed that only these should be told off to throw up rude little daub huts with sodded roofs in which to sequester their brides—if any could be persuaded to have them.

To her relief, Tara was permitted to go on the raid. She had pleaded vigorously, but still was astonished when Sigefert agreed. Her goal was to make sure the kidnappings were as humane as possible, and she wondered how she could disapprove of the plan so deeply, yet work so wholeheartedly toward its success. For Sigefert's sake, she decided. For his survival.

The planned target number was some sixty women, to satisfy all who wished wives—and as many, belike, as were likely to be obtainable in a quick raid. The strength of the raiding party was thrice that number, and four boats were taken, to provide room for their anticipated return cargo.

Tara found herself again in Gormsson's longboat. He came along, the only Dane, because his knowledge of the area was vital to guiding them to the most promising landing point. They had delayed until after spring planting, so the majority of Agder's able-bodied men would be off pillaging, or upland pasturing the cattle. They hoped thus to confront fewer fighting men, and spill as little blood as possible on either side.

Four Gokstad ships crept along the darkened coast with oars muffled, and crept into the remote Agder inlet. A main group would strike the village before dawn, while smaller bands would infiltrate nearby farms, to snatch the cream of their young womanhood. Each man bore not only sword and buckler, but also a blunt cudgel to stun any lads or oldsters who proved troublesome, without wounding them seriously. Tara was at the collection center, where the bound women could be looked over, to eliminate any unsuitable prospects before they were loaded onto the vessels. It was a post of little danger, which was why Sigefert had not objected to her request to join the raiding party.

When the first captives started trickling in, hands tied behind their backs, ropes secured about their necks, Tara was agonized at how terribly young they were, scarce fifteen or sixteen years, but in the next moment she recalled with a start that she had been no older when she killed the outlaw at Dewi Sant. One was even younger than the others, and Tara concluded she was best left behind—but when she made her decision known, groping through the language difference, the girl shook her head violently in the negative. Astounding though it was, she was choosing a terrifyingly unknown future rather than separation from her companions.

Then the captives began arriving in greater numbers, and there was no time for feelings. Tara did contrive to inquire of each girl if she had a husband, and she left behind four whose mute nods told her they did. Two more were so heart-wrenchingly young she could not harden herself to the deed, and these also she bade stand apart. Despite the unmistakable smell of fear emanating from the rest, and despite the terror showing plain on their faces, she could sense an inexplicable excitement, as if the very enormity of their plight created a fascination for the unknown adventure awaiting them. No matter what fear they felt at their uncertain future, she decided, they would be freed at one stroke from the deadening drudgery of their present existence—just as Gormsson had predicted.

The community's resistance was broken early, and little blood was spilled on either side. With few casualties and a successful mission behind them, the atmosphere in the fleet was one of heady exhilaration. Other than the oarsmen, Tara and Oddune were the only ones from the fortress in the boat carrying the women. When the fleet cleared the headland and hit swells, Tara recognized the fear and misery induced in the captives by the craft's motion. The seas were no rougher than normal, but she recalled the agony of her first voyage, and set out to ease their fears as best she could.

Selecting a prisoner who looked more mature than the rest, Tara cut her bonds and took her aside to explain the situation. The woman was tall and sturdy, with pale blonde hair escaping below her tattered kerchief. She followed Tara to a space under the prow, wide-eyed and trembling, then set her jaw and the shaking ceased. She regarded Tara with unblinking eyes of pale blue. *Just like Gormsson's eyes,* Tara recalled, *that day we met on the Ponthieu beach.*

Hoping her speech was understood, she explained to the captive that they were Danes from the fortress at Lindholm Hoje, and that they sought wives, not thralls. She emphasized that no one would be forced to take a man unwillingly. Pricking her own wrist with her dagger, she swore a blood oath to Freya that after a year, if any woman found no man to accept, and wished to go home, she would be returned to Agder unharmed.

The Norwegian woman was conveying Tara's message to the captives, when there was a cry from Gormsson's lookout.

"A sail! There is pursuit!"

Tara and Oddune sprang to the rail and looked aft. In the distance were two longboats, surely too small a force to engage them with any hope of success. Oddune thought the same. "They are not giving chase to us," he said. "They are coasting toward Kaupang. This is a chance encounter. But they see we head for Denemearc, and will know we are not Swedes. We cannot leave them to spread the word. Gormsson must take them!"

Gormsson must have decided the same, for shortly there came a hail from his boat, bidding them proceed with their cargo while the other three boats moved to intercept the strangers.

The homecoming was poignant. Evidently the woman Tara spoke with had explained the situation to the others, for they showed little outright terror, but much interest in the soldiers crowding the banks as they sailed up the channel. The men cheered lustily at sight of the rich harvest of females crowded in the waist of the ship, and ran alongside, pointing and shouting. Tara cut the women's lashings before they disembarked. I will not have members of my sex in bonds before the men they will choose in marriage, she vowed.

"We cleared a barrack for our guests," Sigefert told her. "And some town women are here to welcome them—if that be the word." He turned to Oddune. "Where are the others?"

"We met two strange craft in the strait, and Gormsson thought best to take them so they could carry no tales. So we must find accommodations for a few more prisoners. They should arrive within the hour."

As indeed they did, but with cargo none could have predicted. Gormsson's tone was light, but his expression was uncharacteristically subdued, as he related how the gods had chastened them for their temerity.

"The two boats carried cargo from Harald's court at Urnes. They had few real fighting men, and the engagement was brief, with no killing. But their cargo is worrisome."

"Cargo? Worrisome? What were they carrying?"

"A young lady and her attendants—nothing more."

"Who is this young lady?"

"Ylva, fairest of the fair—only daughter of King Harald Haarfager of Norway!"

CHAPTER 27

"I know not what alchemy you worked on the women, Tara," said Sigefert admiringly. Whatever your potion, it was wondrous effective to achieve such progress in not yet two months. How many are still not bespoke?"

Of the sixty-six women, fifty-four had taken husbands, most already occupying their rude—but fast being made more livable—cottages, others doubling up awaiting completion of their own homes. Two more were yet in the agony of choosing between competing soldiers, and three ill-favored ones were bottom-fishing among the less desirable candidates. Only three had resolutely rejected all offers and were holding out stubbornly for returning to Agder at year's end. This option, hastily offered at the outset, but now recognized as risking near certain disclosure of the kidnappers' identity, was to be avoided at all costs, and Sigefert had been pressing Tara to dissuade the three from this choice.

"By Odin, girl, you're an odd mix of man-hard and woman-soft. What sort of masters would we be, if we left it to thralls whether to remain in servitude or nay? We must do whatever it takes to change their minds."

"I will say it yet again: these women are not thralls! I gave these women my oath, and you made no objection when you were told so. If no suiters can sway them, by all that's right they should be able to return home when the year is out!"

"Ah, well." Sigefert thought the fight, though essential to win in the end, could safely be put off for another day. "A year's a painful spell to stay unbedded. I wat all three will be happily couched ere snow flies." He counted on his fingers. "But your tally sums to but sixty and two. Is it still the same trouble?"

"Aye, still. But there are signs the lady weakens, and once she does there's little doubt her three handmaidens will follow. I see the longing looks they cast at some of your strapping young officers; their desires show plainer on their faces than they know."

The trouble of which Sigefert spoke concerned the Royal Princess Ylva. When taken captive, she and her three highborn attendants were bound for Oseberg to conclude betrothal arrangements to a Swedish Prince, and her imperious fury at being so summarily interrupted had not lessened. Sigefert was equally disturbed, knowing Ylva's royal Sire would stop at no effort to discover the miscreants responsible, and launch an immediate armada to avenge the mortal insult—to him, no less than to his issue. The Norwegian monarch might conclude the expedition had been lost with all on board, save for two awkward facts. One: word of the Agder raid would reach him, and he'd be forced to the logical conclusion that the raiders had intercepted his daughter. The other: with Lindholm Hoje abuzz over the distinguished captive, it stretched credulity to believe the news could long be contained.

"You say she weakens—how so?

Tara smiled at him, and he realized anew how deeply he cared for this beautiful and complex creature before him. "Can you not see what lies beneath your nose? Gormsson."

"Gormsson? But that's impossible! A Prince Royal cannot wed a thrall."

Tara looked her disgust. "Is 'thrall' all you can speak? Ylva is a Princess of West Norway! Her line to the throne is e'en closer than his, for it is her own sire sits the throne."

"Well! That would be interesting!" Sigefert fell silent, thinking on this happenstance. "And a happy outcome, if aught comes of it. Harald could scarce claim we'd enthralled her, if she weds a Danish Prince of her own free will." Satisfaction showed plain on his face. "How may I help him press his suit?"

"You can leave be," answered Tara dryly. "Let him do his own courting! Belike he has more skill at it than you." A quick smile softened her critical tone. "I've little doubt he'll win her heart ere long—or at least her hand, for I misdoubt the stony-faced maiden has a heart. It is the others puzzle me—the three who never waver in spurning any marriage at all."

Privately, she resolved to try once more persuading them to abandon thoughts of the likely drear homeland they'd left, and make their lives in Denemearc—as she had done.

The three stubborn women, notable mainly in being more mature than their sisters in exile, were housed still in the temporary barrack set up on their arrival. Initially crammed with the refugees, it now held only the as-yet unmarried captives. Ylva, in deference to her high birth, had the end apartment, her handmaidens just outside her door, and they kept as strictly aloof from the three lowborn bondi women as their close confinement allowed.

On entering, Tara spotted Gylfion sitting apart from the others. She had been the one Tara selected on the raiding craft to take a reassuring message to the others, and though she kept mostly to herself, Tara knew she'd played a significant role in stemming their despair during those first frightening days. As Tara drew near, she put her work aside and looked up in respectful silence. Her deep inner strength could be sensed, and Tara longed to penetrate her reserve and see what she held so close inside.

"I've spoke with the Jarl about you," she started, "and he wonders that you've no wish to marry." The Norwegian woman remained silent, making no effort to address the implied query. Her expression was hard to fathom; certainly not resentful—rather gentle and serene, but undergirt with an unshakeable certainty.

"Why do you not take a man, Gylfion?" Tara asked impulsively. "Is there one you loved at Agder? Were you betrothed?"

"No, Lady." Gylfion's quiet response made Tara ashamed of her prying, but a sudden suspicion prompted her to persist.

"Are you promised to the Church, Gylfion?" she asked softly.

The woman's face lighted up. She is beautiful, thought Tara. "Yes," she replied simply, and her gaze lowered.

Tara sat down beside her, wondering how to express the half-formed thoughts tumbling through her mind. "I was a Benedictine Sister, Gylfion," she said at last.

The woman looked at Tara in stunned astonishment. "You?" Her expression showed her disbelief.

Tara took Gylfion's hand, suddenly transported back to her grim sojourn, imprisoned in the convent. What passionate resentment had assailed her! What naked hate for Mother Prioress, who was to become an unexpected ally. How long ago and unreal it all seemed now. Her own serenity and trust had been a long time developing, she realized. Was it her belief in a higher order of things, or just because now she had Sigefert? But Gylfion had needed no man to bring her to peace, Tara realized. Coming back to the present, a daring thought was forming in her mind. "It may seem hard to believe, seeing me accoutred like this," she told the woman, "but I spent a year in the Convent of Dewi Sant in Britain."

Gylfion looked up again. "Would it be right to ask…?"

"Why I left the order? Many reasons, Gylfion. Mother Prioress thought me unsuited. I was next in line for a throne, and thus in a sense bespoke. I felt no call to serve the Virgin." Her mind called up scenes of Sister Pebligia's garden, her shameful whipping, her killing of the outlaw. "And other things," she added. "But may you tell why you feel called to the convent?"

She sought no cloistered life, explained Gylfion. Her felt mission was the spreading of God's holy word, and to do that she wanted to live amongst the people…assist them to know the word of the Lord.

"Only in Norway, Gylfion?" Tara hazarded. "Or could it be done as well in Denemearc?"

"God is everywhere. He will show me where the need is greatest."

"If it should prove possible, would you serve as a Lay Sister in Lindholm Hoje?"

"I would—if I could be brought to feel the need is there."

Tara thought of the raw frontier settlement, still in its rude growing pains, lacking in every civilized grace. "Need there is in plenty, Gylfion," she said feelingly. Mayhap even too much for any ministering to cope with, she thought but did not say.

Learning that Gylfion's two disciples, Hyrrokin and Gudrun, had the same call to serve the church, Tara decided, then and there, that naught would be allowed to stand in the way of this project.

And naught did. Sigefert initially refused, in scornful disbelief of their motives, but Tara was used to his resistance to new ideas, and knew she could overcome it in the end. However, on this matter he was adamant, and his rigid stance began to color her attitude toward him. Matters came to a head one night in the chamber, when they had come up from the Hall, and Sigefert hastily stripped off his clothes. "'Fore the gods," he growled, "would that toasting never end? I could think of naught but your tender body awaiting me!" He strode toward her in breathtaking nakedness, scooped her up, and tossed her on the pallet. "Curse these buttons!" he growled, fumbling to unfasten them. "I'll put you in a shift henceforth, sweet love."

Tara rolled off the bed in irritation, of a sudden unwilling to be partner to his heedless lovemaking. If he could not accommodate her regarding Gylfion, she'd not accommodate him in bed—e'en though his surpassing tenderness when she submitted was forever new and wondrous. She stood across the bed from him, stiffly unyielding, daring not glance his way lest her resolve evaporate.

"What in Freya's name has got into you, girl?" he demanded. "Have I turned of a sudden so distasteful?" He started around the bed, but she halted him with raised hand. "Stop!"

Surprised, he halted. "What ails you this night, Tara?" he demanded. "Are you bewitched?"

"Not bewitched—angered! I must jump to your bidding whene'er you say, but you've got no regard for my wishes. Bed down alone this night; you'll have none of me!"

"I'll have you when I want you, girl, and best you not forget it!" But his words were empty, and he made no move to carry through. "What wishes am I disregarding, then?"

She told him, wondering nervously how he'd take her importuning thus on the brink of his lovemaking. To her surprise—and vast relief— he roared with laughter. "Odin's wounds, Tara!" he cried cheerfully." If it means so much to you, you've got your wish. She can have her accursed mission, and much good may it do her. Now, have done—there's a limit to my patience!" As his urgent fingers struggled again to undo her fastenings, she could not forbear an inward smile at her new found power over this impetuous giant who loved her so deeply.

The idea of a mission in their remote outpost appealed to Tara strongly. Recalling the uncomplaining devotion of many sisters at Dewi Sant, and the impact their unswerving faith made on her, she was determined these refugee women would have their chance to put their pious resolve into practice. "They'll get no help from the fortress, mind," Sigefert warned. "Let your Christian god feed and clothe them. Do not look to my soldiers for any aid!"

The soldiers may not have helped coax the tiny mission into existence, but their women did. Gylfion's project plumbed a deep well of faith among the Danish wives, plucked from the comforts of Jelling to brave this northern wilderness outpost. The notion of Jesu's word spoke amongst them brought strength and inspiration. When Gylfion invited Tara to the tiny chapel for Easter, she was astonished at the size of the congregation that pressed at the walls and overflowed into the road, and was impressed by the solemnity of the service. "With no priest, we say the Sacramental prayers together," Gylfion told her, a hint of longing in her voice. "Though it's no true Service, it brings comfort to the women."

"How did you get this chapel built?" Tara asked after the service. The building, though small, was well made and equipped with sturdy new benches. Gylfion wore no somber habit or starched wimple, but a brightly colored kirtle and apron, and her fair hair hung gracefully down her back—like a halo, thought Tara, recalling the unsightly cropped heads of many Dewi Sant sisters at the wash troughs. Religion should impose no requirement for ugliness, she mused, profoundly moved by the simple attire and unassuming manner of the three women.

"The Lord provided," smiled Gylfion, in answer to Tara's question. "But we helped Him all we could. And of course, Jarl Sigefert sent us the materials and benches. We could never have started without his blessed help." She touched Tara's hand. "Will you ask him to visit us, so we can thank him properly? He has never seen what his generosity wrought."

And never will, guessed Tara. But then, she'd never dreamt he'd help build their chapel. There was much about Sigefert she still had to learn.

Gormsson had been laboring valiantly to overcome Princess Ylva's resistance to his suit. "I trow she's decided long since to have me," he declared to Tara. "But a Princess cannot take the first freebooter who tosses her a friendly smile, or a lecherous one. I've few illusions about Ylva, you know," he went on in a more serious vein. "No need to warn me. She's a spoiled shrew, and it will be Loki's own job whipping her into shape—though I mean to try, and even to get some pleasure from it. Who knows? She may prefer a stern, unbending man to her milksop of a Swedish popinjay."

Tara smiled, trying to visualize Gormsson a tyrannical husband. Then she recalled his bold stance back on that Ponthieu beach, and decided he could hold his own with the vixenish Ylva.

In the event, Gormsson did win Ylva as his bride, and their wedding released her maidens to take husbands of their own, restoring Tara's status as the only female within the parapets.

That very status of hers rekindled the old controversy. Of Sigefert's devotion she now had no doubt; his lovemaking was so ardent she was left breathless. Never had she dreamed of such happiness! Yet they could not marry. King Gorm himself must approve a fortress commander's marriage—it was the oldest of the fortress laws—and raising the question might divulge the well-kept secret that she lived now within the fortress walls. That was a violation not even a Jarl could commit, and keep his head on his shoulders.

"By Odin's blind eye, girl," Sigefert demanded, "what boots it if some words be mumbled over our heads? Would you love me the more? Could I hold you dearer?" He shook his head in perplexity. "Can you not cease fretting on what cannot be changed?"

"Then you prefer it be said you share your bed with a soldier?" she demanded irrationally, hurt and angry. Her rational mind knew naught was gained by harassing him so. In truth, it did make scant difference, except that she longed for a ceremony, to sanctify her position as more than chattel to her passionate giant—and to certify to all that he was hers alone, forever.

Far more pressing was the question of whether Harald Haarfager would learn of his child's fate, and seek retribution. None doubted how massive his response would be, once her captors were identified, for his solemn compact to ally his lineage with the Oseberg royal line had been thwarted, and honor was dearer than life itself. His attack, if it occurred, could come from either end of the Limfjord, or overland from the north, so watch must be maintained in all three directions.

"I've little fear for the fortress," concluded Sigefert, discussing the matter with Gormsson and Tara over the Second meal. "He would need thirty longboats for any hope of success. But I fear their hitting the town. They could level it, and seize all the women, ere we could muster

a defense—and we'd lose the advantage of fighting behind our ramparts. That argues that he'd hit from the east. I don't suppose,
Gormsson, your bride has any idea how he might strike."

Gormsson's smile was humorless. "None she's confided to me. I can
tell you one thing sure—she's had no chance to get out word of her
whereabouts. We watch all who have contact with her, and she's made
no sign of being aught but a faithful and obedient wife. Not as obedient
as I could wish, but she learns."

Tara suggested they station longboats in town, to evacuate the resi-
dents if danger should threaten, and to her surprise Sigefert pondered
her idea. "But we'd need eight to ten boats," he concluded, "and that
many lazing crewmen with naught else to do but get in trouble, when
the fortress cries for more labor."

"Teach the women to row them."

Such a thought was akin to heresy. Longboats never had women as
crew, and objections were raised furiously when it was discussed more
widely. But lacking an alternative, it was arranged so. The initial trials
had the frustrated instructors pulling their hair, but within a month the
women's performance would suffice for emergency evacuation.
Lookout towers went up along the Kattegat to the north, and it was
decided invaders could be sighted in time.

Summer gave way to fall without sign of invasion, and the defenders
began to hope Harald had heard naught. It came as a rude shock therefore, when a lookout galloped in to report a fleet nearing the estuary, but
the alarm was tempered at word that there were but three boats, and
coming from the south. Tension ran high nonetheless, and the evacuation
longboats were loaded and ready, when the little flotilla turned out to be
bringing Gorm's emissary.

When brought before Sigefert, the courtier would say only that he
was to fetch Gormsson back to Jelling for consultation, and Sigefert's
increasingly angry questioning failed to elicit any hint of the purpose.
"Will Prince Gormsson return, when his accursed conferring is done,

then?" he demanded, irritation and a vague apprehension rousing his temper more than would be considered seemly in front of a royal emissary in other circumstances, but the unruffled nobleman could do no more than assure him that Gormsson would indeed return promptly.

Tara awaited her chance to see Gormsson alone. "Dear loyal friend," she cajoled him, "I've a favor to ask of you."

"Ask away, girl," he replied fondly. His friendship with Tara had not at all abated after his marriage. "A vial of unguent? Some silver broaches? The moon and stars? Ask and it's yours."

"I want you to take three Norwegian women with you…"

"A most pleasing errand! Pray tell me more."

"…and take them to a Christian bishop, and have him administer their vows of Sisterhood into some Order. Persuasion of the strongest sort may be needed, but I've great confidence in you. And be sure to bring them back safely," she added. Gormsson agreed at once, silently vowing that he'd do a thousand times more than this trifling task to please the lovely Tara.

"I don't like its smell, Tara." It was early morn, and Sigefert lay at her side after a sleepless night. "Why send for Gormsson, with no word to his commander what it portends? There can be but one meaning!"

"You leap too swift to that conclusion. I can see many reasons for a man to wish the company of his grandson." And pray he does not press me to name one, she hoped fervently.

The hope was futile. "Name me some," he demanded angrily.

"Well…he's got wind of Gormsson's marriage, not knowing he'll wed a princess."

"And would not that be a disaster?" Sigefert snapped. "Gormsson explains by confessing we just happened one day to kidnap King Harald's Princess!"

"No, no, I didn't mean that." She'd only made matters worse, adding that worry to the ones already plaguing him. "He may want a progress report on how construction is proceeding."

"And does he not read those I send each month? No, my girl, he plans to replace me, by Gormsson or another, and summons his grandson home to fashion the plan."

Naught she could say eased Sigefert's mind—particularly as she agreed with him. Let Gormsson return with such orders, and where would she and Sigefert go then? She thought of her earlier suggestion that they return to Britain, and his cogent reasons why they could not.

Regrettably, the party's return from Jelling failed to dispel the pall of uncertainty hanging over the fortress, or allay the fears Tara now shared fully with Sigefert. Gormsson turned their queries aside, assuring them it was but a fond grandparent's desire to see his favorite grandson, but dissembling was never his strong suit, and his clumsy efforts fueled their apprehension.

"It is clear something's afoot," said Sigefert in an angry exchange with the now taciturn Gormsson. "You've no wish to share it, or more like, Gorm forbade you. Very well, I will put it from my mind, and try to do my job. When you decide to say more, you know where to find me." Gormsson remained mute, and acutely uncomfortable.

In an effort to compensate somewhat for the strained atmosphere, Gormsson related to Tara how he'd pressed the Court Bishop mercilessly, to the point that Gylfion and her two partners in religion took their vows in a miraculously accelerated ceremony, and returned in a blissful state of certified grace.

It distressed Tara almost more than she could bear that the old cameraderie with Gormsson was no more. She pressed him privately for any hint of what lay ahead. "I've no wish to cause you trouble with any assignment you've received," she said apologetically, "but Sigefert has earned the right to know if he's being replaced, if for no other reason than to give him…us time to plan where we'll go." He remained mute, his face anguished, telling her more clearly than if he'd spoke that a serious danger to Sigefert portended. "I'll press you no further now, but when you decide our long and close friendship has its obligations, our anxiety will ease." She rose abruptly and left, sparing him the acute distress of being unable to respond.

As a respite from worry, Tara asked Sigefert to take her to Lindholm Hoje. "Time we broke free of this accursed fortress for a time," she declared. "Else I'll be weighed down to the breaking point, and you as well."

Sigefert reacted angrily, as she'd expected, to any hint that his spirits were fraying. "I am no puling child, to be shielded from truth lest it fret me! I've no time for such a trip."

To get him away, she blamed her own restlessness, but with Sigefert so beset she had to choose her words carefully. "You need be gone but two nights," she urged. "Sure Gormsson can handle matters for so short a period, young or not."

The moment she spoke, she regretted her words. "Aye," he said bitterly. "And why not? He will succeed to command soon, and I'll be…" He broke off abruptly, and she wanted to bite her tongue, for she knew his thoughts as she knew her own. It grieved her deeply to see so fine a fortress commander reduced to a sleepless and uncertain state induced by Gormsson's silence. Knowing how painfully he chafed under his burdens, she vowed all the more to insist on a change of scene, and to her relief he finally agreed to the outing.

When Aggersborg was lost to view behind them, Sigefert's spirits rose noticeably. With the sun breaking through the clouds east of the fjord, they walked their horses along an inviting stretch of beach, watching the wavelets erase their hoofprints. Tara reached over and slipped her hand into his. "None following could guess we came this way just a moment earlier," she observed.

He looked back. "It shows how we might hide our tracks when we flee," he commented, in a poor effort to make light of his fears.

Sister Gylfion's overflowing pride in the robe and wimple proclaiming her new status illuminated her face. "Your thoughtfulness is beyond believing, Princess," she said, as she made them welcome. "How strange that abduction into thralldom could bring such happiness!" She turned to Sigefert, who stood embarrassed at Tara's side. "And this church you made come true, Jarl. I've no words to thank you!" Shyly she looked at Tara. "May I show the two of you about?"

The tiny church, with its larger main part and two small wings, nestled in the grassy square like a jewel. One wing served as a surgery by day and living quarters by night; when they entered, Gylfion introduced Sister Hyrrokin, who was bandaging the arm of a sobbing child, and told them the primitive facility was the town's only apothecary. The other wing was outfitted as a library and workroom, with papers and parchment spread on the worktable. Tara was amazed at the quality of writing and illuminating. "It is but a start," said Gylfion with quiet pride, "but we become more skilled with practice. Certificates, marriage compacts, legal papers—we do them all. We've become scribes for half the town. Few missives leave Lindholm Hoje but are writ in our little library." She lifted up a document, to show how they'd corrected the terms without harming its appearance, and challenged Tara to find where it was altered.

Gylfion implored them to spend the night, assuring them they'd be comfortable, and Tara stopped Sigefert on the point of declining. "Can you not see," she pointed out later, "how she aches to make recompense for accepting so much? We'd be most cruel to refuse her gift."

Tara woke early, and stepped into the chapel, to see the three Sisters kneeling at the tiny altar. On impulse, she tiptoed in and knelt beside Gylfion, surprised and awed at the peace that stole over her in the quiet solemnity of their surroundings. Gylfion rose, and took Tara's hand to lead her aside. "I feel unhappiness in you, Princess," she said. "Would it be wrong to ask what troubles you?"

Tara found herself pouring out the whole story of their uncertain status in Denemearc, the pressures that led them to kidnap wives, the disastrous mischance of Ylva's abduction—and now the near unbearable worry about Gormsson's instructions. "I've urged our secret leaving," she confided, "but the Jarl thinks it craven to desert his post, e'en though his post soon may desert him. So we stay, knowing not what danger brews, mayhap until too late." Impulsively she threw her arms about Gylfion, weeping silently. "Oh, Gylfion—I'm so affrighted! You think me a warrior, but you don't see inside."

Gylfion pressed her face against Tara's flushed cheek, and urged both of them back to their knees. "I will ask the Virgin's guidance for you," she whispered. "Pray with me, and she will find a way out of your misery." Searching her memory for words long unused, Tara prayed.

With no other plans, Sigefert thought to ride out to a coastal watchtower he'd never seen. The weather turned threatening early on, but he insisted the blow would moderate soon.

Instead of moderating, the wind grew until the horses' heads were lowered against the buffeting blasts. They were moving along a promontory bordering the sea, when Sigefert reined in his mount. Following his pointed finger, Tara saw the wreckage of a longboat upended on the jagged rocks below. When she turned back to ask what they should do, he was halfway down the face of the cliff.

The wreckage told its own stark tale. The boat's seams had started, much as Gormsson's had done on the race up the Channel, and it had foundered in the Kattegat's frigid waters. One by one, the frozen crew members must have lost their holds, and the implacable sea had taken their bodies into its depths. Tara and Sigefert poked through the splintered flotsam for any bodies or identifying signs, with no success. They had turned mutely away from the tragic tableau, when some impulse caused Sigefert to return for a final look. It was then he spotted the leathern case they had overlooked, lashed to a broken stub of mast, all but hidden by the tangle around it. The fastenings were frozen tight and caked with verdigris, but he managed to open it at last, and unrolled the oiled silk protecting its contents.

It was a message from the Court, sealed with the Royal Crest—and addressed to Gormsson. The penalty for breaking a royal seal was death, but without hesitation Sigefert slit it open, and they sought out a tiny cym in the rocky coastline, to shelter them from the wind while they spread it out to examine it.

Sigefert looked at Tara bleakly. "It is what we expected," he said in a hard, taut voice. "Our work at Aggersborg…all we've built…all we've done for that accursed Gorm—all as naught!" he dashed the epistle angrily down, and Tara hastily rescued it. "Curse him! Curse Gormsson! May their bones burn eternal in Loki's fires of the Otherworld!" He turned away, staring unseeing at the roiling ocean.

Tara skimmed the document as best her command of the written word permitted. The meaning was starkly clear. King Harald Haarfager had learned the identity of the raiders, had assembled troops for an invasion, and had laid down an ultimatum which Gorm was in no position—and belike no mood—to reject. And Gormsson was directed to execute it.

When the first spring thaw softened the ice on the Limfjord, Gormsson's Danes would seize Sigefert and his chief officers, and deliver them in chains to the King of West Norway!

There was a final catastrophic instruction. Gormsson must acknowledge receipt by courier to Jelling, so Gorm could be sure his orders were not intercepted, but reached their destination.

They rode back toward the town, enveloped in gloom. "We'll not have time to plan our escape," said Sigefert glumly. "The western reaches of the Limfjord must be ice-free if we are to reach the Northern Sea, and Gormsson is instructed to make his move before that occurs."

"Can your Northumbrians not resist, when the Danes seek to arrest you? True, they are outnumbered, but not by so much. And they will be fighting for their lives."

"You forget, Tara. Many of my Vikings have taken wives, and will balk at leaving their soft couches for the uncertainty of winning free—and beyond that, for the uncertainty of finding any safe haven in Britain. Less than an hundred will join my standard. Gorm's plan must be based on some such calculation." He smashed his fist upon his thigh in frustration. "Just one month more is all we'd need. If the order told Gormsson to move after spring planting, instead of after the first thaw, we'd have a fighting chance. Just one month more!"

Spring planting! And why not? It seemed as if some conscious power thrust the bold thought into Tara's mind.

"We can do it!" She fairly shouted the words. "Gylfion! The library! If you wish it to say 'spring planting', I'll grant you your wish!" She spurred her horse to dash ahead, leaving the bewildered Sigefert to chase after her.

"But of course, Princess—it can be changed." Gylfion's quiet confidence, and immediate acquiescence when she learned what portended, were as a tonic to Tara, and even Sigefert's depression lessened. "Tell me the words once more."

When the missive was rephrased, to direct that the arrest be made only after spring planting, the Royal Crest duplicated with exquisite care, and the freshly bound document within its oiled silk resecured inside the leathern case so cleverly that it might never have been removed, Gylfion made a hesitant suggestion. "Thee's a fisherman in the town whose wife we saved, and the babe too, when she delivered early after a tumble. He aches to repay us for this small kindness. If he takes the case to the Military Commander in the town, letting it be thought he found it caught in his trawl, who would question his tale?"

Who would? And none did. Two days after their return to the fortress, a courier brought a package for Gormsson's eyes only. And within the week, Sigefert's picked men, keeping secret watch along the Limfjord estuary, noted the clandestine departure of a longboat—the message to Jelling that the orders were received and would be carried out. Orders, though Gorm was not to know, that called for arresting Sigefert, not at first thaw, but after spring planting.

Sigefert bade her lift a triumphant horn with him, when word of the longboat's departing was sneaked to their apartment. "We celebrate the blind fortune that brought us both the missive and the one person who could rephrase it," he said, with something of his former spirit. "We cast our good deed on the current, and the tides returned us recompense an hundredfold."

Tara touched her horn to his, reveling in the lifting of his morale— knowing, e'en as she echoed his toast, that it was more than blind fortune.

It had to be but another intercession of the gods, guiding her inexorably toward the destiny that was writ for her!

CHAPTER 28

Never had a winter dragged on so interminably! The deep snows and bitter cold limited outside excursions to necessary hunting forays for food, and the enforced confinement brought Tara into frequent contact with Gormsson. It was painful, having to speak and act as if all were well, whilst aching inside with the distressing knowledge of his duplicity. How could such a charming nobleman be transformed into so despicable a turncoat, to friends who had trusted him, who had cherished his friendship—who e'en had rescued him from shipwreck? Tara could but wonder if ever again she'd be able to put her trust in another. An evil spell seemed to descend on all rulers—and would-be rulers—making them reject any gratitude, any friendship, any shread of decency or honor, that might conflict with the malignant lure of a throne. I'll not be such a ruler, she vowed!

"Are we doing right, Sigefert?" He was awake, she knew. She could sense his sleeplessness beside her, feel his distress. Since the day they unrolled that fateful missive, he'd been quitting the hall after a hasty sup, lacking stomach for the carousing and bonhomie in which both had participated. In partial recompense, she had to admit, they had a time of rare privacy to talk things out. Her Sire and his beloved Queen had talked so each eve, and Tara knew that bond of sharing their problems had made their marriage more precious and enduring. She had come to terms for now with her status as half-wife, feeling this was no time to press Sigefert, though knowing its conflict with the plans of her

Celti gods meant difficult decisions ahead. She had the wisdom to understand that these days with Sigefert, tempering her uncertain future with near unbearable happiness, were bound to end. It was but a precious and fleeting interlude in her life, and she would continue to savor every golden moment as best she could.

"Are we right to keep silent with Gormsson?" she asked yet again. "How if we say we ken what his orders be, and ask him to understand we must save ourselves? I'll remind him the plan to raid Agder was his, so by rights Gorm's anger should fall on his grandson." She had another thought. "I could let it be the gods brought me a vision of Gorm's scroll."

Sigefert pulled her closer to him, their bodies as one in the darkness. "That would never succeed, my dear love. Gormsson is not a fool. He has scant faith in gods and goblins, and if you reveal any knowledge of the message, he'll ferret out the truth. That bondi who will say he dredged it up from the sea has not the wit to withstand skilled questioning. Gormsson would learn what we did all too soon."

Reluctantly, she agreed. Despite Gormsson's past closeness, despite how he'd all but laid his heart at her feet, he now was an enemy. But if King Gorm sought to placate King Haarfager for his daughter's kidnapping, why did he not offer up the real culprit—he who'd proposed the raid that actually abducted his daughter, and who'd taken her as thrall to his marriage bed?

She answered her own question. Gormsson was of the royal line, and kings never offer up their own. Some whipping boy is tossed on the blazing pyre of kingly hubris. Belike King Harald Haarfager could wish naught better for his precious Ylva than union with the royal line of Denemearc—the end result of her abduction—after an easy gesture by Gorm to salve her Sire's stiff-necked hauteur. And Gorm was twice blessed, for not only was his delicate problem solved with the stroke of a pen, but he would rid himself of Sigefert whilst retaining his useful followers.

Why not foil Gorm's scheme by smuggling word to Harald that Gormsson bore the real blame? It could be done easily enow—just contrive that one of the handmaidens finds her way home, bursting to relate the true story that Gormsson had captured the royal barge and ravished Ylva. She'd be a convincing witness, bound in self-interest to protest that they'd all been wedded against their wishes. Why should Tara not protect Sigefert and herself thus?

Again she made answer to herself: she could not. Gormsson had been a friend once, and she wanted no part in sentencing him to Harald's mercies. And as well, she wanted to believe no kingly command could turn him against them. He was in a painful quandary, squeezed as he was betwixt loyalty to his grandfather and affection for the two of them—but in the end Tara could not accept that he could turn on Sigefert in this despicable way, order or no. She wanted to trust in his essential goodness—and he could trust hers. She'd not betray him to save herself!

In any case, spoke a small voice inside her, King Harald had no interest in who actually did the abducting. His pride wanted salving, and Sigefert would serve as well as Gormsson. Better: why sacrifice a prince—who would make an excellent match for his daughter—when a nobody lay to hand? Belike he knew already it had been Gormsson, and cared not a whit.

One unexpected benefit accruing from the dreadful situation was the closeness engendered between Sigefert and herself. With none to trust, and none to care, but each other, they were bound in a deeper intimacy, born of need, and discussed their problems as equals. Almost equals: when she urged him to put his trusted officers on alert to start planning their escape, he was vehement in his refusal.

"They'd show their anger at Gormsson in an hundred ways, no matter how they sought to act otherwise," he said impatiently. "You know how hard it is for us, and I suspicion e'en we do not deceive him in full, or prevent him from seeing things are not quite as they were. My officers are not mincing courtiers, bred to scorn the truth; they'd be at his throat within the week, on one or another pretext. We must bide a while, Milady."

Tara could see the right of what he was explaining, and made no further effort along these lines. "Then when must they be told? What we plan is at the same time a delicate project and an exceeding large one. We cannot do it all ourselves. You need help on this. How soon will you tell them, if we're to be ready when the ice breaks?"

"Not until the last moment. A week before we go, not earlier. The less who know the better. Men cannot reveal, even under duress, what they do not know. E'en you must not know too soon."

Winter was waning before Sigefert reluctantly shared his plan with Tara. The day was cold, their breath crystallizing on the air, as they galloped across the north plain. The sun shone in a cloudless sky, the crisp snow glistened like tiny diamonds on the frozen ground, and despite the gravity of their plight, the clear beauty of it all lifted Tara's flagging spirits. They carried bows, to show a purpose for the outing, and already two snowshoe hares and a whitetailed vixen had fallen to their shafts.

They pulled up, well out of sight of the fortress, and she moved close to him in unconscious support. He had been restless from prolonged physical inactivity, and she knew the process of escape planning provided a lift to his spirits. She had not realized at the start how enormously difficult it would be to maintain normal relationships with Gormsson, and belike Sigefert had the right of it that e'en now he suspected they'd be planning flight. Gormsson knew Sigefert was no fool, and none but a fool could fail to deduce the significance of the summons to Jelling. Belike he did not know they'd seen Gorm's fateful missive, and for certain he'd have no slightest suspicion how they'd altered it. But it was too much to believe that he was not now keenly on the alert to their movements.

"But how can he foil your flight, knowing not when or how it might take place?" demanded Tara. "His boats—can they not be disabled just before we leave?"

"I plan as much. He will credit me with doing that, and a shrewd adversary would be readying a backup plan to give chase. I know that, and he'd reck that I know it. But what form could such a plan take?"

They evaluated three escape routes—west on the Limfjord to the Isle of Mors, then northwest around the Isle, then south—dragging boats across the neck of land to the outer bay—e'en the precarious eastern route, which Gormsson would reck only a madman would choose—to probe for weaknesses in each. One by one, they considered other alternatives, only to discard them as foolhardy at best, or completely unworkable at worst. Day after day, they examined ways to elude such a cunning adversary, sorrowing as they did that a man of Gormsson's honor and past warm friendship could stoop so low.

More in desperation than real hope, Tara proposed that they seek to make Gormsson think they would go east, whilst actually going west. To her surprise, Sigefert did not pooh-pooh the idea. "It would be a masterly stroke, save for knowing how to do it," he declared. "Have your Cymri gods told you how it might be done?" Thus challenged, she proposed they explore east by boat—forgetting in her enthusiasm that the Limfjord was iced over—or by sledge, which Sigefert rejected as too heavy-footed to deceive. But his mind, triggered by her thought, came up with a scheme to schedule an eastern trip when the ice cleared, ostensibly to inspect the Kattegat defenses now the invasion season was at hand, but actually seeking to plant suspicion that it might be the escape route.

"We'll make as if we plan to leave from the landing stage, but secretly have a longboat hid in the creek east of Aggersborg, as if planning to flee the night before." His enthusiasm grew as he talked. "We'd arrange for Gormsson to get wind of the hid boat, with its full provisions, and keep secret watch to learn when it departs. But when he gives chase and o'ertakes it, he finds but a boat full of his own Danes, sent on some fool's errand to the town, knowing naught more.

"And how does that help us?" But she was beginning to comprehend.

"Our real escape fleet would be hid to the west, of course. And at his pursuit to the east, we'd embark to the west. All it would give us would be an unhindered start, but we can't expect the moon. A good start is the most we can hope for, and that would be a gift from the gods."

As the day approached, it became crucial to break silence and start enlisting confederates. They'd use a 'pyramid', Sigefert told her: he and Tara each enlisting two, these each finding two more, until the force was as complete as it was likely to get. "But how if it leaks out?" asked Tara. "Do you not fear some little leak that will give our plans away to Gormsson?"

"That is my hope—because the plan we will give out is escape to the east. Just one more way he might be deceived. Let him hear! We have to take care that he does hear."

With their flight scarce two weeks off, the suspense became near unbearable. Sigefert revealed the plan to Oddune, who in turn and with great care enlisted the help of a few trusted conspirators to form the advance guard. They'd assemble and load boats in extreme secrecy, hide them in a network of swamps well west of the fortress, and disguise their access channel so no sign of the hideout showed from the fjord. It was clear that Sigefert and Tara themselves, and Oddune as well, could take no part in this enterprise, since they'd be watched too closely, and the hardest part was the frustration of enforced idleness whilst the operation was proceeding. Once they put the pyramid plan in effect, four days before departure, the die would be cast, and the venture in the hands of their gods, for better or worse.

Tara took to riding out each morn, seeking with little success to alleviate her restlessness with exercise. On one such excursion, she spotted someone amongst the trees, and reined in to see what portended. To her surprise, it was a woman, and Tara dismounted to approach more closely, hand on her sword.

It was the Princess Ylva, wife of their nemesis, Prince Gormsson!

A turmoil of thoughts raced through Tara's mind. Her first thought was that Gormsson had put his Princess up to some mischief, and she told herself to believe nothing and tell nothing. Despite their mutual residence in the fortress, the two never had conversed, and Tara wondered not only why she was there, but how best to greet her. Ylva solved that problem by initiating the conversation.

"I have hoped we would meet, Princess," she said, seeming oddly timid for one reputed so arrogant. So Ylva had sought her out—and in this remote spot! But why?

Seemingly apprehensive, Ylva confided that she dared not let her husband learn of their meeting. "The Agder women say you promised any who wish to return at year end would be free to leave. I wish to return to my home."

"Return home? You?" Could this addle-pate truly wish to leave her handsome mate, one destined to sit a throne? Could she e'en think Tara would believe so obvious a trick? "Why do you wish to return, Princess—the true reason? How can you hope I'll believe you? Is your man mayhap cruel to you? Does he beat you…deny you food…lock you in?"

"Oh, no, no…he is a good husband! None could be kinder. But I miss my home. Every night I cry." She seemed to be trying to look sad, but was not skilled at acting.

"Why do I not tell your husband. Sure he will not hold you against your will." Suspicious though she was of the clumsy excuse, Tara realized how fortunate they all would be if Harald got his daughter back, safe and sound—instead of Sigefert's head.

Ylva recoiled as if struck. "No! You must not speak to him! He's…he would…" She stammered confusedly, and Tara decided she'd not been rehearsed for so direct a question.

"Tell him your wishes, Princess Ylva," advised Tara. "He will do whatever you ask. He is a good and honorable man, and that is what was agreed. Now I'm sorry, but I must return to the fortress." As she turned to walk away, Ylva grabbed her arm frantically.

"Wait! You must help me!" Her disappointment seemed genuine, but its cause was unclear. "Can we not meet here tomorrow? I pray you come, at the same time."

Tara reluctantly agreed, and again turned to go. On impulse, she suddenly looked back, in time to catch a hastily extinguished expression of gloating triumph on Ylva's transparent face.

"You must know Gormsson's put her up to it." Sigefert thought that much was clear, but was as puzzled as Tara about what he sought to gain. That Ylva was being candid, and that Gormsson truly knew nothing of the meeting, they rejected out of hand. Tara thought longingly of Atheurin, e'en cleared her mind and waited a time for a sign, but naught materialized, and she knew the two of them were on their own.

"Is there any way we could turn Ylva around?" she mused aloud. "Realizing he sent her, but offering her summat she wants so strong she'll have to play double traitor to get it?"

"You tell me. You're a woman. What would the brainless jade want so powerfully as that?"

"If I read the Princess aright, she loves none but herself. Gormsson was the best catch here, and a good catch anywhere, but how if we contrive somehow to offer her more?"

"What's in our power to offer? What's in your mind?"

"Belike she knows Gormsson's orders are to deliver you to her Sire, which is of small concern to her. But say we made her believe Harald knew it was Gormsson took her, and now she willingly shares his bed? And learning as much, Harald's vengeance now settles on Gormsson—and on her, for craven submission to her captor? What might she likely do then?"

"Turn on her husband without an instant's hesitation, to save herself. E'en join with us, if we offer her a way to escape to Norway, showing her father she was an unwilling bride—with the side-effect that he now demands Gormsson's head, not mine." He frowned. "But how to bring her to so unlikely a conclusion—make her believe such a fool's tale?"

"It's not so unlikely. Gormsson himself abducted her—swooped down on her craft bound peaceably for Sweden, and cruelly snatched her whole entourage away. He forced her into marriage, near enow. But the question remains: how make her think King Harald knows this?"

Both were silent for a period, trying to puzzle out a way. Suddenly Tara cried out. "Sister Gylfion! She'll write us a letter, from Harald to Gorm. And another from Gorm to the fortress commander—to you! Belike you see what these letters would say."

Gylfion was reluctant to be party to such outright forgery, until Tara explained that she and Sigefert would die painfully, unless the deception enabled their escape. She turned to with a will then, her documents so artful Tara vowed Gorm would think he'd writ them himself.

Ylva, still waiting behind the tree, panicked at the sight of Sigefert with Tara, and had to be calmed sufficiently to give heed. "We've something here to interest you, Princess," said Sigefert, in what he thought passed for a gentle tone. "Something of which your husband has kept you ignorant, to save his own life at the expense of yours." Ylva's eyes darted desperately about for some way to escape, then reluctantly took the documents as if they were poisoned. As she read, she suddenly gasped aloud, and a look of terror beyond her ability to simulate told of her willingness to credit her father's harsh threat. The papers fell from her trembling fingers.

"Prince Gormsson sent you to Tara with his story." Sigefert's voice was accusatory. "He told you King Harald wanted me, and I would try to escape. And he was right—then. But your father since has learned the truth of who abducted you, and demands Gormsson be delivered into his hands." He paused. "Mayhap you can guess what lies in store for you, who went willingly to Prince Gormsson. He wants you as well, to do we know not what to you!"

He stopped for his words to sink in, then went on. "Gormsson does not know I have these orders from his grandfather, but he fears they may come soon. Can you not see—he uses you, to trick our escape plan out of us, when we have no need for escape, so he has excuse to kill me before I get the orders to arrest him—orders I now have. List to me, you

silly child. Harald will have you both soon enow, and your own fate will
not be pretty!"

Tara found herself actually pitying the pathetically sobbing Ylva. She
put her arm around the girl's thin shoulders. "Do not fear, Princess," she
said consolingly. "None of this is your fault. We will see you free from
your husband, whilst there is yet time. We will get you home, and when
your father learns you fled from Gormsson of your own free will, he
must disbelieve the tales his spies have told him about you."

Ylva looked at her pathetically, a trace of hope dawning on her tear-
streaked face. "How?" she wept. "What must I do?"

"List close to me," said Tara sternly, her distaste for a woman so
willing to betray her husband mingled with an unexpected pang of
sympathy. "And you must do exactly what I tell you!"

CHAPTER 29

A light misting of rain helped to mask the movements of the group creeping noiselessly through the trees that bordered the river. Ahead, a fading loom on the horizon marked the moonset, and soon the darkness would be almost total. To all but the selected few who'd positioned the longboats, the way was completely unfamiliar, and without the moonlight to show the path it would be all too easy to lose the way and waste precious minutes getting back on track. They'd been on the march for five miles already, but Sigefert had not dared risked a closer hideout for the boats. Oddune was in the lead, having learned the route, and Sigefert brought up the rear, both to be on the guard for any of the party who might wander from the path and to pay close heed behind for any sounds of pursuit.

Any chase so soon was unlikely, if Ylva's vow that Gormsson had quaffed a full horn of sleeping potion could be credited. She stumbled along now with the escape group, after having sworn to Sigefert that she left him sleeping like a babe. But her manner was oddly restless, and Tara was all but certain she'd played them false. Whether true or false, it was far too late to deal with that now, and Tara forced her mind off the matter—and to the memory of another night's excursion that had led her farther along the path of her destiny.

Vividly she recalled the foray from the Gloucester encampment to scout Alfred's forces. The atmosphere had been equally oppressive with danger, only then it came from ahead, from the Saxon foe. This time the danger was from behind, mayhap at their heels e'en now, from their former allies become enemies. How sad, she thought in sorrow, that conspiracies of kings could force friends to become foes against their will. This time, if the gods willed it, there'd be just a silent escape in the deep of night, with no bloodshed, no slaughter of long-time allies.

But did the gods will it?

"These woods affright me," Ylva whimpered, miserable in the penetrating damp. "Where are we? Whence came all these great trees?" She shivered uncontrollably. "What is our path?"

In that moment, Tara knew for certain that Ylva had betrayed them. She looked for the open moors of the eastern route, which had no 'great trees'. Gormsson was not drugged on his couch, but deploying his cohorts to give chase. Ylva alerted him before she left! Through her terror, she's finally harnessed her paralyzed brain sufficiently to note the forest and marsh on their route, and to realize that these would not be found on the eastern plains. Belike she's on the edge of screaming for help! Tara eased her dagger, ready to stifle aborning any shout or other disturbance that could give them away. No doubts assailed her at what must be done. Ylva had sworn by all her sacred gods, and spilling her blood would be on her own head. Tara whispered a quick message to the warrior just behind, and he slipped back to warn Sigefert.

Ylva was looking about in growing panic; with little doubt she was seeking to catch sight of rescuers. It was abundantly clear the overwrought girl would not keep silent much longer. Keenly alert, Tara moved at once to a position where she could reach her instantly.

Princess Ylva's already fragile composure was undone. She was on the verge of rushing blindly into the woods, a scream forming in her throat, when a strong hand was clapped over her mouth, and she felt the chilling pressure of a keen blade hard against the blood vessel pulsing beneath the soft skin of her throat. She twisted about, and froze in terror as her sudden movement caught the blade, and she felt a trickle of hot blood on her neck. She was pulled roughly off the narrow trail, ghostly figures filed silently past, and her terror mounted. She stiffened in horror as the realization hit her that she was being abandoned and helpless in this Stygian darkness, at the mercy of the grim creature behind her. Her trembling legs threatened to collapse, dizziness assailed her, her senses reeled, and she collapsed unconsious on the ground.

When they broke clear of the woods, Tara made out the two boats, already pulled from their swampy hideouts, drawn up and ready on the beach. The crews swarmed aboard and manned their rowing thwarts, the sleek hulls glided out on the water, and the fateful voyage was begun.

Ylva had been bound and gagged while still unconscious, and Tara now lashed her wrists to a thwart. She sat in a comotose silence, head collapsed on her chest, eyes closed as if in denial of her situation. She was an utterly pathetic figure—and her very presence an unwanted complication. But her base treachery freed them from any obligation to help her return to her homeland, e'en if there was any feasible way to do it. They'd set her ashore when they put to sea, to be found eventually by Gormsson—or not, as her gods willed.

When the boats were well underway and pulling strongly, Sigefert came forward to tell Tara how fortunate they'd been so far, quit of Aggersborg and underway without interception. To her intense surprise, he lifted her off her feet, whirling her around in an unwonted display of feeling stronger than she'd ever seen in him. "This night is the birth of a new life for us, love," he declared. "Thanks to Gorm, we do what I'd not had the wit to do on my own: go home." Planting his lips on her unprotesting mouth, he kissed her so hard and long she was left gasping. "The world lies at our feet, lass!" he said exultantly. "The great Northern Sea calls to us, deep water will flow beneath our keel, and the ocean lanes lie open to our passage!"

The skies were lightening when they reached the eastern point of the Isle of Mors, and must choose the north or south route. Oddune brought his boat alongside to learn the decision. The plan had been to go north, but with Gormsson like to be on their heels, speed was more vital than deception, and on the broad south fork they could make much better time.

"Do you disremember we took all his oars?" asked Oddune. "Do we worry too much that he'll o'ertake us? Is Gormsson then a storm-god, to catch us without oars?"

Sigefert shook his head. "Count not on his depending on the one set. I wat he has our scent, has long had his replacement oars hid away, and will gain on us, for his longboats will be fully complemented. I say he recks we'll take the southerly way and will take that himself. Reason would tell us, then, to take the northern channel and cozen him. If you find naught to fret you in that decision, bid your Northumbrians put their backs to it, or our freedom is forfeit!"

After two arduous hours of rowing, Sigefert called halt, and all hands rested on their oars, chests heaving as they gulped in the invigorating air. Were they fully manned, replacements in each boat would have rotated as oarsmen and the flight continued without let, but they'd not dared approach too many Northumbrians in their escape planning, lest word leak out, so the advantage this gave the pursuers was unavoidable. Dried fruit and nuts were passed along the line, and the boats lay to, drifting slowly downstream.

To their right, on the north shore, a small settlement came in view, and people could be seen gathering on the bank to watch. Sigefert seemed disturbed, and Tara asked why.

"That's Thisted," he said. "It lies on the west road from Aggersborg. If Gormsson sends mounted scouts, they'll learn we took this route, and can better intercept us." When Tara remarked that Aggersborg had not horses enow to carry many fighting men, he explained. "Horses can cover four miles to our one, and a Prince of the Blood can requisition help any place from Odin's Sound to Norrejyske Horn, and bring a hornet's nest about our ears, if he knows where to sting us. Even if he didn't already know that we came west, he'll know now."

Of a sudden the escape, which Tara had thought all but won, had turned problematic. "What will you do?" she asked, dismayed.

"I've little I can do, lass, save keep going. You can call up your Bard, if you've a mind."

With pursuit now seeming all but certain, Sigefert reasoned Gormsson's fully manned boats would take the faster south route around the Isle of Mors, to intercept them where the two routes met at the south of the island. He'd been studying his map of the Limfjord, and called Tara to look. "So we'll try to confound him by not reaching the intersection at all," he said, pointing. "There's a place just before the two routes come together, where the north shore narrows, and the marshy ground makes it easy to pull the boats. If the gods be with us, Gormsson will not know it's possible to cross there, and we can drag our boats over to Nissam Bay which fronts the ocean, and never reach the intersection. He'll await us there in vain."

Gormsson must indeed not have known, as they landed unhindered. Tara was reminded of the Great Portage in the Dnieper River, for they lightened the two boats and set towing lines for the slow drag across the isthmus. They crossed without incident, and were vastly relieved to be waterborne again. Tara felt a welcome release of tension, which lasted until Sigefert spoke.

"We can take any of three paths across the Bay now. Straight westward, to the Horns that open to the sea, is but a two-hour pull, but mightily exposed if Gormsson is in the Bay before us. Hugging the north shore of the bay provides concealment from him—but not from the road his horsemen will take. The long way around the south shore of the bay gives us the best concealment, but will take all day or more, and if Gormsson has not entered the Bay yet we'll waste valuable time getting through the Horns ahead of him." He looked at Tara, not quite ready to ask her advice outright, but with the unspoke question in his eyes.

Tara turned fiercely on her prisoner. "It's time you speak the truth, Ylva!" she rasped, and drew her dagger purposefully. "We know you told

Gormsson all. I asked Sigefert to spare you, but he's for slitting your throat, slowly. Did you ever hear the screams, when King Harald inflicted the slow death on a traitor?"

Ylva's reddened eyes widened in horror, and Tara saw the hysterical scream rising. She clapped one hand across Ylva's mouth, and with the other grasped the hapless girl by the throat.

"You've but one way to save your miserable life, Princess. Tell me, here and now, is Gormsson after us by water? Lie, and your body will feed the fishes before he takes us—and the death will not be easy!" She released her hand slightly, that Ylva could answer, but the terrified Ylva seemed incapable of speech.

"Speak, wretch, if you put any value on your miserable life!" Tara's hand closed again on Ylva's thin neck, cutting off her breath momentarily.

"He…he thought you would go this way. I told him east, as you bade me—but he…he did not believe. He will come…this way…west."

"And the sleeping potion? You did not put it in his mead, did you? Did you?"

"N…no… I could not deceive him; he knew all." The answer was torn from her, as if she was convinced Tara knew everything. She dropped her head, awaiting the expected thrust.

Tara had no further time for the conniving creature, and hastened to tell Sigefert that Gormsson almost surely was hard on their heels— possibly out on the Bay already, though probably still behind them. They must take the southern loop around the Bay, but could not risk it until darkness, meanwhile praying that some ill chance would not place them across the entrance to the bay just as their pursuers were coming through.

They holed up on a bit of beach short of the perilous channel, and dragged the boats into the rushes to pass the time until dark. Tara suggested she and Sigefert take a turn through the woods for game. When they were out of earshot, he stopped and turned her to face him.

"I have no gift for words, as some do, to tell you what lies in my heart, love," he said huskily. "That has ne'er been my way, as well you know; you've chided me for it oft enow. But I would speak now, lest events o'er-take us and it goes forever unsaid." He paused, groping how to say what lay heavy on his mind, and she had a swift premonition what it might be. "You are more to me than all else in this world, Tara, and I want no future without you at my side. No, hold!" as Tara, deeply moved, started to reply. "I've a question to put to you. If we win through the Danish and Saxon thickets that lie ahead, and reach Northumberland, will it be enow for you? Can you be content there, lass?" He looked pleadingly into her eyes, as though by sheer intensity of his stare to drag a favorable answer from their liquid grey-green depths.

The question, coming so hard on his moving declaration, was oddly unsettling. Until it was put so bluntly, she'd not thought of any future past eluding Gormsson and then Alfred, but of a sudden he asked her about a whole lifetime, and she knew not how to answer.

"You hesitate, Tara." His voice was full of understanding, as if he knew the problem troubled and confused her. "Can it be two futures clash in your mind, and you cannot find a way to make the twain one?"

What prescience made him decipher her dilemma so well? Sigefert was life itself to her, and she could envision a future apart no more than he. She ached with all her being to give up her pretensions to greatness, subordinate herself to his greater strength, and find safe haven within the warmth and security of his protection. If they fought through to Northumberland, she knew she could find complete happiness as his loving wife, serving his every wish and desire, and achieve complete ful-fillment as a woman in the passionate heat of his love.

But the call of Cymru was the call to duty, and too strong to gainsay: the private vow she'd made to Sire to realize his great dream for Dyfed, the sacred quest to which the Celti gods had dedicated her, the stirring Cymri heritage Atheurin had pledged her to fulfill...

And crowning all that, her own undeniable ambition to be something more than just a devoted wife and faithful thrall to a man—in short, to be a Queen.

But she could not have both. Would she be content to go to Northumberland, stifling the call of destiny, and make a new life with the man she loved? Or would she, when the newness palled, find herself aching for Cymru and all that life meant? Would the poignant tug of her homeland, and the clarion call of her destiny, prove too strong—e'en if it meant farewell to Sigefert forever?

In her perplexity, she overlooked what might have tilted the balance—Clydog's claim on her. But that thought did not come, and she kept silent, knowing not how to answer.

"I thought you'd see it thus," Sigefert said finally, in resignation. "While we stayed at the fortress, your heart was mine alone—and mine yours. But in Britain, you'll hear the call of your homeland, and though I'll still be yours, you'll be mine no longer."

"Sigefert...no!" His bleak expression wrung the sharp cry from her, and she clung to him desperately, hot tears coursing down her face. "You must never say that! I love you with all my being! Never, never, could I endure life without you!" But deep in her inmost heart, another voice was calling.

The hazardous transit across the channel mouth, seeming so fraught with peril, was made with no encounter. Did this mean Gormsson must be delayed more than they'd guessed—or more like, was he already out on the bay and setting up his blockade of the Horns? Morning twilight found the party well out along the narrow spit of land forming the southern arm enclosing the bay, to end as the southern Horn of the exit through which they must pass to gain the Northern Sea. The terrain offered scant concealment, but by scooping out depressions in the sand for boats and crew they were hid from sight of passing craft. From this vantage point of temporary safety, a patrol was dispatched by land to scout the area around the Horns—their sole escape route.

Sigefert accompanied the patrol, and when they returned he called the Northumbrians together for a council. "A massive force guards the Horns," he reported. "Longboats are beached on both the Norrejyske and Gotland shores—ten or more each side. Any attempt to force a passage through such a force would be suicide. We'd make them pay dearly for our deaths, but that's not our aim." He paused to look around the stolid group. "Gormsson'll not break his blockade for two or three weeks—and then only to search the Horns closely. In the end, if we stay here, we'll be hard put to stay hid. Waiting sits ill, but I see no better course."

There was an instant uproar. Delay after delay had gnawed at the men's spirits and their manhood, and there were shouts for an immediate frontal attack. Few voices favored the waiting Sigefert espoused, in what must seem a futile hope that time would show them a better course. He's bound to give in to the majority, thought Tara. But he is right! E'en if one boat, by some miracle, should win through, it would be o'ertaken at sea. A deep lassitude crept over her, an indifference to the crucial choice that could mean life or death to them all.

"Well, lass, have you aught to add to the clamor?" Sigefert's eyes seemed to beg her to call up a miracle. Half-heartedly, she cast about for a suggestion, some experience from her past that could suggest a solution to their problem.

From her past...her past...

She was transported in imagination to the long voyage to Byzantium. In her mind's eye she was creeping again in the shallows past the citadel of Kiev...spiriting away the Petcheneg's horses at Aifor...stabbing the pagan with her concealed dagger in the Hippodrome...rolling the boats overland on logs at the Great Portage...

Rolling the boats overland on logs!

She rose, lifting her hand for silence. Some special quality in her stance seized the attention of the bickering Northumbrians, and one by one they slowly fell silent, until there was no sound save the calling of sea birds and the plash of wavelets spending themselves on the beach beyond the dunes.

Then, quietly, she explained her plan to them

CHAPTER 30

Although the procedure Tara set forth for transporting the longboats was perfectly clear, the tools for accomplishing the task were not available on the bleak and windswept spit of land where they found themselves. What were needed were massive logs on which the boats could be rolled across the arm of land separating the bay from the ocean, and the nearest trees that could provide such logs were in a stand of timber more than a mile to the east.

The weary Northumbrians, ready for a hard-earned sleep, were forced to draw on their now dwindling reserves of energy, and trudge east to the wooded mainland to find and fell the large trees suited for their purpose. They were trimmed of branches, stripped of bark, and scraped with sea shells, to produce six large cylindrical rollers capable of supporting their two longboats. These were rolled into the water, and willing hands lashed towing lines borrowed from the longboat rigging to each log, so they could be towed through the shallows back to the campsite.

It was a grueling travail, necessitating back-breaking digging and grading to level the dunes and tussocks blocking their passage, and at times it seemed the Norns were against them and they must give up the impossible effort. But they kept doggedly at it, and at long last, as the gloom of night was fading into dawn, the near-impossible passage was accomplished. They were across the isthmus at last, and could dip their tired feet into the welcoming waters of the great Northern Sea. By unspoken agreement, all dropped in their tracks, made rude beds for themselves in the reeds, and slept.

In the early light of dawn, the horizon was empty. No craft—enemy or otherwise—was in sight, and the first few to wake had dived into the waves to refresh themselves, when a soft call came back from a swimmer well out from shore. He pointed urgently northward and started swimming back, and all eyes searched the ocean in that direction, but could see naught. When he reached the beach, he reported what he'd seen.

A blockading longboat, resting on its oars, lay offshore just around the bend. It could not be seen from the beach, but it was there! And if there were one, there would be more! The question for Sigefert was clear: how many other blockading craft were on patrol, and where were they?

Hastily they pulled back to take stock. If just one picket lay offshore here, it lay within their capabilities to attack and sink it, but if it was only one in a long picket line of ships within view of each other, the problem would be far more difficult. Before any action was taken, they'd have to know exactly what they faced.

Sigefert dispatched patrols at a run, north and south along the beach, to learn what they could. When they returned, the news for once was good. No other craft could be seen in either direction. But there was no knowing how long this fortuitous state of affairs would last, so fast action was of the essence.

But they must not just charge helter-skelter toward the lone picket, for it could flee east near as fast as they could pursue, to give warning that would bring down Gormsson's whole flotilla on them. No, the two Northumbrian boats must close from east and west at the same time to intercept. Cursing the inevitable delay, Sigefert ordered half his force to drag a boat once more, around the point and well to the east of their prey. When this dreary task was completed, and search by every eye disclosed no sign of other craft, the two longboats were launched simultaneously and rowed at breakneck speed toward the lone picket.

It might have escaped them, had it not hesitated too long in deciding to turn and flee from superior force—and when it did flee, as it turned out later, it had too few oarsmen to make best speed. The ill-defended craft was taken in short order, though the brief fight was bloody in the extreme. Ylva, now shrieking in terror, was dumped amid the wounded and dead, to await rescue or death by exposure as her gods chose.

The Northumbrians, smothering the defenders by boarding simultaneously over both rails, sustained relatively few casualties, but the four slain included Guthram, Sigefert's trusted navigator—a tragic mischance that would prove critically important.

The need for getting clear of the area as quickly as possible was so compelling that Sigefert set a course due south, rather than heading more westward toward Britain as Gormsson would expect. He sought thereby to put maximum distance between them and any pursuers, which was understandable in the circumstances, but a decision he was to regret bitterly later.

Tara woke to brilliant sunlight, opening her eyes to Sigefert's cheerful smile. He stood above her on the stern sheets, legs widespread, large hand firmly grasping the steering oar. She reveled in the strong set of his jaw, the steady look of his clear blue eyes, his competent way with the helm in the long quartering combers—his expression happier and more carefree than she'd ever hoped to see.

But holding their southerly course so long was strangely disturbing to her, though she could not have said why.

"We head for Normandy," he announced. The twinkle in his eye told her belike he jested, but she wondered. He'd long resisted return to Britain, lest Alfred seize and hang them all as pirates. Could he really think the Viking Duke Rolf, that shadowy Dane who'd carved out a kingdom from the land of the West Franks, offered surer welcome than his own countrymen, despite their token allegiance to Alfred?

"You actually think he'd welcome your foreign Northumbrian band?" she asked.

Sigefert shrugged. "That's a strong word: 'welcome'. Ask rather, would he suffer us to join his standard as Gorm did, instead of putting us all to the sword. And my answer to that is plain—I know not."

"My senses tell me you hope to cast your lot with him, in spite of your doubts. Do my senses deceive me?"

He shook his head in the negative. "I plan no such thing, love; the risk is too great. Better we seek the demons we know, than trust unknown ones on a foreign shore. I've had enow of negotiating with foreign monarchs for service in their cause. I've had enow of begging! Besides," he added teasingly, but with a quizzical expression, "if you cannot tell whether you'll bide with me in Northumberland, sure you'd never stomach going outside Britain itself."

She had to admit the justice of his many-sided comment. Sigefert deserved a decision from her, whether she'd stay with him or no. She could not call to Atheurin—e'en if she reached him, which was doubtful, he'd only talk her back to Cymru. This was a decision on her alone.

But what would her decision be?

At midday the sky was leaden, and the sun obscured. Sigefert fumbled with the unfamiliar solerstein, but shortly threw it down in disgust. "Cursed be that witless Dane who chanced to fell Guthram," he swore. "None but he knew the key to this accursed device! We'll have to find our course by simple reckoning."

Tara felt a sense of unease. A skilled navigator was deemed crucial to Vikings; lacking one who knew to read the sun and stars, their course was scarce more than guesswork. Steer too high, and they'd strike the barbarous land of the bloodthirsty Picts; steer too low, they'd chance falling in with Alfred's patrol. They had to be right!

Sensing her doubts, and realizing their cause, Sigefert sought to reassure her. "We will land a patrol by night when we hit the British coast, and bid them reck out where we are." The process sounded most haphazard, but Sigefert had sailed these seas many times, and belike had carved on his mind the coastal terrain of his homeland. She determined to put her foolish fears aside, if she could, and enjoy the voyage.

And enjoy it she did. Both her seasickness and her terror of the unfathomable deep were gone, and she realized they had blinded her to the untrammeled majesty of the open sea. Far from being a watery wasteland, it fair teemed with living creatures. Great blue whales, near as long as their boat, rose from the depths to join them, swimming lazily alongside with their great inscrutable eyes on these strange intruders. Oft she saw on the horizon a thin column of spume, marking a whale spouting vapor from his blowhole. Large sleek fish sported ahead of them, riding their bow wave, darting beneath their keel to come up on one side or far astern, and soar aloft in graceful arching flight, then dive cleanly back into the rollers. Menacing gray sharks swam just abaft the curving sternpost, evil eyes glaring balefully at the steersman. Flying fish rose in sudden swarms, some e'en landing in the boat to be seized at once for the food stocks, taking to the air as if in escape from an unseen predator. Sea birds kept pace with them day and night, squabbling over food scraps by day and oft huddling in the rigging by night. Transparent creatures, more plant than animal, pulsated aimlessly in the waters, and great amorphous patches of sea grass housed vast colonies of tiny crabs and fishes busy at their unknown pursuits. With the winds holding fair, the crewmen passed the time fishing the deep green waters, hauling up bizarre denizens of the depths to be marvelled at, and at times added to their burgeoning food stores.

"Shorebound folk refuse to credit the deep seas with such peace and beauty," mused Sigefert, sitting with Tara just aft the dragon-head prow, looking across the water. "They ken only the seashore, where dying ocean waves crash and spend themselves on the shelving sands, and the sea-gods dump their broke rubble. The dreams of such as they tell them naught of the great peaceful creatures who dwell in the depths, or the quiet of the ocean far from land." His expression was tranquil, and she detected a mistiness in his eyes. "I would we might sail out here forever, Tara, shedding the cares of the land, bound for the edge of the earth."

This emotional side of Sigefert kept Tara silent, unwilling for the spell to be broke. He was scanning the horizon intently, as if seeking to catch sight of unknown or mythical lands beyond the sea. "We sailed to the north a few years back," he reminisced, "and fell in at sea with a foreign Viking force. As we approached, we found ourselves so even matched that we eschewed thought of battle, and came together for a parley. The leader of those long-traveled Norseman was an explorer calling himself Bjarni, son of Herjulf."

Sensing from Sigefert's far-away look that he relived the occasion in his mind, Tara kept her silence, and he went on.

"He was a great talker, and painted a grand picture of a fair land far to the west, across an ocean so vast the Northern Sea is but a pond beside it. It came to him in a vision, but he knew not how to reach it. He had three ravens, and released one each day. The first returned to the ships and the second also, but the third did not, so he steered along that one's flight path, and came on the land of his dreams. He saw hills green with grass, valleys laced with flowing streams, skies fair and bright—and great herds of game so tame they came up to the boats on the beach. Some of his men wished to remain, but he had places to go. Yet he longed to return one day." Sigefert paused, seeing it in his mind as he'd never seen with his eyes. "And I caught his fever, and I wished to go there, too." He looked down at her, his eyes misting again, but his eyes were not on her alone— he still saw that bright far-off land across the seas. Then she saw his eyes focus on her. "How if we go there together, lass?"

The question was half-jest, she knew, but she sensed a thread of seriousness running through that tale of far-away lands. It was as if he dreamt of spiriting her off, away from the problems awaiting in Britain, to carve out a magical existence where they would be inseparable for all time, with the world shut out. And I want the same, she thought, weeping inside. But the world cannot be shut out. It is here, and we are in it, with problems to be faced. She knew not what to say, but reached out, taking his hand in both of hers, and pressed it against her breast in a gesture of intimacy and love.

Lacking the skills of his lost navigator, Sigefert could not be sure of the landfall they sought at the Tees River mouth, or how to steer to get there. "If I make our position right," he told her, expressing a confidence he was far from feeling, "we'll make land at Durham or the river mouth on the morrow. How good a navigator I am, we'll know after scouts go ashore."

Shortly after noon next day, an excited cry rang out from the mast-head, and all hands searched the horizon. Soon the misty coastline rose slowly from the sea, as if reluctant to show itself. "We be home, Tara," said Sigefert in quiet triumph. "The lazing days are done. Time to make our way on in. And time for you to think how you'll decide—which way you'll go."

Despite their eagerness to hit the shore, Sigefert cautiously waited for dark to move in and land the patrol, with orders to seek out a farmer who could tell where they were, then truss him up if he seemed likely to spread an alarm. "Best we take the safer way of just slitting his throat," said the grizzled patrol leader, but Sigefert exploded at that. "These be our countrymen! Would you harry the land of your birth?"

The patrol returned all too soon, shouting ahead to ready the boats before pursuers were upon them, and the boats shoved off the instant the scouts dived on board.

"Blast!" Even as the longboats beat hastily off the shore, Sigefert tried to decipher what had happened. Saxons could not be so far north! Mayhap outlaws, but how did his men allow themselves to be surprised by such? When they slowed offshore for a parley, he and Oddune checked survivors, to discover that three of the scouts had not made it back, and the three who survived had not had a chance to learn what had happened to them. The mission was more than a failure—it was a catastrophe. They must have been seen when they landed, dark or no, by an unseen force lying in wait.

"What now?" demanded Oddune, his voice devoid of feeling, but Sigefert knew he was ice cold inside. One of the missing men was his younger brother.

Sigefert thought fast. The hamlet whose faint lights flickered on the skyline north of them must be Durham, so the Tees estuary lay just to the south. There was no time for deliberation; they must get into the Tees and safely upriver fast, lest one of the missing patrol had leaked word of who they were, and news galloped down by courier to the Saxon fleet massed in the Wash. He must decide, and now!

"Turn south. Make for the Tees River. And pull!"

Little did Sigefert suspect the magnitude of his navigational error. That first day's southing had taken them down much farther than he'd recked. That initial miscalculation, during the time of their euphoric inattention born of their miraculous escape, had not brought them to land north of the Tees, as he'd decided, but perilously far south in Danish Mercia. And now, each stroke of his oars was bringing him nearer the Wash, that body of water where Alfred's North Britain patrol was based.

Tara was assailed by doubts that refused to abate, and confessed her fears to Sigefert. "We'll reach the river in half an hour," he assured her. "If we don't raise it within the hour, I'll turn north and scout the shore once more." Mayhap he was right, but still…that inner voice…

"The river mouth!" Sigefert's tone was triumphant. Following his finger, she made out a scarcely visible sheen of light reflecting from some inland waterway. "Now are you and your fearful gods satisfied at last?" he chided her.

He'd been right, and she wrong—if it was the Tees. Mayhap Atheurin was no longer in tune with her, thinking she had abandoned Cymru. No! she cried silently. I've abandoned naught! He'd have to give her time, to work out of the confusion as to her fateful choice. She'd not fail him, or Cymru…ever!

In Sigefert's euphoria, he failed to make sure Oddune saw him turn upriver, but forged confidently on, unthinking. "Will we rendezvous with the other boat?" asked Tara. Her intuitive sense was still warning that all was not well, but she was reluctant to dampen Sigefert's excitement.

He laughed. "I confess I'd forgot him, in my enthusiasm for reaching home. We'll wait for him to come up with us." As he spoke, a call came from the bow lookout: "Boat, ho!" and Oddune's boat came alongside to port, materializing out of the dark. Then, inexplicably, another came alongside, to starboard.

Not until the grapnels fell, their wicked points biting into the gunwales, did the terrible truth come home to them.

Lion-heads!

Unexpecting, cumbered with oars jammed through thole pins, no weapons or helmets to hand, overmanned four to one by Saxons leaping down from the lionhead ships, they made an unequal battle of it. Many were slain at the outset, before the Northumbrians comprehended that these were Saxon fighting men, not Oddune's crew. Most fought desperately before they were overcome, but a few, stunned by the hopeless odds, had not the will to continue.

Sigefert's maddened sweeping blows dispatched the first two Saxons to reach him. Then an arrow caught his sword arm, and as he transferred his sword to the other hand, the butt of a Saxon lance to his unhelmeted head felled him to the floorboards.

Tara, standing in the prow, alerted by some sixth sense, had her blade drawn. The first man to spring aboard stumbled, and died from her thrust to his stomach ere he could regain balance. Before she could withdraw it, another was behind her, and swiftly she whirled to confront him, but her hilt caught on his cuirass, and her faithful sword spun away out of her reach.

Weaponless, save for the small dagger against her thigh, she watched the Saxon draw back for a mortal thrust. This was the finish, she knew, but she was unafraid. It seemed, somehow, as if she were in a dream.

Calmly she faced him down, looking deep into his eyes, reading there his indecision, his momentary reluctance to kill one waiting so strangely quiet for the blow. He's not faced such an enemy before, who looks death in the face so, she thought. But she must make a move, as her strange inaction would scarce suffice to hold him back for long!

She raised her right hand, carefully lest a sudden motion break the spell, made the old Druidic sign of peace and brotherhood, and extended her hands toward him, palms upraised in the chivalric symbol of friendship. She stood thus, motionless, a smile of friendship on her face, looking him directly in the eye.

A sudden fear of the unknown chilled his stomach, arresting his attack. What manner of person was this? Uncertain, he contented himself with gesturing her to follow, to enter the lion-headed craft. Relieved that the critical moment had passed, but strangely serene, she did as he bade.

When the lion-head bearing her was underway, she listed to the talk of the Saxon near her, who spoke unaware that this foreign Norse devil could understood his tongue. Sigefert was thought to be the pirate chieftain they'd been seeking these long months, and all with him Danish pirates. Despite trying to hear all that was said, she could not learn whether he had been killed, but the strongest feeling came to her that he lived. She heard, too—or it came to her somehow—that they would be taken at once to Winchester.

To the court at Winchester! The court, where they would be tried as pirates—and where it would be the gibbet for them all!

CHAPTER 31

What followed was little more than a blur to Tara. The dispirited remnant of Sigefert's force was shackled roughly and spread through the three boats with scant attention paid to the Northumbrian's wounds, and the little flotilla with its cargo of prisoners started out at once on its interminable trip to Winchester gaol where almost certain execution awaited them all.

Her rude cell was cramped and moldy, but Tara realized with a pang of remorse that the damp unlighted dungeons beneath Sire's Menevia Castle were even more stark. Naught at Winchester surprised her, nor lifted her flagging spirits. As soon as they made shift to patch up the prisoners' most urgent wounds, their trial took place—brief and foreordained, judging them pirates from Normandy harrying the coast. The trial judge's sole focus was on Sigefert as leader, and so slight attention was paid the other captives that her sex was not detected. The hasty trial was her first chance to see Sigefert since their capture, and she'd been looking forward eagerly to meet with him and see how he'd fared, but it was not to be. The moment sentencing was pronounced, they were returned to confinement to await the gallows.

Once back in her cell, Tara forced herself to take stock of the situation, her attention focused on escape to the exclusion of all else. The walls offered no hope of breaching, and the tiny hole of a window was far too small for egress, even had its bars been removed. The only hope was persuasion, and that meant somehow deceiving or winning over a gaoler. Knowing Atheurin would scorn her for not exhausting all efforts to help herself, she would have to devote all her thoughts and efforts to the supreme task at hand, and only hope for success.

Of the three gaolers she'd seen in the passage outside her cell, just the morning guard, a youth she'd seen make a sign of the cross earlier, gave promise of being approachable. He was a Christian, and she must work on that. Forcing her mind to concentrate, she combed her memories of Dewi Sant for aught that could serve as a starting point. She might contrive to employ a suitable prayer in some way that would impress him. Its meaning mattered little—she'd be working only on his senses and emotions, what he thought he heard or saw through the door grating. Hastily she went through the half-forgot litany, considering and discarding this or that ceremonial figment. In the end, she was left with but one possibility, and that a hollow reed on which to lean her hopes of deceiving the young guard. But she had no other weapon at hand, and Atheurin would expect her to do her best.

Out of the youth's view, with fingers so clumsy she could but half-control them, she cobbled up a crude religious disguise that might pass muster in the cell's dim light—if the gods looked favorably on her poor efforts. Adjusting it as realistically as she could, she peered out at him through the grating.

"Veni creator spiritus, my son."

He could not suspect an infidel pirate would know his tongue, so at first he looked about him in complete mystification for the source of the words. Almost as an afterthought, he glanced at the cell door—to see, with awed surprise coupled with apprehension, the beauteous face of a nun! For a moment he stood irresolute. This must be a miracle! Unconsciously, he crossed himself. What was happening? Was the Blessed Lord speaking to him? Was he chosen?

The divine vision spoke again. "Open to me the gates of Justice, my son. May merciful God nourish you with His grace, and may Christ, our divine teacher, grant you His light."

The words rang true. This was no Viking devil trying to deceive him. He'd heard such in the Holy Service. But coming from this prison cell housing naught but foreign pirates...? He stood transfixed and dumb, his brain in a whirl.

"Is it not better, my son, to be free within the caring walls of Mother Church? Art thou not obedient to Christ, the Good Shepherd? Answer with your heart, my son."

Through his awed confusion, the last question found its way to him. With what seemed an infinite calm, the heavenly creature waited silently to hear his response. "Oh, yes!" he all but whispered, unthinking, controlled by emotion.

"Go thee, then, and bid the Reverend Father come with no delay, my son. Thy eternal soul hangs in the balance. Go!"

The note of command in the spirit's sweet voice galvanized him into reflexive action. He spun at once on his heel, forgetting the duty to remain at his post, in palpable eagerness to obey. Tara hastily pulled off the makeshift wimple and headpiece, and composed herself as patiently as she could manage, to wait.

In minutes, the guard was back, with a priest. The latter's open countenance was irritated and skeptical. Of course he disbelieves, thought Tara; how would he not? But some part of him remembers withal that there is much betwixt earth and heaven passing human understanding, and he does not quite dare to scoff at a miracle, however improbable.

The cell door was flung open, and the two stared past her, looking for they knew not what. She must seize the moment.

"This is the gate of the lord, Father," she intoned piously. "The just may enter."

The priest recoiled as if struck in the face. "What are you?" he demanded hoarsely, his ruddy face paling. "Where did you learn those words? "Would you make a...a mockery of...?" He stared in bewilderment at the creature before him, standing so stolidly in its drab uniform. Again he questioned, "Who are you, pirate?"

"I have received the yoke of the Lord, and bear His burden which is sweet and light." Tara spoke softly, in a gentle tone, befitting a novice, but wildly unbelievable from the lips of this foreign barbarian who lived only for rapine and foul murder. But the creature was continuing. "I ask thy protection, Father, and thy help to accomplish my mission."

The priest, taken completely aback, stared intently at Tara, twisting his reddened hands to collect his waning courage, until some thought or power seemed to bring him to an abrupt decision. He spoke to the guard, fighting to hold his voice steady. "Release the Viking to my custody, and rebar the door firmly." He turned, beckoning her to come with him.

When they were seated in his cramped and chilly chamber, the priest spoke, trying to regain his fragile composure. "I know not who you are, or if ye be man or demon. I know not what evil spirit blasphemously whispered the rituals into your ear. But I shall find out! So speak, pirate—or whate'er ye be!"

How must she approach this man of God? His features, not those of a rigid ascetic, and lacking the flabby softness of the cloister, bespoke one who would seek to serve his Savior righteously—if only she could show him the right. She prayed he had sufficient will to stand against the King's judgment, and intercede on her behalf in the name of Mother Church. Belike she should mount a frontal attack, shocking him at the outset with the truth.

"I am no Danish pirate, Father, but a British woman. My name is Tara." As his features stiffened, and he gaped in astonishment, that she knew could turn to angry disbelief any instant, she hastened to complete her revelation. "I am a Princess of the Blood, heir to a throne in Cymru, which is a province of your own King Alfred!"

Then, with a mighty effort, he regained composure, and set about questioning her, first broadly, then in detail. This was no stupid prelate, and she was relieved that there was no need to deceive him. Taking pains to avoid his snares to trap her in falsehood, she told how they'd left Denemearc as fugitives, under Royal edict of death, bound in peace for Northumbrian sanctuary. They knew naught of Norman piracy, for they'd been in Denemearc these six years past. Unable to shake her story, but now understanding that no satanic creature stood before him, nevertheless he remained openly skeptical.

Taken by a sudden thought, he leaned forward to put a question, and she knew by his expression that her answer would be vital. Pray the gods grant me power to answer aright, she breathed silently.

"You say the Bishop at Saint David's sent you to the convent?" Pray tell me, then, who was Bishop there before him?" He sat back, his expression that of a cat who waits intently at the mouse hole.

Who was it? She'd been so young when he left! How could she know? But this suspicious prelate would not credit a plea of youth. Her answer must be correct.

Hazily, she recalled a sea voyage. A trip to Brecon…to Glamorgan Castle…to the High Court. Sire had received some ill news there. News so serious he'd been forced to promise her to Clydog! News, he said, of a betrayal…betrayal by someone very dear to Sire…

Betrayal? But who…?

Then, without knowing how, she heard the name in her head: Asser! But who was Asser?

"That Bishop was Asser," she answered confidently, scarce knowing she spoke, or how.

The priest sprang up, eyes bulging. "How did ye happen on that name?" he demanded roughly. But she knew the battle was half won.

Why did he ask of Asser, Tara asked herself. How could he know who'd been a Cymri bishop close on eighteen years back? Then it came to her somehow, what Asser had done in betraying her father.

"He came to King Alfred's Court. As his Scrivener."

And she saw belief growing in his eyes.

The date of the hanging was set, but still the priest had not returned. Despite her powerful belief that the Celti gods could not let her hang, she began to lose confidence. With but two days of grace left, she ceased eating or speaking, and sat lifelessly, shutting out the present, thinking only of the grassy glade where she had communed so oft with Atheurin.

She was shaken rudely awake in what seemed the deep of night, and dragged from her cell, by two guards cloaked and spurred for riding. They hurried her up the narrow stone staircase, and to her great surprise bundled her unceremoniously into a finely appointed coach. She heard the click of the latch, and the coach rattled across cobblestones, down a rutted street, and through a maze of buildings. A clatter of hooves betokened a substantial escort.

The buildings on each side thinned and disappeared, and they were passing through the countryside. She could see gaunt trees, and empty fields silvered by the moon, and once a stone watchtower standing stark and ghostly on the moor.

She dozed at last, until hands were laid on her again, and she was hustled through passages dimly lit by guttering pine knots. She was led up flights of stone steps, and around a balcony like one she remembered when escaping Glamorgan Castle, and finally shoved through a door into a commodious chamber. Was this where her mysterious journey would end?

Where was she?

A quick glance around the room disclosed no one else. Within an alcove at its far end stood a small table, and the feeble light from a shaded lamp at its center illumined out a dim circle on the tabletop, but did little to relieve the stark blackness of the room. She started tentatively to approach the light, when a slight movement made her draw back in alarm.

"Sit down, my child."

Startled, she peered toward the sound, and saw now why she had missed him, for he was garbed all in dark cloth, and his face was in shadow. He motioned her to a seat opposite him.

His words had possessed a quality that both impressed and reassured her. She cast her eyes down, not to seem forward, and awaited his pleasure—with scant doubt as to who he was.

"Please tell me your name." His voice now was full of warmth, and she knew he bore her no ill will.

"I am the Princess Tara of Dyfed Gwlag in Cymru, Your Grace."

"Indeed." An aura of security emanated from him, reassuring her again that she had naught to fear.

"Whence did you come, Princess Tara of Dyfed?"

Finding no way to make any clear answer in few words, she found herself relating the long, convoluted story. He listed without interrupting, until at last she fell silent.

"And your father—what was his name?"

"King Llywarch, Your Grace."

He showed no surprise at the title she accorded him. "And your mother?"

"Queen Gwenwed, Grace."

"Whence did she come?"

"From Eire, Grace. County Meath in Eire."

"And your name—how came you to be named 'Tara'?"

"I was named in memory of Tara Hill, where my mother was born."

He settled back, relaxed, as if her replies pleased him, and she had the strongest sense that all would be well. After a time he bent forward, and she knew somehow that her answers to the remaining questions would be crucial.

"You remember when I left Saint David's, Tara?"

"I remember what my father told me, Your Grace. And I recall visiting the High Court, and there learning you had gone. It all happened close on eighteen years past."

"Why did your father think I left, child?"

She hesitated, ashamed to recount Sire's anger at a desertion he could not comprehend.

"Your abashed silence speaks for you. Tell me, then, why you think I left."

The question surprised her. How could a babe of but four years ken such matters? But his expression demanded an answer. Confused, she tried her best to think how to respond.

"Why, Your Grace, I..." The shaded light hid her face, red with embarrassment. Then, to her amazement, she found herself speaking, directly and with a strong feeling of confidence.

"You left to save Cymru."

He stood up then, and drew her from the alcove to the main part of the chamber. "You are indeed the Princess Tara. None but a Princess of the Blood could know these things. You are right: I did indeed heed the call to Alfred's Court that I might help in some small way to avert the endless years of warfare I saw stretching ahead. My mission has borne fruit, though grievous slow and parlous it has been. With your return, the last piece falls in place, and my small crusade is well nigh complete. If the Lord should wish to take me now, I go to Him in peace."

Gradually, she came to understand the rightness of his words. Though he looked to Jesu, and she to the ancient Celti and Druidic deities, she knew he followed in his way a beacon full as strong and true as the one that guided her.

"I would tell you, Princess, of my conversation with your father, the King, and your sainted mother, when you were a swaddling babe and I came to Menevia for your christening. Your mother, a beautiful creature she was." He paused, savoring the memory. "She had a promise from your father that you'd be rightful heir, as if you'd been a prince. But King Llywarch, thinking she'd bear him a son in the end, gave the promise lightly. I read on her face, poor creature, as could Sir Gruwent, that you'd be the only heir. When I anointed you with holy water, I whispered a special prayer that you'd prove a worthy ruler." He saw her tears start, and waited quietly until she collected her feelings.

"I can see, not only from your stirring tale, but from your stalwart carriage and the honesty in your eyes, that you have met our expectations and more. My prayer was answered."

"How did you know I was in Winchester Gaol, Your Grace?" she asked, when the turmoil in her heart had stilled somewhat. "Did the Father I spoke with come to you?"

"No, my child. He fear'd to take your story to his superiors, lest they charge him with blaspheming. He fretted long on the matter, and asked for heavenly guidance which did not come, and in the end kept his own counsel."

His reply astonished her. "Then how did you learn...?"

"It came to me in a dream, that I would find you imprisoned there. I like to believe that the pastor's troubled thoughts on the matter somehow were conveyed to me by a higher power. In any case, I sent a holy man at once to question the dominie and ferret out the truth of his encounter with you. I knew he'd not in sooth seen quite what he related, but his fanciful tale was confirmation enow of my dream, and I had you brought here to Chippenham." He led her to the door. "And now, my child, you'll be returned to Winchester, but you are under no immediate peril of hanging, nor your comrades. In the meantime, I must intercede with King Alfred. Then you'll be sent for—my sacred word on't."

On her return to her cell, she noted a different morning guard. When Tara asked for the priest, he came at once, his attitude almost as if he responded to a royal summons.

"Thank you for attending me, Father," she said, when the cleric appeared at her cell door. "I've a favor to ask of you. Pray get word to Eorl Sigefert. Inform him I meet with King Alfred before the week is out, and advise him to be of good fettle in his mind." The priest stood irresolute for a moment, and she took a more forceful tone. "I beg you, do not displease his Grace with your dalliance. Be sure the Eorl receives my message forthwith."

Prodded into action by his recognition that the command emanated from one born to authority, he scurried off, and she was relieved to know that Sigefert could breathe easier, though belike in wonder at what manner of deity she'd invoked to importune the Saxon King.

No less a personage than the Lord High Sheriff himself appeared in her cell to escort her to the waiting carriage this time. Belike he ached to ask why his monarch sought out a Viking pirate, if he durst—and if he could conceive that the prisoner spoke his tongue. Tara could only hope her venture would not end in ignominious return to his custody, for hanging.

Despite her nagging worry that all might not turn out well at Chippenham, her second trip was vastly more pleasant than the first. This time she made her way in daylight, and could see carefully tended greensward and stately trees along the road, and woodsmen busy at their gardening. So absorbed was she at seeing for the first time the Saxon countryside that it came almost as a shock when the landscape changed abruptly to cottages and public buildings. She compared this panorama of Chippenham with the settlements she'd known in Cymru and Denemearc, to the great discredit of the latter. Only Byzantium, of any metropolis she'd seen, could surpass, in the quality of streets or elegance of structures, this city where the Saxon King held court. No, she corrected herself—not the Saxon King, but the British King. For if any ruler had the right to claim sovereignty over these Isles, it was Alfred. For the first time, appreciating the might and reach of the powerful monarch summoning her, Tara was afraid.

The carriage entered the keep to find Asser waiting. "You are in good time, Princess," he told her, escorting her inside. "Refresh yourself, but we must hasten to the Throne Room."

She addressed him by his former ecclesiastic title, but this time he corrected her. "I am Bishop no longer," he said. "My proper title is 'Court Scrivener.'"

The title was unfamiliar. "What is its meaning, Your Grace?" she asked, before she caught herself. Belike the term 'Grace' was improper as well.

If so, he made no comment on it. "The Court Scrivener makes shift to be Private Secretary to King Alfred. Some would add the title 'Royal Chronicler', since I maintain records of the reign, in addition to preparing letters and documents." His face relaxed in a warm smile, and Tara understood how her mother and father could have so loved this man. "In writing, I exert some small influence over his affairs, though King Alfred is not one to be led about by his underlings, or indeed by anyone. He knows his mind, and a powerful mind it is. But we dally. Hasten to fresh your appearance if you wish, and I'll call for you within the half-hour. And have no fear," he added with a reassuring pat on her head. "King Alfred has no wish to harm Dyfed's heir."

Asser's last remark, comforting though it was, astounded Tara. It flew directly in the face of beliefs so stoutly held by both her father and King Cadell. They swore the Saxons were implacable foes of the 'Wealhas', with all the calumny that invidious soubriquet of 'outsider' implied. Could she—could all of them—be wrong?

Her heart pounding with excitement at the coming incredible event, she followed Asser to the Throne Room, and her critical meeting with the King. Just outside the door, Asser raised his hand for her to bide. "I should have told you earlier, Princess Tara. King Alfred has been unwell for some time. He had hoped at least to see you, but has been advised by the chirurgeon that it will tire him excessively. You will meet another."

Another! Who else could it be? "Who, your Grace?" she asked uncertainly, still holding to the familiar title.

"His son, Crown Prince Edward."

Edward! She pulled back in horror. Her mind flew back to her encounter in the Black Mountain, when the craven Clydog had abandoned her to the Saxon scouting party. And when the personable young Saxon noble, thinking her a wench brought along for pleasuring, sought light-heartedly to press his attentions on her.

And she had stabbed him!

She had cruelly and with deception stabbed the man she now would petition! The man who was no less than Britain's Crown Prince—the one-time enemy who held her life in his hands!

"Come, Princess." Asser thrust her ahead, and she found herself in the Throne Room, on the verge of confronting Crown Prince Edward.

"So this is the valorous Valkyrie of whom you've spoke, eh, Asser?" He sat, not on the throne itself, but beside it on a plainly carved bench. Surprisingly, he rose as they entered, and approached them with easy informality. "I'd not take her as a maiden, garbed so; but then, you've regaled me with her exploits, and I'd be surprised to see her in maidenly dress." He turned his attention to Tara, smiling pleasantly. "Step forward if you please, Milady. I'd fain have a closer look at the gallant Viking who's a Cymri Princess beneath."

Asser prodded her forward, whispering, "Pray respond, Princess. Do not hang back speechless. Prince Edward would hear from you."

So prompted, she managed to find her voice. "I am most honored, Sir Prince," she quavered. "You are most kind to see me."

"Ah, yes. To be sure. But in actuality, I cannot see you. Step out from the shadows, pray."

Her heart pounding so she wondered he could not hear it, she stepped into the bright light about the throne.

Edward scrutinized her, puzzled. "Do I not know you, Milady? Have we not met? Have you, perchance, visited us at Chippenham?" He took her chin gently in his hand, tilted her head back and to each side, then released it. "I've seen that beautiful face before, that I'll swear to."

Tara turned toward Asser, seeking his help to rescue her from the perilous moment, but he made no move. "I...I've not traveled to Saxony, Sir Prince. Mayhap you..."

Edward raised his hand for silence, while he stared intently into her face. Too intently...

Suddenly recognition showed in his eyes. "I think I've got it!" He shouted out the words. "In the Black Mountains of Glamorgan...in a tent. Yes, in a tent. And you...you..."

He broke off, and a deep bellow came from his throat. She knew, in that instant, that he had recognized her as the one who had stabbed him...

And that her fate was sealed!

CHAPTER 32

Tara, her head high, stood proud before the furious Edward. As a Prince of the Blood, sure he'd have to accept that a princess must resist profanation of her person with all her efforts. How could he vent his rage on her for having fought back? Would he not think the better of her for refusing to submit supinely to his advances. If he could not understand as much, she'd accept no favors from such as he. She'd return to Winchester and death, with her honor intact!

But simply giving up without any effort to patch things up somehow, without seeking to make him understand what had forced her to act as she did, would mean abandoning Sigefert to his fate. Try as she might, however, she could find no words that might persuade him.

She half-turned, thinking of naught save that she must leave, but Asser grasped her arm and sought to turn her back again. "What do you do, my child?" he whispered urgently in her ear. "Are you daft? He has not dismissed you! Take care not to offend this man, lest he think you undeserving of his favors."

His favors! To escape such favors was just the reason she'd drawn dagger on him that unfortunate day! Reluctantly, in obedience to the holy man who'd baptized her, she raised her downcast eyes to the Prince's face—to be dumbfounded beyond imagining! Could it be…was it possible that…?

Yes, against all odds, beyond doubting—Edward was indeed roaring…
Roaring with laughter!

"I'd not have credited you with the effrontery to come before me and petition thus, did I not behold it with mine own eyes," he said, when he'd regained sufficient control to speak. "Not every day do I suffer a request for clemency from one who plunged a dagger into me." He glanced in jocular mood at Asser. "You must enter it in the Historical Archives of the Realm, Scrivener."

Tara's relief, dispelling at once her deep apprehension, was so far beyond words that she knew not how to respond.

"Before you pinked me with your little bodkin, I took you for a common camp wench well knowing what she was about, albeit a most sightly one. But it made scant sense, as I thought on it later, for such a one to be in soldier's garb. And I wat few drabs would possess such skill at arms—or with riding my stallion of those days, who allowed few but myself in his saddle." He laughed again, but ruefully, rubbing his cheek. "It's been my experience an angry woman is more like to unsheathe a vicious set of claws."

She knew she must respond, if only to express her sincere regret for having injured him. "Sire, I meant you no serious hurt. I was but a lass then, and deeply affrighted. I fear'd to be murthered, and sought but to save myself."

"You've no call to beg pardon, Milady. I was the enemy, and you my prisoner. No soldier but would have done the same. I accept full blame for letting your beauty blind me to your poinard. When my troopers patched me up, they could scarce smother their smiles and whispers. Any grudge I might bear would not be for your courageous defense, but for the ridicule you made me bear back in the Officers' Mess."

His last words had a strange effect on him, for as he finished speaking his eyes opened wide and his smile faded, as if the recollection of that episode had awakened a sudden thought. Tara could not fail to note the change in his demeanor, and waited nervously for what the unpredictable young Prince would say next.

"It comes to my mind, Milady, that there may be summat you can do for me. If you can do this small trifle, I'll count the slate wiped clean." He hesitated a moment, and she saw that he was thinking if he should say more, or turn the matter aside. If she read aright, he'd decided to keep to his original track, for he continued. "If not…well…" He shrugged, a smile returning, but beneath it she sensed the carefully veiled, and mayhap unconscious, hint of a threat.

"I would be honored to do what you ask, Sire," she answered at once, thrusting her worry aside, anxious for the enormous gift of his favor. "You've but to say it, Sire, and if it be in my power, you may count it as done."

"Capital! Capital! It's well within your power—indeed a trifle for a gallant such as you. I dine shortly with my Eorls and others, officers who ride with me on campaign. Some of them are the ones who scoffed back then, at the notion of a lass besting me. I'd but have them look you over…" His tone was diffident, and she realized that, for all his power of life or death, Edward hesitated to make this request of her. "Wouldst sit by me at table tonight, Princess?"

The gathering in Chippenham's Great hall minded her of that heady experience in Carmarthen Castle, when first she dined with Dyfed's uchelwyr and won their allegiance. But in this Royal Dining Hall, she was not leader of the foregathered nobles, but more of an oddity for gawking at—a maid who purported to fight as a man. But she did fight as a man, and oft better, for she could list those who'd died at her sword. She had ample reason to hold her head high, in this or any other assemblage!

When she grasped the reality of Edward's invitation, she begged leave to retire and make her toilet. The Prince sent the Chatelaine along, availing Tara of all facilities for feminine adornment. Now ensconced at Edward's side, cynosure of all eyes, she was as well bathed and perfumed, as appealing to the eyes and enticing to the imaginations of the group assembled, as all the artifices of the bower could contrive. She wore her distinctly unfeminine Viking attire, partly since she had naught else, but mainly because she recked that Edward's wounded pride would heal the better if she appeared as warrior rather than maid. Knowing not what was expected of her—how she might prove Edward's stabbing was no reflection on his manhood—she was nonetheless completely at ease amid these high-born nobles who'd been vying for her favor so engagingly. I've come a long way from my childhood days, she realized.

"Asser's revealed summat of your exploits, Princess," Edward told her as she took her seat. "The hair-raising voyage to Constantinople, abduction by the despicable Emperor of Rome and slaying his gladiator, besting your Viking berserker in a death duel, bearding the Norsemen in their very stronghold to steal their women—e'en overcoming two ruffians bent on stealing the Convent's plate." His unabashed admiration was plain on his face, but she knew the evening's success depended on earning the whole Court's respect for her prowess. She could not stand and publicly recite her exploits as he'd just done in private. Most would consider her a braggart and many simply would not believe—and in any case she could not bring herself to do it. How, then, could she prove herself, as the Prince clearly desired?

Even as she rose to acknowledge each toast, her brain was groping for a way to show his officers that they, too, might have suffered the same wound from her as did he. Edward made light of it, but she could see that his vanity was pricked, and that the unthinking jests of his officers still pained him. Incredible as it was that a Prince could be sensitive, Tara doubted not that his clemency easily could hinge on her ability to drive those taunts back into their throats.

But how? E'en were her sword not sequestered in Winchester gaol, she scarce could stab a royal carouser to prove her mettle. She had won over the uchelwyr at Brechnor's Castle by toppling Wulfdune, but most credit was due his wine. Krohgarn she'd defeated by unfamiliar dueling tactics, but the Saxon dueling style was similar—and e'en had she stomach for such a confrontation, for no purpose save vanity, bloody combat in the Great Hall was unthinkable. The outlaw who fell to her billhook at Dewi Sant had been caught unaware, knowing naught of her martial skills. The ruffian in Menevia forest was a crude swordsman. The great lout, Grosseteste, in Aber Castle's tilting yard, had...

Of course—the quarter-stave tourney!

As she smiled and conversed, Tara's mind worked furiously to recall the details of that joust—the stratagem that made Grosseteste lose his head. Could the same work as well here: maddening her opponent beyond prudence? Quarter-staves were not lethal. Yes, if a showdown of some sort must be, such a joust would be preferable to any other.

But could she prevail? Or would she fail ignominiously, and dispose Edward irretrievably against her and her cause? She must not, could not, fail!

At meal's end, an officer rose ponderously to his feet. "We hear rumors, Milady, that beyond being fair to look upon, you're monstrous dangerous with weaponry withal." He was a beefy man, red of face, heavily muscled but running to fat. In a few years, excess flesh would weigh him down, and excess living blotch his face. He must have been a dangerous antagonist once, but she could see that his abilities now would be dulled by years of soft living. She studied him with heightened interest.

Not receiving a reply, he continued. "Hast ever faced a true man, my lass? Has that pretty body posing as a Viking ever known a real antagonist? Were not your brave exploits—the tales of which are beginning to weary me—won against doltish bumpkins?" His tone was intentionally rude, his smile scornful.

She'd been right—this one would serve. Stirred beyond prudence by the wine, he'd need little to be goaded into fury, e'en in the presence of his Prince. "Aye, Milord," she responded mockingly. "They were in sooth just such doltish bumpkins as he who stands before us here."

His scornful smile turned to a scowl of hot anger. So high a lord was unused to facing such open insult. "You take me as easy a conquest as those in your past, do you?" His eyes turned calculatingly toward Edward, all but including him in such 'easy' conquests. He'd scarce dare so unveiled a slur, had not wine dulled his judgment. Pray Lug—and pray Odin for good measure—his skill with the quarter-staff be equally dulled!

"You'd be passing easy, in your state, Eorl," she said, taunting him. "Wouldst challenge me, that your comrades might witness your drubbing?"

Of a sudden, at her provocative words, all talk ceased. Her challenge hung starkly on the air. The Eorl hesitated, discomfited, not intending this impasse—suddenly recalling that she was his monarch's guest of honor. Around the hall, many voices were loudly urging him to pick up the gage Tara had thrown out, or take his seat. He might have shrugged off the raucous importunings even then, until some expressions of mock sympathy for his supposed fears goaded him beyond enduring.

"I offer you challenge then, Princess, to joust with you here and now, the Prince permitting, with whatever weapon you find suitable to a woman's strength!" Belligerently he looked about the Hall, staring down those who would mock him.

"I accept your challenge, Sir Eorl, if the Prince be willing. If you be not too infirm or easy winded, I select the quarter-staff."

His livid expression betrayed rage at the open slight to his manhood, coupled with bemused surprise that his careless words had brought things to this pass. At Edward's nod of acquiescence, menials hurriedly cleared an area before the main table, and the Weapon Master hastened off to find staves.

"You need not proceed with this, Princess," whispered Edward, his tolerant smile erased by the swift turn of events. "I admire your gallantry, as does the whole assemblage, but you've no call to suffer painful injury. I need but say this charade has gone far enow, and no dishonor will attach to the names of either."

Strongly tempted to accept his generous offer, Tara tried to read his expression, and thought she saw disappointment there. She'd be unwise to presume on a generous offer that he'd been reluctant to make, leaving him keenly disappointed, mayhap e'en resentful, that she'd not shown his officers her martial abilities. No, she'd best not take advantage of that seeming escape, lest it prove dangerous to her future.

"Nay, Sire," she said, more firmly than she felt. "I've been challenged before your Court, and cannot take the craven's path out of it. By your leave, I'll let it proceed." The gratitude in his eyes told her what store he set, not only by the encounter, but more—by having all in the Hall see her prevail against a dangerous opponent.

Facing off against the Eorl, awaiting the gage, Tara felt two emotions conflicting within her. One was the fact of her surprising inner calm as she faced the affray, born of her growing experience and success with the number of altercations she'd had to face over the past few years of her turbulent young life. The other was her dismay at seeing the familiarity the Eorl displayed at handling the quarter-staff, as if from extensive recent experience with its use. She had not expected this, and realized more than ever that she must bring his blood to a boil early in the bout, if she was to induce him to abandon caution. She must find a way to do so at once, e'en before they started. But how?

She addressed Edward, as he was about to drop the gage, taking care that her words rang throughout the Hall. "Fear not for the Eorl, Sire. Though belike he's far past his manhood, and his aging bones easy crackt, I'll take care to smite him only hard enow to teach him manners."

The naked taunt she flung in his face took immediate effect. "By the Rood!" he roared, his face scarlet, "look to your own defense, you strutting jade! I'll give you a lesson you'll not soon forget!" Unable to contain his fury, he swayed restlessly, clenching the staff so hard his knuckles showed white. "God's wounds!" he fairly shouted at Edward. "Drop the gage, Sire!" The gage fell as he spoke, and the bout began.

Despite his rage, the Eorl still appeared to retain full control of his senses, and Tara knew she must infuriate him beyond reason if she hoped to prevail. But if her insulting remarks would not work, what else could she do? She watched him intently, balancing on the balls of her feet, poised to move on an instant's notice.

He was shifting his grip to the end, belike readying a mighty sweep that could knock her senseless or worse. She feinted back, luring him to follow. He took the bait, but with a speed she'd never have credited him, lunging forward with arms extended, swinging too powerfully for her to parry. But she did not try to parry. She sprang straight at him, bypassing his staff to slam into his body with a thud heard throughout the Hall, and drove her staff like a spear, with all her lithe strength behind the thrust, deep into his ample stomach.

To her dismay, he shook off the painful thrust as if she delivered a love tap. Amazingly quick to readjust, he swung his own staff swiftly around to smite her stingingly in the back, and backed quickly away. Warned by the sudden hardening of his biceps, she dropped sideways onto the floor, avoiding his wicked backhand sweep, and rolled away clear. His reverse, intended to bring the bout to an end, met no resistance, and he stumbled to keep his overbalanced body from falling. There was a sprinkling of laughter at his discomfiture, and his strenuous efforts to recover balance.

She saw then, growing on his reddening face, the start of the unreasoning fury she sought. Shamed before his peers by this strutting female, he trembled with open hatred. Now his eyes, smouldering, shifted almost imperceptibly to focus on her waist. She hesitated to read overmuch in so slight a shift, but taken together with his widespread stance and changed grip to the center of the shaft, it could signal a murderous drumbeat of alternating right and left blows. His enormous strength, she knew, would overpower any straightforward parrying defense she could mount, so she must devise an unorthodox defense he could not anticipate. She had little time to come up with a strategy, and for a moment her brain seemed to have failed her. But the Eorl inexplicably gave her the precious time she needed to collect her thoughts, by taking too long to readjust his stance. By the time his jaw muscled tensed, she had settled on her hazardous plan.

Her rearward leap this time, an instant before he moved, was no feint. Not anticipating this action, he failed to pursue enough, and his furious flurry of blows was spent vainly in the air. So, she observed, surprisingly quick though his movements were, his mind was less so. Once committed to an attack, she concluded, he would follow it through doggedly, and rely on his superior strength to overwhelm her defenses. Pray Lug she read him aright!

He recovered quickly, and his eyes warned of another similar attack, but if he'd adjusted his strategy this time to suit what she'd done before, he'd drive hard forward to circumvent her expected swift retreat. She readied her response, knowing the heavy risks it entailed. If she read him wrong, she'd be critically vulnerable, belike badly injured or worse.

Again his jaw muscle hardened, and he erupted into motion. Instead of retreating, she dropped instantly to her knees, well knowing the risks she ran. Then he was upon her, the cruel shaft flailing so close above her head that it riffled the tendrils of her hair, and the sweating mass of his body started to bend her backward. She rammed one end of her shaft between his thick ankles and, in the instant before she would be overborne, grasped the other end firmly and threw her body sideways against it with every ounce of her strength. Overborne from his unstoppable momentum, his ankles inextricably entangled in the shaft, the Eorl's attack turned to a desperate struggle to disengage his feet and maintain his balance.

His efforts were for naught. As the awed assemblage watched in silent fascination, he wobbled precariously, grasped desperately for the corner of the table, and crashed heavily forward to the floor like some great mortally stuck boar.

As he lay on his stomach, momentarily stunned, Tara sprang lightly up, lifted her quarter-staff high, and brought it down in a stinging blow on his exposed bottom.

The mortified Eorl struggled awkwardly to his feet, shaking his head to clear his brain, and looked about dazedly for his opponent, but the deafening cheers disoriented him and he could not get his bearings. Where was the accursed girl? He spun around, suddenly fearful she would creep up behind him. Then he saw her, seated calmly beside the Prince. And heard, to his eternal shame, the resounding plaudits of his fellows, shouted out for the accursed witch who had bested him so soundly.

"I've no further need to excuse my stabbing at your hands," said the exuberant Edward, when they had retired to his seating chamber. "Granted a blind fortune awarded an overweight adversary to you, but sure he was not one to be taken lightly."

"Oh, no, Sire," objected Tara. "That was no blind fortune awarding him to me. I selected him."

"What do you mean?"

"I let him see me looking at him, as I whispered in your ear, and betimes laughing as if taking him an object of ridicule. By meal's end he could not contain himself for aching to give me a lesson."

"But your whispers to me…they did not concern him."

"Ah, Sire—but he did not know that."

Tara had thought to return to Winchester for the release of her Northumbrians, or at least bring Sigefert the happy tidings that no longer were they taken for pirates, but Asser dampened any such hopes.

"The King's pardon, arranged by Edward, applies only to you," he explained. "In his eyes, you were an unwilling captive. Since your shipmates turned out not to be the Norman pirates his fleet sought, he's stayed their hangings. But mindful of Sigefert's earlier depredations with Hasteinn along the Thames, Alfred thinks to let them cool their heels in gaol, at least for some period of time."

"But when a war is concluded, are not all combatants at peace, free to pursue their affairs? Were not the Danes worthy and honorable foes?"

"Worthy, mayhap. Honorable…not for the most part. And in many wars, down through the sweep of history, the losers are executed to the last man. In time, Alfred will free them, but he cannot be pushed. It was no simple task, I may tell you now, to persuade him to release even you, Princess. He did so chiefly because you are heir to Dyfed, and your father the King will not live forever." He took her hand. "Sometimes you must trust in the Lord, my child."

"What will the King do with me?"

"What he deems nearest your heart—and what will best further his plans for Britain. Send you home."

Home! She had not dared to hope for so much. At long last…she'd be going home!

At his incredible words, it suddenly came to her, in a glorious rush of emotion, how long and eagerly she'd ached to roam the hills and forests of her homeland once more. To see the massive grey stone of Menevia Castle…savor the beloved sights and sounds of the place where she was born…bask in the warm welcome of the faithful servitors she'd abandoned, when the siren tocsin of glory sounded in her ear. And best of all—to see Sire once again!

Sire—what of him? She blushed with shame to realize how seldom, during her years in Denemearc, she'd given thought to the loving man who begat her, and engendered all her triumphs by his enormously generous decision to accept her as his heir. Though she'd been forced to focus on her own survival, still she'd been woefully remiss not to look back in gratitude for his enormous gift. E'en when she was back in Britain, just over the Hafren Channel from Sire, she'd been so distraught by her sentence of hanging that she'd had no thought for him—how much she owed him. She savored in memory how he'd given up his lifelong dream of a shining young prince, and unreservedly given his support to a mere girl. And, she belatedly realized, above all else, how very dear he was to her!

So at last, no thanks to her, but through the farsighted vision of a hated enemy, they would be reunited. Too much had happened, too fast, for her to take it all in.

True to his word, Alfred—or Edward, more like—provided transport to Milford Haven, giving her no time to sort out the confusion of thoughts and hopes seething within her, dumping her unceremoniously on the landing stage to take ship before she was well prepared. She had left home a raw child of sixteen years. Six years later—an eternity later—she was being rushed back home as a woman grown.

Despite her firm determination to remain calm, Tara was taut with anticipation when she spotted the carriage and outriders at the Milford Haven pier. Any moment now, Sire would be running forward to meet her! With a sudden unaccountable shyness, she could not think how to greet him, so did not quit the royal barge to meet him halfway, but waited for him to cross the pier and come to her.

But strangely, his big well-remembered frame was not among those approaching. Then belike he planned to welcome her privately in his carriage, in a homecoming greeting just between the two of them. Emotions suddenly running high, she sprang from the deck to run past the greeters, headed for the waiting coach, fumbled with the catch, threw open the door...

But the carriage was empty. Confused, and bitterly disappointed, she demanded of the stranger leading the escort where he was.

"The King was unable to come, Princess," he said stiffly. "He awaits you at Menevia Castle."

She did not recognize the young knight, and suddenly wondered if this was an omen—a signal that she'd find none she knew at her home! If so, it was an unbearably heavy price to pay for her long absence. She felt a quick sense of foreboding. Her knees were weak, she had difficulty controlling her thoughts, and tears pricked behind her eyelids. She'd thought this would be a time of joy, but instead it was becoming one of worry, wondering what infirmity prevented Sire from coming to meet her.

Her apprehension was worsened by the gloomy confines of the carriage, and she wished a mount had been brought for her, but forced herself to sit quiet and endure the stiff formality. She vowed that when she was Queen, never would she travel inside a carriage like a prisoner.

When she was Queen? The title felt empty, as if she had ashes in her mouth. She was not a queen, but only a child coming home. But she'd be seeing her beloved homeland with different eyes—eyes of an experienced woman. A woman who'd never thought of herself as Queen, or e'en the stress of homecoming. How could she handle the enormous responsibilities of being a Queen, if that day came? No, not 'if'—when that day came, for come it would. She wanted not to be a Queen!

Her gloomy train of thought made her wonder anew why her father had not met her, after this long six-year absence. Belike the delay was of little moment, she tried to tell herself. Soon they'd be relaxing in Mama's bower, each overflowing with tales to bring the other up to date, telling all that had transpired in those long six years. Would she meet Sire's expectations? Her emotions overcame her, and by the time the carriage rattled over the old drawbridge she was weeping. Breathless with anticipation, she jumped out, and looked excitedly about for her first glimpse of Sire's sturdy form.

But he was not there in the keep either.

A stranger, coming up to her, introduced himself as Seneschal, which was absurd—he was not Sir Gruwent! Another stranger purported to be Captain of the Guard. She wanted to expose them both as imposters and frauds! But Gruwent, they told her, lay at rest in the churchyard, and Tellicho—squat, bull-necked, loyal Tellicho—was out to pasture on some farm. And old Brigidea? Dead. Tara's dread grew, as she followed the new Seneschal up the cold stone stairs.

They took her to Sire's bedchamber, and she steeled herself to seeing him indisposed. But she was disastrously unprepared for the gaunt figure lying supine in the great bed. They had propped him up to face the door, and a welcoming smile illuminated his drawn face when she came into his view. Tears streaming unabashedly down her face, she rushed speechless to his side, and reached for the wasted hand lying on the coverlet.

His eyes were the same, as was the warmth in his voice. "It's more than life itself to have you home, Tara, love," he said feelingly, his simple greeting belying the depth of his emotion. "I've lived for this moment, lass! You bring this old cold pile of stones alive again." He made as if to say more, but his voice turned too husky for speech, and he fell silent.

"Oh, Sire," she choked. Then, somehow, she found herself in his arms. The smell of sickness was heavy in the closed room, but for one shining moment he was the Sire of old, his strong arms wrapped about her, enfolding her, shielding her from harm.

Then the moment passed, and with heavy heart she steeled herself to face the stark reality of her homecoming.

Later, in Mama's bower, at the hour of eventide when the two always had their talks, Sire was brought in, and bundled up in his huge chair, and tried to tell her what had taken place in her absence. "Everything has changed, Tara," he lamented. "In Dyfed, and in all Cymru—and not for the better. New faces here in the Castle are everywhere, half of them strangers to me. Near all of the old ones you'll remember are gone. I try to keep up the tilling and harvesting as we've done always, and to maintain the estates—but I tire too easily…" Reading beneath his gloomy words, Tara pictured tasks grown too numerous and taxing for him, urgent work undone, fields lying fallow, the old order breaking down. He fell silent, head bowed, as though just reciting the dreary litany of ills was too tiring for his failing strength.

So was this why the gods had brought her home? Was her destiny here, assuming all the responsibilities for which she'd been selected heir, becoming Sire's right arm, doing what he no longer could? Was it her task—no, it was her task—to restore the realm! How could she have allowed herself to sail off heedless with Sigefert? Her rightful place must be here!

Sensing something of her thoughts, Llywarch looked keenly at the strong Viking maid he'd sired, and a fierce pride lighted up and warmed his drawn countenance. "You've grown up finer and far stronger than I could have dreamt, Tara," he declared. "You've mastered your destiny— I see it plain in your stance. No prince could make me prouder! Forsooth, the years were mightily kind to you."

She took pride in his words, putting aside how unkind the years actually had been. It was not the time to dwell on the past. Her strength and ability were critically needed here, and she vowed to give of them in fullest measure, to help Sire, and to preserve the realm.

He told her that the crops had been bountiful, but mainly for the bugs and rodents. He recounted resentfully how heavily Clydog had levied on Dyfed's men-at-arms, to the point that his own palace guard was well below strength. That detestable Clydog again! For six years she'd not heard the hated name. Thinking on it, she realized how cruel a tyrant he was, and how hated by his subjects high and low—giving no thought to Cymru, holding his throne by fear alone. She learned, somewhat to her surprise, that his signing the treaty of submission to Alfred had been the final straw turning the nation against him, to the brink of open rebellion.

"But Sire," she asked, confused, "is not Alfred's suzerainty of some small benefit to Cymru?"

Surprisingly, he nodded. "What you say is indeed true," he agreed. "The day is past when Cymru can go her way alone. But Clydog has made no effort to explain this to his subjects—indeed, I misdoubt he understands as much himself. He acted solely for selfish and craven reasons, to hold on to the throne and protect himself." Tired by the emotion, he leaned back, his face drawn, and Tara's heart ached for him, and for the man he once was.

"Clydog may find himself dangling on a rope soon," Llywarch continued after a long pause, as if talking to himself. "Precious few will there be to mourn him."

Just like Clydog, she thought contemptuously, to act in utter disregard of his subjects. Then she forced herself to address the burning question. "Belike he's taken a wife by now…?"

Llywarch's eyes were closed, and he was silent so long she thought he slept. But she had to know, so she repeated the question more urgently.

"I regret with all my heart what I must tell you, Tara," he said at last, in anguished tones. "Clydog was informed by the Saxon court of your return... and..." Again he fell silent.

"And what, Sire?" she demanded, a cold hand clutching at her heart.

"He has invited you to Brecon...no, he has summoned you to Brecon...to become his bride. I'd sooner this tongue were torn from my throat than tell you, lass..." He dropped his head on his chest, the picture of utter dejection.

Were it not for the certainty that Clydog would avenge himself on her father, she'd flee Cymru at once, to make a life elsewhere. But she could foresee his vicious reaction plainly, and though her stomach writhed at the prospect, she could do naught in the present circumstances but come meekly at his beck. She prayed—to Atheurin, to the old gods, e'en to the Catholic bishopric that had served her so ill—that some happenstance be conjured up to prevent the abominable union, but there was no answer, and no sign was vouchsafed her. Never had she such need of help! Oh, Atheurin, do you not hear my call? She felt that such an excess of grief and hopeless despair would drag her into madness.

The dreadful Clydog awaited her in Glamorgan's keep. She'd planned to show a docile manner, to soften the hateful encounter, but he had no thought for aught she said or did. "What is your excuse for this delay, wench?" he demanded truculently, yanking her off the horse so hard she near measured her length on the sward. His bloated pig-eyes, dulled by drink, seemed to gleam in anticipation of marital delights awaiting him. "So you make your monarch wait for you, like some swineherd, do you?" He noticed her garb, as she knew he would, and frowned. "You still affect that absurd costume, do you? By Lug, we'll soon have that stripped off, and you in proper women's garb!" Not deigning to inquire about her trip, he half-dragged her through the postern gate and into the Castle.

To her enormous relief, he thrust her into the cheerless Bower, and abruptly left her. Tara waved the waiting women silently aside, needing solitude to cope with her bitter thoughts.

The days of preparation that followed were dull agony for her, immersed in unrelieved misery as she was. Princess Meuriga, now Sister Rhiannon of Saint Catwg Convent, had been summoned as her Attendant of Honour, and she tried to lift Tara's shattered spirits, but her mindless homilies were fragile dikes to stem the sweeping tide of Tara's anguish.

"Thee must not dwell on the carnal side of marriage," she admonished primly. "Think on the good that thou canst do as Queen, ministering to the poor and sick, serving the Blessed Virgin…"

"Nonsense, Meuriga," said Tara bluntly. "There's more to this blasphemy of a union than visiting cottagers. Do you not know your brother is mad? I swear by all the gods—or by your Blessed Virgin, if you wish—if he handles me rudely once more, I'll slit his throat!"

Meuriga's reaction to the desperate threat was unexpected. "Yours will not be the only such threat, my sister."

The wedding day dawned gray and overcast, matching Tara's black mood. Her entreaties to Atheurin had elicited no sign. No help would come. Naught could prevent the marriage. She sank into death-like apathy, oblivious to the eager ministrations of her handmaidens. Her spirit was far away, out with Sigefert on the open sea. Events at Glamorgan Castle could not touch her any more. She stood, numb and unseeing, letting the women clothe her in the bridal robe, and attach the filmy veil to hide all but a provocative hint of her frozen face. She heard not the delicate giggles, saw not the sidewise glances, as they thrilled over her lacy garb for the nuptial couch. Her heart a block of ice, she allowed herself to be shepherded to the garlanded pavilion. She neither saw Clydog nor wondered that he was not there, but simply waited with total lack no interest for the ceremony.

An ominous, almost inaudible, undercurrent of sound was born within the depths of the watching multitude, became noticeable, and gradually swelled. She took it for part of the hoary ceremony of marriage, and closed her ears to it. It grew, competing with the hum and bustle of the audience, until the attendants and officials in the wedding party were falling silent to listen and wonder. Irresistably it grew, becoming louder and more insistent, until it was a frenzied angry roar, drowning out all other crowd sounds, too overwhelming to ignore.

Not until the knights hustled her hastily and unceremoniously into the Castle was she snatched from her lassitude, realizing that something was terribly wrong.

When the reinforced palace guard with their staves finally made shift to clear the bailey, and the horrified Sheriff hastily mustered men to restore an uneasy calm in the cantref, she at last learned the truth.

The tinderbox of unrest that had seethed throughout the kingdom, at which Meuriga had hinted without fully understanding its explosive potential, had needed only a spark to ignite it beyond control. The deep hatred Clydog had engendered by his cruel and oppressive rule, and brought to a boil by what his subjects saw as cowardly submission to a foreign sovereign, needed but a time and place to boil over. It was Clydog himself who unwisely provided the unintended time and place for subjects from near and far to foregather inside the very palace walls, and the opportunity was too great to let pass. A carefully rehearsed and grimly purposeful group, posing as a suddenly uncontrollable mob but arriving armed with pitchforks and billhooks, overwhelmed and brushed aside the ceremonial guard. Before reinforcements could be called—if, indeed, anyone could be found who wished to make such a call—they dragged a shrieking Clydog roughly to the square, hoisted him to the gibbet, and shouted out furious imprecations upon him as he kicked and choked his despicable life away.

Oh, Atheurin, breathed a suddenly rejuvenated Tara thankfully—you did not fail me!

Through her euphoria, a sudden disturbing thought struck her. Knowing naught of the roots of the riot, she fear'd the rioters would scarce differentiate between King and Queen, and in their present mood her life would be forfeit in an instant if they caught sight of her. She raced to the Bower, fear lending wings to her feet, ripped off the despised wedding gown, and quickly threw on her other clothes. The terrible event had stripped the numbing mists miraculously away. Her mind once more was clear and alert.

She was confident she could manage, but realized she knew no one in the Court with power to help her escape through the doubtless sealed gates. No one, save a gallant former companion who once thought well of her—if only, by Lug's grace, he was assigned to the Castle still. She must find out, and quickly. It was Pumphrey—Sir Pumphrey, the light-hearted knight with which she'd ridden out on patrol from Glamorgan Castle the day she encountered Edward. Breathless, she dispatched all her handmaidens to scour the Castle urgently, find Pumphrey, and bring him here.

And find him they did. As soon as he entered the Bower, starting to express condolences, she interrupted with a command that he stop wasting time, and assemble a troop at once to escort her through the gates and to Menevia Castle.

"But Milady," he demurred, surprised at the request from a newly bereaved. "I cannot…"

"I recall you were ever bold, Sir Pumphrey. I did not think you quite so bold as this. You ignore an order from the affianced bride of your monarch?" The steely threat behind her chilly smile demolished his doubts, and within the hour they were through the Moot, and in the safety of the encircling woods.

As she rode up to Menevia castle with the party, its air of serene peace contrasted strikingly with the chaos she had left at the High Court. Her relief at the tyrannical Clydog's timely death, with all its implications for her future, was profound. Bursting with newly charged energy, she could scarce wait to immerse herself in Dyfed's affairs, and start helping Sire set things to right. She ached to make a start on relieving him of the burdens that overwhelmed him so. Her heart sang at the exciting prospect of throwing herself wholeheartedly into these long overdue tasks. As well, she thought more soberly, she would be occupying her mind and tiring her body, taking her thoughts off Sigefert. As she entered the keep, she could scarce wait to bring the good news to Sire. It was with great excitement and high anticipation that she reined in and sprang from her mount.

Strangely, the Prior of Roch Dinas met her at the postern gate, almost as if he expected her. His expression was lugubrious. "Thanks be to the all-seeing wisdom of the Lord that you return just at this time, Queen," he intoned gravely. "Let me offer my deepest sympathies to you in your hour of great bereavement." He reached gravely to take her hand, but she managed to busy herself with the reins to forestall the intimacy.

He was continuing. "In the midst of life, we are in death…"

She acknowledged his greeting briefly as she hurried past him, seeking to cut off whatever colloquy he had in mind, musing how his sanctimonious expression would change could he know her eternal gratitude to whatever gods had created her bereavement, and how little sympathy she merited. Clydog's death had been her blessing, and to even let it be thought otherwise would be a hypocritical falsehood.

Then she came to a halt, puzzled. How could news of the assassination have reached Menevia and the Prior e'en before she arrived? She'd left Brecon within the hour of the grisly event, needing a special clearance even to pass the gate, and they'd ridden posthaste. None could have arrived earlier.

And another puzzle: the Prior had dubbed her Queen.

She turned back to him, grasped his shoulders, and spun him abruptly about. "What meant your tender of sympathy, Father? Wherein am I bereaved?" Then she waited, on tenterhooks, wishing him not to utter the words she suddenly knew would come.

"Why, your father, the King. He passed on to the Eternal Kingdom early this morn, Milady." He put the tips of his fingers carefully together, and recited sonorously,

"The King is dead. Long life to the Queen!"

CHAPTER 33

Tara woke with the early morning sun in her eyes, and for a moment, poised between sleep and consciousness, she was back at Aggersborg. She felt beside her for the reassuring bulk of Sigefert, but her hand encountered nothing. Nor did she breathe the warm, vital smell of his strong body. She wondered, drowsily, where he was. Then the events of the previous day came rushing back, and she turned over with a groan and covered her head with the pillow. It was her first momentous day as Queen Tara of Dyfed Gwlad, Laird of the Skomer and Caldey Isles, Defender of The Faith, Ruler of the Southern Seas—and a very unhappy young woman.

For a time she lay so, curled up and motionless in the immense bedstead, willing oblivion to come once more. But the storm of emotions, which led last night to a bitter and uncontrolled flood of tears, and pervaded her exhausted slumber, returned like a physical blow with her waking, leaving her limp and heavy of heart. The relief and exultation she had felt at her escape from marriage to Clydog had changed to shock and grief at her father's death. And the ever-present worry over Sigefert, the uncertainty of their joint future, and the sudden burden of queenship for which she was woefully unready, formed a cumulative crushing weight. She had nowhere to turn, no way to marshal her confusion of thoughts, and no strength for the effort to sort things out.

She sighed wearily and sat up, dishevelled from her fitful night. The maids would come all too soon, to awaken her for an early start on the day's dreary burdens. No, she realized—none would presume to enter the royal chamber save at her summons. She was the Queen, and all would be vastly changed from her old existence. Mayhap when this first day was done, her life would be easier to bear, she hoped, and stepped out onto the cold floor.

The funeral was an occasion of sadness and bitter regret for her, its solemnity tugging at her heart unexpectedly. Her six-year absence had been a cruel burden to lay on Sire. How much it had contributed to his fatal illness Tara could only guess, but recalling the love and warmth of his welcome e'en as he lay on his death-bed, she felt cruelly unworthy. Never had she doubted his affection for her, but from this new perspective she realized what a kind and just father he had been, and how deep ran his respect and admiration for his daughter. What other king would have suffered a female to come out of the bower, and be brought up as a prince? Standing there in the old chapel, she thought back how his willingness to bring her up as he would a male heir had molded and enriched her life, and expanded opportunity for her future. She recalled his lofty dreams for Dyfed, dreams he'd neither time nor knowledge to bring to fruition, and sorrowed that father and daughter had not worked together on those aspirations before he died.

Silently, with her heart too full of emotion for the release of tears, she made him a sacred vow: you, and your glorious dreams for your people, will not be forgot, my father!

As Tara forced herself to watch the dreadful finality of the massive stones being set to wall off his tomb, she felt that they were walling off her past as well. She closed her eyes, and breathed a heartfelt prayer for her magnificent Sire, inside his bleak sepulchre, separated from her forever—and for herself, that she might find the wisdom and strength to rule as wisely and mercifully as he. When the service was over, she turned abruptly away, trying to purge from her mind those dark shadows of the past. Heavy responsibilities awaited her, and she must find the heart and strength to meet them. Or mayhap the very burden of responsibility would bring its own therapy, helping to chase the ghosts back into their otherworld hideouts.

The new Seneschel, Sir Wegered, was shorter than Gruwent, and lacked the old knight's grace and sober dignity. His dark stubbly hair stood straight up, and together with his slightly protruding eyes and sharp nose gave the impression of a surprised marmoset. A pointed beard sought vainly to confer an aura of dignity. He was industrious in his palace stewardship, almost to an annoying degree, and Tara sensed that he was not popular with the staff. He was reputed a doughty knight, though for what exploits none seemed to know, and was eternally eager to help her, sometimes to the point of harassment. She had not realized how much she would miss Sir Gruwent's knowing counsel and self-effacing courtesy. Tellicho, too—replaced by a stiff and taciturn stranger.

They are all gone, she thought sadly, every one. The Queen is the stranger.

She was not entirely right in thinking all were gone. She learned as much when she took the Seneschal to inspect the storerooms, and asked why the meat stocks were so scanty. Her question seemed troubling to him, and at Tara's impatient persistence he was goaded into an odd response.

"The wood is bewitched, Milady," he blurted out at last.

"Bewitched? What can that possibly mean?" Her scornful tone, and the disbelief on her face, drove him to defend his words.

"Aye, bewitched. None knows why, but my thought is the Bard. He's laid on a spell, and game is become cursed hard for the woodsmen to raise." He looked extremely discomfited.

"Atheurin? Is it Atheurin you mean?" Tara felt her heart give a sudden lift, and start to beat faster. If only she could see Atheurin right now!

"Aye, Milady. They do say…"

"Where is he?"

"No man can say for sure. His chamber in the Castle has lain empty since the King was stricken. Sometimes woodsmen catch a glimpse of him in the forest, but no one…"

"Why do you say he has laid a spell on our woodsmen? How can you know as much?"

"Because, Milady, the very day he left marked the day our woodsmen took no more game. From that day hence, we've brought in nor beast nor fowl, either with bow or snare." He spread his hands, embarrassed but holding to his story. "It could be naught else but a spell."

Tara was not surprised. When Atheurin wished to be unavailable, no force of beaters could find him—it might even be, she thought, that where he went no human could enter. She dismissed the Seneschal, and returned to her counting house to ponder this odd tale. She did not ridicule what Wegered had told her; on the contrary, she was sure it was true. What puzzled her was its purpose. An idea came to her, and she resolved to investigate.

Early next morning, she had the women bring the masculine garments she had foregone since her coronation, and ordered the groom to saddle her father's big bay. She rode out alone, disregarding Wegered's professed fears for her safety, knowing she'd learn naught with him in tow. The way seemed unfamiliar, with old landmarks not to be seen, so she let the red-brown stallion have his head. It was enough that she was alone in her beloved forest, keenly conscious of the tiny scamperings and twitterings that made the woodlands come alive for her. Riding beneath the great oaks and graceful beeches, relieved for the moment of pressing cares, she was once more the little girl who years ago had ridden so wildly and joy-ously along those hidden paths and byways, chasing her destiny.

Well into the morning they proceeded at leisurely pace through the wood, following a trail she could not see. When the horse stopped, in a small clearing surrounded by a circlet of ancient oaks, and turned his lordly head to gaze expectantly at her, she looked about. She felt a tug at her memory, sensing something familiar. Then, miraculously, she saw the opening in the thorn hedge, and recognition flooded back.

It was Presceli Cromlech—her cave of the Mabinog!

Breathless with anticipation, for she knew not what, Tara dismounted to scramble through the narrow opening and down into the old cromlech. The light was dim in the forest glade, but she could make out the ancient stone altar, unchanged since the terrified child once sought sanctuary here. The memory of her excitement and fear was sharply fresh. The cave seemed both damp and musty at the same time, its far reaches invisible in the gloom, but Tara never had felt danger here. She knew she'd come home to a welcoming place.

Of a sudden, she felt a friendly presence near at hand, meaning her no harm. She turned, feeling the familiar pounding of her heart, knowing who it must be.

"The gods brought you safe back, and in good time, as the Mabinogion prophesied. Welcome home, to the throne, Queen Tara of Dyfed!"

The years fell away instantly, and she was a child again, as though she'd never left, as though she'd lived in these glades always. The comfort at seeing her old friend and tutor was overwhelming.

"Oh, Atheurin, Atheurin," she breathed. "How terribly you've been missed! How oft I've longed for your help, to ask you what I should do. How oft my memory has brought me back to our times together in the forest!"

Impulsively, she threw her arms wide and extended them toward him, tears of relief and of wonder on her cheek—and he came near, but did not touch her outstretched hands. "I, too, have missed those times," he said, his voice low and musical. "My thoughts were ever on you. Never were you alone." He paused. "I think you knew as much, in times of trouble."

Tara looked silently into his shadowed eyes, knowing he spoke true, despite the many troubled times she'd thought herself cast adrift and alone. She'd lacked faith, she now knew with sudden clarity; whenever her need was desperate, he'd vouchsafed her a sign. It came to her that the Bard must have been her rock of stability, her never-failing source of inspiration and succor through those turbulent years. "Yes," she said simply. "I did have you at my side always, Atheurin, my good friend. Never had I cause to be afeard."

She looked at him with new eyes, knowing this. He'd not changed in appearance; if aught, he was younger. Or could it be I'm older, she wondered. His body was slim and lithe under its soft deerskin habit, and even in the gloom his curly hair gleamed with gold and brown, as if from an inner fire. His eyes were deep pools, and shone redly, as do the eyes of wolves about a lonely campfire deep in the woods. Truly he was ageless! Here in the misty shadows, she was quite prepared to think him immortal.

The thought prompted a question. "And how did you know I was back?" The moment she asked, she knew the answer.

"I watched your travels in the flames. I was beside you when the seas raged. I shared your cell in Winchester gaol. I rode with you down the rivers of the Rus, and over the great inland sea of the Byzantines. I saw through your eyes, felt the sinews of your arm when you fought for honor or life. I was ever with you." He smiled, and inside her there formed and grew a feel of complete security.

"I brought you back, my Queen, to fulfill your destiny."

She could not say how, but knew he spoke the truth.

"Will you not ask why you have been brought home? Would you not know the high purpose you are destined to fulfill?"

Mesmerized by his tone, she heard her response, though she knew not what strange force had impelled her to say it. "I know what purpose I serve."

He smiled at that. "I think perhaps you do not quite know, though a part inside you knows. But no mind—you shall know anon, when the call comes."

She wanted to say more, express her appreciation more fully. "I felt you with me when I was in peril—I ever did. And you kept me always from harm. I owe you my life. Tell me, how may I thank you?"

"Your life is thanks enow. That, and what you will do for your country. The old gods are steadfast in their plans for you—and for Cymru."

She remembered why she had sought him out. "Tell me, Atheurin, why the woodsmen find no game? Whence came this spell that shields the creatures of the forest?"

He laughed again. "And what else would have brought you to seek me out?"

She let that pass unquestioned. Sure it took no spell to make her want to find her dearest friend! But he'd not given her a full answer. "Then there is some deeper purpose in this meeting?"

"Aye, there is." He tilted his head toward the altar, and Tara turned to look, but the great stone was bare.

"On the altar that gave sanctuary to the small child that day long past, there now lies a scroll, bearing an ancient Mabinogion. Take it, keep it with you, against the day of need. It foretells the time Saxon and Cymri will become one people, united against a greater danger the gods foresee but are helpless to quell." He indicated the altar once more.

She looked again, and this time imagined that the dank stone was suffused with an eerie glow. She turned in some alarm to Atheurin, but he had vanished. Then, strangely unafraid, she approached the altar. The glow transformed itself into undulating waves of iridescent color that seemed to pulsate, to be alive with shimmering emerald, carnelion, ice-cold sapphire flame. Feeling herself in a trance, she reached out her hand toward the melting stone, and her hand was bathed in an unearthly glow of blood-red incandescence. She saw her face reflected in the top of the altar, distorted, luminous, floating unattached, as the shapes ebbed and flowed, and changed to scintillating ribbons of seething color.

Her hand, beyond her control, touched the iridescent stone, absorbing as she did an aureole of radiance. There was a flash, and she drew back, dazzled by the intensity of light. Then it was over, her eyes cleared, and she was staring at the stone altar as it was before, damp and dark in the dim of the cave. The vision was gone—but where she had touched the glowing stone there now lay a tightly-rolled scroll, heavy with age-old dust. She picked it up and fingered it.

How she got out into the daylight, Tara did not remember. She was in the clearing, on a dew-specked patch of grass. Warmed by the sun, surrounded by the melodious warbling of countless birds, she wondered if she had dreamed the vision—but looking down, she saw she still clutched the ancient scroll. A peace she had not known for months stole over her. The dread and heaviness were replaced by a sense of strength and purpose. What was in the scroll she knew not, but for the moment it was enow that she had a calling, and naught would swerve her from fulling the prophecy. Henceforth, she would dedicate her life to what the gods foreknew. There was a larger plan, in which she'd play a critical role, and she was content now to place her life in the way of the greater destiny.

Now she knew how she must answer Sigefert's question to her, when their paths crossed again, hard though the words would be to utter.

When Tara emerged from the shadowed wood onto the Common, she met a panting and flustered Wegered, who looked his vast relief that she was found. "Oh, Milady," he greeted her, "great affairs are afoot! A messenger from the High Court awaits you."

And what else might the gods find to put before me, she wondered. A king's messenger was not oft the bearer of welcome tidings. Was Atheurin's prophecy starting so soon? She touched the stallion's sleek flank with her heel, exulting at the power unleashed at her bidding, and thundered across the Common toward the palace.

When the weary messenger had delivered his tidings, and been sent to a welcome meal and a soft couch, she summoned the Seneschal. "It comes from the Imperial Council," she told him. "They proclaim a

Royal Convocation to select a High King, and all the minor rulers are ordered to proceed there with all dispatch."

"When do you leave, Queen?" His voice was unsteady, and she looked at him in surprise. What does he know, or surmise, of what's afoot?

She thought a moment. Naught was pressing to delay her, and unless she went speedily the Council would meet without her. "I would leave in two days, no later," she told him. "The ships will take that long to ready. We must move quickly."

She caught his look of excitement, and thought it best to nip his hopes in the bud. He hoped to travel with her, but she could not bear his company for so long.

"I will leave affairs in your strong hands, Sir Wegered," she said tactfully. " It is not meet for Queen and Seneschal to be absent at the same time." She avoided his look of regret, but hardened her heart. The journey would prove arduous enow without the constant irritation of the fawning Seneschal.

In the event, the trip proved uneventful, and the Menevia force arrived in Brecon just before twilight of the third day. The Castle was crowded to bursting with delegations from all the Cymru gwlads, and Tara was relegated perforce to a cramped little chamber, but she welcomed the privacy that gave her a breath to put the rush of events into perspective. She thought again and again of Atheurin's mysterious words in the cromlech. What was the 'high purpose' she was destined to serve? Did the gods intend her to take some action in the Council meeting? If they did, how could she know what it might be?

Giving up such bootless speculation, Tara turned to readying herself for the evening ahead, wondering how the other rulers would receive her. Some few might approve heartily of a gallant female, but she was sure others would scarce credit her right to attend such a portentous convocation. She began to brush the shine back into her thick golden tresses, the familiar task reminding her of her womanhood, with all a woman's hopes and longings. She ached painfully for the feel of

Sigefert, his strong companionship, his counsel and understanding, the intensity of his caring and his love. She wanted to rush headlong from the queenship she had not sought, but the strength which had come to her in the clearing held steadfast, giving her the resolution to put aside the hopeless yearning. She bound up her lustrous hair with care, imagining she was prettying herself for him, and went serenely down to the banquet hall, to join the members of the Imperial Council for their feast and crucial meeting.

Her entrance created a small stir. This was her first appearance since her coronation, and her return, coincidentally at the precise time she was needed to assume Dyfed's crown, seemed to these superstitous monarchs to smack of godlike intervention. She was at once the center of an admiring coterie, stimulated more than a little by her stalwart bearing and stunning looks, but some stood apart as if grudging such honor to a woman, however young and beautiful. Discomfited by the adulation, she was relieved to see Ystrad Towy's king, and broke free of the crush to thread her way over to Sire's oldest friend.

She was warmed by King Brechnor's unfeigned pleasure at seeing her again, and gave in to a strong impulse—was it planted by the gods, she wondered—to ask if she could join him at dinner, but as she wanted to be with him anyway, she put the matter from her mind. As they renewed their old ties, she noted with pleasure that Brechnor was unusually alert, despite being ten years older than Sire. She was saddened to think her father might have been here, hale and hearty as the rest, had she not been away so long. But mayhap her absence had not been to blame, and in any case tonight was no time for such regrets.

She turned the conversation to Alfred, and Brechnor expressed his views forcefully. "A fight with the Saxons would be madness for us," he declared. "Many are the same Celtic stock as we, and they have no wish to invade Cymru. Far better them than the Danish pirates, who would rape and pillage. These hotheads be mad to think we can stand against the Saxon might! They see not our need for staunch allies, when the Danes harass our coasts again, as they will."

"You must know, Sire," she said, perplexed, "I lived six years with the Danes, and came to think Alfred a bitter foe. It is hard to turn about and embrace Saxons as saviors."

"But did not Alfred return you safe to Deheubarth? And did not the Dane cast you from his shores, seeking to kill you?"

Tara realized how close his questions hit to the truth. It was indeed Alfred to whom she owed her life, and Gorm who would have thrown them to the Northmen. But she was not ready to concede so readily. "It was Edward, the son, who freed me, not Alfred. I have no quarrel with Edward, Milord. Alfred is the one I came to hate."

"Then it is of Edward you must think, Tara; Alfred is a dying man, and little he does will bear on our future." He looked at her keenly. "Tell me, lass—think you to rally Dyfed behind this union with Saxony?"

His words jogged her memory to think of the scroll she carried. Brechnor could be trusted, and the matter was urgent. "May I speak to you of private matters, Sire?" Impressed by her seriousness, Brechnor bent his grizzled head to hear her.

She was unsure how to start, but time was fleeting. "I have an ancient Mabinogion to show you." She knew not if Brechnor could read, but decided to act as if he could, and unrolled the fragile parchment before him. "This came from the old ones, from deep in an ancient cromlech on Presceli Top, and foretells our future. It bids us cast our lot with the Saxon, lest we be swept away by the whirlwind." She thought it necessary to explain. "The whirlwind of which it speaks is invasion, by some alien force of which I know naught, but which threatens our future. I know not how to bring it to the attention of the Council."

"How came you by it?" The old king was not looking at the scroll, but intently at her.

"It appeared before me, in a blaze of fire and color, on the cromlech altar. It was not there when first I descended into the cromlech, but of a sudden appeared. It is from the gods, that I'll swear, and they wish me to use it—but I know not how."

Brechnor stared at her for a moment, his face perplexed at first, then turning inscrutable. His eyes dropped to the scroll, and his face gradually lighted up. If he could read it or no, Tara could not say, nor did it matter. It was as if its message flowed like a stream into his mind. "Why, child," he exclaimed, "this is the sign we've long awaited. The assemblage must see it! But we must pick our time with care, lest the hotheads shout it down before its true import can reach them." He crossed himself, and made the old sign of protection against Manawyddan fab Llyr. "By Teutates, this old scroll may yet carry the day for Cymru!" He reached for a joint and carved off a generous piece. "Let us get on with our meal. We will think about what to do when the time comes."

The Council meeting went badly for the forces of conciliation. Burly King Liathan of Gwynedh was strongest in his denunciation of craven surrender to the Saxon, supported loudly by the rulers of Powys and Lleyn. Of course, thought Tara, these three kingdoms would not be first to feel an invading Saxon thrust. They had not eyes nor brains to ken the importance of incorporating Cymru into a strong Saxon empire, against the day the Norse or some other foreign power inevitably would sweep down on them again.

Liathan was on his feet, shouting down those who opposed his views. "We are not craven taeogion, to bow down before these popinjays," he roared. "We are Celt, boasting a lineage from the great Cunedda Wledeg himself! Who are these Saxon dogs, that they dare to outface those with such a heritage?" His words were compelling, Tara had to admit, and the spell of his ringing voice was swaying many. He had no reasoned arguments, nor need for any. His appeal was to emotion, which was running strong in the Hall this night.

Prince Gialwor of Llewn rose to lend support. "Why fear we the Saxon?" he shouted. "Ne'er have they breached our border. It is they who should fear us! They are one with the cowardly king, Offa, who built his great Dyke between us to hide behind. We need not fear these Saxon swine—let them rather fear us!" He sat down to a roar of approbation, more from his appeal to Celtic pride than to reasoned argument, but the atmosphere was charged, and Tara knew appeals to logic would be shouted down.

She rose to her feet nonetheless. She had to try. She made an effort to get the attention of the Council, but none paid her any heed. How do I get them to listen, she thought, discouraged. How can sense be knocked into these stubborn heads?

It was Brechnor who provided the way. Springing to his feet with a celerity she'd have thought impossible, he lifted her lightly on the table with a strength few could have surpassed, and as his dramatic action caught the nobles' attention, he spoke. "Queen Tara of Dyfed would be heard!" His voice did not seem loud, but it rang from end to end through the Hall, and quiet fell over the assemblage.

He's given me my chance, thought Tara nervously—my only chance. It must be grasped immediately, lest it slip away. Lug be with me; help me to grasp it!

"Royal Sires," she began, surprised how firm and clear she spoke. "We are assembled to select a new ruler for Cymru, not to decide on a peace with Saxony. But it seems the first will not be concluded until the second is settled. You have heard that King Liathan of Gwynedh favors the Dane over the Saxon. I would ask him, has he ever been prisoner of either Danes or Saxons? Mayhap that would have told him what he seems not to have learnt, nestled safely in his castle at Glynnog, in the far—and safe—reaches of Gwynedh."

Liathan sprang to his feet in a rage. "Are we to heed a puling maid telling us how to wage war? Will we judge her a fine statesman, for her time spent in Danish bedchambers and Saxon gaols?" He looked scornfully at Tara. "Tell us, great Queen, what valiant feat of arms did you achieve among the Danes?" He looked about triumphantly for acclaim, and some cheered him, but many did not.

Tara thought furiously. I have little time to sway them, for they are ill disposed to attend a woman. It must be now, or I have lost them forever!

"Let the brave King Liathan know, though it matters not to the rightness of this matter, that I held the rank of Jarl in Denemearc—an Eorl. Let him know I commanded a great fleet, that fought its way to Byzantium and back through a hostile land, that I bested a gladiator in the Roman Emperor's Hippodrome..." She paused, to heighten the effect of her next words. "And that I have killed men as bold as he, with this sword, in fair fight!" She glanced down the table, seeing Brechnor's son, Wulfdune, staring at her, entranced. Mayhap she should add that she'd bested a king's son at wrestling. No—that would be an insult, and it could lose her Brechnor. She should stop with what she'd said.

Her bold speech brought some cheers, and more laughter at Liathan's expense, but all too soon the kings and princes would tire of her, and grow impatient. Now, she thought. Now!

She pulled the scroll from her tunic, and raised it, that all might see the old script. "This scroll contains an ancient Mabinog prophecy for our nation—for Cymru. It came to me on a Druidic altar in a sacred place, and there is magic in it. It bids us unite with our countrymen against the Northmen, or we are lost. List to what it says, that you may know what the old ones foretell!"

Liathan was on his feet again. "What bookish sniveling is this for fighting men?" he cried, scorn dripping from his lips. "How came this posturing wench by such a great and powerful screed? Why would the old ones entrust it to her, and not to a mighty warrior king? I say her sniveling scribe cobbled it all together for her, back in his cell in Menevia. I say cram it down his lying throat!"

There was shouting at that, too. Not all of it was favorable, but Tara could feel her advantage slipping. She had played her only card, and it would not suffice. Oh, Atheurin, she called silently—where are you?

There was a muted rumbling outside the Hall. She heard it, and Brechnor heard it as well, but the others seemed not to notice. It swelled in intensity, like distant thunder rolling across the dark hills, and now the diners were falling quiet to listen. Tara closed her eyes, and prayed to the three mighty gods of the Celts to stand with her.

A great crack of thunder blasted through the Hall, shaking the socketed torches, and smashing goblets on the banquet board. There was a searing explosion of lightning, shooting through the narrow embrasures, blinding in its intensity, illumining the vast room as with the noonday sun. Tara stood transfixed, the scroll still held aloft in her upthrust hand.

For years to come, minstrels and balladiers would sing their lays, immortalizing what took place then. The Hall fell dark again, and there was a total stillness, as though the very ether was transfixed with anticipation. Then, through some unseen opening high amid the rafters, soared a snow-white falcon, glowing in the darkness as with its own inner light, fierce staring orbs gleaming blood red. Propelled by the audible beat of its powerful pinions, it traversed the length of the hall, its eye locked on the tableau below. Swift as an arrow to a target, it plunged down to where the young Queen of Dyfed stood, and landed on the upthrust scroll. For a time it stayed so, motionless—as the tales related in years to come, it may have been as short as an instant, or as long as an age—then slowly unfurled and spread its mighty wings, and sprang aloft. The beat of its great pinions roiled the air, as it flew swiftly the length of the Hall, soared up into the rafters, and disappeared from sight.

Dazed, Tara looked about. The assemblage was motionless, as if frozen in time. Her hand holding the scroll stretched aloft still, and she could not muster the power to lower it. For a vast time, the eerie stillness endured.

Then there was movement. King Brechnor rose majestically from his seat, strode swiftly and purposefully to the dias, and spoke. His voice was strange, as if some inner being spoke, and his words rang through the chamber so powerfully that none could have shouted him down. But none had any mind to gainsay him.

"O noble Cymri Monarchs," he called out portentously, "we have seen a miracle! We have received a true sign from the gods, and the power of this sign any of you questions at his peril! Members of this Council, we all have been shown from on high where lies the true path!"

He drew his sword, kissed the hilt, then took the blade in his hand and thrust the handle toward Tara. "Kings and Princes of the Realm, join with me! Rally ye to High Queen Tara ap Llywarch map Ceorle, Monarch of all the great nations of Cymru!"

The silence ended then, as if by the sundering of a dam, and all were on their feet, proffering their swords, shouting out their allegiance. Tara, stunned by the swift march of events, looked at Liathan. His sword was drawn with the others, and he waved it high. A stunned look transformed his face, and involuntarily he joined in the swelling chorus of cheers.

The signal from the gods was far too powerful for any man, king or commoner, to deny!

Tara, High Queen of Cymru! This was what Atheurin meant by his portentous words in the cromlech. Here was the 'high purpose' that she was born and dedicated to serve. Her throat choked with emotion, but her countenance firm, Tara found the strength to grasp the sword Brechnor proffered, and hold it aloft. There was a hush, and she stepped from the table, holding the old Maginogion that, in the event, none had needed to read.

Her head held high, she walked slowly and solemnly to the dias, to claim the crown being pressed upon her by acclamation, and fulfill her destiny.

CHAPTER 34

Despite the bloated staff of the High Court—stewards and under-stewards, butlers and under-butlers, panters, pimenters, chamberlains, ushers, and a score of others in a huge jumble of officialdom—there was no Chatelaine to see to the Court ladies and overgrown household staff, no Seneschal to manage the sprawling palace enterprises, no Commander of the Guard, and neither Chancellor nor Privy Counsellor to provide seasoned advice and oversee affairs with other kingdoms.

Desperate to find a trusted subordinate at once, Tara summoned Sir Pumphrey, and with no ado invited him to be her Equerry. "Belike you have noted the parlous state of our palace," she began. "It seems Clydog attended to naught but himself. This commission will bring you endless work, and a growing roster of enemies. Your reward, if you consider it such, will lie in knowing we work to better the realm. If you decline, it will but testify to your good sense."

She must have plucked the right chord, for his acceptance was immediate. "Conditions in Cymru have disgusted us all, Highness. Sir Oresten exerted a modicum of control over a hapless King, but since the old man died…" He went on, discussing in detail the problems not addressed, with a depth of understanding that surprised her, until finally she was forced to halt his recitations, so that they might get on with their overwhelming task.

"My contempt for our late king is as as vast as yours, Pumphrey, though I confess I'd not realized he had let his demesne deteriorate so woefully. Your words add more urgency to our task. Our first business, then, will be to find two replacements for Sir Oresten."

"Two, Milady?"

"A Seneschal to bring order to the chaos you describe, and a Chancellor to advise on affairs of state. They are separate tasks, and call for different skills. I've been gone too long to know who might fit, so I stand in need of your best advice. And we must select a Guard Captain, a Privy Counsellor, and a Chatelaine. And be assured," she smiled, to soften the impact of her words, "I sorely need your counsel, but I must make the final decision."

Painstakingly, Queen and Equerry built a slate of candidates. She realized anew the price of her long absence, for her list of those she knew totalled scarce a decade. Despite her distaste for Eorl Skomer, he did have solid abilities at managing—and his Countess was more able than he. Brechnor's son, Wulfdune, would be a solid lieutenant if there were enow of his sire in him. Sir Rhydder had been staunch once, and belike was yet. She catalogued all those whose paths had crossed hers: Tellicho—retired, but strong and capable yet...Sir Aelfgan...Lady Agrinore...the Countess...Eorl Tenby...Sir Rhydder...Ugri...Rhiall...Cadfan...all she could recall. Pumphrey's far larger listing was set out with recitation of strong and weak points.

A candidate for Dyfed's empty throne must be found forthwith, and Pumphrey suggested Clydog's younger brother, Prince Hywel. Thrust to the background whilst growing up, he'd gone to study at the Catholic Court in Old Rome. Despite the ever-present risk of developing a future pretender to her own throne, just now she was more interested in competence than any fancied machinations. He was reported honest and sagacious, and she decided to invite him back to Brecon for a closer look.

Exploration of the situation for each of the candidates disclosed a few surprises. Skomer was dead of apoplexy, and his Countess had sequestered herself in an apartment in Dewi Sant Convent. Tellicho was both hale and available. Sir Aelfgan's health was poor. Eorl Tenby's capabilities proved too meager. Ugri, amazingly, had become Eorl Ugri, and ruled Aber Castle. Lady Agrinore was in ruddy health. And Crosbey...

Tara felt a clutch at her heart, as she realized how she'd have welcomed into her service his keen mind, unswerving loyalty and buoyant disposition. What a splendid Seneschal he'd have made! How tragic a loss, to Cymru no less than to her, of that good and perfect knight. She asked Pumphrey to leave her for a spell, and sat alone to muse how it would be if Crosbey were by her side. Almost she could see him, here in the Counting Room with her...making her problems his...advising her...reassuring her. And loving her.

Loving her!

And how would that impossible situation play out? With a sense of shock, she realized that her bittersweet reverie had excluded Sigefert completely. E'en had Crosbey not been killed—not selflessly laid down his life that she might live—he could never have been her Seneschal. The close relationship that would have entailed—being in daily intimate contact with one whose unswerving friendship had ripened into warm and passionate love—yet ne'er able to give way to the emotions seething within her, would have demanded a measure of restraint far beyond her strength. Confused and distraught, she summoned Pumphrey back, and steeled herself to get on with the suddenly dreary task of choosing.

When Pumphrey appeared in the doorway, looking so stalwart and loyal, his countenance clouding sympathetically as he sensed her distress—so like Crosbey in his dedication to her service, she realized—she saw him suddenly in a different light.

Here was her Seneschal! Here, unrecognized, right before her eyes. She knew, from the period at Glamorgan Castle before they marched buoyantly off to the disaster of Gloucester, that he was possessed of a clear head and a strong sense of duty, and his recent analysis made plain that he understood the problems and complexities of managing the Court estates.

"I've good news for you, Sir Pumphrey," she told him, with the ghost of a twinkle in her eyes. "We've found our Seneschal."

"Indeed, Milady?" Belike he was miffed, that she'd chosen without his recommendation, but naught in his cheerful expression betrayed as much. "Who is it to be?"

"You."

Within the month, preliminary selections were complete: Hywel as Dyfed's King, Lady Agrinore as Chatelaine, Sir Rhydder as Guard Captain, Tellicho in the sensitive new post of Privy Counsellor, Skomer's Countess as Chancellor, and a host of lesser appointees.

Tellicho was first to arrive, and Tara was delighted to see how fit and alert he seemed. The aging but still vigorous Captain was near tears of joy to see his young mistress in this grand position, and after they had commiserated on Llywarth's death, they got down to cases.

"I recall how you impressed me on the march to Gloucester with your understanding of affairs," she told him. "That depth of knowledge is nowhere to be found here." She outlined what she hoped to get from her new Privy Counsellor.

"No need to tell you I'm honored, Princess," he said, using the old title. "But I'm only a simple soldier from a minor kingdom. I've no experience with high statecraft, and the ins and outs of a High Court. I might be of scant help." But the glow on his face belied his words.

"If the gods permit, the High Court will have done with ins and outs. It needs a plain-speaking man of sense, one I can trust. If you'd like to come help me, the post is yours."

The Countess arrived almost as soon as Tellicho, and she, too, held her years well. Her bearing, as she swept into the Solar, was regal, and her deep curtsy was executed with a faintly mocking air. Still the grand lady interviewing the young page, thought Tara, resolving not to be put off by such puffery.

"It was good of you to come, Countess." She indicated a seat at her side. "No doubt my emissary informed you of what we have in mind."

"I admire you, Princess—forgive me, Queen. I always predicted that you'd go far. Allow me to say you've exceeded e'en my lofty expectations since last you came to see me. At that time, as I recall, you were recruiting young Crosbey to your banner. How sad he had to die as he did—so young, so much ahead of him. What cruel jests the gods play on us!" She looked narrowly at Tara as she spoke.

"Yes," responded Tara, unwilling to be drawn into that discussion. "But we do not meet to speak of friends. Our business today is with one another, and we both must speak frankly. I am close onto asking you to be my Chancellor, but with serious reservations, which I am hoping you will dispel before we can come to any agreement."

The Countess inclined her head slightly, not speaking.

"Let me tell you first, that I understand you well—at least I think so. A friend once told me that two competing forces struggle for mastery within you: one good, the other not. The same friend warned me never to trust you."

"Interesting," murmured the Countess. "And belike quite close to the truth—but perhaps not completely. Do I know the lady?"

Tara smiled faintly. "I think not. It was a gentleman, in fact. But let me continue. When you and the Eorl graciously responded to my plea for assistance, I was not quite honest in that request. In fact, I acted so in fear of my life."

"I told my Lord as much. He thought otherwise, not crediting you with so much maturity. In the end, you deceived me as well. But I'm intrigued—if you did not trust me then, how can you do so now?"

"Things change, Countess. The Eorl had prospects of a throne then, and I may have stood in his path. That is why I contrived to be seen as a help, not an obstacle. But your Eorl is dead, and you have no prospects I can obstruct. Do I state things accurately?"

The Countess's expression was enigmatic. "Pray continue, Milady," she murmured.

"If you see no advantage in doing me harm, I make use of your considerable talents with no danger. I would like to do so now, if we understand each other."

"And what am I to understand of you, my Queen?"

"Simply put, Countess, if you serve me well—nay, say rather, if you serve Cymru well—you will be a respected senior member of the High Court, in a post worthy of your talents."

"And if I do not?"

The menace behind Tara's faint smile was not lost on the Countess. "If you play Cymru false in any way, great or small, you will regret it keenly," she said simply. The two women regarded each other steadily for a long moment, and it was the Countess's gaze that fell first.

She rose, holding out a dry hand to her new High Queen. "Then we understand each other well, Your Highness. And really, we are not unlike, you and I. I have always had a motto, and it may be yours as well: Carpe Diem—Seize the Day. Since it serves me well to serve you well, and since Convent life grows tiresome, I will seize the day, as you ever have done so well. You will see me here within the fortnight." She curtsied again, but without mockery this time. "And now, Milady, permission to retire?"

She turned back for one last comment, as she reached the door. "My congratulations, Queen Tara. You have read me well—then and now." The door closed softly behind her, and she was gone.

The interview with the Lady Agrinore was more pleasant, concluding with her delighted acceptance of the post of Chatelaine. Tara thought to ask Sister Rhiannon—Meuriga—to return to Glamorgan Castle and lend some assistance, now that Clydog was no more, and was gratified by her enthusiastic acceptance of the invitation.

Tara was delighted at the immediate rapport between Tellicho and Pumphrey, and recalled nostalgically how Tellicho had taken to Crosbey the same way. Could it possibly be, she mused, that the gods have implanted something of Crosbey's essence into Pumphrey, enabling her to reach beyond the grave, and receive help and guidance from one who had loved her so dearly? Of course not, she thought disgustedly, answering her own question. The gods had better to do than that, and she had no time for enticing fancies. But still…she wondered.

As the new team settled into its tasks, Tara hardened heself for opposition from those deprived of their former perquisites and easy ways, but few mustered up courage to confront the fiery young monarch. She threw herself wholeheartedly into the gargantuan task of shifting the household's direction into more effective paths, driving herself mercilessly, seeking to expunge the spectre of Sigefert in Winchester gaol. She spent sleepless nights inconsolably lonely, without him beside her to share her hopes and assuage her fears, to enfold her in his strong arms, and engulf her in the passionate tempest of his love.

Oft she thought of travelling to Chippenham to intercede for him, but was dissuaded by Asser's warning not to push Alfred. All she could do was wait for his release, that they might meet once more before parting forever—he to his path up in the north, and she to the endless tasks laid out for her, both by her high destiny and in conformance with her own ambitions.

Then came a welcome break in her drudgery, in the person of an emissary from the Saxon Court. The news purported to be sad, but she took heart from it. Alfred's tenuous hold on life had broken at last, and she was commanded to Edward's coronation. She prepared for the trip with keen anticipation, not knowing what she might accomplish, but taking it as an omen—a sign that after all the heartbreaking delay the gods could be taking pity on her. Embarking for the voyage across the Hafren Channel, she could not rid herself of the hope that somehow she would be reunited with her beloved, though recognizing in her moments of sober realism what an unlikely outcome that would be.

Her flotilla landed at Avon on the Wessex coast, ironically the area where Sigefert had put her ashore, a lifetime ago, to scout for news of Arthur. But what had changed? Sigefert was a Saxon enemy then; he was an enemy still. No—one thing had changed: he was a free enemy then; now he was in a Saxon gaol and under sentence of hanging. Trying to put aside such unwholesome thoughts, she stepped ashore and into the waiting carriage.

She'd thought Edward might receive her, but instead a young cleric waited, with word only that Asser would call when she'd shaken off the dust of travel. Quelling her impatience—for what, she could not have said—she forced herself to make a proper toilet and don seemly garb, to be presentable if the opportunity came for an audience with Edward.

Asser reminded her that he'd never seen her bedecked in woman's finery, and with her lustrous hair flowing loose down her back. "Allow me to compliment you on a regal beauty, Queen," he said in courtly manner. "I'd near forgot the many sides to your personality." He bowed low and continued standing, until she suddenly realized with a start that he awaited her permission to sit. So much for the attributes of rank, that a senior churchman and statesman like Asser should defer to one scarce more than a girl. She must take care lest the privileges of high rank turn her head.

She wasn't sure that his remark about the many sides to her personality was flattery, but decided to take it so. "My thanks for your gracious comments, your Grace," she acknowledged. "You were most kind to welcome me, knowing how eagerly I seek any tidings you may have."

"I must disappoint you to some degree. I have no real news such as you hope for. Your Vikings are at no immediate risk, but the decision to release them has not been made. You must realize that events have piled in on the new King Edward, and he cannot at one time get to all of them. I have naught to counsel save continued patience." Tara's face must have shown her deep disappointment, for he continued. "You have reason to expect favorable resolution in time, I am certain. But that time is not yet."

If this learned man were certain it would be favorable in the end, then how would it profit her to delay her petition further? "I will see King Edward, and petition him," she declared. "My mind is settled on it."

"Such premature action would be nigh disastrous at this turn of affairs," Asser said gravely. "You would be well advised to rely on my opinion on this. I know Edward far better than you. He can be fair, even generous—oft extraordinarily so, for a royal person—but in his own time. He must not be pushed."

"But is he not grateful to me? Did I not run some risk of injury to show his officers how he…" She broke off, knowing what a trivial thing she'd done in the grand scheme of events. Her duel was naught to him but an evening's foolery, no matter that she'd risked a broken head. Asser was right.

He had more to tell her. "The new King would meet you after his coronation. Do not let it raise your hopes, for he's unlike to speak of this matter. You'll be there as Cymru's monarch. I felt it needful to warn you, to adjure you under no circumstances to importune the King. He'd take it most ill!" Not until Asser had received her half-hearted promise did he depart, leaving her dispirited and with no least notion how to help the Northumbrians and her own true love.

The pomp and display of the Coronation were of no interest to Tara, and she was relieved to return to her chambers. She waited impatiently for Edward's summons, but the day passed without word—as did the next, every dreary moment of it. Not until the third day did his equerry run her down.

Despite her low spirits, she was surprised and flattered at the warmth of King Edward's greeting. "I apologize abjectly that you were delayed so grievously," he told her, motioning her to be seated. "It's really surprising that I'd little notion what vast quantities of trifling matter devolve on a monarch, particularly one just crowned. I've been kept busy from first light until midnight and later. It was good of you to wait."

Precious little choice she'd had! "It was my pleasure, Your Majesty," she said graciously. "You were kind to grant me audience at all, in your present estate."

"I vow you impress me more and more, Milady! You left our Court a scant few months past, a wandering Princess from a minor gwlad. You return as Queen of all the Wealhas."

"Wealhas, Sire?" She knew the invidious Saxon name for her Celtic countrymen—'Outsiders'—but her pride would not let her accept it passively, e'en from the High King of Britain.

She was glad to see the faint flush of embarrassment on his face. "I apologize, Milady," he said ruefully. "It is an unfortunate soubriquet, and one not to be used henceforth in our Court. But pray accept my congratulations on your succession. There's none I'd sooner see on the throne of Cymru."

"Thank you, Your Majesty," she acknowledged. "The throne came open quite suddenly, when the former King…died."

"We've had some news of that, but the versions differ. Perhaps you'll enlighten me as to what truly transpired."

"His subjects murthered him, Your Majesty."

"But why? Kings take a great interest when one of their number is killed by his own people. What was his terrible crime?"

"He signed the Treaty of Accord and Suzerainty with Saxony, Sire," she replied without hesitation.

A humorless smile came to his lips. "I reck I invited your plain answer. So they dislike the two nations settling their squabbles peaceably, do they? And you—how do you see it?"

She thought how best to respond. Six months ago, she'd have opposed it violently, with her life if needs be, to prevent such an unequal union. But Asser's words about Alfred's long-range vision for Britain had influenced her mightily, as had the ancient Mabinogion scroll as well as Brechnor's words. Now she was at the point of deploring the pig-headed chauvinism of her stubborn countrymen that had kept hostilities alive so many years. So much more could be done in a nation at peace! Sire's dream for Dyfed, multiplied tenfold over all Cymru, could be realized only without the wars that sapped the realm's vitality, and killed the young flower of its manhood.

"I favor it, Your Majesty," she answered, in a strong and sincere voice. "Some day, when you've more time, I'll recite to you all of my reasons." She was gratified at the answering smile of appreciation that lighted the young monarch's face.

They went on, discussing the problems she'd encountered on taking the throne, comparing them with what he faced here, finding much in common. The time sped by, and as she realized how long she'd occupied him, she rose to leave.

But he was not quite finished. "I've one more matter to address, Milady. You may find it a touchy subject, but we must speak on it. The matter of your marriage..."

She was startled, not taking his meaning. "My marriage, Your Majesty? I plan no marriage."

"A ruling Queen must have her Prince Consort. You'll find it cursed lonely, not to say unseemly, to sit the throne with none at your side. The monarch must be privy to one voice that speaks with no hidden motive or hope of preferment, one person to provide the most delicate counsel. It is our pleasure, indeed our strong wish, that you be married soon."

Tara was too dismayed to reply. How to explain that the only man she had any wish to wed languished in Edward's gaol—and that if she could not have Sigefert, she'd have no man.

But the King awaited her reply.

"I...I...there is none I would wed, Your Majesty," she stammered.

"None, Milady?" He feigned surprise. "We would have thought many in your realm, stout young fellows of noble birth, would leap at such a chance." His tone was so jocular that Tara had the uncomfortable impression that he poked fun, enjoying her discomfiture.

"I know of none, Your Majesty," she replied stiffly, hating the discussion.

"Such is scarce to be credited!" He appeared to be considering. "A Saxon, then. Many of my nobles witnessed your tumbling of Eorl Mandred, and I'll testify you caught the fancy of all." He rose briskly, signalling an end to the audience. "We'll see what we can find, Queen Tara. Place your trust in us to find you a mate without peer, and that right soon!"

"No!" The refusal burst unbid from her lips, and she recoiled in dismay at her temerity. But she must not let this well-meaning man force an unwanted groom upon her!

The King looked surprised, but she drew courage from his apparent lack of anger. "That is, I...Sire, I can never marry!" She spoke brokenly, vexed at the tears welling from her eyes.

"And why is that?" His tone was strangely sympathetic. "Why cannot a beauteous maiden take a likely man of her choice?"

She could not meet his intent gaze. "Because I care only for one I cannot marry," she whispered. Now he'd likely draw the story from her, and she'd break her word to Bishop Asser.

"What lout is this who'll not have you?"

"Oh, it's not that!" she cried, anguished. "When he is free...that is..." She cursed her loose tongue, which she prayed had not prejudiced Sigefert's chance for release.

Edward struck the table, a look of triumph on his face. Tara trembled; did he guess it was Sigefert? She must throw him off the track, lest he take her answers as importunings. He must not think she was opening the question of Sigefert's pardon!

"I mean, Sire—it is not my destiny." She could scarce speak for fear and distress. "Our two paths do not cross, Sire."

"Destiny!" Edward's tone was scornful. "Believe me, destiny makes a cold bedfellow Milady. Belike your man has scant concern for destiny when you're near him." He laid his hand on her shoulder with surprising gentleness. "Let us have no more talk of 'destiny'. Tell your reluctant swain you'll have him, else we'll find you a better man, who'll not care a whit about 'destiny'. Hah!"

Tara found herself outside the audience room, with an impression of an almost mischievous expression on Edward's face as she left. Preparing for the homeward voyage, she was in such a fever of anxiety for Sigefert's safety she scarce knew what she did. Edward would force her into a marriage, but how can he, when he must know he keeps in gaol the only man I want?

Or does he know?

Somehow, the hours passed, and she was in the carriage for the seaport. She tried to put from her mind Edward's last words, but they kept intruding. Would he in sooth force her to marry a proud and insufferable Saxon nobleman, who belike could find no other to wed? Was she to be sentenced to spend her life in a loveless match, fashioned only for reasons of state? While the one she loved...

Oh, Sigefert! Sigefert! Why cannot you be beside me? Her heart was close to breaking with the pain of her longing. Edward's words came back to her, his scorn for 'destiny'. Did he truly believe she was letting her destiny guide her in this?

Hearing her mind expressing the thought—as if she were outside herself, listing to another—she sat bolt upright with the shock of a sudden revelation. She had been letting her destiny guide her! She had been about to accept that she had no choice in life, that events could not be altered to fit the imperative of passion—of a passionate love as strong as hers for Sigefert!

No! she cried inwardly, her face hardening with resolution. The gods cannot—do not—ask that of me! There must be room in the plan for my wishes. I will not be a pawn! I will have Sigefert! We will work together, and overcome whatever would threaten our happiness.

But every turn of the carriage wheels was taking her farther from Sigefert, and she might never see him again.

So preoccupied was she when they reached the landing, she paid no heed to the shadowy crewmen, noticed but did not take in that it was not her flagship, but an unfamiliar lion-headed craft, with a regal cabin into which she was ushered. A separate part of her brain registered, without comprehending, that it must be no less than the Saxon Royal Barge. Nor did she look up as they cast off the lines, swung the ship out to breast the current, hoisted the big sail to catch the fair wind. In spite of her gloom, she felt a moment's release as the breeze ruffled her hair, taking her back in memory to when they'd left hated Denemearc and driven into the sparkling waters of the great Northern Sea—and e'en further back, to a dim recollection of riding with Sire out of Milford Haven, as a tiny child, feeling the flung spray on her face.

Almost she could imagine she was with the Northumbrians again. There stood the helmsman, standing so erect in the stern sheets, so vital and alive, gripping the tiller so confidently. He could be Sigefert, watching the wind and and the sail and the water, guiding the ship, taking her home. Taking her back to Cymru, to rule by her side, a strong and resolute adviser, her full equal in preserving the realm. Taking her back, to warm her empty bed with the intensity of his caring and devotion, to keep her forever secure in the undying passion of his love. Taking her back, to be as one with her forever, in a shared life of eternal bliss!

The vision faded and disappeared, as the impossibility of her fantasy came cruelly home to her. She bowed her head hopelessly, her eyes awash with bitter tears of despair.

Something made her lift her head, and she looked again at the helmsman, more intently than before. The gods were punishing her for striving to escape their net, by playing a cruel deception on her—for they made his stance incredibly like Sigefert's. The resemblance was more than extraordinary, far beyond chance similarity. What cruel sorcery was this? Her eyes were betraying her, playing her hateful tricks. She rubbed them...looked more intently at the silent figure...looked again.

Then, in a rush of glorious awareness, she understood Edward's quixotic insistence that she find herself a mate, his perverse inability to comprehend her objections—the wondrous gift he was tendering her. All in a moment, with a blinding certainty, she knew!

It **was** Sigefert!

Utterly flustered, she was at a loss what to do. Sigefert must have recognized her when she boarded—how could he not? More, when his release was being arranged, they must have told him what was planned, else why would he and the rest of the survivors know to man the Royal Barge, know where to set their course?

He knew—all of them must have known—the identity of their passenger.

Then why was he not handing over the helm to another, rushing furiously through the open door of the cabin, clasping her in his arms as if never to let her go?

Suddenly she understood what it must be; how completely their positions were reversed.

When they fled Britain so long ago, she was homeless, terrified, in an alien environment where her own painfully learned skills counted for naught. He was the powerful Jarl, leader of a fierce band of Vikings, in his own element. She had crept unwanted aboard his longboat, forced to cast herself on his mercy.

How different the situation now. He was the homeless castaway with no prospects, she the powerful High Queen on whose mercies all of them were cast. Released in her custody, with the pitiful remnants of his force, seeing himself as little more than a slave. Small wonder his pride made him hold aloof from her.

But did he not feel the intensity of her love and desire for him? Could he not feel it, e'en now? Had she not made it clear, in an hundred ways, back in Denemearc?

Yes, back in Denemearc!

But they were not back in Denemearc now. Here he was a commoner—a fugitive Viking pirate—and she a High Queen. Suddenly she understood, and felt a rush of sympathy for him, in his uncertainty and distress. How could she explain? How could she persuade this proud Jarl to accept the changed situation?

She stood in the door of the cabin, facing him. "Oh, Steersman," she called. "Pray give over the helm to another, and join me in the cabin." She saw him stiffen, hesitate, then beckon to one of his men to relieve him. Slowly, reluctantly, he stepped forward and stood stiffly at the door to the cabin.

"Sigefert!" She could stand no more. "Do you not know who I am?"

He remained silent so long she wondered if he had heard. "You are Queen," he said at last.

"I am no such thing!" she said, abandoning her plan in her intense frustration. "I am Tara! Are you bewitched, that you do not remember someone by that name?"

His frozen expression softened almost imperceptibly. "I once knew such a one," he said stiffly. "She is gone."

Torn between anger and distress, Tara waited for him to say more. The silence grew more oppressive, but she was determined to wait him out. Finally he spoke again, though not saying the words she wanted to hear. "Is there anything more, Queen? May I return to my helm?"

Tara felt a swift apprehension. Was she misreading his stiff manner? Was it more than just discomfort at her lofty estate? Had his long sojourn in gaol given him time to choose between the two competing futures? On the one hand, did he envision a life with one who had been his alone, but now would be a busy monarch, while he idled the time away on the sidelines, only one of many distractions to her? On the other, imagining himself savoring the carefree seaborne existence of his dreams, sailing off to new and exotic lands across the Western Ocean, shedding the shabby and inconsequential cares of life on shore?

Had he chosen the latter?

No! She was finding trouble where it did not exist! Resolutely she put the devastating notion from her, sprang to her feet, went directly up to him, and grasping both his hands in hers, put them about her. Gathering all her courage, she confronted him with the terrifying choice she could scarce bear to speak.

"If your love for me is gone, Sigefert, you've but to say so now, and I'll bother you no more." She gulped with the enormity of what she was saying, but pressed on. "If you still have love for me, then take me in your arms, and show me how much!"

There was an awful moment of uncertainty. Then she found herself suddenly pressed against him, his arms enfolding her in a crushing grip. Over the frenzied fluttering of her heart, she could feel the rapid beating of his against her. He kissed her hair, her eyes, her cheeks. As his lips found hers at last, she gave herself over passively to the urgency of his love, near to swooning with the miracle of it.

"Tara! Tara, my dearest love!" he whispered huskily. He picked her up and carried her, unresisting, back into the cabin.

"You are no Princess, no Queen, no High Ruler, my love," he told her, when their reunion had been cemented with the intensity of their caring.

"Then what am I?" she asked softly, knowing the answer. At this precious moment, she was all woman, loving and desiring him, long deprived of him, despairing that they'd ever be reunited, hungry for his nearness, living only for him.

"You are still Tara, my dearest love—the maiden who has filled my dreams every night since we parted." He leaned back against the pillows. "And from whom never will I be parted again!"

"And can you be content sharing the throne, fretting over the cares of running a kingdom? Will you grow restless in that life?" Her tone was light, but her questions were deadly serious. She had to ask, to remind him, from her new found realization of the frustrations and never-ending burdens of rule, just how trying that life could be. She waited in dread for his answer.

"I will be at your side, my love, helping you where you need help, devoting all my efforts to the fulfillment of that destiny of yours, in this strange wild land that you seem to love so much. I will rule with you, support you, keep you from harm." He paused, as if suddenly uncertain. "If you agree."

She took his hand in hers, and pressed it to her cheek. "I agree," she said blissfully. "How could I not?"

THE HISTORICAL
BACKGROUND TO TARA

Tara is a 'docudrama', true to the documented history of real people and events but bringing history's gaps alive through the breathtaking exploits, martial skill and passionate nature of a stunning Celtic princess striving to achieve the high destiny foretold by her old Druidic gods.

West Saxony

Alfred the Great (849-900) assumed the throne of West Saxony in 871. In 894 the 80-boat force of a 330-boat Danish fleet under Hasteinn was chased from the Thames estuary by Alfred's larger 'lion-head' ships. A splinter force under Sigefert escaped up the Thames to Gloucester (remains of a Roman defensive wall circling the encampment still exist), where it allied with a force of Celtic patriots from Wales, to defend against Alfred. Alfred's son Edward laid seige and overran them, but some Danes escaped to sea again under Sigefert. (Tara aged 16). In 899-900 Alfred's fleet captured 20 of Sigefert's ships, tried the Viking crews at Winchester, and hanged them all as pirates. (Tara aged 21-22). In 900 Alfred died and Edward assumed the throne. (Tara aged 22). (W.D. Hassall's MEDIEVAL ENGLAND AS VIEWED BY CONTEMPORARIES (NY, Harper & Row, 1957) quotes extensively from THE DEEDS OF ALFRED, by Asser, Monk of St. Davids, who was Alfred's Scrivener.)

Wales

In the ninth century, Wales was called Cymru, and Pembrokeshire was King Llywarch's Dyfed, whose Menevia Castle (in the story) was at Haverfordwest. His daughter Elen (Tara in the story) became Queen of Dyfed on his death in 903. Bishop Asser, of Saint David's Cathedral in Dyfed, was brought by Alfred to his Court about 882 (Tara aged four).

The sacred mountain of Presceli Top, 15 miles NW of Haverfordwest, contains a neolithic burial chamber 3500 years old named Pentre Evan Cromlech, reputed home of the Tylwyth Teg (goblin folk). Carmarthen (Brechnor's castle in the story) is the old Welsh settlement of Caerfyrddin, on the site of the Roman fort of Maridunum or Bryn Myrdden, connected by the Towy River to Carmarthan Bay. (R.M. Lockley, WALES, London, B.T. Batsford, 1966). Tenby lies on the mainland opposite the 500 acre Caldey Isle. Milford Haven was a fishing center. (H.V.Morton, IN SEARCH OF WALES, NY, Dodd/Mead, 1932). The Brecon (Brechnoch) Beacons (that guided Tara back to Glamorgan Castle) are true landmarks, rising 2900 feet. Mathry is the site of Aber Castle (where Tara was page and squire) and of Carreg Samson Cromlech. A gwlad is a shire or minor kingdom, a cantref is equivalent to a county, and a tref a village. A uchelwr (wyr) is a noble freeman, a grwda a lesser freeman such as a priest or bard, a taeog(ion) a villein or serf (tied to the land, but with certain rights), a caethwas a slave. Bards were poets and songsters, preservers and teachers of the old Druidic principles, and sometime seers or advisors to kings and others in power. Some sixth century bards: Talhaern, Bluchbard, Cian, Taliesen, Aneirin and Myrddin (origin of name 'Merlin')

In the fourth century, Roman commander Magnus Maximus (enshrined in Welsh history as Cymri leader Macsen Wledeg, erroneously termed 'Emperor of Rome') came to Britain to restore order, built the Roman fortress of Segontium that is now Caernarvon, and married Elen Luyddog, daughter of Cymri chieftain Caratacus (Caradog). In 383 he withdrew to fight in Gaul and died there. Elen of the Hosts (so named for the armies she led) returned with son Constantine to defend her welsh dominions, adopted the Maximus Red Dragon symbol as a Cymri banner, and eventually controlled much of Wales. Many roads (e.g. from Neath to Brecon) are called Sarn Elen (Elen's Road). Llywarch named daughter Elen after her. The Welsh were Cymri (fellow-countrymen) and their nation Cymru from when they united against English invaders. (David Frazer, THE INVADERS, WALES IN HISTORY, Cardiff, Univ. of Wales, 1965; and Geoffrey Ashe, QUEST FOR ARTHUR'S BRITAIN, NY, Praeger, 1968).

King Rhodri, called Rhodri Mawr (the Great, or High, King), ruled from 844 to 878 (Tara born in 878), founded the princely houses of Gwynedd and Deheubarth in South Wales, and shortly brought Powys and Seisyllwg under his control. Ultimately he ruled all Wales except Dyfed, Brecon, Gwent and Glamorgan. He had two sons, and at his death in 878 his son Cadell ruled in the south (our area of interest in the story), and his other son Anarawd in the north. Cadell had three sons: Hywel (the eldest), Clydog and Meurig (daughter Meuriga in the story). Hywel ruled as High King from 916 to 960, and was known as Hywel Dda (the Good). He married Elen (our Tara), thus adding Dyfed to his kingdom. He and Clydog jointly ruled Seisyllwg. The real Clydog in fact was killed by his own subjects; the reason is not known.

Cymru accepted the Pope and Roman practices of Christianity in 768, but the religion was interwoven into Celtic and Druidic cere-monies. The Catholic Church adopted many of the old holy days, but overlaid the meanings and forms of worship to comport with the Catholic faith.

Wales is rich in old castles, some restored, the rest as preserved ruins. Two are of interest to the story—the Brecon area (our Glamorgan Castle of the High King), and the Haverfordwest area (our Menevia Castle in Dyfed where Tara was born).

Brecon area: the site shows evidence of habitation some 5000 years ago. Northwest of the town is the remains of Pen-y-crug, an iron-age fort. The Romans built a 5-acre fort, Y-Gaer, two miles west of Brecon, shortly after they first arrived in 50 AD, and occupied it for some 2½ centuries. A local ruler probably took it over in the 5th century. The castle, whose extensive ruins survive, was built by Norman Bernard de Neufmarche in the late 11th century.

Haverfordwest area: a strong stone castle was built here by the Earl of Pembroke in the mid-12th century, and history reports a visit by Archbishop Baldwin in 1188. The town was defended by walls encompassing the castle as well. Extensive well-preserved ruins survive.

See Web Site *www.castlewales.com/cow_art.html* for excellent views and information on these and 30 other welsh castles (including Eorl Tenby's castle)

Denmark

The name 'Dane' was first recorded in 550, and the land was dubbed 'Denemearc' by King Alfred in 890. Harald Haarfager (whose daughter Ylva is abducted in the story) was King of West Norway and later all Norway (860-933). King Gorm (Gorm the Old) unified Denmark and ruled from (860-935). Gorm's son was Harald Blatonn (Bluetooth) Gormsson (story borrows the name Gormsson for Gorm's grandson).

Hedeby was a trading center at the base of Jutland on the Baltic, for trade routes from the Baltic along the Dnieper and Volga Rivers. Ribe was a trading center on the west coast. Jelling, in central Denmark near the east coast, was the royal necropolis. Aggersborg was an early fortress in north Denmark, on the Lindholm Hoje waterway from the Kattegat to the North Sea.

Women of that day enjoyed high status, legally and actually, being permitted to manage property, own land, and sue for divorce, and with complete authority in household matters.

The Varangian Way (Viking trail down the Dnieper to Miklagard)

Gotlanders founded the first Norse trading colony in the Baltic, near present-day Liepaja. The Dnieper Route went through the Baltic and Gulf of Finland to Aldeigjuborg (Staraya Ladoga) on Lake Ladoga, thence down the Volkhov River to Holmgard (Novgorod) and the Lovat to Gnezdova (Smolensk), down the Dnieper River to the Black Sea at Berezany Island (at Odessa), and across the Sea to Miklagard. Downstream of Kiev were seven rapids spanning 50 miles. Aifor, the fourth rapid, required portaging cargo and dragging boats over the rock-filled shallows. Berezany, at the delta to the Black Sea near Odessa, was a permanent center.

Vikings were the Rus or Rhos (from 'Rodr' or rowing road), and the eastern Vikings the Varangian Rus. Cities like Smolensk, Novgorod and Kiev then were ruled by Viking chieftains. Archeologists have uncovered 28 levels of log-paved streets in Novgorod.

Byzantium

The Capital City of New Rome (variously Miklagard, Byzantium, Constantinople) was the major trading city, and some Rus expeditions numbered in the hundreds of boats. Vikings termed Miklagard the 'city of gold', and its bay the Golden Horn from the abundance of fish.

Emperor Leo VI of New Rome reigned from 886 to 912. The Roman army of this period numbered 120,000 men, and was considered the most efficient in the world. An elite force, mostly Norse, was known as the Varangian Guard. (Some authorities hold that this force was not specifically designated the Imperial Guard until a century or so later) By the time Tara visited there, the Roman fleet, though still powerful, was in decline. The chief warships were triremes (three banks of oars), called Dromons, some with sails. They had up to 230 rowers and 70 marines, had war engines on turrets, and bronze Syphons (catapults) for throwing Greek Fire. Miklagard was one city the Vikings (the Rus) never managed to capture.

ADDITIONAL REFERENCES
TO THOSE CITED ABOVE

Britain: ENGLISH MEDIEVAL BOROUGHS, Beresford & Finberg (Towota, NJ, Rowman & Littlefield, 1973)

EVERYDAY LIFE IN ROMAN ANGLO-SAXON TIMES, Marjorie Quennell (NY, Putnam, 1959)

HISTORY OF ENGLAND, V1, David Hume (Phila, E. Littrell, 1828)

HISTORY OF THE ENGLISH SPEAKING PEOPLE; THE BIRTH OF BRITAIN, Winston S. Churchill (NY, Dodd, Mead, 1956)

LIFE AND WORK OF PEOPLE OF ENGLAND, Hartley Elliot (NY, Putnam, 1931)

SOCIAL HISTORY OF ENGLAND, Asa Briggs (NY, Viking Press, 1983)

STORY OF CIVILIZATION, V4, Will Durant (NY, Simon & Schuster, 1950)

STORY OF ENGLAND; MAKERS OF THE REALM, Arthur Bryant (Boston, Houghton-Mifflin, xxxx)

Wales: ABBEYS, M. R. James (Garden City, Doubleday, 1926)

AGE OF CHIVALRY, F. G. Vosburgh, Ed. (Wash., Natl Geographic Society, 1969)

CATHEDRALS OF ENGLAND AND WALES, T. F. Bumpus (Edinburgh, Dunedin Press, 1927)

THE CELTS, Joseph Raftery (Cork, Mercier Press, 1964)

MONKS, NUNS AND MONASTERIES, Sacherell Sitwell (NY, Holt Rinehart, 1965)

THE NUNNERY, Dorothy Charques (NY, Coward-McCann, 1960)

THE NUNS, Marcelle Bernstein (Phila, Lippincott, 1976)

PAGE BOY FOR KING ARTHUR, Eugenia Stone (Chicago, Follett, 1949)

SQUIRE FOR KING ARTHUR, Eugenia Stone (Chicago, Follett, 1955)

Vikings, Danes: DENMARK, PREHISTORY, Bent Rying (Copenhagen, Royal Danish Ministry…, 1981)

HEIMSKRINGLA: SAGAS OF THE NORSE KINGS, Snorri Sturluson (NY, Dutton, 1930—written by Sturluson 1223-1225)

HISTORY OF THE VIKINGS, Gwyn Jones (Oxford, Oxford Univ Press, 1968, '73, '84)

LEGENDS OF THE NORTH, Olivia Coolidge (Boston, Houghton-Mifflin, 1951)

THE LONG SHIPS, Frans G. Bengtsson (London, Fantana Books, 1956)

MYTHS OF NORTHERN LANDS, H. A. Guerber (NY, American Book Co., 1895)

SCANDINAVIA, Hammond Innes (NY, Time, Inc., 1963)

SHIPS AND WAYS OF OTHER DAYS, E. K. Chatterton (London, Sidgwick-Jackson, 1918)

STORY OF THE IRISH RACE, Seumas MacManus (NY, Devin-Adair, 1921)

THE VIKINGS, F. R. Donovan (NY, Amer. Heritage via Harper & Row, 1964)

THE VIKINGS, Rudolf Poertner (NY, St. Martins Press, 1971)

THE VIKINGS, Howard LaFay (Wash., Natl. Geographic Society, 1972)

THE VIKING WORLD, James Graham-Campbell (New Haven, Ticknor Fields, 1980)

THE VIKING WORLD, Jacqueline Simpson (NY, St. Martins Press, 1980)

Varangian Way, Byzantium: BYZANTIAM, AN INTRODUCTION, Philip Whitting (NY, NY Univ Press, 1971)

THE BYZANTINE EMPIRE, ROME OF THE EAST, Merle Severy (Natl. Geographic Magazine, Vol. 164, No. 6, Dec. 1983, pp 709-767)

HISTORY OF THE BYZANTINE EMPIRE, Enno Franzius (NY, Funk & Wagnalls, 1967)

VIKING TRAIL EAST, R. P. Jordan (Natl. Geographic Magazine, Vol. 167, No. 3, Mar. 1985, pp 278-317)

General: THE WARRIOR QUEENS, Antonia Frazer (New York, Knopf, 1989)